MW01131180

PETER MACK PRESENTS

The Seduction of Ayana Cherry

Sequel to A Neighborly Affair

A novel
By

Peter Mack

Includes opening chapter of the sequel
Ayana Cherry & The Tabernacle Glorious

authorHOUSE®

AuthorHouse™
1663 Liberty Drive
Bloomington, IN 47403
www.authorhouse.com
Phone: 1-800-839-8640

© 2010 Peter Mack Presents, LLC. All rights reserved.

No part of this book may be reproduced, stored in a retrieval system, or transmitted by any means without the written permission of the author.

First published by AuthorHouse 10/26/2010

ISBN: 978-1-4520-7084-1 (e)
ISBN: 978-1-4520-7082-7 (sc)
ISBN: 978-1-4520-7083-4 (hc)

Library of Congress Control Number: 2010912283

Printed in the United States of America

This book is printed on acid-free paper.

Certain stock imagery © Thinkstock.

Because of the dynamic nature of the Internet, any Web addresses or links contained in this book may have changed since publication and may no longer be valid. The views expressed in this work are solely those of the author and do not necessarily reflect the views of the publisher, and the publisher hereby disclaims any responsibility for them.

PETER MACK PRESENTS

www.petermackpresents.com

For

Toccara

For believing

PART ONE

Stacy & Percy

"Our demonstration must match our expectation"
- Peter Mack

CHAPTER ONE

Stacy didn't know how to feel about the way the rising horizontal stream of light seeping in through the sheer peach curtains, announced a new day. They were parted in such a way so as to allow a narrow slice of sunlight across the torso of Marlin's muscular deep brown chest. She'd watched the burgeoning glow rise from the foot of the bed, creeping along the flower print comforter, until it reached the chiseled stomach of her husband.

She was transfixed by its glow, her eyes moving to Marlin's shuttered eyes. Behind the long dark lashes and the shiny lids, his eyeballs roamed as if he were in deep thought. She watched his sharply defined face closely; the way his wide full lips gently touched each other, revealing the occasional stab of his thick pink tongue to the soft part at the center of his lips.

There was something new in his face. Something that she could not quite grasp a hold of; something that she felt she should be feeling as well. She'd at first thought that this new brightness in his face was because he was back on the football field; but when that glow had passed there was a new glow that had to do with something that felt more intimate.

He stirred as the warm shelf of light caressed his neck and touched the underside of his chin. Stacy followed his strong hand as it slid along his stomach and disappeared beneath the comforter. He'd exhaled, his torso rising and falling slightly with this movement, his lips parting slightly as he grabbed his erect meat, lifting the comforter to form a tent. He stroked himself slowly, his face turning away from Stacy's glowing eyes.

She hadn't yet figured what her feelings should be about his private moments. Again, he's seemed to regain his sexual appetite with his return to the football field, but when he made love to her it felt as if he were thinking of someone else. The familiarity and tenderness with which they'd made love before moving to Indianapolis, before his injury, before she was the only one working and supporting them both, had been replaced by something foreign and impersonal.

Still, she remained dedicated to keeping him satisfied. She wanted to prove everyone wrong about her. They said that she was a typical professional athlete's wife. They said that she would divorce him when he was injured and released from the Seattle Seahawk. She couldn't yell loud enough for them to understand that she really loved him. Hadn't she proven this by supporting him through rehab? Why should she feel guilty because she'd gotten a good opportunity and he had to follow her across the country? She tried to make him comfortable every chance she got. But lately...

The fresh sunlight crawled across his flared nostrils and pulled at his sloping eyelids. She reached out to pull the comforter away from the stake wrapped gently in his fist. When she looked back to his eyes they were watching her.

"Good morning," she greeted him huskily, pushing away her curiosity about what or who he was dreaming about.

Marlin's dark brown eyes were smoky with passion. They changed depth and color as he focused on his wife. He seemed to only now realize that he was grabbing his swollen joint.

"No!" she said, reaching for his hand as he pulled it across his stomach. "Keep going," she urged him. "I enjoy watching." She smiled crookedly, her almond shaped hazel eyes twinkling in the early morning light.

"How long you been up?" he asked, stopping short of "watching me sleep."

"Not that long," she answered before looking back to his deflating erection. She was committed to keeping him satisfied. Though she felt him pulling away as of late, she was determined to prove everyone wrong. Their marriage was for real and would last until death parted them.

"You want me to finish that for you?"

Marlin raised his arms and cradled the back of his head in his palms. He looked down the length of his body as she leaned over him and wrapped her thin lips around the tender head of his dick.

Stacy closed her eyes in concentration. She worked hard to get this part right. She was glad that he allowed her this attempt after a four-day suspension; she scraped her teeth across the ridge of his helmet. She opened her mouth wide and licked the base of his flaccid joint tenderly, enjoying the feeling of him growing inside of her mouth. His muscular thighs tensed under her as she sucked him slowly and carefully. She reminded herself not to get too excited and accidentally cause him pain. She twirled his fleshy nut sacs between her fingers, taking the caress of his hand across her petite ass as a sign she was doing a good job. She moved with his urging, settling over him as her pulsing pussy lay over his chest. She exhaled over his shining member as he pushed a thick finger past the fine brown hairs on her pussy into her warmth. She moaned as she sucked on the swollen head hard, making his body jerk.

"SUNNY!..." a whining voice called out, causing her to jump, scraping her teeth over Marlin's dick. The result was a flurry of activity that found him bucking her from the bed and landing her on the hard wood floor.

"Gotdamn, Stacy!" Marlin shouted, jumping from the bed holding his dick as he strolled towards the bathroom, ignoring the familiar blur of thick black hair and chocolate limbs outside his window.

"SUNNY!" came the voice again, this time an octave lower, perhaps having heard Marlin's complaint and the slamming bathroom door.

Stacy made no move to rise. She felt like she could stay there and cry until her entire naked body shriveled up and disappeared through the tight cracks of the floor boards. She tried and tried and tried, but every time she came close to feeling like they were back to where they'd started, there was something new added to the mix. He'd said that he didn't mind when her father needed to live with them. How could he say no when she was paying all the bills? Still, she included him in the decision so that his pride would not be threatened. She'd told him how her father had been abused in the assisted living community. He would only stay with them long enough for her to find a safe place for him to live. It had been a week and her father had successfully thwarted every attempt she made to satisfy her husband. Of course he had no way of knowing the distance between them of late.

"Blimey HOTTENTOT! Sunny! Pray tell why I'm left to ROT!" he screeched in his sing-songy southern voice laced with sugary lemonade being sipped on a wide wooden porch. He had a voice that reminded the listener of a simpler time of horses and general stores behind a blacksmith.

"Here I come daddy," she called back, lifting herself from the warming floor. It was not enough that she let him come live with her, but he never seemed to sleep at all. He was not the man she remembered from her childhood or even her college days. She remembered him as an outgoing silent man who didn't suffer fools. The last five years had changed him, beginning with her mother's death and then the slow deterioration of his eyesight. Stacy was still not sure how much of his mental rot was genuine or manufactured. Sometimes she felt as if he were playing one long con and everyone, including his only loving doting daughter, was being taken for a ride of extreme sympathy gathering.

"Sorry about that," she said to Marlin as she opened the bathroom door. She saw a glimmer of anger in his eyes through the mirror as he looked to her sharply. His cheeks were fat with mouthwash. He spit a frothy mix of toothpaste and Scope into the sink.

"Don't worry about it," he assured her, resigned to the fact that she would never win a medal for sucking dick. He ignored the way she sat on the toilet, her piss streaming loudly into the bowl, while resting her chin dejectedly in her palms. *Let her feel some kind of way,* he thought to himself.

"SUNNY! Blimey fool I am to think you care!"

Marlin smiled at this muted insult, looking back to Stacy as she remained seated. "I'll see what he wants."

She forced a tight smile. "He probably wants the curtains opened."

"Then that's what he'll get," Marlin replied cheerfully, having shaken his earlier pain, as he stepped from the bathroom.

The flush of the toilet followed Stacy to the door where she pushed to close it. She stood naked before the full length mirror and admired her petite frame with its palm-size breasts, tight ass and slim hips. She rubbed her stomach tenderly, wishing that there was life forming inside. *Maybe this would bring us closer together,* she thought. Maybe the boy that Marlin spoke less of now would bring him back to her in a way that would assuage her insecurity. Like a much needed crutch she leaned on the fact that she was a beautiful, cultured, corporate executive to return a bounce to her step as she grabbed a silk robe from a hook on the wall.

The living room was bathed in light, the rays bouncing through the finely appointed space; a lighting on the crystal center piece on the glass dining room table before cascading across the gold framed photos atop the fireplace ledge and settling on the lean figure of her father; he sat ensconced in the plush leather easy chair looking blindly to her now. He gathered his collapsed lips together in preparation for what he wanted to say. The effect was that of a man trying to chew cotton.

"Good morning daddy," Stacy said as she skipped past the dining room table and glided to where he sat in the living room, glancing quickly to the porn scene on the plasma screen before leaning to kiss his roughly stubbled face.

He leaned away just as she drew near. "Pigeon beak!" he yelped out.

"Happy pop ain't happy at all." He looked to a spot above the plasma screen where a large dark-skinned woman was riding a slim white man with abandon. It was no wonder that she didn't break his body in half.

"Yo Grump! How many slices you want?" Marlin asked from the kitchen.

"What are you making?" Stacy wanted to know.

"Never mind you that. The boy got some pig and some chicken eggs. Why?" her father asked with a twitch of his lips, his small head suspended on a narrow, wrinkled neck the color of hot bronze. Wisps of sparse gray hair stood from his round skull. He had the fine, pointed features that Stacy inherited. Her light caramel color came from her mother. She had his hazel eyes, too, but with the cataracts attacking his left eye and seeping into his right, the effect was of a man with marble colored eyes that changed color in varying degrees of light; right now they were a light gold color shot through with sparks of cloudy white.

"I'm hungry too daddy," she said in her most innocent, girly voice. Grump shot both hands out in front of him as if waving away a batch of flies.

"Tell me what's happening on the box. Why they stop humping?" he wanted to know. "Put the whole pack oink oink in there son," he called, his face turned skyward.

"It's over daddy. The credits are rolling."

"No no no," he motioned when Stacy moved away from him. "It's another one coming, too. This is the good one," he said gleefully while rubbing his weathered palms together. The flannel pajamas hung loose from his thin body except for the bulge that sat in his lap like a coiled snake, stretching the fabric so that it bunched up suggestively.

The smell of bacon soon wafted into the living room. The house was coming alive. "It's time for you to get to the white folk. You ain't hungry Sunny," he said with a toothless grin. "You never eat." He reached a bony arm out until she found her way within his grasp. He pulled her to the side of the easy chair and let his fingers drum against her hip bone.

"Did you sleep well, daddy?"

The sun bathed his leather tough skin, making it glow as he lifted his chin to her question. "I'm all alone marshmallow."

Stacy felt her heart being squeezed. "I know, daddy. It's just hard finding someone to trust."

"Blimey!" he hissed, pressing his strong fingers into her body. "Fine stroke of luck a pretty cotton tail make me a happy pop."

Stacy rubbed her palm soothingly across the short tufts of gray hair on his head. "I don't know about a pretty cotton tail, but I'll get someone to look in on you. Want me to come home for lunch?"

He was shaking his head slowly as the new porn movie burst to life with fresh moaning and flesh smacking. A muscular black man had a white woman, dressed as a nurse, bent over a white leather couch. He pounded into her with abandon. Stacy briefly wondered if the long shining dick was going into her ass or pussy. "No no no. Don't leave them white folk for me. Happy pop be okay Sunny."

"We ready to grub Grump," Marlin said from the door of the kitchen. He held a pan of scrambled eggs in one hand and a spatula in the other. Sometimes Stacy felt that he was simply biding his time for the way he looked to her with an amused expression.

"Make my grub will ya Sunny," Grump said distractedly, his attention now directed to the plasma screen where a new smacking sound emanated from the same muscular black man slamming into a new woman who'd recently stepped into the house dressed as a DirecTV service provider. She was naked, except for her blue hat pulled low to her eyes as she bent over the wooden dining room table, her long blonde hair crashing forward with each hard thrust. Grump tilted his head at an indirect angle as if there was a spot in his left eye that allowed him to see what was happening.

Stacy left him to his naughty past-time and traipsed into the kitchen where Marlin was busy preparing breakfast. She stopped at the door and leaned against the frame to observe her husband. He'd slipped on a pair of Colts training shorts that hugged his powerful thighs and gripped his tight ass. He moved about the linoleum floor gracefully, his skin tight over flexing and taut muscles. How could she be so lucky? She hates to think that their love could ever end.

"He tell you he lonely?" Marlin asked after sliding a healthy portion of eggs onto a white plate with gold trimming.

Stacy exhaled lightly. "Yeah. I wish I could be here for him myself."

"You gotta trust somebody, babe."

"I know." She was next to him now at the counter next to the stove. "The weekend went by so fast. What time do you have to be at practice?"

"In about an hour."

"I'm really proud of you," she said, rubbing her hand along his arm as she looked to him tenderly.

"Thanks, babe." He held up a plate of bacon and eggs. "You hungry?"

She smiled. "Daddy was right. I'll just grab something at the office."

"Suit yourself," Marlin responded as he moved past her. As he stepped into the dining room with a plate of food for her father, her mind grabbed at a comfort that awaited her at the office. More often this comfort was becoming more appealing, wearing against her resolve and conservative upbringing; it represented a sweet rebellion that she was not sure she wanted to exact for fear of what hidden emotions it would unearth.

CHAPTER TWO

The numbers weren't matching up. Expenditures far outweigh income, yet the balance sheets were still showing profit. The smiling faces of the white people around him seemed to be mocking him, waiting for him to make a career ending mistake. It was as if everyone was watching and waiting for the nigger to fall face first into the soft mound of camel shit set before him. He felt the pats on the back and heard the compliments, but they didn't match up with the results of his hard work. There was something wrong with the balance sheets. His perky young secretary seemed unaffected by the inconsistencies and pretended naiveté when there was some important accounting record that went missing. It was all he could do to keep from yelling out...

"Percy ... Percy, honey ..." Sherrelle gently nudged her bare thigh against his leg, the soft cotton a barrier to the spontaneous sex she so wanted. He'd interrupted her own dreams and self pleasuring with his incessant murmuring about the something not being right with the numbers. She'd ignored him long enough, and then found it was impossible to concentrate.

Percy jerked awake and sat upright in bed, his breathing labored as the smiling faces dispersed from his mind's eye. He looked around wildly before settling his gaze on the curious, deep black eyes of his wife beside him.

"Are you okay?" she asked with a hint of passion in her voice, the memory of her orgasmic vision still fresh between her legs. She could smell the sex seeping from her moist pussy; it glistened on her finger tips as she brushed them against his pajama top.

Percy was untouched by the way her full mocha tinted breasts heaved with her shallow breathing; the way her long dark hair hung to the pillow as she leaned on one elbow didn't move him in any kind of way. Her supple skin, glowing soft and tender in the early morning light didn't force him to reach out and touch her the way it used to do. The numbers weren't adding up and the laughter was growing louder.

"What time is it?" he asked in frustration, looking to the bedside clock. With his recurring dreams he was at least waking up on time.

"Was it another bad dream, baby?" Sherrelle asked in barely a whisper as he swung his legs off the side of the bed. She'd thought to rub him across his back in an effort to interest him in early morning sex, but thought better of it. He was already off the bed and staggering towards the bathroom.

The numbers aren't adding up, he thought to himself as he pulled his retreating member through the opening of his pajamas. He watched the deep yellow stream part the blue toilet water absently, thinking of what the dream could have hinted at. Fighting against this complex puzzle was the smoky image of his wife; her scent was making itself known in his being, drawing his attention back to the bedroom like some mysterious calling.

His eyes scanned quickly across his image as he turned from the toilet. It was true what Sherrelle said about him during their latest argument; he did need to start going to the gym; his stomach did resemble a wayward ring of fat; his shoulders did slope as if pounded on with heavy hammers; he had developed dark rings around his eyes. He'd responded simply that this was the price of his achievement in the white man's world. The look she gave him in response was enough to make him spin, grab up his briefcase and head out the front door for work with renewed anger at the way boxes of clothing were strewn about; she had the audacity to think that she could successfully operate her own clothing business.

He peeked into the bedroom and studied her relaxed expression as she lay back on the bed. Jealousy moved him forward while her hands moved slowly between her spread legs under the silk comforter.

"Why do you insist on doing that?" he asked, standing beside the bed. The question didn't come out as he intended and was grateful that her smoky eyes opened to him with a mischievous invitation, ignoring his judgment.

Sherrelle held Marlin's image in her mind as she lifted the comforter for Percy who quickly shed his pajamas, his hot-dog sized penis dancing out before him as he slid onto the bed beside her.

It had been two weeks since she'd met Marlin at Dahji's house and shared an intimate kiss. Her entire body felt alive and active; sparks of electricity spreading to the edges of her nerve endings only to burst as he held her in his arms. It had been something that had to happen after her continued voyeurism.

Percy kissed her tenderly on her hot cheek in what Sherrelle knew was to be a short form of foreplay that would end with him shuddering to completion only minutes after his dull intrusion.

She'd never expected for Marlin to be at Dahji's house, though she was pleasantly surprised. It was the second time they'd found themselves away from their front yards or her peeking into his bedroom window as he made love to his wife; the first was just after she'd received her first shipment of HoodSweet apparel. It was Peaches who suggested that she bring the clothes to Applebottoms to sell to the exotic dancers.

As scheduled, Percy was climbing between her legs, careful not to crush her fingers as she pressed against her swollen clitoris, eyes shut tight in concentration. His hanging pouch of a stomach pressed softly against her working digits as he slipped through her warmth. His breathing came short against the side of her face as she tightened around his joint and pulled him inside.

The night was like a fairy tale. Marlin had just received confirmation that he'd made the Colts football team. Sherrelle was truly happy for him. Marlin had shown nothing but enthusiasm for her and the burgeoning clothing business she was introducing to the world.

It was no use. Her fingers were being crushed by Percy's stomach. It was a shame, too. For a petite man to have such a hanging paunch went against the laws of nature. She'd long ago ceased in mentioning this oddity to him; he'd simply reply that this was the cost of success. He would go on to remind her that it was because of his success, working long days in a glass office building, that allowed her to drive a Jaguar and enjoy her lavish lifestyle of brunches, manicures, and endless shopping. And it was for this very diatribe, masking his arrogance, that prompted her to answer the ad on MySpace about representatives to treat HoodSweet women's apparel as their own.

The night at Dahji's penthouse was a huge success. The beautiful women who'd come at Dahji's invitation loved the clothes. They all posed sexily for the website Dahji was putting together and videos to accompany the national advertising campaign. Amidst the excitement of a new situation for everyone involved, she was made to feel – if only for one night – that she was all that mattered to Marlin.

Percy huffed in her ear, his familiar murmur of how she felt so good coming out in a hot rush. He shuddered on cue before collapsing with a loud sigh onto her breasts.

"Are you done?" she asked in barely a whisper, frustrated that he'd succeeded in chasing Marlin from her thoughts while proving to be a calculated failure in pleasing her. She lay limp under him, forcing his spent joint from her pussy, the effect making him shudder as he was released from her warmth.

He rolled slowly from her and watched as she scooted to the edge of the bed and pulled on a pair of white boy-shorts and wife-beater. Her full breasts and ample hips and ass pushed against the thin cotton as she stomped from the room, the smell of sex trailing her.

Percy did not see the way her ass bounced hard from the room because he'd closed his eyes to the ceiling to bathe in the glow that spread throughout his body. Her attitude didn't break through his own selfish pleasure to reveal her frustration with his performance.

When the phone rang Percy was stepping from the shower. He'd hopped in not long after Sherrelle left the bedroom. He'd let it ring several times, thinking that she'd answered it after the tenth ring. It had to be at least ten rings; it felt like four when he first wondered where Sherrelle was. Then the ringing began anew. *She must be outside,* he thought to himself as he remembered how she'd dressed leaving the bedroom. He was thinking about how he'd chastised her before about going outside dressed in the same manner as that of a prostitute when he picked up the phone from the bedside stand.

"Santiago residence," he said as he moved towards the bedroom door.

"Percy?" replied a syrupy voice.

"This is he." The living room was bathed in early morning light, its sheen brightening the brown boxes that were stacked neatly around the living room. Sherrelle had succeeded in making their home into a warehouse.

"Hiiii. This is Ayana." There was a pause for recognition. "Ayana Cherry. Sherrelle's niece from California!" she said brightly.

Percy tried to place her face, but the voice didn't match the young girl who had come to their wedding seven years before.

"You mean Sharon's little girl?" he asked as he peeked through the living room curtains. Sherrelle was not at her car parked in the driveway.

"That was a long time ago. I'm all grown up now. It's the milk." There was a suggestive edge in her sexy voice. Percy wondered what prompted this call after so many years. He remembered her mother as a beautiful, flirtatious woman who lacked Sherrelle's southern hospitality. Sharon said the first thing that came to her mind, never mind how rude or poignantly observative it was; like the time she pointed out how she doubted he would be able to satisfy her sister Sherrelle and that it was a good thing he had money. She'd said this after the wedding in front of the women Sherrelle was most close to in her family; they'd smiled graciously and begged him to forgive Sharon for her mouth and not to pay her no mind; she was from California, they said as an excuse.

"Hey Ayana," he said, forcing a smile as he headed towards the kitchen. "How are you and your mother?"

"She's fine," Ayana sighed. "Where's Sherrelle?"

"I'm looking for her right now," he replied as he stepped through the kitchen door, nearly expecting that she would be gathering breakfast from the refrigerator.

"Oh, I forgot about the time difference. Tell her that I was returning her call and ..."

Percy didn't hear anything after that because his attention was arrested at the sight of Sherrelle bursting through the back door. Her face was flushed and her eyes blazed like hot coals. She stopped short just inside the back door with her hand to her heaving breasts, gulping air to collect herself.

"Hello?" Ayana said into his ear.

"What happened?" he wanted to know, stopping at the threshold before the service porch as Sherrelle leaned on the washing machine, her mind searched for the reason she'd given him the last time he caught her in this post-voyeuristic state. The image of Marlin getting his dick sucked was fresh. This was all she needed. She'd watch him for so long. She wondered what it was that Stacy was thinking about as the sun slowly crept up along his body.

"Is it the snake again?" Percy asked, giving her the reason on a silver platter. He'd believed this the first time.

"Yeah!" she breathed out, bringing her hand to her mouth, stifling the laughter threatening to spill forth. It was funny the way Marlin bucked her to the floor. She must have bitten him again. *What a shame*, she thought to herself.

Percy was caught between the sight of her fat pussy bulging against the white sheer cotton of her boy-shorts, her inflamed nipples pressing darkly against the ribbed wife-beater, the glow in her eyes, and the snake that kept reappearing behind their trash cans.

"Who's on the phone?" she asked, having recovered and feeling flush.

She moved close to him, enjoying the confused reaction that the heat of her body caused. It amazed her that he hadn't yet figured out that she'd been creeping to watch the neighbors have sex. He was clueless to his deficiency and how much this mattered to her.

"Ayana," he answered simply, holding the phone out as she stepped over the threshold. Her fingers brushed against his warmly as she took the call.

"Hey little girl," she said as she moved to the refrigerator. Percy watched her as he moved slowly towards the door. He wondered what it was she'd called her young niece about. Sherrelle laughed gaily at something Ayana said as she poured herself a tall glass of orange juice. Percy held the wall as if preventing himself from moving totally out of the kitchen. His curiosity was piqued when Sherrelle confessed that she needed help. She turned to him then and smiled big, turning on the sex appeal that prompted his marriage proposal seven years ago. He took this as an invitation to wait until she got off the phone so he could find out more.

"Oh no girl ... What else did she say?" Sherrelle asked into the phone as she leaned against the counter with her arm under her breasts, making them bulge and adjust firmly.

Percy let his hand slip from the wall. He could hear about this later. He had to get ready for work. Sherrelle's melodic laughter followed him as he turned into the dining room. A slow fire burned in his stomach. In his fat stomach. How she could turn him on and off with a simple glance or twisting of her lips angered him to no end; yet there was no defense against her seduction. He'd known early on that she had control of his heart, but the grip had loosened some when he'd moved her to Indiana and provided a good life for her. He'd been dealt some better cards, but with each new hand she was able to detect his tells and fold when necessary. It was as if she were simply biding her time until something better came along, but he doubted that there was anyone who could provide the kind of lifestyle she was used to. Besides this he held private comfort in her upbringing. Every married couple in her family had been married since college. They didn't believe in divorce. With a new burst of girly laughter his interest was piqued anew as to the nature of Ayana's phone call.

When Sherrelle walked into the bedroom Percy was straightening his woven silk tie over a crisp white Hugo Boss button-up. "You look nice," she said, walking to him and wedging herself between him and the mirrored dresser. Her hands replaced his on the tie knot. The scent of her made him inhale deeply. Her hair hung to her shoulders in thick, loose waves. Her eyes, with thick dark lashes, were lowered in concentration as she adjusted the tautness, her delicate fingers brushing gently under his chin with her slow maneuverings. He wanted to know what the phone call was about, but didn't want to break the intimate spell she'd cast so effortlessly with her presence.

"Is it okay if Ayana stays with us for a couple months?" she asked softly, her eyes rising to meet his. She brushed her fingers along the length of the tie and dropped them to his zipper. He jerked behind the cage at the motion of her touch.

"Is everything okay with her?" he asked, enjoying their closeness. He absorbed every second she was wedged between him and the dresser drawer, her body thick like molasses and twice as thick.

Sherrelle lifted her hand back to his chest with his question. This was a subtle withdrawal that worked to dispel any further questions. "I could use some help with my business," she offered with her palms on his shoulders. The effect gave Percy an inflated sense of his brawn. He briefly felt that there was no need to go to the gym as Sherrelle had directed him so many times before. He felt compelled to apologize for not being able to give her the time and attention he knew she needed. That must be it, he reasoned; she's lonely with all the hours he was away and wanted some company.

"Help with what?" he wanted to know.

She deprived him of her closeness with this question, slipping away from him slowly while she dragged her fingers across the protruding paunch of his stomach.

"With my business," she answered shortly, stopping to rest her weight on one leg and her hand on her hip. His eyes traveled over her body and for the first time he realized she was barefoot. Wet blades of shining grass clung to her slender ankles.

Oh that, he said to himself as he turned to the mirror again, reaching for the knot of his tie. "I thought your friend Peaches was helping you with that."

Sherrelle ignored the way he emphasized her friend's name and referring to her business as "that." Instead she moved back to him, prepared to smooth out his ruffled feathers.

She blocked his way as he turned to reach for the suit coat slung onto the arm rest of the linen cushioned chair in the corner. "She has her own business to attend to. She can only help me so much. I need more help." This last was said with a reminder of the success he'd ignored the first time she gladly shared her latest triumph. She read his insecurity clearly then and now as she looked into his light brown eyes set into a small, tan face.

"For how long?" he asked, relenting under her challenging gaze. She was past begging him for the marital sex that should have been written in the contract. Now she focused her attention on getting in a position to make a new situation for herself if the need arose.

"Just a few months." Her voice was soft and sweet, coupled with a light caress down the length of his arm, careful not to squeeze too hard and expose the need for him to lift a heavy weight or two.

The thought of having two women in the house didn't make him feel any kind of way; except that if it were a nephew he knew that he would have been dead set against him living under his roof.

"When does she want to come?"

Sherrelle smiled, moving her body into his so that her breasts rest lightly on him. "Later in the week."

He recognized her gratefulness in the way she pulled against him, wanting to reward him with what he was sure would be great lovemaking, but there were numbers to make right at the office. He couldn't stay to give her what she wanted.

"Thank you," she said in a low voice after he said that he was late for work and kissed her on the forehead.

"Just make sure she knows not to bring any boys into my house," he said as he walked away from her.

Sherrelle didn't answer, standing still in the far corner of the room as he stepped into the hallway and turned from sight. She smiled with her achievement. It would be great to have Ayana come to live with her. She didn't realize how much she missed being around family until she thought to call her sister Sharon.

Sherrelle was headed for the shower when the front door closed. She was capturing the image of Marlin lying in bed getting his dick sucked by his wife, her pussy twitching with the recent memory.

CHAPTER THREE

It was a morning filled with advertising and marketing meetings. As the senior assistant to the head of the marketing department at the Sloan Advertising Agency, which generated half a billion dollars in revenue annually, Stacy was on the fast track to a Vice President of Marketing position. She'd only been recently promoted to senior assistant to the Vice President of Advertising & Sales. These were heady times, fraught with shallow potholes and fragile, duplicitous friendships on the road to a titled position.

She'd successfully orchestrated a PowerPoint presentation to show the executives her idea for the recently procured contract for GAMETIGHT men's apparel. The back story on the clothing line was that it was formed by an idea to show the authenticity of the clothing by showcasing the author as a come-from-nothing-to-something original. The idea of brand marketing the author along with the clothing was received enthusiastically, along with the proposed tag-line "REAL.SEXY.URBAN.BOSS."

When Stacy's boss walked into her office she still had the story board of the marketing campaign spread across her desk.

"That was great Stacy," Rebecca sang in her proper New England accent. Slim and lithe, Rebecca Deneuve was grace personified. She wore black Chanel or Claiborne suits to match her coal black eyes and raven hair; all of which contrasted starkly against her pale skin that seemed to glow under the bright lights of Stacy's office.

"Thank you," Stacy responded with a wide smile, no longer surprised at how Rebecca seemed to suck in the air with her arrival. "I'm glad that you supported me on this," Stacy added as the graceful woman sat in the chair before her desk, her long fingers folded over her narrow waist.

"It was easy, Stacy. You did all the work plus it's a great product. Finally we have something authentic that can reach the urban market with the potential of reaching every corner of every house in America." With this Rebecca clenched her thin fingers into a fist, the knuckles turning white with the pressure; her platform bracelets jangled together with her motion.

Stacy tried to control her enthusiasm; not only for her impending success, but for the feelings Rebecca awakened in her. The properly coifed woman had to know that her resolve was weakening against her occasional, subtle suggestions that Stacy allow her to advance her career.

Rebecca suddenly stood from her seat. "Come on. Let's get some lunch." The invitation was not lost on Stacy. In this environment a lunch date meant more than the food that was to be consumed; there was a position to be gathered; a power play to be made; a seduction to be employed.

"I'm starving!" Stacy exclaimed, remembering that she'd skipped on the scrambled eggs and bacon Marlin had prepared.

Stacy felt as if she'd already been promoted by the way her coworkers greeted her as she walked alongside the very respected and feared Rebecca Deneuve. Through the plush lobby – with its most successful ad campaigns adorning the walls in Technicolor and prosperous smiles – she was congratulated for her demonstration. Though most hadn't attended the meeting, word of her performance traveled like a bullet through the high-rise building of chrome and glass.

She basked in the glow of compliments from coworkers – some of whom would love to see her fail, but dare not reveal these feelings in front of Rebecca - as they rode the elevator to the food court located on the seventh floor of the fifteen floor building.

"How about Italian?" Rebecca suggested, motioning to the Olive Garden restaurant as they stepped from the elevator into the cool, brightly lit food court of stainless steel and white formica. The Olive Garden sat tucked into an airy corner behind fragrant indoor flower beds.

"Sounds good to me," Stacy replied as she fell in stride with Rebecca through the entrance of the cozy restaurant. They'd missed the rush of the lunch-time crowd and found a secluded table near the rear of the restaurant. They were partially obscured by hanging plants which met flowers planted along the headrest of the horseshoe-shaped booth.

"Let us have a bottle of white wine and almond salad please," Rebecca said to the smiling red-haired waitress when she appeared at their table.

Stacy didn't mind that the bossy woman had ordered for her. She reasoned that she was going to order a salad anyway. Stacy smiled with agreement when the waitress looked to her for her approval.

Rebecca sighed softly as she reached her hand across the table, beckoning for Stacy to meet her touch. "I am so proud of you," she said when Stacy's cool hand landed in her palm; she squeezed the slim fingers tenderly before releasing her. "There was really only one person you needed to convince."

"Really?" This was news to Stacy. She was under the impression that the suits needed to sign off.

"Really. That person was the publisher of the novels that got the author his clout, Karen Mitchell."

"The beautiful Jamaican woman?" Stacy asked in surprise. She'd heard Rebecca greet Karen, but had no idea – though she was impressed by her regal bearing – that she was the publisher.

"I bet you thought she was an accounting higher-up," Rebecca said with a certain mischief. "She didn't want you to direct your presentation to her."

"Good thing, too. I might have stuttered my way through if I had known." Stacy smiled bravely with this, glad that Rebecca shared her humor.

"I doubt that very seriously. You were terrific. I'm considering putting you in charge of that Phat Farm account. They have a new line of fall apparel coming out."

Stacy was beyond words, thankful that the waitress arrived with the bottle of wine and the almond salads.

"But don't worry, Russell will not be in the room and since it's an ongoing account I can give you a few pointers on what they might be looking for," she added after the waitress poured the wine and retreated discreetly after Rebecca assured her that they would be needing nothing more.

"That's incredible, Rebecca. I don't know what to say." Stacy's heart beat wildly with the opportunity that was being handed to her. She met the pale woman's steady, dark gaze as she toasted the raised glass before her.

"You don't have to say anything. Tomorrow we'll go to the Doubletree Inn and show them what you have."

"Tomorrow?"

"Yes, tomorrow. Is there a problem?" Rebecca Deneuve wanted to know, her black eyes blazing with mischievous humor.

Stacy nearly choked on the almond lodged in her throat. "But ... this ..." she stammered.

Rebecca raised her perfectly trimmed eyebrows in question, patiently waiting with amusement, while Stacy gathered herself.

"It's just such short notice," Stacy said with a bit of fear.

Rebecca waived her off. "After what you did today? You could come up with something right now if I needed you to, I bet." Her smile was reassuring.

"Well, I'm glad that you have so much faith in me."

"It has nothing to do with faith. You can do this in your sleep. Don't worry. Before the meeting we'll go over the presentation together. It's connect the dots, I promise."

Stacy tried to hide her nervousness, exhaling slowly as she lifted the stabbed salad to her lips. She was vaguely aware of the undercurrent of sexual tension being emitted by the calculating woman across from her. If it were a man who'd given her this opportunity and promised to go over the details at what amount to be a hotel, she'd be alarmed; but there was something intriguing about what Rebecca – a woman she found seductive – was offering her. Was this the way that promotions were handed out? *Why me?* She wondered as Rebecca prattled on about how this was only the beginning of a very lucrative working relationship between the two of them. She nodded absently when Rebecca complimented her on her professionalism and attention to detail; attributes that made her both very valuable and attractive; this last was said with a glint in her eyes as she winked across the table at Stacy, the crooked, rouged smile one of impending mischief.

***

She like the way the amber light cast a soft glow across the glass and chrome city-scape; the way the descending sunlight reflected off the mirrored high-rise buildings was intoxicatingly powerful and seductive.

Stacy steered the Lexus Coupe along the raised highway, braving a ticket as she sped along in the fast lane. Grump was making it a habit of calling an hour before she could safely leave the office; his complaints were always the same: He was lonely, hungry, and needed his eyes cleaned out. And, as usual, she would leave half an hour earlier than was fashionable, but no one said anything about this since she was the new favorite in the office.

Mary J. Blige sang powerful ballads about claiming a divine reward after a hard struggle, serenading her as she relaxed in the plush leather, her mind catching snatches of her conversation with Rebecca over what turned out to be a two-hour lunch that warranted another bottle of wine and platter of aged cheese. Yes, her husband was doing great, she'd answered when Rebecca inquired about Marlin in training camp. She could only agree when the raven haired boss demanded that she be given tickets for home games, though Stacy had not thought that far ahead. Then there was the surprise mention of how everyone in the office wanted to know why Stacy had not invited Marlin to one of their monthly office parties. This, too, had made Stacy think of how selfish she could be when it came to her career. She'd responded that Marlin hated playing dress-up, but knew this was a lie. She had to admit to herself that she never felt quite secure enough – at work or home – to upset her delicately scaled balance by mixing the two. Marlin had mentioned this to her before and she shrugged it off, not ready to deal with it; but now it was becoming apparent that this was the root of her problem with having any real emotional connection with the man she loved; the root of why she allowed Rebecca to insinuate that they spend time alone tomorrow in a hotel room before a marketing meeting. New feelings were emerging that warranted her attention and clarification; though she was committed to her marriage and silently vowed that she would learn how to suck dick if that's what it took. Oh, and to include him more often in her professional environment, but that could come later.

She didn't know what to make of the jolt of electricity that shot through her body and settled between her legs when she saw Sherrelle leaning into the trunk of Jaguar parked in the driveway. She silently envied Sherrelle's coffee colored beauty. She was the kind of beautiful that epitomized Foxy Brown in the ghetto. Shapely, with long black hair and full features, she seemed to have everything together. Stacy could only be so lucky to be able to shop all day and have a husband who provided everything.

Damn bitch! She hissed to herself. Your shit is tight, too, so quit looking for reasons to feel sorry for yourself, she added as she pulled into the driveway beside Sherrelle, who looked up with a smile and wave as she balanced light blue Tiffany bags along her wrist. The latent jealousy in Stacy was pleased that Marlin had not made it home from practice yet.

'Hi neighbor," Sherrelle called out as Stacy emerged from the Lexus. "You are killing that skirt suit and I love that shirt," she added.

Stacy smiled appreciatively, proud of her bold move to wear the ruffled silk shirt under the lavender suede skirt suit. She jerked her head subtly as she rounded the back of the Lexus so that her diamond earrings could twinkle under her stylish cut that stopped at the bottom of her ears. She was about to compliment Sherrelle on her dress, admiring the way her smooth thighs escaped its uneven hem, when the throttle of dooky-brown Toyota Camry pulled to the curb in front of Sherrelle's house. The noise gathered both of their attention as the car coughed and died at the curb.

"Damn girlfriend," Sherrelle whispered as Peaches meekly emerged from behind the wheel.

The slender, light-skinned woman with the flowing burgundy hair did not match the automobile. Stacy had seen her driving a stylish Chrysler 300C and thought then that it might have been her boyfriend's car and maybe he was a rapper or dope dealer. Peaches had that look about her, though she was beautiful and finely dressed in the best every time she'd seen the jeweled beauty. Watching her wave with feline grace as she planted high heels over the concrete, Stacy thought that she naturally offset Sherrelle's more stable demeanor. Peaches was a little unpredictable in a glamorous way.

"What's up bitch," Peaches said cheerfully as she air kissed Sherrelle. "My baby sick," she pouted as the Prada purse dangled across her arm lightly.

"She more than sick. That heifer's ill," Sherrelle replied with an amused giggle. "I don't know why you just won't buy you a new one." With this, Sherrelle turned to Stacy. "She's tight as frog pussy and that's water proof."

Stacy smiled, marveling at their friendship, wishing that she had a friendship as close as theirs obviously was.

"Hi neighbor friend," Peaches said as if noticing her for the first time. "Tell Marlin that I'll be at all the games," she added with a mischievous glint in her gray eyes.

Being in the presence of these women sparked some long forgotten sense of freedom and sexuality in her. She'd spent so much effort in curbing any natural hood appeal in order to be politically correct and corporate friendly that it was not until now that she was reminded of what she'd sacrificed.

"So how's everything going for your father?" Sherrelle asked, sensing Stacy's fawning discomfort, knowing the question was a good one when her expression brightened with more familiar territory.

"Oh, he's getting used to the change of place," Stacy responded, trying to keep her eyes averted from Sherrelle's luscious cleavage; the diamond heart pendant rest softly between her plump, cinnamon mounds. Stacy figured that she must have left earlier in the day.

"Don't he be lonely there all by hisself," Peaches complained, her eggshell colored forehead wrinkling with the question. "I know I would," she added.

"Well, we have to find someone to look after him..."

"Oooh!" Peaches said wide-eyed, tapping Sherrelle on the arm. "Ain't Ayana coming out here? She can help him out, right?" Then she looked to Stacy before Sherrelle could answer. "How much do something like that pay. I might look in on the old man myself." She grinned with this as her shoulder nudged Sherrelle's for agreement.

Stacy was thinking of a more professional situation and was thankful when Sherrelle mentioned that she was sure Stacy had somebody in mind already.

"Yeah. We're working with an agency. He has special needs," she added with sympathy.

Peaches was interested. Special always was something she was attracted to. "What kind of special needs?" she wanted to know, any hint of being a caregiver gone from her voice. She was simply being nosy now.

"He's blind and generally grumpy," Stacy answered.

A cool breeze swept over the trio of women, blowing Sherrelle's cotton dress up, revealing the soft flesh of her upper thighs. Stacy's heart raced with the quick glimpse, embarrassed by her own attraction.

"Oh, the sun is gone!" Sherrelle said as if she were the only one properly equipped to notice such an occurrence. "Well, don't be a stranger neighbor. Come by sometimes so I can show you my new line of clothes."

Stacy bought a wife-beater and a pair of boy-shorts from her a week earlier, but with her petite frame they didn't have the same dramatic effect as they did on Sherrelle when she'd seen her in a pair at the mailbox. She couldn't bring herself to put them on for Marlin knowing that he'd seen the same pair on a much more shapely frame. "Sure. Maybe this weekend," she answered with half a heart.

"Okay. I got something new that I know you'll like," Sherrelle assured her as she closed the trunk and secured the delicate Tiffany bags in her hands along with the flower print canvas purse that Stacy admired for the large gold Gucci buckle.

"Bye neighbor friend. Tell your father that a beautiful woman said hello," Peaches called as she followed Sherrelle up the driveway.

Grump was sitting in the dark save for the flickering lights of the porno movie dashing across the top of his head; his chin was slumped into his chest. He jerked up suddenly when Stacy closed the front door.

"Sunny?" he said, pointing his sharp nose in her direction.

"Yes. It's me daddy. Why are you in the dark ... And why do you have your pants around your ankles?" she asked, dropping her purse and briefcase to the couch and turning on the lamp beside the leather chair he'd made his permanent area to sleep and recline while watching porno movies.

"Fine stroke of luck you catch me with my pants down," he said with a soft chuckle. He wasn't embarrassed at all. Stacy inhaled deeply at the sight of the thickly veined swipe resting between his bony legs. She looked up to his gray blind eyes. There was a small smirk on his lips.

"Daddy ..." she whispered, not wanting to ask him what he was doing to himself in her leather chair.

"Thas a good one right there," he said, pointing to the screen. "Sit for a spell. Might do you some good," he suggested after she'd successfully pulled his khakis under his butt and snapped them closed around his thin waste.

"I have to make dinner. Aren't you hungry?"

He was tapping at the air beside him, signaling the chair on the other side of the lamp stand. "Might do you good. How was work today?" he wanted to know, forcing her to let out a deep breath of resignment and have a seat.

"Work was good daddy," she replied as she looked to what was happening on the plasma screen: A petite, beige woman was on her knees while a man's thick penis dangled before her. She was looking to where his eyes must have been as he lengthened before her. Stacy's breath caught at the sight of a massive dick as it reached its full length and smacked across the woman's chin. Stacy explained in a hoarse whisper how she'd been tapped for a promotion as the woman kissed the swollen head tenderly before sucking on it softly with both hands cradling the heavy weight of muscle.

"Never any doubt," Grump said quietly as the soft, twirling music of the porno washed over them.

Stacy paid attention to how the woman's tongue occasionally slid across the wide base of meat before her lips caught up. *Wow*, she thought to herself, thinking of what effect this might have on Marlin.

"And tomorrow is a big day. I've been entrusted with the Phat Farm account," she said in a husky voice as the woman slowly swallowed the thick sausage, the side of her jaw sucked in tightly. This was something new to Stacy. She never thought to actually suck hard. She'd thought that simply having the dick in her mouth and sliding it in and out was enough. She didn't know whether to be mad at Marlin for not telling her how to do it right.

"That's that RUN DMC fella that owns that," Grump said.

"RUN who?" The woman was sucking faster now, her lips gripped tightly along the length of dick. The man's hands came into view, running through the woman's short afro in pleasure, guiding her along his legs tightening and moving into her as she continued to swallow him. His meat left her mouth shining and pulsing before it disappeared between her lips again.

"The rap group. He was the brains," Grump said, throwing his hands out in front of him so that Stacy's attention was distracted.

"Oh," she agreed, her eyes shifting back to the action. Filling the screen was the woman's thick, tight lips as they pulled his skin along with each sucking motion. The action had been slowed down so that it was possible to see the concentration on her face and the muscles tensing in his thighs in preparation for a climax. Stacy was vaguely aware of Grump nodding beside her as the woman squeezed tightly over the pulsing meat, cream spilling from the corners of her mouth, as she continued to milk the juices from him.

Damn, that was intense, she thought to herself as the woman popped off his shining dick to lick what dribbled out like a lollipop. She sucked dick as if she thoroughly enjoyed ... NO ... loved it.

"Fine play pigeon beak. Told you it would do you good," Grump whispered, his opaque eyes staring to a spot over her head.

CHAPTER FOUR

The numbers still were not adding up and it was becoming frustrating. There had to be some kind of mistake. Someone was playing a cruel joke on him. Percy pulled together last quarter's numbers in search of the error, but could find none. It had to be some kind of joke, but the way the Chief Financial Officer had casually mentioned the possibility of an indictment, he knew that there was something more serious going on than he was possible of or had the wherewithal to execute. He had the sneaky suspicion that he was being set up to be some sort of fall guy. He could see it now: Being led through a phalanx of photographers up the stone, white federal courthouse steps, by a battery of sharply dressed – sharper than him – attorneys that would bankrupt him whether or not he went to prison.

He needed all the help he could get. Someone with ears in every corner of the accounting firm. He was quickly learning that Vice President of Domestic Partnerships – a title recently conferred on him at the quarterly meeting – was nothing more than what he did before; and that was the accounting for American companies that thought it wise to outsource this possibly criminal activity – even when it was done right. The only plus was that he inherited a perky blonde secretary who thought he was special in every way. She seemed genuinely interested in his frustration and was a loyal warrior in helping him to make sense of the mess he found himself in. It was inevitable that they would come to feel close. And he didn't feel any kind of way that he found himself following her small Honda hybrid to her apartment after a long day of document scanning and shredding.

Carrie had come to be his lifeline to sanity. She made him feel whole again where everywhere else – including home – he was made to feel inadequate. He was nearly ashamed – nearly – to admit that he'd come to enjoy the youthful look in her soft blue eyes and the way she brushed stray strands of blonde hair away from her smooth face. He'd become entranced at the sight of her creamy breasts when on occasion she'd wear a low cut blouse. And she smelled like fresh flowers on a hot summer day whenever she leaned over him to examine a fine point of a document. He needed her in more ways than one. He needed her to feel whole again and as a salve to ease the pain of his burning frustration.

The large apartment complex was fronted by a large cobble stone framed sign that announced the well manicured units as "Heavenly Manor Condominiums." The white-washed, two-story buildings formed a semi-circle around a grass area complete with a lone swing set. He followed her to a pair of parking spaces in front of a wide glass door at the center of the complex.

When Carrie stepped from her car he noticed how the moonlight made her skin glow. She smiled to him as she bounced around the front of her car, taking his hand in hers as if they'd been dating for years.

This was the first time he'd decided to come to her place; this after many invitations. Before now they'd shared countless nights of light flirtations over accounting ledgers and financial statements. It was her confession that she found him to be a very handsome man – and promise to keep whatever developed between them a secret – that melted his weak resolve to follow her home. He'd privately fantasized about what lay at the top of her long, smooth legs and the tenderness of her pert nipples that always seemed to find a way to imprint their shape through any blend of fabric.

"It feels funny being away from the office like this, hunh?" she asked after she keyed the entrance code into the panel beside the glass doors. They opened with a soft hissing sound as if allowing them into private domain reserved for the well deserving.

"Yeah, kinda," Percy responded, noting how his hard soled Ferragamo shoes sunk into the thick hallway carpeting. Her soft giggle was a comfort to him, dispelling any reservations about going further.

"Here we are," she announced once they turned left into an amber lit alcove with a tall wooden door at its center. She let his fingers slip from her palm and opened the gateway to some promise that was communicated by the way she smiled as he passed into her lair.

After she closed the door behind her she pointed to the spacious kitchen to their left, artfully furnished in stainless steel.

"There's wine in the frig. Pour me a glass will ya...? They're in the cubbard above the counter ... I'll be right back. Make yourself comfortable." As she said this she'd slipped her high heels off and padded into the dimly lit living room that smelled of pine, and pressed a button on a small silver component atop a wide screen television which sat under a portrait of a woman who reminded him of the Queen of England. He wanted to ask who the woman was, but Carrie disappeared down a hallway while R. Kelly's voice blasted behind her.

He found it interesting how uncomplicated the homes of white people seemed to be compared with black folk. The décor was finely picked and uncluttered. He found the wine amongst a carton of cottage cheese and a basket of strawberries. He grabbed a Heineken from the door, wondering if her boyfriend – did she have a boyfriend? – had left it. He couldn't remember her talking about anyone special.

The dining room was occupied by a simple glass four-seat table with a bowl of brightly colored marbles as its center piece. R. Kelly sang of how a woman made him fall in love – he hadn't meant for this to happen. The beat began to relax Percy, dissolving his inhibitions as he stepped into the small living room. A snow white bear fur lay helplessly before the couch on the thick beige carpet.

- you made me love you baby / the power of love you see / there's a whole new world for my eyes to see / so much joy darlin / you put in me / and now the sun is shinin where there used to be rain oh lawd / and no more loneliness / no more hurt / no more pain / you made me love you / you made me love you babe / you made me love you babe / you made me love you babe / I was minding my business / you made me love you babe / you made me love you / somebody listen / it's like going to church y'all / it brings peace ... joy ... strength ... -

"You like that don't you?" Carrie asked in a sultry voice, appearing at the edge of the hallway in a bright red teddy. She stood with one foot atop the other, posing against the frame of the archway.

"Yeah. That's nice. Can't go wrong with the master of sex." He didn't mean to say sex, but there was something in the way her eyes searched his face that twisted his tongue. It was all he could do but hold her glass of wine out to her as she strolled seductively to him. She wedged herself between his legs and looked down at him as she sipped slowly.

"You found my beer," she said with mock accusation as she gestured for him to take the glass of wine from her hand. She then grabbed the beer and took a nice swig.

Percy was hypnotized by her near transparent neck as she tilted her head back and swallowed, the small knot in her throat rolling with each gulp. When she brought her head forward he took a sip of wine to tear his eyes from her slender neck. His hand brushed against her warm leg as she moved forward between his knees.

"You need to relax. I think you worry too much," she said, reaching for the knot in his tie that Sherrelle had pulled tightly that very morning. Carrie's hand felt lighter than his wife's. Sharper. Weaker. Her very presence felt as light as a feather.

"It's kind of hard when your neck is at the point of an ax."

She smiled with this. "I've seen this before. They just want to see how you handle the pressure. You didn't do anything wrong did you?" she asked cryptically, forcing his mind to step through the fog of seduction and look at her anew. There was a keen intelligence behind her soft exterior.

"Of course not. You would be the first to know," he scoffed.

"Good," she said, her bubbly tone returning as she loosened the tie and pulled it from his neck. With it deposited to the floor she deftly worked at the buttons on his shirt, exposing the small balls of hair congregated at the center of his chest. Now he wished that he would have listened to Sherrelle's complaints about him not shaving. He'd responded that he was a man's man. With her loud guffaw he was more determined than ever to keep his small outcrop of hair positioned like taco meat in the middle of his undefined chest.

"I like it," Carrie said, rubbing her hands through the rough patch before bending over to lick his fleshy nipples. The effect was something new and exciting. Sherrelle had never licked his nipples, not even when they were first married. A low grumble escaped his throat as she trailed her tongue around the soft mound before sucking on the raised center with a quick jerk. The cool air washed across this sensitive spot when she raised up to admire the sensation she'd caused in him.

"You like that?" she asked, grabbing for the wine glass held delicately out to his side.

"You said you'd seen this before."

"What?" she asked, losing some of her sensual allure as she placed the beer and wine glass on the low table beside the couch.

"This accounting mess. Is this something that happens a lot?" he asked. Percy had been with the firm all of two years and had not heard of this type of situation before.

"A long time ago," she answered evasively with a toss of her blond hair. She situated herself between his legs again and reached for his belt buckle as she explained that the man who'd occupied his position had resigned. "He was a real cheese bag," she added with a scrunched expression.

"Did he do anything wrong?" Percy wanted to know, lifting his butt so that she could pull his pants down over his legs.

"Did your wife buy these for you?" Carrie asked, pulling hard at the band of the paisley print, silk boxers Sherrelle had indeed gotten for him. "They're cute," she added with a snap of the elastic.

Percy didn't know whether to feel aroused or suspicious, but he did want to know why his predecessor resigned. "So what happened to the cheese bag?"

"Mindy in Payroll accused him of sexual harassment." This was said quickly as if to show her impatience with his questions and hoping that he could put the dots together himself; but there was still some gaps in the story that left Percy more confused than ever.

"Payroll," he mumbled absently, trying to remember who Mindy was or if she was still with the firm. These thoughts danced across his mind as Carrie mentioned the nice curve in his 'cute little Richard.' She grabbed him between her fingers like a cigarette and pulled on him slowly. Percy's arousal soon pushed his suspicion out of the way, allowing him to grow between her fingers.

"That's better," she moaned as she kneeled between his legs and took him into her mouth. Her hair fell along his inner thighs and brushed against his skin with tender strokes. Her mouth was soft and her touch gentle. Somewhere along the way she'd wet her finger tip and reached under him to poke at his ass hole. A thrilling sensation shot through him, making him rise on the couch. Carrie giggled over his lap, the dick still in her mouth and her finger probing the soft lining of his butt hole. She pressed just inside the rim and made a short burst of cream squirt from his dick.

"Oooooww!" Percy whooped in surprise, his body feeling tingly all over. Carrie continued to suck. He was surprised that he had not deflated.

"Tonight is your night," she said as she raised from him and turned around. Percy could not believe his luck. Carrie raised the silk teddy, exposing a small, creamy ass. She spread her cheeks and backed onto him, her ass hole lubed warmly with KY. She slid onto him slowly as he gripped her waist with trembling fingers. His body was on fire as she squeezed him inside of her hotness.

Percy grit his teeth as the tight hole worked along his joint. In the dim light, R. Kelly singing of being a perfect groom, he was mesmerized by her glowing ass as it swayed sensuously in small circles onto his lap. Her soft moaning and tossing of her golden mane added to the pleasure. Through a passionate haze her tossing hair became a blur of gold and her groans became proof of his manhood.

***

The time spent with Carrie had succeeded in accomplishing nothing of what he hoped. She'd deflected any further mentioning of anything related to the office. She assured him that everything would work out and he should not worry. This last was said as she shoved him into the shower of cold water and wouldn't let him turn the hot water on. She'd knelt before him, his balls retreating from the cold and taken him again into her mouth. This had been an odd sensation, one he began to enjoy once her mouth warmed him from the middle outward.

And there was the added feeling that he'd made his situation only worse. She'd seduced him in a way that subtly revealed her dominance. He'd never been with a white girl and had to admit to himself that the experience was enough to make him want more. She'd made him feel briskly alive, flirting with danger; it was a danger that was centuries old, distilled into his bloodline by assassinations and lynchings. Even more dangerous than this was the real life possibility that Sherrelle would find out. How? He couldn't say, but she had a way of seeing things that weren't present; like the time he'd gotten a raise at work; she knew about this before he walked in the door. Later, when he found the courage to admit that she was right and ask how she'd known, she responded that it was in the way he walked from his car.

Percy reminded himself to walk as he'd always walked when he turned the motor off. Marlin's Escalade was parked at the curb next door. Percy smiled to himself when he tried to mimic Marlin's graceful stride and upon seeing this Sherrelle had reminded him to be himself. It was amazing how she saw through him at every angle.

Percy knew that Sherrelle was in a good mood when he stepped through the front door. Though he enjoyed her new sense of joy, he tried mightily not to feel threatened by her new business enterprise. Empty boxes were stacked in front of the fireplace. An assortment of brightly colored clothing was folded and sorted neatly on the couch, coffee table and floor. He'd thought that this was a not-so-serious thing and had blown it off as a fad, but there was no denying her drive. There were enough sexy clothes in his living room to fill a specialty section at the GAP.

He inhaled deeply, the scent of strawberry wafting through the house.

He recognized this as the bubble bath she would no doubt be soaking in. The soft voice of Diana Krall sang over a smooth jazz horn, pulling him through the dim living room and towards their bedroom.

"Hey baby," he called towards the parted bathroom door, dropping his suit jacket onto the foot of the bed. He loosened his tie in an effort to appear fatigued from a long day of work.

Sherrelle did not answer.

He crept slowly towards the bathroom door and peeked to the large Jacuzzi tub, its scented bubbles boiling over her shining, chocolate skin. Her eyes were closed and her breasts swayed gently back and forth, dipping into the frothy water; they shined in a way that made Percy blink and take a hard swallow. Seeing her this way was worth the price of admission. Her lips were pursed in thought, the pink tongue reaching out to lick along the pulpy ridge of her bottom lip.

He stepped from his hard soled shoes and eased silently on nylon coated feet into the bathroom. Candles lined the back shelf along the large tub, their lights flickering across her body and stabbing at the ceiling with hot licks. He watched her, careful not to take too many steps. Her shiny neck arched slightly under the pulsing flames as her lips pressed softly together. Her vibrant body swayed subtly with her knees spread over the roof of bubbles. Her tender arms disappeared into the valley between her legs. Her breasts were pressed together like tight mounds of dark caramel. Her arms flexed with her self pleasuring.

There was a break in the music, the jazz horn dying slowly. Percy felt vulnerable, not knowing whether to announce himself or take two steps backwards out the door. His heart raced with indecision and the memory of his adultery. Now he was presented with a wife who was masturbating, igniting his passion and jealousy. *What ... Who was she thinking about?* he asked himself.

Sherrelle gasped, her soft moan muffled by the bubbling bath water. She opened her cloudy eyes slowly and turned to Percy. She observed him without comment, her face glowing and flush with completion.

"Hi," he choked out, his mouth dry. He was suddenly aware of his stooped shoulders and the looseness of his stomach under her cool gaze.

"Hi yourself," she replied in a low voice, bringing her hands to her stomach so that the white peaked bubbles moved around like icebergs.

Even in the dimness of the flickering candle light Percy felt as if he were under a powerful helicopter light. He scooted to the toilet and sat down, Sherrelle's lowered gaze on him steadily.

"Busy day at the office?" she asked, and he was thankful for this. He wouldn't have been surprised if she'd asked if Carrie's finger felt good in his ass or if he enjoyed the way she licked from his balls to his ass, his legs spread like rabbit ears after the cold shower.

"Yeah," he breathed out demonstratively. "They're making it hard for a black man." He didn't know what to make of the slow smile that turned one side of her lips up, pointing to the dimple in her cheek.

"Really? ... Is it hard, baby" She sloshed the water again, bringing the frothy bubbles back to life as she moved them over her breasts.

"Yes." And it was true. The sight of her shiny brown skin did something to him. He wanted to please her in an effort to erase his indiscretion.

"Ain't nothing worth having easy," she said in finality, having decided something that he had no clue about, while standing from the water. Her shapely body glistened as water dripped from her full breasts and the fine hairs on her pussy. She was pointing to the pink cotton HoodSweet bath robe tossed onto the wicker chair by the door.

"Oh," he gasped when he realized what she wanted. He had to tear his eyes from her beautiful body, his dick making a small tent in his pants as he stood to retrieve the covering.

She was smiling when he turned back to her. "You should really try to make it home earlier. I could have made dinner for you. Are you hungry?" she wanted to know.

He was, but not for food. He sat on the toilet as she stepped from the bathtub. "You are so beautiful," he whispered, reaching for her hip and guiding her to him. He reached his hands into the robe and palmed her smooth ass, bringing her closer to him so that he could bury his face in the dampness of her pussy. He inhaled deeply. Her hands rest lightly on his head as he breathed into her, massaging his scalp. She was thick and warm in his grasp.

"Is this what you want, baby?" she whispered, caressing his ears as she spread her legs for him.

Percy answered by jabbing his tongue into her sweet pussy, the hairs tickling his nose, and tasting her nectar. She gripped his shoulders for balance as he sucked away the bath water and replaced it with his own moisture.

"I love you," he murmured into her muff, feeling the warmth of her soft thighs pressed against his cheeks. And it was true. He knew that his lovemaking was lacking, but if there was one thing he could do, he could suck her pussy. He could make her moan softly and shudder in his grip with his tongue lapping at her clean, hot flesh. He wrapped the swollen knob between his lips and sucked on it tenderly until she creamed onto his tongue. He loved her this much.

CHAPTER FIVE

She wanted so much to show Marlin what she'd learned from the porno movie the night before. She thought she was doing a good job, but soon after she'd started he was fast asleep. It was all her fault, she'd reasoned. She should have followed her first mind and braved his sweaty balls when he first stepped in the door; but no, she'd waited until he showered and eaten; and after this was a long talk with her father about sports. She'd waited patiently, becoming frustrated that he'd ignored her hints of how horny she was and what she wanted to show him before he came to bed. Admittedly, it was late and he'd had a hard day of practice, but still she thought her new skills at sucking dick would have kept him awake.

It was a new day now and morning sex was the best sex after all. She didn't waste time watching Marlin sleep. She slipped her hand beneath the comforter and grabbed ahold of his thick meat.

He really must have been tired, she thought to herself as her fingers stroked him softly and the morning sunlight crawled over his rippled stomach. She still had not told him about the great day she'd had at work for fear that she would reveal that hidden desire Rebecca planted deep within her. What she did say was that today she had an opportunity to pitch to Phat Farm for an advertising campaign for their new fall collection. He had a mouth full of hamburger when she'd said this and simply nodded, his jowls fat and hungry. The magnitude of what this meant was lost on him, so she thought.

She leaned over his muscular body and slipped the soft head between her tight lips. She sucked hard one good time, feeling the pressure of her jaws tightening. His skin was loose over the stiff meat as she pulled her lips tightly over the stiffening joint. He stirred under her heavy suction.

"Ey," Marlin grumbled awake, rising slightly to look down the length of his body. Stacy hungrily attacked him, diving down to the base as he stiffened inside of her mouth. She wanted to prove that she could do it right; and by his reaction she knew she had at least gathered his attention. He reached over to caress her curved back, rubbing along the satin material of her nightgown.

"Mmmm," he moaned, leaning up to watch. His eyes moved to the window and there she was. Sherrelle. Her concentration was focused on Stacy's attention to his shining manhood. He grinned knowingly, his dick pulsating inside Stacy's mouth at the sight of his beautiful neighbor.

"What the ..." Stacy gasped, having looked up from her performance and seeing Sherrelle dart from view. A sharp squeal of pain shot through the window behind her.

"What's wrong?" Marlin asked innocently, feeling ever more aroused.

Stacy looked from the window back to him.

"Did you see that?"

"Naw. What?"

"I think Sherrelle was outside our window," she said in astonishment, her mind rewinding to what her neighbor must have seen.

"For real?" Marlin asked, soothing his wife's consternation in the hopes she would finish what she started.

"Yes. For real. You didn't see her? She was looking right in here at us." There was a flash of heat shooting through her body.

"She was just probably emptying the trash, baby. Don't worry about it." His suggestion fell on deaf ears. Stacy pulled away from his touch and stomped towards the window. She looked across the small fence separating their property. On Sherrelle's side was a lush row of rose bushes that bloomed brightly under the morning sun.

"SUNNY!" Grump yelled out. Marlin threw his hands up and lay back down. He knew it was all over. Stacy pulled the curtains together and stood to face Marlin.

"You didn't see that?" she asked, dumbfounded.

Marlin feigned sleep, turning his closed eyes away from her. He didn't bother to pull the comforter above his waist. His limp meat hung to one side across his muscular thigh.

"SUNNY! Gosh DARNIT! My eyes hurt!" her father called out to her.

Stacy began to question what she saw. Maybe her neighbor was just walking along the side of her house and ... Or maybe she was pruning her roses. How did she get to the side of the house when the trash can was in the back yard? Was it trash pick-up day? It was Tuesday.

"Marlin. It's trash pick-up day!" she announced, now believing that Sherrelle must have been pulling her trash can to the front of the yard.

"I'll get it," he mumbled without opening his eyes or turning his head.

"Surely this must be a matter of no concern! SUNNY!" Grump called out again.

Stacy grabbed her robe and moved towards the door before her father yelled out again. She did not see Marlin's dick rising again. She could not know that Sherrelle's visit had aroused him more than any mouth trick she could perform on him.

Grump was seated in the leather chair, his blind eyes in the direction of the plasma screen where a woman was taking it in her ass. Her face was screwed up in painful passion.

When Stacy stepped within arms length he reached out and grabbed her roughly, halting her inquiry as to how he was feeling this morning. "My eyes!" he hissed, turning to her then to show the gray orbs shining with a filmy mucus that pooled at the rims of his bottom lashes.

"Oh daddy!" she cried out both from the pressure of his grip and the sight of his ghastly eyes. She'd initially thought to suggest that he take a bath to wash the sour smell from his body.

"Any chance you can ease my suffering?" he asked, shoving her violently away from him. Stacy stumbled backwards in fright. So much had changed about her father since she'd last seen him. She was a little frightened at the transformation.

She hurriedly retrieved the saline solution from the bathroom cabinet and returned to find him staring towards the screen. She wanted to ask if he could actually see the three men filling the woman's every opening, but he would have recognized her meanness. "Okay daddy," she said instead, her voice pliant and obedient. He looked to the ceiling and prepared his eyes for the swabbing.

"That feel mighty good Sunny," he said beneath her arms, his forehead raised to the ceiling.

"Want me to give you a bath before I go to work?"

"Some things a man has to do for himself, pumpkin. You go on and tackle them white folk like that good education taught you." Here was a remnant of the father who'd always told her she could accomplish anything she set her mind to. Her touch was gentle over his eyelids, appreciative of his unpredictable nature taking a turn for nurture.

"Feel better?" she asked, making one last wipe across his face with a damp towel. He smiled his toothless grin.

"Yeah. That'll do fine." He shot his arm towards the screen. "That do you any good?" He chuckled wickedly with this question. On the screen the woman was now being pummeled in her ass hole as she stuffed two dicks into her mouth. Her jaws looked as if they held large jaw-breaker candy in each cheek. Her lips were stretched wide and tight.

"I don't think so daddy," she answered with a sad shake of her head. "That's nasty. How do you know what's going on?"

"I can feel it," he answered cryptically, his body quivering as if he were in a blizzard. "Now go get them white folk. They don't like niggers to be late." His expression turned somber as he returned his concentration to the screen.

"You don't want any breakfast?"

"I got it," Marlin announced as he crossed into the living room wearing a snug pair of Colts training shorts. Stacy turned to him suddenly, wanting now more than ever to take him back into the bedroom and make love to him. This was her way of keeping him close. She tried not to privately hope that he would hurt himself and need her again. She'd like the closeness they shared when he wasn't occupied with his career.

"Yo Grump, what you feel like this morning?" Marlin asked, stopping next to Stacy and throwing his heavy arm across her shoulder. Stacy accepted the short peck on the forehead, wondering what had made him so chipper. There was still the nagging suspicion in the back of her mind that they were being spied on. Marlin had shrugged her concerns off as if they did not matter.

"Pancakes," Grump announced.

"Sound simple enough," Marlin said, looking to his wife's upturned eyes. She was observing him with private thoughts.

"It's trash day, " she said in a low voice, the tenor not so much a reminder to set the trash out, but a question to the reasoning he'd so readily agreed to as why Sherrelle was at their window.

"Got it," Marlin assured her as he spun towards the kitchen. It wasn't until he'd lifted his arm that she realized how good it felt across her shoulder.

"Well, I better get ready for work," she sighed, her body registering with a short thrill something she was looking forward to. As she walked through the room and disrobed for the shower the feeling became more intense, heat pooling at the center of her body.

Today is the day, she remembered. Not only is it the beginning of a fabulous opportunity, but the forbidden fruit Rebecca spoke of would be offered today. She was excited and angry; excited at the unknown and angry that something she knew was being lost to her despite her best efforts.

***

His sleep was interrupted throughout the night by a mix of erotic dreams and nightmares. They merged together on occasion, playing tricks on his mind, but more often they either pleasured or tormented him as soon as his body allowed sleep to possess him again. There was a common theme throughout the night. Sex with white women. The dreams would begin innocently enough. There would be a banquet-style dinner by candle light and the blonde, blue-eyed woman would enter from a far door like an angel on roller skates. She would smile lovingly and invite him to dine with her. On the table would be roast duck, golden turkey, and sliced ham. On the walls were lined portraits of white men in curly wigs who sat upon high-backed chairs; they looked upon the scene with slight grins.

Other times this same scene would play out, only with a different ending. Instead of the passionate sex that followed a sumptuous meal, the white woman would glow increasingly more aggressive. She would grow small horns at the top of her forehead and her eyes would glow red. Her teeth grew sharp and if she was sucking his dick she would nibble on him softly, the pain increasing until he was forced awake, or the golden turkey and the roast duck would come alive to the delight of his dinner companion. The birds would attack him mercilessly until he dripped blood onto the white linen spread on the table. The white woman would howl with laughter, her piercing screams forcing him under the table where he cowered from her taunts. She pounded on the table, calling to him sweetly to return to dinner, promising that the fowl would behave.

Percy snatched sleep between bouts of this madness; so that when he woke up he was mildly surprised that he'd overslept. Sherrelle was not beside him. He vaguely remembered her slapping him across his shoulder when he'd lashed out in sleep. He couldn't be sure if he'd hit her or not, but was sure of her anger and the kick of her foot. She may have said something about sleeping in the spare bedroom, but he couldn't be sure.

A sharp pain shot through his temples as he swung his legs from the bed and planted his feet on the hardwood floor, warming from the sunlight that streamed in through the open curtain. He rubbed his hands over his face while trying to wake up properly and make sense of his strange night of dreams. He listened for movement in the house, but all was quiet. *Where is Sherrelle?* he wondered as he lifted himself groggily from the bed.

"Sherrelle?" he called out, with a new pain in his side as he turned into the hallway. He rubbed his thigh at the spot where she must have kicked him. Then why did his knee hurt, too?

The spare bedroom was bathed in bright light. The powder blue Tiffany bags lined on the flower print ottoman at the foot of the canopied bed caught his attention. Last week he'd addressed the many Nordstrom's and Macy's bags lining the floor in front of the closet, his argument being that she was spending money for no reason other than to empty his bank account. She'd responded then that she'd spent mostly her own money, which turned out to be $250 for a pair of shoes; a fraction of the $3,800 he tallied by the receipts. Now here were more purchases as evidenced by the dates on the receipts in the small designer Tiffany bags. Silk scarves. Platinum Tiffany bracelet. Diamond and gold bracelet. Platinum toe ring. Crystal finger bowls. *What the hell?*, he thought to himself, suddenly angry. There were over $8,000 in charges here.

"Sherrelle!" he called out more forcefully this time as he turned from the bedroom. A sharp pain stabbed at the center of his eyes, making him stop at the entrance to the living room. The clothes that were stacked on the couch had disappeared. He wondered where they'd gone. Had she sold them already? She was doing better than he thought in this small clothing business. He didn't know how to feel about this. He was too preoccupied with the torment of his dreams and the scandal that was plaguing him at work. *Whether asleep or awake there is no escaping the hell,* he thought to himself as he stepped through the dining room, headed for the kitchen.

He was just inside the kitchen when he heard Sherrelle's yelp. She was just outside the kitchen window. He leaned over the sink and caught a glimpse of her as she ran past. He looked towards the back door and waited for her to burst through with panting breath.

"Owww!" she hissed, stumbling through the service porch and standing before him as if he were not looking to her with wide, curious eyes.

Percy was deciding whether he should renew his criticism for the way she was dressed, complain about her new Tiffany purchases, or ask what she was doing outside in the first place.

"I cut myself on the rose bush!" Sherrelle complained as she ran water over her hand. She was aware of Percy's stare, wondering if he could guess at the way her body felt. She was sure that her pussy bulged against the material of her boy-shorts. She was sure that her nipples were inflamed, pressing hard against her halter top. Sure that her bare, flat stomach was hot to the touch. She had to stop peering through her neighbor's window. Now she'd come close to being caught by his wife.

Percy was shaking his head as she rubbed at the bloody cut with wet fingers. "You're going to infect it," he said finally as she lifted her ankle to the sink to get a better look. The sunlight streamed over her shapely leg as the water coursed over it in small rivulets.

"It's a small cut," she whispered, rubbing her leg gently.

"If you put on some pants you wouldn't have to worry about that."

"If you get up and take the trash out I wouldn't have to do it myself," she replied quickly, dropping her leg hard to the floor. She stood facing him, the image of Stacy's lips sliding over Marlin's dick still in her mind.

Percy rubbed his temples as his eyes shut tight. "Baby, how much shopping did you do yesterday?" he asked, his eyes popping open with a frown. She crossed her arms and leaned her hip against the sink.

"Am I on a budget now?" she asked with a hint of venom as if daring him to say it was so.

"Eighty-five hundred dollars, Sherrelle?"

"How you know I spent your money? I got my own money," she announced.

"Then why didn't you spend it? I saw the receipts. Do I have to take my credit cards back?" As soon as he said this he wished he hadn't. Sherrelle stormed past him, knocking her shoulder against him roughly.

"I don't give a fuck about your money! I was getting some stuff for Ayana if you have ... " Her voiced trailed off as she stepped quickly from the living room and disappeared into the hallway. Percy stared out of the window thinking that he didn't need this right now, yet he had to answer her anger.

"So now you don't GIVE A FUCK?! You're so busy hanging out at the strip club with Peaches you're starting to sound like ... He'd turned towards their bedroom and realized she'd gone into the spare room.

"Take your fucking money! Now you don't have that to control me with!" she screamed, emerging from the opposite end of the hallway, her fingers thrusting forward. The green, white, and blue credit cards sailed through the air like small frisbees. She turned around just as quickly and slammed the door behind her.

"What ..." Percy whispered, his eyes following the trajectory of his

American Express card. It landed at his feet. He wanted to argue that Ayana wasn't worth eight-five hundred dollars worth of merchandise, at least not using HIS money.

"Baby," he whispered, opening the bedroom door slowly after seeing her folded in a fetal position on the bed. He went to her and sat down. When he reached out to touch her bare back she inched forward away from his touch.

"Get away from me and take your money with you," she huffed out.

"Don't be like that, Sherrelle. I didn't mean it like that. But I just don't think that you should spend so much money at this time. It's a really difficult time right now at work." His voice was soft and pleading.

There was no answer from her.

"And please don't think that I don't support what you're trying to do with your business. I support you in that. Do whatever it is ..."

She sat up suddenly and turned to him with red-stained eyes. A shallow stabbing piercing his stomach to see her cry. "You don't act like it," she whispered, allowing him to reach out and brush a thick black curl from over her eye.

"I'm sorry, baby. I'm just under a lot of pressure at work right now."

"You're always under pressure at work and you always take it out on me." Her eyes were big and her mouth was in a puffy pout. She was the little girl that needed him to take care of her. All of his resolve to be angry with her evaporated like dew under a burning sun.

"I apologize. Forgive me?"

She smiled a little, giving him a small reward for his compliance. "I'll think about it."

He shrugged his shoulders, glad that she didn't retreat when he leaned forward to kiss her on the thick curls swirling over her forehead. Her eyes were partly obscured by soft tendrils of hair, giving her an exotic appeal.

"And you're right. I'll give her a little at a time and see how she acts."

"Isn't she supposed to be working for you?" he asked, feeling they were on their way back to normalcy. He hated confrontation.

"Yeah. I just wanted her to look good doing it. Maybe I should have discussed it with you first."

"Well, that would help. When is she coming?"

"Tonight." Sherrelle replied, enjoying the look of surprise on his face. She'd successfully thrown him away and pulled him back. She was in control once again. "Is that okay?" she asked.

Percy nodded his head quickly as if he'd been caught in a private thought. "Yeah. That's fine." He tapped her on the ass before standing from the bed awkwardly.

"What's wrong with your leg?" she asked.

He massaged his hip. "I don't know. You kicked me last night." He hobbled to the door in pain.

"You were tossing and turning all night. Am I going to have to sleep with Ayana from now on?" The expression on his face made her smile.

"I'm following you wherever you go," he replied mischievously.

"Ohhh," she began, bringing her fingers to her lips. "I didn't know you had that in you. Can you handle that?"

There was not a reply that could be a good one in this instance. He simply shook his head, not wanting to jump into the sticky web she'd spun for him after narrowly escaping her wrath. He felt a small success at having been able to depart with his secret rendezvous with Carrie being unknown.

"Good boy," she called after him. She could not see him smile wickedly as he walked through the hallway. *Yeah. Good boy,* he thought to himself, with a fresh hunger for white pussy coursing through him. He didn't want to be good. He wanted to be bad. He wanted that feeling of recklessness Carrie had introduced him to. He wanted to know what it was she promised to do to him with a hot whisper into his ear.

CHAPTER SIX

It wasn't often that she'd meet Percy at the same time when leaving home. He must have been running late because his BMW would always be gone when she stepped onto her porch. She'd never really paid much attention to him. She knew that he was successful and that his wife didn't have to work, but beyond that she knew nothing about him.

But seeing him this morning, with Sherrelle's spying still on her mind, she looked closely at the slight, sharply dressed man. She'd slowed up to observe him step from his porch. He looked to be preoccupied. She was struck by how similar they were in dress and mannerism. She suspected that he was also tortured by having to subdue his natural blackness in order to succeed in corporate America. Yet here they were side by side, next to their foreign luxury cars, dressed in foreign name-brand clothes, going to work in companies that did global business. She wondered if he was satisfying his wife sexually; this would explain her voyeurism.

They exchanged pleasantries, each saying hello and assuring the other that the day promised to be a good one. He seemed surprised when she mentioned Ayana's pending arrival, confessing that it was only the day before that she'd called since the wedding. This gave Stacy the impetus to ask – because she didn't know – how long he and Sherrelle had been married. "Seven years." "Wow, that's great," she'd responded, adding that she and Marlin were going on six years. Big smiles were exchanged before Percy politely bid her to be well.

To be well. That is an odd way of saying have a nice day, she thought to herself. For the way he didn't compliment her in the way that any responsible man would, she thought that maybe she'd picked out the wrong suit.

Nonsense. Marlin said it was fine. Looked good on her in fact, he'd added when she paused for more. This only added to her opinion that something was on Percy's mind. Even when mentioning Ayana, he seemed to be absent from the conversation. He didn't seem to notice that their trash can hadn't been rolled out to the curb.

The closer she got to the Doubletree Inn the more intense became her anticipation, and the less she thought of her neighbors. She could not be concerned with them. Not now. Not when the thrill of success and rebellion beckoned.

The parking lot shined under a bright morning sun, its gleam bouncing from the chrome and fresh paint of luxury cars. Stacy recognized the 911 Porsche coached by Rebecca and pulled in beside her near the edge of the Doubletree Inn. She checked her scarce make-up (eyeliner to highlight the light brown of her eyes) and cherry-scented lip gloss before exiting the Lexus Coupe with her leather briefcase. She inhaled deeply, saying a silent prayer to herself *(Lord please make me good)* before stepping under the veranda that spanned the entrance.

***

There was a lot on Percy's mind. He was married to a woman who seemed to be oblivious to the fact that he didn't earn as much money a day as she spent. Added to that was the growing mystery of her newly discovered fascination with masturbation. He'd showered and dressed before calling to Sherrelle that he was about to leave. When she didn't answer he figured she'd fallen asleep or returned to her anger for him. Either way he was late for work and couldn't be bothered. He was just outside the front door when he remembered his briefcase. He'd turned back, and when he stepped into the hallway he heard a soft moan. When he looked towards the spare bedroom he could see Sherrelle's legs parted at the end of the bed. He crept slowly down the hallway, his heart beating fast and his manhood challenged. He got close enough to see – without her seeing him – the large dildo she glided in and out of her pussy. Anger gripped him because he had the feeling this sex had nothing to do with thoughts of him. He turned from the scene in disgust.

With everything else going on at work, the nightmares that plagued his sleep, and his most recent sexual indiscretion, he didn't think he would be able to function if his wife wasn't happy. He knew he was out of his league, but felt that if he at least kept her happy then that would be enough. Maybe there was something else besides the sex that he was not able to provide.

And the business with this clothing company really began to wear on his patience. She was spending more time with Peaches at the strip club than she did at home. He couldn't remember a time when they'd eaten together at the dining room table. But this wasn't entirely her fault, he reasoned. He'd been getting in late every night for the past two weeks.

He didn't notice that the trash wasn't at the curb until he turned away from the house. *What was she doing outside then?*, he'd asked himself in confusion. And now her niece was coming to live with them. Maybe it would be fun having someone else around.

He'd arrived to the office late, a cheery Carrie welcoming him at her desk just outside his office door. There was the secret of their lovemaking in her eyes as she handed him his messages.

He was frustrated more than ever. The numbers still weren't adding up. He felt as if he were waiting for a mighty hammer to fall on his head. There was nothing he could do to stop its fall and the inevitable splitting of his skull. There was a new financial report before him that he'd hoped would shed light on where a missing $1,000,000 disappeared to. This was only the latest in a series of missing million dollar sums. When he'd voiced his concerns earlier, he was assured that the accounts would balance out in the next statement. They had not. And now he was being blamed for the oversight. His eyes hurt and the rows of numbers began to blur together.

His desk phone beeped. "Mr. Santiago. Mr. Maxwell is here to see you." Carrie announced. *Great,* Percy thought to himself. This couldn't be good.

"Send ..."

"Percy!" Mr. Maxwell said as he entered the office before Percy could finish his sentence. Percy wondered if the sunlight streaming in through the window behind him had this same effect on him as it did on Vernon Maxwell. His mocha-colored skin seemed to drink in the sun. His smile was bright and wide.

"Hello Vernon. How's it going?" Percy asked, watching as the tall, broad-shouldered man walked past him and stood at the large picture window overlooking the city below. He was one of three blacks working in the firm, though he was considered to be untouchable. With an Ivy League education, proper speech, and a beautiful blonde for a wife, he had completely crossed over. Now he turned to Percy, his eyes narrowed for inspection. He had a plain slope of a forehead that was accentuated by the way he smoothed his short wavy hair back. His graying temples gave him a distinguished air. Percy wondered what he wanted with him. Though he was a Vice President, he wasn't directly connected to the Accounting Department.

"How are you taking it?" he asked. Percy didn't want to answer too quickly. The wily man could have been talking about anything. It was widely rumored that he prospered because he was willing to do to other black men in the company what the white men didn't want to risk a lawsuit over; namely firing and demotions. Vernon Maxwell was on the Executive Board.

"I'm good," Percy answered, hating the way he had to swivel in his seat to face the man. He felt vulnerable now that he was turned away from his desk. Vernon was nodding, his thin lips pursed tight as he looked around the office.

"How long has it been?" he asked.

"How long has what been?"

"Your employment here ..."

"Just a little over twenty-four months. Why ... What is this about, Vernon?" Percy asked, needing him to get right to the point.

"Well," Vernon began as he leaned against a tall bookshelf so that Percy had to follow him with his eyes. "Apparently there's been more ..." He paused here, looking out the window at a passing airplane. "Discrepancies in the financial records. We've been notified that an independent federal auditor will need your records."

WE? Percy asked himself. *Who is WE?* "I only did what Geraldo instructed me to do," Percy said, aware of the whine in his voice. He was angry. Vernon lifted his palm to him.

"Hold up ... Don't get bent out of shape. No one is saying that this is your fault."

"No one is SAYING it?" Percy nearly shouted in return. If he weren't gripping the armrests of his chair so tightly he would have shot to his feet. He wasn't sure what he would have done next so he was glad of it.

Vernon was unaffected. He'd no doubt been the agent of change and bad news many times before. "No. Our first priority is to find out where the money went. Then we need to find out who's responsible for putting it there."

It all sounded simple enough to Percy. He knew he didn't have the money nor was he responsible for where it might be. He was just using the accounting system left to him. He didn't trust his tongue to speak. His eyes followed Vernon as he stepped towards the door with graceful, slow strides as if he were in thought.

"Is next Monday too soon?" he asked when he reached the door, his hand on the chrome lever.

"For?" Percy asked in confusion. He was genuinely lost as to what his role in this was.

"The accounting ledgers."

"I can give you those right now," he announced.

Vernon smiled mischievously. "No, that's okay. Not now. Deliver them Monday. I'm sure everything will be okay." With this he stepped through the door. With the door ajar, Percy watched him stop at Carrie's desk. Her soft giggle wafted back to him at something Vernon said. Then he leaned out of view, his hands shoved into his pockets. There was another giggle. Then he was standing again. He looked back to Percy and winked with the same broad, bright smile.

Percy didn't realize how shallow his breathing was until Vernon was out of sight. His office felt suddenly very cold. He shivered. The desk phone beeped.

"Mr. Santiago," Carrie said.

"Yes."

"Are you okay?"

"It just got cold in here."

"Maybe I can help," she replied excitedly.

It was a strange feeling seeing her now that they'd been intimate with each other. There was a private knowledge they shared. She was more attractive to him now. Her stride was more self assured as she closed the door behind her and glided quickly around his desk. She kneeled between his legs and unzipped his pants.

"I want you so bad!" she hissed, deftly reaching in for his joint and pulling it between the zipper.

She was so quick and determined all he could do was grip the armrests for the ride. Her hair was pinned up in a tight bun so that he could see clearly the way her small lips wrapped around him and sucked him to hardness. The phone rang as she slurped him hungrily and was transferred to voicemail. Percy briefly thought that the call might be Vernon Maxwell or someone else no less meaningful. Maybe they would wonder why voicemail was picking up and take a stroll to see what was going on. But they would be too late. The way Carrie was bobbing and twisting on his dick she would be back at her desk with that same innocent smile when they approached with an inquiring gaze. The mere thought of this excited Percy and it was no more than four or five good sucks from her tight mouth before he spasmed between her jaws.

He was still recovering from the assault when Carrie stopped at the door, after replacing his spent organ, to say that she had a special treat for him after work.

CHAPTER SEVEN

All of Stacy's concerns were forgotten. Only the thrill of a successful conference remained. Rebecca had been right and very helpful in putting together a fashionable presentation that represented the Phat Farm lifestyle. She had no idea that she would have the use of a graphic designer to help translate her ideas to the screen. This was Rebecca's surprise. Not only this, but that they would not be alone in the suite (which Stacy foolishly assumed) before the conference.

Throughout the demonstration she felt Rebecca's energy reaching to the front of the room, urging her on with confidence. She was angry with herself for giving too much attention to the possibility that she would disappoint her mentor. She reminded herself that she should have more confidence in herself.

Afterwards she graciously accepted cheers and thanks from everyone involved. Rebecca was at her side, filling in the blanks and giving her all of the credit. She found herself sipping champagne and eating shrimp casually during what turned out to be a festive affair. Rebecca solidified the account and tied the loose ends with Stacy as an observant appendage. She would know more the next time, or as she'd heard Dahji tell her husband, "You know better you do better."

It felt like the end of a long and very exciting day when Stacy returned to the suite; yet it was barely after three in the afternoon. She couldn't believe that the day was almost over. She wished all of her workdays could be a fashion conference. She could get used to this.

"That was absolutely INCREDIBLE!" Rebecca cheered, closing the door behind her and bounding into the room with a bottle of Moet in her hand.

"Yes. That was ..." Stacy was saying until Rebecca stepped close and placed her hot lips to her open mouth. She was startled by the sudden intimacy, though she had to be aware that it was coming. Her arms were stricken, shooting downwards as Rebecca loosened her lips and sought out her tongue.

Like melting ice Stacy wilted under her soft touch, feeling Rebecca's warm fingers trail up the center of her back. She found herself reaching for the spaghetti strap on Rebecca's shoulder. She lowered it slowly, revealing the creamy, pert breast underneath. She cupped it warmly as Rebecca moaned with champagne breath and bubbly tongue in her mouth. The effect was intoxicating itself without help from the buzz of spirits and accomplishment she was already feeling.

Rebecca let her lips slide away. "You were fantastic," she whispered with Stacy held close. They looked deeply into each other's eyes with a silent attraction.

"Thank you," Stacy responded and leaned in for another sensuous kiss. Soft tongue. Sweet breath. Tender skin. The feeling felt like completion. Something she'd been missing all along. She moaned under Rebecca's touch.

Then they were apart, silently observing one another as each disrobed the other with slow pulls of linen and cotton fabric. There were soft caresses over each other's body as if mapping the journey their mouths would take. They shared equal parts economy-size breasts and petite frame.

Rebecca lowered her head to take one of Stacy's nipples into her mouth. Tenderly she licked around the raised bulb while her finger found the opening between her legs. Stacy returned the favor, enjoying the feel of Rebecca's shaved skin.

The bottle of Moet was thrown to the bed. Rebecca used her now-free fingers to run through Stacy's hair. They were held together tightly like Legos as they fell over to the bed.

Rebecca opened the Moet and poured some over Stacy, the bubbly coursing and fizzing over her breasts and pooling in the hollow of her stomach.

"You are fantastic," Rebecca whispered, leaning on one elbow, looking over Stacy. She then lowered her lips to Stacy's hot breasts and sucked the champagne away. She trailed her tongue down the river of Moet and slurped the shallow lake that pooled in her navel. Stacy squirmed, moaned, and rubbed her knees together in ecstasy under the attentive touch of experienced fingers.

"Does that feel good?" Rebecca asked, her lips shining with champagne as she looked up the glowing length of Stacy's body.

"Ummmhmmmm," she replied, her tongue flicking across her lips and her eyes shut tight.

"Thought so," Rebecca said as she kissed her navel lightly. She trailed her tongue down the center of her body and found the moist hotness between her thighs. She kept one finger inserted in her pussy as she licked across her growing clitoris. Stacy moaned with satisfaction.

Slowly Rebecca crawled up the length of Stacy's body, pecking her tingling skin along the way. Stacy waited hungrily for the taste of her tongue, sucking on it slowly when the sweet flesh was between her lips. The feel of Rebecca's shaved pussy, its tingling stubble, against her own sent shivers through her body and cream pouring from her throbbing pink snatch. Rebecca met her with her own warm pouring, the new wetness coating the small space between them as they ground into each other.

In a haze of perfumed body aroma and passion they kissed, licked, stroked, and caressed one another atop silk sheets. They found their lips pressed snugly to each other in the 69 position, their knees cages for movement; their tongue lapped up the sweet cream they excited from one another.

This lovemaking was the most thorough Stacy had ever experienced. She didn't want it to end. The passion subsided slowly as their energies were transferred between bodies. With slow kisses along sticky skin they found themselves in each other's arms as the sun lowered itself from the sky and cast a red glow over their glowing, intertwined bodies.

***

There was comfort here; like an oasis from everything that seemed to crowd his thoughts. Here was a place that he could feel like a man who mattered. Nothing frustrated him here. He'd gone about the rest of his day behind the desk in a stupor of anger and boredom. If it weren't for Carrie's marvelous throat and promise of a special treat at the end of the day, he would have been left to replay over and over again the mysterious conversation he'd had with Vernon Maxwell. He would have spent the remainder of his day trying to decipher the coded messages and vague innuendo. He had no belief in Vernon's words assuring that he had nothing to worry about. He believed more in Carrie's optimism.

When Carrie appeared at the edge of the hallway the wine had done its duty. He was relaxed deeply into the couch, his tie loosened and the top button undone. He'd thought to reveal himself more, but enjoyed the way she did this. He enjoyed the way she stood in front of him with her scent before his nose as she looked down on him. He was wrapped in the slow jazz and sultry voice of Norah Jones; she was waiting for the shining sun, not knowing why she didn't come.

"You like?" Carrie asked, posing in a pair of black stockings and garter belts. Her breasts heaved above a black satin corset, the tie-strings a shiny vinyl that was long enough to drop past her waist and obscure the fine blonde hairs on her bare muff.

"I can't really see from there," he said casually, noticing the oddly shaped short whip, its handle bulging and ridged in the middle. She slapped the leather strips into her palm gently. He didn't know whether to be frightened or aroused.

Carrie strolled on bare feet with swaying hips to where he sat on the couch. She smelled of jasmine. Her hair fell to her shoulders in long, swirling tendrils dipping into the cleavage of her creamy breasts. "How about now?" Her blue eyes glowed with sensual appeal.

"Yeah. That's nice. Real nice." His eyes moved from her crooked grin to the short leather whip with the oddly shaped handle; it reminded him of a pregnant worm, its center thickest in the middle and growing smaller in roundness towards the edges.

"This is your treat," she announced with that same crooked grin as she held out her hand.

Percy dutifully followed her through the hallway, the smell of incense growing stronger as they neared the dimly lit room ahead. Her ass cheeks shined like two halves of a moon.

The small room was dominated by a round bed with thick, shiny throw pillows thrown about. There was a lone candle flickering on a low wooden dresser, its mirror facing the bed. Carrie turned to him.

"Vernon is a prig," she said as she loosened his tie. "Don't you agree?"

In response Percy grabbed her in his arms and kissed her hard. She relaxed in his embrace, allowing him to press into her. He breathed heavily as he gripped her ass and shoved a finger into her hole.

"My goodness!" she hissed with wide eyes after she was able to break from his embrace. Percy was already shedding his trousers and tossing his socks away. He stood before her naked, ready to pounce.

"Not so fast," she said, her voice taking on a commanding tone. She planted one foot on the bed and swung the whip at him. "Lick my kittie cat."

Percy smiled, feeling aroused in a way he thought was impossible. How could she know that he'd secretly dreamed of being dominated? This was something he could not share with Sherrelle. He didn't know ... He hadn't heard of any black woman who enjoyed dominating a man; at least not a black man; at least not in bed.

"Lick it softly. She likes to be licked softly," Carrie instructed after he'd kneeled before her.

Percy did as he was told. The whip touched lightly on his back with an instruction for him to go deeper. Then it swooshed onto him a little harder with another instruction; this time for him to suck her clit. He obeyed, the fine hairs damp against his nose. And when she was ready for him to lap at her kitty like a good dog she smacked him over the back – harder this time – with the whip. Percy's joint strained mightily out in front of him. The whip came crashing down onto his back again when he stroked himself for relief. She didn't want him to touch himself.

He followed her with his mouth intact as she turned to the bed and lay on her back. She spread her legs wide and swung the whip over his back with an instruction to suck her kittie good. He obeyed. His tongue darted in and out of her soft mound with loving care, his back tingling. There was some relief as his dick met the soft sheets. He ground himself into her bed without notice until the whip came crashing over his back again. She didn't have to say anything. He stopped grinding her sheets.

"Yeesss," she moaned as his face was buried in her pussy. She gripped his ears and guided him to and fro. Her thighs quivered as her center grew hot.

Percy inhaled her scent deeply, enjoying the whims at which she commanded him. The whip touched freshly scarred skin lightly, making him wince in pleasure. When she creamed onto his face he forced his finger into her butt. She shook violently and then shuddered as if suffering from some sort of spasmic attack. She called out his name several times and encouraged him to continue, which he dutifully obeyed.

"Do you want to fuck me" she asked hotly, her voice a ragged whisper. Percy's breathing came short. He croaked out a low grunt.

"How bad do you want to fuck me, Mr. Santiago?

"Bad," he answered, taking a break from his oral duty.

"Tell me you want to fuck me."

"I want to fuck you."

"Tell me you want to fuck me good," she said, raising the whip with a lazy hand. It flopped onto his back helplessly.

"I want to fuck you good," he replied.

"Fuck me please Mr. Santiago. Fuck me good." Her face was arched up at a crooked angle, her creamy neck stretched and exposed as if she were expecting to be bitten by a vampire. Percy eased into her wetness and sunk to her hot depths. She moaned her agreement and rubbed her hands across the raised skin on his back as if reading Braille.

"Do you like that," she asked, squeezing herself over him.

"Yeaaah," he groaned, her body flushed and sticky under him. Her thighs burned as they wrapped around his waist. She rotated her hips into him so that he reached her depths in a hypnotic motion. Their taut stomachs met with a slapping sound. With every motion she huffed hotly into his ear.

"Yes. That's good fucking," she panted. "That's good. That's good."

Yes. It was good. Percy was near delirium. Her body seemed to merge with his own. There was a constant burning at his core that would not find its way to release. Without warning he felt the cold intrusion into his ass hole. He was too caught up to stop and investigate what this strange and good feeling was. His body was on fire. There were parts of him that opened up that he didn't know existed.

"Come on. Give it to me," she hissed, her arms wrapped around his hips. With each thrust she worked the end of the whip into his ass hole. He seemed to grow larger inside of her, pounding into her with an aggression not his own. His breathing was hoarse as he worked to chase some elusive explosion. Her wrists worked the oddly shaped whip handle with precision to help him along.

"Yes. Yeeesss. That's it. Come on Mr. Santiago. Give it to me good," Carrie demanded, her legs spread to the edges of the bed. She was totally open for him as he slid in and out of her. His back arched powerfully and his hips bucked with such force that she began to yelp out in pain.

The sounds coming from Percy were not his own. He could feel nothing outside of the center of his body. His ass hole expanded to receive and his dick enlarged to punish. There was a vortex of passion that propelled him forward unconsciously.

Carrie hissed and struggled to maintain her effort. She encouraged him with soft whispers to "let go."

"Let go. Let go. Come on Percy. You fuck me good. Yes. You fuck me good."

He grit his teeth and shoved into her with two more powerful strokes before exploding. He yelled out and strained into her, gripping the handle of the whip in his butt while he streamed and shuddered inside of her.

"That's a good fuck," she whispered softly into his ear after he'd collapsed onto her hot, wet body. That was so good. I love it when you fuck me good." Her panting breath whistled past his ear.

Percy did not hear a word she said. He rolled from her and lay on his back with his mouth agape. He could feel his spent organ touching his thigh. And the leather strap was next to him, the acidic smell of it wafting into his nose. He was amazed at himself. He felt as if he'd gone to Mars and overheated with his re-entry back to earth. He was vaguely aware of the burning sensation across his back, the silk sheets cooling some of the hot pain.

CHAPTER EIGHT

And they talked. For an hour after they'd made love to one another they cuddled and talked. At every whispering and quiet moment some part of their bodies met. They lay in one another's arms secure in the after-glow of their passion, a beautiful culmination for a successful day.

Stacy could get used to this as well. *Power,* she thought to herself. The feeling ran through her loins like a mighty river. She had no regrets with her rebellion. She felt freed of some invisible restraint; a restraint that pulled her along to satisfy everyone around her. Now she'd satisfied herself and it felt pretty damn good.

It was just after sunset when she turned onto her street. There was a small gathering at the curb in front of her neighbor's house. She was thinking that she was early enough to make a nice dinner for her husband and afterwards make love to him slowly and tenderly. She wanted to show him a new part of her that had been revealed. She wanted to transfer her experience with Rebecca to her marriage bed. She recognized the gold trimmed smile of Dahji, his hair hanging in long waves to his shoulders. There was a tall woman standing with her back to Sherrelle as she lifted a Coach bag from the trunk of her Jaguar. Stacy'd never seen the man who was leaned against Dahji's maroon Range Rover. He was slim, dressed in tailored slacks and a white, silk button-up shirt. The gold strands of his hair hung bone straight to his shoulders. She was trapped in the easy gaze of his light-brown eyes as she turned into her driveway. Dahji's Range Rover was squatted at the curb where Marlin usually parked.

"Don't start no mess Ayana. And come get your own bags," Sherrelle was saying as she dropped the black Coach bag to the ground.

"Auntie, that's Coach!" the pecan-colored woman said, reluctant to tear herself away from the attention of Dahji, who'd turned to Stacy as she pulled to a stop near the porch.

"I was just saying to myself – Dahji McBeth ... this garden sho need a rose – and here you are," he cheered grandly.

"Hi Dahji," Stacy responded with a smile. She looked from him to the woman lifting the Coach bag from the cement. On her slim frame were ample portions of titties, hips, and ass; all encased in a nylon body suit as if she were on a track team. She had the long hair that a weave provided, its strands shiny – apart from the duller, black hair closer to her head – and curling like stiff nylon when it parted over her narrow shoulders.

Dahji waved her over. "Come on over here and meet your new neighbor folks!" His slender frame held the expensive silk as if on display. From the olive green gators to the Rolex chain and diamond pendant hanging beneath the open collar of his mustard-colored shirt, every detail was carefully tended to. It still surprised her that this man was responsible for getting her husband a spot on the Colts football team.

"Hey Stacy" Sherrelle said, stepping from the Jaguar as a signal to Ayana to get the rest of her stuff.

"Hi." Stacy received Dahji's inspection bravely, wondering if he could sense her recent rebellion. There was a glint in his eyes and his mouth was crooked into a half smile.

"I see she made it, hunh?" Stacy said, looking away from Sherrelle's gaze. She wasn't ready to question her about looking into her window.

"Yeah. She's here. I don't know for how long with that attitude," she replied.

"That ain't nothing but flavor!" Dahji volunteered. "She just need something to occupy her time." With this, Ayana looked their way for the first time as she pulled a small suit case from the trunk.

"I don't need to do nothing but stay away from you," she said with a roll of her tight eyes.

Dahji never looked at her. Instead he turned to the man leaning on the Range Rover. "That right there is my uncle Prince Sweetwater. He come all the way from California."

Stacy waved, noting the twinkle of diamonds on his slender pinkie as he let his fingers dance before him.

"Do y'all have a Rally's out here?" Ayana asked, returning to Sherrelle's side. In her glance to Dahji she'd scanned Stacy with narrowed light brown eyes. Stacy wondered where she arrived from. It had to be a place that valued fake eyes, fake hair, and plenty of attitude.

"We have something better than that," Sherrelle began. "We have a refrigerator full of food that you can cook. And stop acting ghetto. Say hi to Stacy. She's our neighbor." Sherrelle's instruction was met with a forced smile as Ayana huffed. She gave Stacy a small wave of hello and turned away. Her ass knocked hard – like two gorillas fighting in a pillow case – as she walked up the driveway.

"Excuse her," Sherrelle said. "She had a long flight."

"Yeah. That air can mess up your hair," Dahji said with humor. "We gon' get her right like algebra." This last was said in a low voice, to which Sherrelle nodded enthusiastically. Stacy felt apart from their familiar banter. Now she wondered what their connection was. Did he have something to do with the HoodSweet clothes she was selling?

"Well, let me get her settled. So, will you be at court tomorrow?" she asked.

Why did they have to go to court? Stacy wondered.

"She'll die if you're not there," Sherrelle replied before turning her attention to the loud beat of drums pounding up the street.

"There go the million dollar man right there and right on time," Dahji announced, turning and placing his hands on his hips. Everyone watched silently as Marlin pulled to the curb behind the Range Rover. He let the beat knock, Too Short shouting "BITCH" every few seconds. He took his time gathering his practice gear.

Just when Stacy was feeling like an intruder at a private party, she was joined by the main attraction.

"See you tomorrow, Dahji. Bye Stacy. Give your father my hello," Sherrelle said hurriedly. She wasn't prepared to see Marlin or the feeling of being observed by his wife while in his presence.

Stacy smiled with a small wave and an assurance that she would give her father the message as she walked away. Stacy had the odd feeling she was avoiding Marlin for some reason. Maybe it had something to do with her looking in their window that morning.

"Marly Marl!" Dahji said as Marlin hoisted the heavy Colts bag onto his shoulder and chirped the alarm on the Escalade. He stopped in front of Prince and pointed a peace sign in his direction.

"Thas my uncle I was telling you about," Dahji confirmed. "Excuse me Ms. Cassidy while I get your husband some important forms to fill out for you alls future."

Stacy nodded her head in agreement and watched the slight man pimp strut around the grass. He grabbed Marlin's hand and whispered in his ear. Stacy wondered what he said as she moved towards the porch. When she looked towards the door she was surprised to see her father's lanky frame silhouetted behind the dark screen.

"Sounds like my kind of people," Grump said when she stepped onto the porch, opening the screen for her entry.

"What are you doing, daddy? ... Being nosy?" she asked, guiding him away from the door. The house smelled sour, his funk taking over what was usually a fragrant potpourri aroma.

"Sounds like that girl is here," he whispered happily.

"Yeah. She's here ... And sassy, too."

"She's just young that's all"

"Young and sassy." Stacy wanted to add "fake," but instead she said, "Want me to run you a bath? You have a taste for pork chops?"

This was a common trick she used, taking his yes to pork chops for the bath. She escorted him past the plasma screen – which show a man dressed as a fireman entering a house of women that didn't appear to be on fire – to the bathroom next to the room he never slept in. His arms felt like no more than bones in her grip.

"How are you feeling, daddy?"

"Lonely. When are you going to get me some company?"

She'd made no progress in this area. "Soon daddy. I'm working on it."

"You need to stop being so particular." He looked up to her while he sat on the small chair in the bathroom. The rush of bath water and lemon-scented bath gel filled the room.

"I did find a qualified man for ..."

"Hocus pocus!" Grump railed, throwing his hands to his knees. "Don't offend your pah pah that way. Ain't no man fingers touch this skin never. Never ever ever." He couldn't see the smile on his daughter's face. "And it ain't funny lemon peezy!" But he could feel it.

She was laughing, running her hand through the shallow water as she said, "I'm going to make some calls over the weekend. I promise. It's just that I've been so busy at work and ..."

"That's how the white folk is when they got you in them buildings. They don't leave no time for yo'self." There was a lull in conversation, the running water swirling and the heat rising into the air before he whispered, "You smell different."

Stacy looked to him with wide eyes, glad that he could not see her expression. He was stretching his neck forward, his opaque eyes searching the air.

"That's some nice perfume, but it's a white woman under it." He said this calmly and relaxed his gaze. "They all got that smell," he added.

"What's going on?" Marlin asked, appearing in the doorway. Stacy's chest thumped hard in her chest with her father's mystic sense. She was eyeing him carefully, afraid of what it was he wasn't saying. He had a satisfied grin spreading his thin lips.

"Well, you can handle it from here," she announced as she rose from the edge of the tub. She flicked the water from her hand into his face as a mild punishment for her embarrassment. He laughed in response.

"What you do to her Grump?" Marlin wanted to know, resisting her tug at his shirt.

"Come on so he can take his bath," Stacy said, pulling him away from the door.

"What's up, babe?" he inquired as she led him to the bedroom.

"How does Dahji know Sherrelle?" she asked once they'd reached the bedroom, trying hard to stay focused with him in front of her. She had an overpowering need to feel him inside of her. She glanced to the window to make sure the curtains were pulled together.

"I told you already that he's helping her with the clothes and stuff."

"And stuff?"

Marlin tried to pull away from her, laughing softly, but she held him tight, stretching his athletic sweater to a point in her grip. "Modeling, Stacy," he answered, stopping to look squarely in her eyes with wonder.

"What's up with you?"

"Why do you have to go to court tomorrow?" she wanted to know. She could smell the salt on his body. There was an outline of perspiration on his sweater that formed a triangle in the middle of his chest.

"Are you serious?"

"Just tell me. I feel like I don't know anything Marlin," she complained.

He let the duffel bag drop to the floor. "Peaches gotta go to court. Something about taking drugs to her boyfriend in jail."

"Really?" Stacy asked wide eyed. She knew there was something mysterious about the glamorous woman in the raggedy car.

"Yeah. So they supposed to go check that out." He was free from her grasp now.

"What does Dahji have to do with it? Why is he going?" she wanted to know, following him into the bathroom as he pulled his sweater over his head. She said nothing when he threw it to the wicker hamper only to have half of it sliding down its side. He quietly opened the glass door of the shower and turned the spray on.

"He got her a lawyer," he replied, bringing his arm back wet and standing to look at his wife. He was seeing her as if for the first time. There was a hunger and loneliness in her eyes. "How was your day? Did the Phat Farm thing go cool?"

She smiled now as she let her skirt drop from her waist and unbuttoned her blouse. "Yes. My day was very good," she admitted. She was done with her questions. She accepted the fact that she would never be able to understand the full range of Dahji's influence. She could only trust that the sharply dressed man he introduced as his uncle was part of the seed from which he'd grown.

"Cool."

"Mind if I join you?" she asked, striding across the tiled floor to him.

"Help yourself." Marlin led the way under the gentle spray of water. He placed both hands on the wall while the spray cooled his aching body, rushing over his head. Stacy eased up behind him and wrapped his sculpted torso in her embrace, leaning her head into his back.

"So you're really on the team, hunh?" she asked softly.

"Final cut this week. I just signed some medical information they needed for the contract."

"I'm really happy for you." She let her hands drop to his hard stomach, stretching her fingers slowly down to his tightly curled pubic hairs.

Marlin turned to face her, the water sliding across his back. He was glad that Sherrelle left the yard before he got out of his truck. It was inevitable that they would find themselves alone again and he still hadn't decided how he would handle that. It would be so easy to grab her in his arms and kiss her again, but doubted neither of them would have the restraint their marriage vows demanded.

"That's nice," Stacy whispered at the rising of his organ. She slid her hands over it and stroked the heavy meat gently. "Can I have some?" she asked in a little girl voice. Her pussy twitched in the knowledge that she would soon have him parting her walls. Though sex with Rebecca was soft and tender, there was no substitution for a hot log of meat tunneling between her legs.

"All you want," Marlin responded as he grabbed her by the waist and lifted her to him.

She wrapped her legs around his waist and gripped his thick neck while lowering herself onto him. The steam shrouded them in mist as Marlin braced himself for her. She let out a short breath as he breached her opening and rolled his hips into her loosening snatch.

She arched her back to receive him better, her fingers digging into the crevices of his muscles for leverage. He was everything that she needed. The thick meat slid into her and filled her. The water held them tight, their skin melting into each other. His strength was beneath her, supporting her from inside and out; his pole holding up her center with small motions of her hips. She buried her face into his shoulder as the swollen head eased in and out of her. Her breathing grew harsh and her eyes were wet with silent tears. He was all she wanted. He was all she needed. She was lost in his embrace, giving him all of her tightly until she felt his muscles jerk and relax. Only then did she hear again the spray of hot water cascading over their tightly joined bodies.

***

Percy's body was on fire. This had to be what hell felt like. The pit of the fire had to be both pleasure and pain. Perhaps the pleasure was in the pain. This is the conclusion he'd come to, though this kind of pain had to be taken in due measure. There had to be some kind of way to get the pleasure without the scars.

What Carrie had succeeded in doing was to get his mind off his troubles. The frustration he'd been feeling was covered over with snatches of their passionate lovemaking. And he discovered she had a wry sense of humor. She'd commented that his skin was like cold caramel as they lay twisted together. He'd never thought of his own skin in relation to candy but the way she pressed her white flesh to his made him see color in a new way; through her eyes he saw that he was as much an intoxicant to her as she was to him; and this was all based on the color of their skin. He'd smiled graciously when she guessed at what candy shade of child they would have together.

Children ... When ... How did that subject get into the equation? *There is always a downside to joy,* he reasoned as he pulled into his driveway. The sight of Marlin's Escalade parked further up the street confused him. Not only that, seeing it was an indication of how late he was in getting home. Grabbing up his red Halliburton briefcase – a gift from Sherrelle – he alighted from the car. He checked his posture and was reminded of the soreness in his back; the undershirt was sticking to him. He hoped it was nothing more than the Vaseline Carrie applied to his wounds as she assured him that the redness and swelling would be gone by morning. It was no use arguing with her about what his wife would say if she saw the welts across his back; maybe this was Carrie's exact hope.

There were fewer clothes in the living room. The brightly colored sweaters, t-shirts and sweatpants now occupied the cushions of the two lazy-boy recliners at the far end of the living room. *At least she was busy,* he thought to himself, privately proud of his wife's determination. Past the dining room he saw Sherrelle cross the opening of the kitchen doorway. She was gesturing with a large wooden spoon as she carried a wide plastic bowl to the sink. She turned back excitedly, both hands under the bowl, on her way back to the other side of the kitchen. She never looked out to the living room when he was standing just inside the closed front door. He was confused as to her energy. She was obviously talking to someone. Then he remembered that her niece was coming out today. The scent of frying hamburger meat filled the house. He was suddenly very hungry.

Percy crept along the edges of the living room and through the dining room, briefcase in hand, and stood just outside the kitchen door. He was bathed in the light of the chandelier over the dining room table.

"That don't matter. What kind of man asks if you have a good manager?"

Percy recognized the chirpy voice of the girl he remembered as a preteen. There was an added element of brashness in her words.

"He's good people," Sherrelle responded. "You just have to get to know him."

"But you didn't hear what he said!" Ayana exclaimed with a sharp laugh. "He must think he some type of pimp or something. Talking about how everybody represents something. Even Taco Bell got reps. They get paid for their services. They wear a uniform. You represent me you wear the finest uniforms and get paid for your services." Here she was mimicking Dahji's slow drawl. Sherrelle's giggles punctuated her lilting tirade.

"Did you hear him tell Stacy that she was ... What did he say?" Sherrelle asked.

"Talking about how he was missin a rose in his garden."

"That's it. That heifer ain't no rose. She's more like a weed!" They shared this joke with howls of laughter.

Sherrelle was still smiling when she turned the corner and saw Percy standing just outside the kitchen door. "What are you doing?" she wanted to know, her face frowned up with what he must have been doing. She looked him up and down.

He jumped in her direction in that split second and she'd decided he was being sneaky. "Are you cooking?" he asked, feigning a pointed interest in who was providing the culinary expertise in his kitchen.

"Dahji McBeth is like the sun. He shine on everything," Ayana sang just around the corner, mocking Dahji to herself.

Sherrelle smiled. "I can't believe you, Percy. What did you think you were going to hear?" she asked.

"Nothing," he replied impatiently. "I just want to know when dinner is going to be ready," he added as he stepped around her on his way into the kitchen. He didn't want to see Ayana as much as he wanted to get from under his wife's appraisal. He felt the welts on his back pulse under her inspection. He felt her silent eyes on him as he turned into the kitchen.

Ayana turned away from the stove, a spatula dangling loosely in her hand. "Hey uncle Percy!" she shouted with surprise as she moved in his direction with her arms wide.

Percy didn't think it was possible to make the sheer, cotton wife-beater more revealing, but Ayana had succeeded in doing this. She'd cut it in half so that it stopped just under her large, jutting breasts; the fat nipples were dark under the fabric. Her small waist and stomach shifted tightly. There was a diamond heart pierced into her navel. It was not the way her long, shapely legs escaped the dark blue boy-shorts that made him feel the way he did. Nor was it the way her pussy pressed against the fabric as if wanting to break out and breathe that moved him. He couldn't admit that it was the way her round hips flared out from a slim waist that scared him. It wasn't the way her toes shined or the ring that hugged the long baby toe that made him swallow. The way her glistening, full lips smiled wide, creating deep dimples in her soft cheeks, and her gleaming, perfect white teeth was not the reason his stomach contracted.

"It's so good to see you," she said, wrapping her arms around him tightly, her soft breasts pressed against him innocently.

Percy winced in pain, glad that Sherrelle was behind him, as his hand lightly rest on the curve of her round ass. She was rubbing her hands up and down his back. He hissed silently under the pressure. This is what caused the various reactions in him at the sight of her coming in his direction. He was in too much pain to feel how her body melted into his softly, rubbing every part of him with a warm, welcoming caress.

Though Sherrelle was silent he could feel the tenor of her thoughts traveling across the kitchen. He had no clue as to what the immediate future held, but he was sure that the beautiful, curvaceously soft, woman-child in his arms was going to be at the center of it all.

PART TWO

Ayana Cherry

Dahji McBeth

&

Peaches

"It is not the quality of the desired object that gives us pleasure, but rather the energy of our appetite."
- Charles Baudelaire
THE END OF DON JUAN

CHAPTER NINE

The romantic voice of Luther Vandross and the smell of bacon finally succeeded in pulling Ayana from her slumber. She stretched like a refreshed feline under the lilac-scented comforter. The sun streamed in through the window over her head, the lavender lace trimmed curtains parted wide.

She blinked her eyes sleepily to her new environment after she turned on her back, the comforter dropped to her waist so that her bare breasts hung free. She was naked beneath the covers as well. The only dressing she wore was a strip of cotton around her head to hold her weave in place. She inhaled deeply, feeling good about deciding to accept her aunt's invitation to come help her out. She'd at first thought that her mother found out about how her trick-of-a-boyfriend was sucking the juice from between her legs on a regular basis. It was a shame that her mother was looking for love when all Byron wanted was to be charged. Maybe her mother was afraid to consider the possibility that her own eighteen-year-old daughter would screw her boyfriend. It was only one time to get him hooked. From then on she'd only let him suck on her marrow. She had to admit she felt a little guilty, but figured since he was only using his tongue then it really couldn't be considered that bad. Besides, as her mother had to realize, it cost to live good in Los Angeles. There was no explaining how her GAP paycheck paid for the clothes, jewelry, breasts, and expensive hair weaves. These things were necessary to match her voluptuous ass. She was tired of looking awkward when what men really wanted was a nice arm piece, complete with all the voluptuous accessories.

Now here she was. It was beginning to be too much. The city was becoming too small. She figured she'd come out here for a minute and figure out her next move. Besides, her aunt seemed to be doing well. She'd grabbed her up a square husband and was quietly milking him dry. Last night, after they thought she'd gone to sleep, she pressed her ear to the door and listened to them argue. It was mostly about money... her spending his money. *Same ol' Sherrelle,* she thought to herself with a silent giggle. And he also wanted to argue about her spending too much time at strip clubs. This was something new to Ayana. She couldn't imagine her aunt at a strip club. She looked like a hood chick and could talk like one if mad enough, but she was more bourgeois than hood. Ayana waited to hear them speak about her. She wanted to know if Percy was cool with her being there, but her name never came up.

She'd gotten up at maybe two or three in the morning to get a drink of water. The window had been left open and the air parched her throat. While walking through the dining room, she was surprised to find Percy asleep on the couch. *Damn,* she thought to herself in the early morning light, faulting herself for missing what had to be the best part of the arguing. But even so, their arguing didn't have the threat of violence she was used to. No matter what he said she never got the feeling that he was going to hit Sherrelle. They argued like television people, and just like television people, he ended up on the couch.

And besides this amusing drama that she felt her aunt was orchestrating anyway, there was the added bonus of the mysterious Dahji McBeth and his uncle Prince Sweetwater. She'd never heard people introduce themselves by first and last names; at least not names as colorful as theirs. She was seriously about to burst out into laughter when she'd introduced herself as Ms. Ayana Cherry. It sounded perfect coming from her lips even though she'd never considered herself a Ms, and her real last name "Jones" sounded too plain considering the circumstances. And she was proud of her aunt for not putting her on blast for changing her last name on the spot. She knew her last name had to be something sexy and fruity. By Dahji's gold trimmed smile, she knew she was on point. It was her duty to act like he was annoying.

This might work out, she thought to herself as she swung her legs from the bed. Keith Sweat was now begging through the speakers. The house was plush. The street was clean with green lawns and fancy cars parked in every driveway. *Nothing but good things could happen from here,* she thought to herself as she pulled on a pair of pink, low-rise HoodSweet sweats and matching half-T. She'd wanted all of three colors, but Sherrelle reminded her that she was running a business. But this didn't stop her from getting at least one of each of the sweat pants, half-T's, boy-shorts, and wife-beaters. Sherrelle had hinted that she'd bought her something else, but she'd have to work for it. Ayana didn't have a problem with this. How hard could it be selling clothes that were hot?

When she stepped from the bedroom, on her way to the bathroom, Percy was coming from the master bedroom at the end of the hallway. He was busy adjusting his tie, so he did not see Ayana at first; then he saw her and a small cloud of lust passed over his face before he could smile innocently and say good morning. It was too late though. Ayana had seen this look before from men who didn't want to be seen as wanting something they weren't supposed to have or were willing to pay for in haste, without complaint or negotiation. The thing that moved them this way had to be possessed, captured, subdued, or conquered in order to satisfy their primal urges.

"Good morning Percy," Ayana replied; his roving eyes making her aware of the fullness of her breasts and the sway of her hips. His eyes stopped momentarily on the small leather Louis Vuitton duffel bag in her hands; it covered the diamond heart pendant piercing her navel. She accepted his short, nervous nod before turning into the bathroom and closing the door slowly.

While staring at herself in the mirror, she whispered, "Please God, let him be faithful to my aunt." The burden was on him. Ayana took no responsibility for his unforeseen actions.

"So, is she going to jail?" Percy was asking Sherrelle when Ayana stepped into the living room. Her body smelled of fresh strawberries, the hot shower making her pecan-colored skin glow a tinted, scrubbed red. She'd prepped her young, tender face with lip gloss and eyeliner. Her hair hung long and lustrous. Percy was seated at the dining room table. If she didn't know any better she'd have thought they made love all night and slept in the same bed.

"Dahji says she might get probation ... Hey you," Sherrelle said, looking to Ayana. "How was your first night in a strange bed?"

Ayana stopped in the middle of the room and closed her eyes. Her body swayed and her head rocked slightly. She began to pop her fingers. "This the one right here," she moaned seductively. Mary J. Blige sang powerfully about being too much to handle.

I'm coming for you / I ain't wasting time / boy all night long you've been on my mind / oh get ready baby cuz I'm on my way / you talk a real good one / but let's see today.

Ayana began to sing, her eyes raised to the ceiling while she wrapped her arms around her stomach.

I just wanna see what you're made of / can you handle me / are you really tight / are you really that tight ..." She was shaking her head in church sorrow as Mary continued without her.

Brothas come and go so what you gon' do / boy this ain't no joke / it's time to show and prove / you can't hide from love / it's too strong / wrap your arms around me and don't be shy / what you feel is a real woman / probably for the first time ..." Ayana belted out as she shook her arms free and stepped towards the table.

You can't hide from love...

"That's my ish right there," she swooned while sitting before the plate of eggs, grits, bacon, and toast.

"We figured as much," Sherrelle replied gaily as Ayana nearly finished the orange juice with one swig. "I see we're going to have to charge you rent," she added.

"How much?" Ayana wanted to know, scrunching up her face in distaste. "What my mamma told you?"

Sherrelle raised her eyebrows in surprise. Ayana had a secret. "How much money do you have?" she asked testily.

"Not much," she responded, returning her attention to the eggs, unaware of the way Percy glanced at her lips as they pressed the fork from her mouth.

"Liar," Sherrelle accused, making Ayana smile as if caught being naughty.

Percy did everything he could to keep his eyes from gluing themselves to the young niece of his wife. *She seem to not know the affect she is having on me*, he thought to himself as he decided it was best to cut breakfast short. "Well, I've got a ton of work on my desk," he sighed, leaving more than half of the eggs and bacon served to him on the plate. He was trying to figure out the best way to introduce Sherrelle to the concept of Ayana dressing more conservatively when the very cause of his discomfort whispered in his direction.

"My auntie says you are an important man at work," Ayana said as she chewed on a piece of bacon. She held the meat loosely between long fingers, the nails clear and manicured to rounded points.

Sherrelle was watching him with a mysterious smile. He couldn't guess what was on her mind if it meant he would save his life.

"Are you late?" Sherrelle wanted to know, slapping Ayana's hand as she reached for the bacon strips on Percy's plate.

He grabbed a final piece of bacon to calm her. "I've got a ton of work," he responded, preoccupied with his chewing as he checked his Rolex.

"So, are you?" Ayana asked before he could step away from the table. He stopped with his legs awkwardly placed one over the other so that it looked like he had to piss.

"Am I what?" He stepped from the knot in his legs and stood so that Ayana had to turn her head to see him. She was not going to let him get away so easily. *Sherrelle used to be this way,* he thought to himself.

"Are you important?"

Sherrelle still had that mysterious quarter-smile on her lips.

"Not really," he finally answered, looking away from his wife to the manufactured light brown eyes of her niece who had sex appeal to spare.

Ayana didn't respond. She simply nodded her head, giving him permission to leave, before returning hungrily to the eggs before her.

"You are your mother's child," Sherrelle said in a low voice after Percy left the room.

"And you come from her mother."

"Well, that may be true, but somewhere along the line Sharon got the hoochie ..."

"Unh unnh, Auntie! Don't talk about my momma like that!" Ayana cried out, poking the clean fork at Sherrelle's dodging arm.

Sherrelle laughed as she stood from the table with her plate in her hand. "Don't think I don't know about how you do. You ain't innocent like you might want me to think, or your momma for that matter." With this she turned to the kitchen, shrugging off Ayana's protests of what she may have known.

"I'm only eighteen auntie," she was calling out when Percy stepped back into the living room. "You look nice," she nearly whispered, making him turn and thank her for the compliment. "You're welcome." She smiled, watching as he walked to the door. *Poor thing,* she thought to herself, *he needs to play basketball and get some swagger.* He looked as if he was trying to remember something and then he turned and called out to Sherrelle.

"Yes," she answered, appearing at the kitchen door.

"Would you mind picking me up a few shirts?"

"Sure, honey. Anything else?"

"Thank you."

"I love you," she called as he opened the door.

"Love you, too."

He seemed anxious to get out of the house, Ayana thought to herself, enjoying the show of television love.

"Have a good day at work." Sherrelle's tone had taken on a mocking quality which was lost on Percy as he waved and closed the front door behind him.

"You are so Lucy Ricardo," Ayana teased.

"I know I am, but what are you?" Sherrelle tossed back to Ayana's delight, her soft laughter following her aunt back into the kitchen.

"So who might be going to jail?" Ayana asked when she walked into the kitchen. Sherrelle was at the sink, her back turned. Ayana was privately proud of her aunt's shapely figure. Though she had on a pair of baggy sweats, there was no denying her tight body. She walked up behind her and lifted the flowing curls that hung to Sherrelle's back.

"My friend Pea ... Girl!" she turned in surprise, her hands soapy and gripping the scrub pad.

Ayana's face was serious as she continued her search. Sherrelle was trapped against the sink while attempting to dodge the assault of Ayana's fingers rubbing her scalp.

"Be still! I just want to see ..."

Sherrelle finally escaped her grasp, wondering at the surprised expression on Ayana's face. "What's wrong with you girl ... Are you on some type of drug?"

"You don't have any tracks. Is that a new technique?"

Ayana flung her arm at Sherrelle helplessly. "Your hair! Where are your tracks?"

Now Sherrelle understood. "Girl, this ain't no weave." She pulled at a thick curl, stretching it over her breast. "This is all good living and proper management."

"Don't hate." Sherrelle returned to her scrubbing.

"Who you say going to jail?" Ayana renewed her line of questioning.

"My friend Peaches. She has a court date today. You wanna come?"

Ayana cringed. "Oooh nooo! I'm allergic to so many white people in the same place. They might try to lock me up for being just damn fine." She chuckled with her joke.

"Get over yourself. How do you know it's going to be all white people?"

Ayana leaned on the counter beside Sherrelle. "What ... So you telling me that the judge, prosecutor, the typist lady, and ..."

"Her lawyer is a sista."

Ayana held up one finger. "That's just one ... And besides that shit ain't gon' keep them from arresting me for being just ..."

"Too damn fine. Yeah I know. Well, I have a shipment coming today so make sure you listen for the doorbell."

"Of what?"

"Clothes. What you think ... Drugs?"

Ayana smiled bravely. "Oh, don't worry. I'll handle the business. Anything else you need me to do?"

"Stay out of my room." Ayana waved this away as if the instruction could not keep her from snooping.

"I'm serious. I'll know, too" Sherrelle warned as she waved a finger in Ayana's face on her way out of the kitchen. "My room is booby trapped."

Ayana followed. "Whatever. So is that all I have to do to get my paycheck?" she wanted to know.

"Nope." Sherrelle disappeared through the hallway, leaving Ayana to wonder what else she would have to do. When she finally entered Sherrelle's room her aunt was already undressing. She'd pulled her sweat top over her head and let her full, dark breasts spring free.

"Don't worry. You'll earn your keep. Don't rush it. Why are you looking at me like that?" Sherrelle asked suddenly, flinging her sweat pants from her ankles. Ayana's eyes scanned her mocha-colored body slowly.

"You have pretty titties. You sure you ain't got no implants?"

Sherrelle laughed in a way that made her body jerk as she rose from the bed. "You are really material. This is all natural," she sang as she slid her hands down her curvaceous body as if on a sheet of air.

Ayana followed her into the bathroom. "Why Percy sleep on the couch last night?" Ayana's voice competed with the spray of shower water Sherrelle was testing with her hand.

"He's been having bad dreams."

Ayana was skeptical. "Bad dreams? What, is he eleven years old?" Steam began to fill the room. Sherrelle's body was obscured by the floor to head three paneled glass casing. The scent of peach shower gel soon burst into the air. *How long has he been having bad dreams,* she wondered. Asking would do no good as the spray of water and heavy steam seemed to drown out further conversation.

When Sherrelle emerged from the bedroom dressed in a brown

pinstripe cotton skirt and blazer, Ayana was sitting on the living room couch looking out to the street.

"You sure you don't want to come with me instead of being cooped up in this house?" Sherrelle asked considerately while adjusting the brown paisley silk scarf thrown casually around her neck, her hair pinned up so that stray strands trailed down her neck.

Ayana turned from the window. "Was that home-girl's husband that just left in the Escalade?"

Sherrelle felt her skin tingle as she leisurely strolled to the front door. "Yeah," she replied, letting the sun shine in through the opened door. She'd looked in the direction of where she knew Marlin's Escalade to be parked. She missed him and the curtain had been drawn together. Seeing him privately every morning was like a fix of dope. Now she was fiending.

"What time you coming back?" Ayana wanted to know, rising from the couch and letting the sun bathe her in warmth. She followed Sherrelle onto the porch and down the steps. "You sure you don't want me to drop you off and get the Jag washed and ..."

"I'll be back this afternoon," came Sherrelle's reply. She looked glamorous behind the Fendi shades she slid onto her nose. The top was lowering itself as she sat behind the wheel.

Ayana moaned loudly, her nose wrinkled. "You ain't right."

"Be ready when I get back so we can go to lunch."

"Okay, but you know you a bad bitch, right?" She looked to her aunt with admiration, her arms folded below her ample bosom.

"It's gotta be in you not on you, boo." With this, Sherrelle backed out of the driveway with a gentle wave.

Ayana watched the back of the Jaguar until it turned the corner. There was no way she was going to court for someone she didn't know. That sounded like going to the dentist and she hated that worse than seeing animals at the zoo. It was all so very depressing. As she turned back towards the house she noticed the hedge of rose bushes as if for the first time. She didn't recall them being so tall and full. They were perfectly trimmed and bloomed.

Ayana stopped at the first rose bush and lowered her nose to the yellow flower. A few feet down was a purple bush of roses. She stopped here and inhaled the fragrant aroma. It wasn't something that she'd intended to do, but her eyes settled on the neighbor's window. Something caught her eyes between the slim opening in the curtain. In the dim living room there was light bouncing off of a still figure. Her heart raced with her intrusion. She looked quickly back up the driveway and instinctively tried to make herself smaller. She searched for an opening between the rose bushes and squeezed through, lightly scratching the back of her hand in the process.

Ayana eased up to the side of the house and raised her head up slowly to the window. There was a lamp stand by the window. Her eyes scanned to the other side of the living room in search of what she thought she saw.

She was right. There was an old, slim man sitting in a chair. He was watching television, the flickering colors bouncing off his shiny brown skin. His face was turned slightly upward as if he were listening to something from a far-off place. His eyes looked vacant. *Is he blind?* she asked herself.

She crouched low again, thinking how wrong it was for her to be peeking into the neighbor's window, but something about the old man intrigued her. He looked lonely and sad. *Did he spend his entire day alone in the house?* she asked herself as she gazed out into the quiet street. Her heart beat wildly at the prospect of someone pulling into their driveway and discovering her at the window.

"One more look," she said in barely a whisper as she raised herself up slowly. She squinted in amazement. He'd stretched himself out on the chair so that his legs were spread wide. His hands were in his lap, a shiny pole held between them. It was thick and misshaped with a huge head. Ayana inhaled with a shock. It was the biggest dick she'd ever seen in her life. It seemed to be alive as the gnarly fingers wrapped it loosely and stroked slowly. He was doing this leisurely as if not really trying to accomplish an orgasm. His head was crooked to the side and up at an awkward angle. *He has to be blind,* she noted to herself with some relief. *Poor old man.*

He'd stopped stoking himself and let the snake-like organ lay across his lap, the cotton pajamas acting as a comforter. He'd turned his eyes slowly towards the window before Ayana slowly eased from his blind view. She forgot about the roses she wanted to pick as she rounded the back of the house and found the back door locked. "Damn."

She prepared herself to pass by the window again, shaking out her fingers and taking a deep breath, the sight of the old man's thick meat fresh in her mind. The way the darkly varnished skin moved over the shaft was permeated in her sight. The large pear-shaped head bobbed in her conscious as she passed by the window with her eyes straight ahead to the street.

Ayana opened and closed the front door in alarm. She stood with her back to the door, her hand over her fast-beating heart, as she scissored her legs across her strumming pussy.

CHAPTER TEN

She couldn't help but feel that she was doomed to a life of hard struggle. She had no one to fault for her choices but herself. Just when she decided that she would leave Tequan and everything associated with him behind, there was this last thing that bound her to him. It was a sad state of affairs. She wanted to be free to pursue what was ahead of her, but this had to be handled first. *Keep* your head up homegirl, she whispered to herself as she sat in the sterile hallway of the Indianapolis Municipal Court.

It was just her luck. She didn't want to do it. She should have broken up with him over the phone, but she wasn't that type of woman. She wanted to bring him what he needed to get paid and let him know that she was moving on with her life. He couldn't have been mad at the trade off. He would have to respect her for that. But it didn't happen like she'd planned. What happened was the worst thing that could happen. She was searched before visiting him in prison, and the guard found the cocaine and weed in her bra. Sure, she was instructed by Tequan's homeboy to keep it in her pussy with a string attached. So it was her own damn fault that she got caught.

The idea of seeing Tequan was worst than being charged with trafficking drugs. She knew he would try to keep her calm and keep her on his team. But the days of being Tequan's girl were over. There was only so much she could take. There was a new life waiting for her and she wanted all parts of it.

"What are you thinking about girlfriend?" Sherrelle asked, tapping Peaches lightly on the leg.

"Where's my lawyer?" she answered with annoyance, ignoring the sharply dressed man passing by with an ogling stare. She rolled her eyes at him on her way to look at Sherrelle. They exchanged a knowing glance. "Niggas will try to get at a bitch in the oddest places," she complained. But who could blame the passing men who looked their way with appreciation. No one would suspect that either of them was here to answer to criminal charges; not the way they were dressed up to look like women rich enough to avoid the drama.

"Like in hospitals," Sherrelle responded.

"Okay? Bitch getting a pap smear and here this nigga is talking about – can I holla at you – Hell naw nigga!" Peaches demonstrated, enjoying the sound of her best friend's laughter. "Bitch could have a deadly pussy disease! A foul discharge." Sherrelle rocked against her with a fit of laughter, begging her to stop. "They don't care. I'm serious!" Peaches added as she let her hand fall on Sherrelle's thigh.

"What's so funny? I wanna know," came a proper sounding voice. Sherrelle was busy wiping the tears from her eyes. Peaches was glad to see her attorney.

"Please. It ain't really funny," Peaches said as she stood from her seat. "Where's Dahji?" she wanted to know, looking past the chunky, peanut butter colored woman. There was no sign of Dahji.

"I just talked to him. He's running a little late, but says to let you know he'll be here," Viola Sparks assured her.

"Where you talk to him at because his cell phone is off?" Peaches wanted to know, never minding the sharp blue pant suit the woman wore. *She could use some off time to go get her hair done right,* Peaches thought to herself, noting the nappy roots of her otherwise long, brown hair.

Viola's eyes turned a darker shade of brown with the question. "He came by my office." Her voice lost some of its warmth, reminding Peaches who needed who at this point.

"So what will happen today?" Sherrelle cut in, thinking that Peaches would succeed in landing herself in jail to make a point if she allowed this.

Viola was more receptive when she answered. "Well, today is simply the preliminary hearing. The Magistrate will listen to what the arresting officer has to say and ..."

"Do I get to say something?" Peaches asked in protest. Viola's eyes moved to her slowly.

"And what is it that you would like to say Ms. Adebenro?"

Peaches was defiant. "It wasn't mine," she replied staunchly.

Viola smiled warmly as if to a child asking why Santa Claus just didn't come through the front door. "Well, this hearing is mainly to establish the fact that a crime was committed and to advance the matter to trial. You can say anything you like at trial if you wish, though I wouldn't advise it."

"She understands," Sherrelle offered with a gentle touch on Peaches' arm. Viola smiled with this and positioned her rolling leather file case behind her.

"Let me go and announce myself. We should be out of here before lunch," she said more friendly this time, cocking her head slightly to Peaches, who smiled in return.

"Fat heffa," Peaches whispered as Viola disappeared inside the courtroom.

"She is the last person you need to be mad at," Sherrelle warned her.

Peaches was still looking to the door where a short white man now emerged. His black suit fit him snug around his large thighs. The white shirt hugged his neck tightly so that it looked like his fat, balding head would pop off at any moment. He struggled to loosen the cheap tie, exposing the police badge attached to his belt. "She went to school with Dahji. I know she fucked him in exchange for representing me," she hissed in complaint.

"I still don't see why you're mad at her."

Peaches threw her arms out shortly and backed up to the bench. She dropped as if the air had been pulled from her. "I don't know," she whined. "I'm thankful. Believe me I am. This shit is just fucked up that's all. I must look like some type of stupid bitch for trying to take dope into a prison. That's like complaining about a parking ticket when you have a warrant for shoplifting." Her revelatory laughter took some of her anger away towards her attorney.

Sherrelle loved her friend with all her heart and realized that Peaches could sometimes be dramatic. She'd let her speak her mind, glad to be her supporting ear. The seriousness of the environment made it hard to sustain laughter. Soon they were reduced to people watching, trying to guess at why certain people were in the courthouse. It wasn't hard to tell who the helpless wife was appearing with small children for her husband; or the young white boy who came with his parents who no doubt had committed some minor infraction like spray painting a wall or stealing a bottle of glue. Then there were the hardened faces of those who stood before the elevator to the upper floors of Superior Court; they were mostly black and mostly women coming to catch a glimpse of their worst halves. Peaches felt sorry for these women. She wanted to scream for them to cut their losses and run.

When the courtroom doors opened and a tall black man in a Sheriff uniform motioned for Peaches, she wasn't sure he meant her. *How can he know who I am?* She asked herself.

"Come on. He means us," Sherrelle said as she stood up. A shot of fright paralyzed Peaches. She couldn't rise.

"Is she okay?" asked the muscular sheriff. He stepped out into the hallway, looking to Peaches with concern as she caught her breath. "Does she need medical attention?"

Sherrelle leaned in close. "Are you okay?"

Peaches nodded as she gulped air and gathered herself. She grabbed a hold of Sherrelle's hand and stepped towards the courtroom as if on a cloud of air.

The courtroom was cold. Her nervousness was eased by the congenial face of the gray haired white man behind the raised bench. He looked to her with patience as she stepped through the swinging partition and sat next to a waiting Viola.

What happened next seemed unreal. The slim faced prosecutor questioned the female Correctional Officer who'd found the drugs on her. Gloria made a few objections and then asked her own questions that seemed to Peaches irrelevant to the charges. She barely noticed when Viola sat back down or the mumbling droning of the magistrate as he summarized his belief that there was enough evidence to bound Ms. Helen Adebenro over for trial to answer.

She barely heard Viola as she explained that this was just a formality. She wasn't trying to hear how motions were going to be filed or that she should be offered a plea agreement in Superior Court. The day for her to return to court felt like tomorrow, though it was two weeks away. She hadn't even noticed that Tequan was not present. It wasn't until she saw Dahji sitting in the back row that the fog lifted from her dreary, haze-filled court date.

Dahji stood from his seat at the edge of the row and accepted Peaches into his arms. She sobbed onto his leather coat, his flowing mane acting as a cushion for her face. He nodded subtly to a passing Viola on her way into the hallway.

"You're late!" Peaches complained, slapping him lightly across the shoulder before wiping the tears from her eyes.

Dahji grabbed her by the hand. "Let's get outta here," he suggested. "It's going to be okay. Trust me on this," he added as he led the way into the hall.

Sherrelle had never seen her friend break down like this; especially not so that a man could see. It was apparent that she really had feelings for Dahji, who held her close to him, tenderly soothing her worry.

"I'm sorry," Peaches said in apology. "You must think I'm silly."

"Naw pumpkin pie. This is something you can't pretend right here. But you gon' be alright." He lifted her chin to him. "Look at me. You trust me?"

Peaches nodded.

"That's all I ask of you. Now let us be about the business of getting ready for the next level. Don't you got some folks to see about that manufacturing and distribution plug? Let's not get snowed in now," he warned.

Peaches straightened up with his pep talk. "You're right. So what's next?" she wanted to know, glancing at Viola who stood near the water fountain talking to another woman dressed in a business suit.

"We right on schedule. We gon' get together like sweaty butt cheeks and squeeze this thang on out like that." With this, he slapped his palms together a couple of times and slid them away dramatically, glad to see her smile.

"You want me to come by later?" she asked, trying to mask her puffy face with some sense of appeal.

"Without a doubt. I'ma be trap checking so hit me up after your appointments and we'll meet in the middle. Sound good?"

"Sounds good," she replied, leaning in for a soft kiss on his lips, glad that Gloria had turned in that instant to see the joining of their lips. She paused for effect and double smacked before releasing him from her light grasp.

"Hey HoodSweet," Dahji called out to Sherrelle as he opened his arms for her. She kissed him on the cheek, noting how good he smelled. "That new shipment come through yet?"

"It should be there when I get home," Sherrelle replied.

"That's the bidness right there," he said, nodding his head. "Y'all gon' need to come by this week for a photo session. And bring that niece of yours."

"She's pretending to be scared of you," Sherrelle countered with a smile. Dahji grinned wide, his gold trimmed teeth shining brightly. "Ain't no need for that. All I wanna do is trim her up and put a crown on her head. Make her a princess."

"I'll see what she says," she promised.

"Thas that then. Time is money." He kissed Peaches lightly on the cheek before strolling away like George Jefferson.

"You are too much drama for a primetime show," Sherrelle teased when he was out of ear shot.

Peaches smiled mischievously. "I know, hunh!" she replied as they stepped into the bright day. "But I guess he told me, hunh? Daddy know how to get his bitch back on the track."

"If you say so," Sherrelle countered. "But I don't care how much you front I know you feel him in a major way."

Peaches swayed into her friend. "Girl, you know I do! He's like some good syrup that I know will give me a hangover, but it's going to be a sweet one, ya know?" Sherrelle was shaking her head sadly, wondering what kind of syrup she was talking about. "Cough syrup! You are so square. Sometimes I don't know why I even bother," Peaches hooted.

"Because I'm like good syrup that you need to stay healthy!" Sherrelle announced proudly, raising her palm for a high five. They were met by the stares of passersby as they laughed together, walking through the parking lot.

"So what's up with your niece?" Peaches asked when they'd stopped at Sherrelle's Jaguar. Though her Camry was parked in the next space, she didn't want to be associated with it for as long as possible.

"She's cool. Ghetto as hell, but she's ..."

"Young and thinks she's grown?"

As if finding a discovery to make her eyes wide, she answered, "Yeah. Exactly. But she's cool though. You'll like her."

Peaches crooked her lips. "That's saying a lot cuz I don't be liking too many bitches."

"So you spending the night at Dahji's?"

Peaches let out a small giggle. "He tried to rewind the tape on a bitch. We too far into the movie for him to start that shit."

Sherrelle wanted to ask what she meant, but there were only so many times she could tolerate being called a square in one day. She pretended to understand, nodding her head slowly.

"You don't know what the hell I'm talking about do you?"

Sherrelle burst out laughing as she admitted she had no clue.

"He stalling on giving me a key."

"The way you was tripping on the lawyer I wouldn't give you one either. You already know he's king dick and his penthouse is like a treadmill for pussy."

Peaches pressed her knees together like she had to pee. "I know ... But I thought I could handle it. I'm catching feelings in the worst way. I talk that shit about not tripping on him doing what he do, but damn!"

"Well, you're going to have to suck it up. You made that bed. That's probably why he's still a bachelor. Can't nobody really handle that shit. They say they can, but that's just in the movies or if you have a billion dollars on some Hugh Hefner type jump off." Sherrelle said this as Peaches was growing more attentive, her neck swinging back in true amazement by the time she finished.

"Well, check you out. What you know about it?"

"Would you agree to live with him if he had another woman there?"

Peaches gave this quiet thought before she said, "If I could choose her. She can't be prettier than me though."

"I know that's right," Sherrelle replied around a bubble of giggles. "Well, let me go. I have to pick up a few shirts for hubby."

"How is your little dick doing?"

"Same as always. Earning money and letting me spend it," she answered with quiet mirth, exchanging a subdued hand grasp with Peaches.

"Okay girl. I'll talk to you later. I'm about to go get that manufacturing hook-up for us."

"Thank you so much girl. This is going to be nice for both of us."

Peaches dipped and swung her long hair as she turned. "Oh. I know," she quipped, looking back to Sherrelle over her shoulder. "I don't do nothing for nothing," she added as she stepped around the rear end of her Camry.

Sherrelle smiled grandly as she slid behind the wheel of her Jaguar, waving as she backed out of the space.

Peaches waited until she'd turned down the aisle before she twisted the key in the ignition. Though Sherrelle had heard her car come to life before, Peaches was still embarrassed by the episode. The car choked and coughed awake, the engine rocking violently until it settled down to a mild thumping rumble.

Yeah, she began in quiet thought, *this is gon' be over real soon. This case is gon' end in probation, which I can handle, and once we get this distribution and manufacturing deal, then it's a whole new situation. Bitch is gon' be the boss then. Nigga can kiss my ass if he think he gon' get some pussy for crumbs.* These thoughts raced through her head as she pulled from the parking lot into the street on her way to Dr. Kim's office. She'd stopped short of swearing off stripping. She enjoyed dancing too much to go that far.

***

Dr. Kim's office was nestled between a See's Candy store and a 31 Flavors ice cream parlor. The effect made the air a mix of sweet confection in and around the doctor's office. The small business park was nearly full due to the lunch-time crowd grabbing a respite from their cubicles and sealed offices.

Peaches let the car die slowly as she pulled into an open space directly in front of Dr. Kim's office. She checked her makeup and hair before alighting from the car, ignoring the looks of pedestrians who also thought it odd that such a beautiful woman should emerge from such a car. Peaches hadn't bothered washing it, willing it to simply die and force her to spend some of that hard-earned money she'd been saving for her dream house; it would have a kitchen window with purple lace curtains and there would be two lemon trees in the front yard.

Peaches often wondered how Dr. Kim stayed in family practice. There were hardly ever any patients in the lobby. *Perhaps he scheduled them in a way so as to keep a relaxed and unhurried environment,* she thought to herself as she stepped to the receptionist's desk. The young, perky blonde looked from behind the tall divider with her usual plastic grin. She would ask Peaches who she was and if she had an appointment even though she'd seen her many times before and no doubt knew the exact nature of her visit.

On cue, Dr. Kim appeared at the edge of the narrow hallway just beyond the desk. It was as if he had a secret sense of Peaches' arrival. He smiled grandly in his white lab coat.

"Ms. Peaches," he said, his face staying smooth and pasty white.

Peaches returned his generous smile as she stepped in his direction, adding extra sway to her hips for the benefit of the receptionist's cutting eyes as they trailed her.

"Good you come. Have very good news for you," Dr. Kim announced after a soft air kiss against her fragrant cheek.

"Well, I'm always in the mood for good news." Her reply came just as they reached an examination room at the end of the hallway. Besides the usual padded exam table there was a leather love seat against the wall. This was a recent addition; something Peaches had said should be added on her last visit.

"Oh, that's so nice. You got the loveseat!" she gushed, rushing over to sit down playfully. She ran her hands along the soft leather while Dr. Kim pulled a leather Louis Vuitton folder from a table drawer. His small, dark eyes beamed from his pie-shaped face as he walked the few steps to hand it to her.

"This is a gift," he announced. "Inside is my cousin Sun Yi address and phone number. He is good manufacturer. He make this luggage," he added, gesturing to the folder in her hand. Peaches was immediately excited. This was good news.

She made her face sad after showing a smile of appreciation. "But he might be too expensive."

Dr. Kim became animated. "Oh no no. We make it okay. You first order free. Then you pay for rest and first from sales. Plus a discount." He smiled wide with his achievement.

Peaches jumped from the couch and hugged the short man to her bosom. "Thank you so much," she whispered in his ear.

"You are welcome." His face was flustered as Peaches held his hand in hers. She then reached between his lab coat and found the zipper on his trousers.

"Have you missed me?" she asked.

"Yes. Very much."

"I can tell," she whispered, having pulled him free and stroked him to life. He was warm and soft in her palm. His breathing was labored.

"You are so beautiful."

"Thank you Dr. Kim. You are always so good to me." With this she unbuttoned her leather vest and let it swing open. Then she slowly unbuttoned the white button-up and let it hang loose, revealing the black lace bra underneath.

Dr. Kim swallowed hard at the sight of her creamy breasts. The effect of her slow-moving limbs, the diamonds on her bracelets and rings twinkling, and her carefully manicured fingers sent waves of dry heat through him. She pulled a pair of Chinese pins from her hair and the lustrous burgundy strands dropped to her shoulders and bounced seductively.

"I've missed you and want you inside of me Dr. Kim," she cooed as she unzipped the back of her leather knee length skirt. It fell to her ankles to reveal the black lace stockings and garter belts. She spread her long legs and placed her hands on her hips, her gray eyes blazing.

Dr. Kim stepped forward silently and gently placed his hands on her shoulders, pushing the shirt and vest from her arms. He then buried his face in her breasts and inhaled her scent while she ran her fingers through his short, cropped hair. Her fingers dipped between their bodies and found his straining joint. She stroked him softly.

"Are you ready to be inside of me?" she asked softly in his ear.

Dr. Kim nodded, allowing himself to be led to the loveseat by the end of his penis.

Peaches sat down and reached into her shallow Chanel purse. She produced a condom and surgically covered his organ with it. Next she applied KY Jelly and rubbed him to full strength as he stood between her legs threatening to climax. She then turned onto the couch, her knees in the cushions and offered her ass to him.

"I need you now," she hissed, reaching behind her to spread her ass wide. This was a delicacy for Dr. Kim. She didn't mind serving it to him because he was as large as a breakfast sausage. She barely felt his entry.

Dr. Kim grabbed her by the hips and humped into her ass hole with urgent, tight strokes.

"Yes. Yes. That feels sooo good," Peaches hissed, bucking back into him with each thrust.

Dr. Kim grunted behind her and pressed his fingers into her flesh. Peaches hissed out in mock pain and squeezed onto his joint roughly, causing him to jerk suddenly, spilling his load into the latex. There were a few more shallow pumps before she relaxed and pushed the spent sausage from her.

Dr. Kim swiveled around and dropped to the couch beside her with his eyes closed in passionate agony. The condom was raised like a flag over his deflated organ. Peaches checked her watch quickly, the deed done, and stood up. Dahji's words of time being money sang in her ears.

When Dr. Kim opened his eyes to her moment she smiled and said, "That was too wonderful. Thank you. I'll see you next week?" As she spoke she expertly pulled on her skirt and buttoned her blouse.

"Yes," he choked out. "Very good."

Peaches leaned to kiss him on the forehead. "It seems like such a long time away."

"Wait." He struggled from his seat, pulling the condom from his weakened shaft and carrying it with him to the table against the far wall. After depositing it into a red plastic container he pulled a thick business sized envelope from the drawer.

"Here. Do not forget."

Peaches accepted the envelope of what she knew was more money than she'd ever asked for. "Thank you, Dr. Kim. You really didn't have to ..."

He waved her words away with a bashful smile, accepting another kiss on the forehead.

"That's so sweet of you, Dr. Kim. Thank you." With this she moved towards the door. He bowed slightly and gave her a short wave before she stepped from the room.

Peaches stepped proudly into the lobby, smiling at the receptionist and telling her to have a great day. There was a tall, handsome white man in a suit who stood as she passed through the front door. She vaguely recognized him from the front row of Applebottoms. She didn't forget a face and if she recalled correctly, he tipped very well for lap dances. She would make a note to give him special attention the next time she saw him.

She said a silent prayer for her car to start with minimal resistance before she twisted the key in the ignition. Sherrelle was right; she really should get another car.

CHAPTER ELEVEN

A pimp's duty is never complete, Dahji thought to himself as he dipped from the parking lot of the courthouse. He could feel his skin growing hives already. Courtrooms made him nervous. The various performances by interested parties nearly made him ill. They all pretended to have as much at stake as the actual person facing jail time. It was enough to make him scratch his neck looking for raised welts of agitation.

It disturbed him to see Peaches break down like that. As much as he liked her flavor, he didn't like to have to work too hard to keep it nice and sweet. But she straightened up with minor instruction. He liked that. *But damn, was she acting jealous of Viola?* he asked himself with chagrin. That was completely out of character for the boss chick that she was. *Maybe the court case was breaking her down and making her vulnerable. You never truly know someone until they have to respond to a crisis,* he reasoned.

Dahji was thinking of making the trip to his favorite eating hole, Haitian Jack's, when his iPhone charmed to life. Mirabelle's smiling face filled the screen, the large Mikimoto pearl earrings giving her waspish appearance a New England pedigree. She was responsible for allowing Dahji space and money to advance his game. Some may have called her a sponsor, but in the years they'd known each other she'd become more than that.

"I was just saying to myself – Dahji McBeth, why has the sun hid itself in the clouds? – and here you are."

"Well, that is so precious. Your flattery never gets dull," Mirabelle replied.

"That ain't flattery beautiful. That's the truth. How are you today sunshine? Missed your call this morning."

She groaned before she said, "I know. I was looking forward to seeing you before ... Did you go to court?"

"Yeah. Building still there, too." He could feel her smile through the phone.

"Is everything okay?"

"It's like a magic trick. Only the person who knows the trick can tell you if it went well."

"Did she get bound over?" she asked with sincere sorrow in her voice.

"Don't fret for her. She's tough as nails and twice as sharp. Tell me about you."

"My day was terrible. I so desperately need to see you," she cried in her pampered way. From any one else Dahji would have taken this as a cry for attention or time, but for Mirabelle this meant something very dear to her was in jeopardy: Money; and by association his very lifestyle was threatened.

"I'm on my way," he assured her.

"Please hurry. I feel terribly alone." Her voice cracked, sounding like she'd leaned away from the phone.

"Dahji will be there to make it better so put a pot of tea on and by the time it whistles, I'll be at your door."

She giggled softly. "I feel better already. Mint or herbal?"

"Herbal sounds good."

"Tootles," she said cheerfully before ending the call.

What is it ... Is it because it's Wednesday that I'm being tested? he asked himself as he made a left for the highway that would take him to Mirabelle. Or maybe it's because the summer is almost over; or it could be some invisible cosmic downpour that makes women seek security by a man's reasoning skills.

Just as he was considering that maybe there was some unknown season for women to become emotional in unison his iPhone charmed to life again.

"Speak on it," he answered. Coretta only recently returned to his life with news that her seven-year-old daughter was his. They'd gotten past the part about how she led her husband to believe that Aryn was his because he had a better job than Dahji. Now, as it turns out, the dude was a criminal disguised as a banker and Dahji had left his job with UPS and was now BAWLIN!

"Hey you," Coretta said in her sexy way. Dahji had to admit that she moved him in a way that still felt like high school. He still hadn't decided what her full angle was yet, but let it roll for the opportunity to bond with his daughter. He wasn't even mad at her for denying him this from the beginning. And didn't fault her at all for calculating ways to divorce her husband when he caught his bit. Knowing all this about her only added flavor to her already seasoned personality.

"Where she at?"

"Right here." There was a transfer of the phone. "Hi, daddy." Aryn's voice was a miniature of her mother's seductive whisper. It would serve her well in life.

"Hey, baby girl. How's daddy's little angel doing today?"

"Good, daddy. We're going to granny house today. Will you be there?" she asked. Dahji suspected the latter part of what she said was at her mother's direction; still, he couldn't deny his little girl.

"Yeah. What time ya'll going over there?"

"What time, mommy?" she asked away from the phone. Dahji heard Coretta answer before Aryn said, "For dinner."

"Sounds good already. Did you have a good day at school?"

"Yep. We made macaroni necklaces. I made one for you and mommy and we made picture families." She stopped abruptly. Dahji wasn't sure if she was still on the phone.

"That sounds like real fun," he said as the landscape beside the freeway slowly merged into one of stately homes and large patches of grass. Only money could buy land for grass. In the ghetto every piece of usable land was covered with a liquor store or beauty parlor. Lately, Magic Johnson was getting in on the act and franchising the same fast food joints that the marinas and suburbs enjoyed. But this area was still too rich for his money. He could envision Mirabelle sitting alone in a room the size of a Baptist church.

"So you'll stop by? Aryn will be expecting you," Coretta said into the phone.

"Don't act like you ain't got a magic trick."

"So what if I do?"

"I'ma have to see your hands when I come through," he replied.

"You might have to do a pat down, too."

"You would like that. So what's the special occasion for the middle of the week dinner at my momma's house?"

"Well, first of all we don't need a special occasion to visit FAMILY ... And second of all your mother wanted to see her granddaughter. Is that okay with you?"

"Well, since you put it like that then ..."

"That's what I thought," Coretta said quickly. Dahji couldn't help the smile that spread his lips.

"So what time are you coming over?" She made it sound like it was her house he was coming to.

"Dinner, right?"

"Right. But what time is that?" she wanted to know.

"What are you the FBI or something? You got somebody in the bushes waitin to assassinate me so you can get to Aryn's inheritance?" When she laughed he was reminded of those long ago nights when they used to make up stories as they lay in bed.

"You crazy. That penthouse and that Ranger Rover together couldn't pay for her Ivy League University tuition. Now unless you got something stashed away that you want to tell me about then I might consider calling the homies and ..."

"YadayadayaDA! See you when I see you. Give my daughter a kiss for me." There was no response.

"Bye daddy," Aryn called out excitedly. "See you later."

"Bye angel. Daddy see you later. Be good and bite your mother on the knee for me. Do it now." She laughed with this as she tried to explain to her mother what her mission was. Somewhere in the excited explanation the call was ended.

Dahji made the final right turn down a shaded, tree-lined street. The houses weren't visible from here. They were secluded behind large shrubbery wrapped around tall security fences. The front lawns provided ample options for a trespasser to be either eaten by Rotweillers or shot dead by private security.

Dahji pulled into the familiar break in trees at the middle of the quiet street. He pressed the appropriate numbers on the digital keypad and the black wrought iron gate hummed open to allow entry.

The mini-mansion stood at the end of a half mile driveway. Dahji had first come here when he was delivering packages for UPS. Mirabelle was distraught when she answered the door. A few kind words and the bulge in his short pants convinced her that he was someone she could confide in. Her deceased husband left her filthy rich and alone.

As he pulled into the circular driveway and stopped behind her powder blue Bentley Arnage, she stood in the large doorway like a miniature doll in a giant playhouse. Her raven black hair hung loose over her slim shoulders. With long limbs and graceful movements, Mirabelle was the epitome of the wealthy widow. The black, nearly transparent silk gown she wore did nothing to alter this view.

"The tea pot has whistled. You owe me dearly for your miscalculations," she sang as Dahji landed on the wide porch. She leaned helplessly against the frame of the door until he closed the distance between them.

"What do I owe you?" he asked as she wrapped her long arms around his neck and stabbed her mint-flavored tongue into his mouth. She ground her hips into him suggestively and moaned with her thin lips working to cover his mouth.

She broke away from him suddenly, lowering her eyes as she brushed at the sleeve of his leather coat. "I apologize. You must think that I am out of sorts." She then briskly turned from him with a flurry of her arms so that the silk of her gown fanned dramatically through the air.

Dahji followed her into the sitting room just off the main hallway. On the walls were ornate tapestries and rare oil-on-canvas artwork by dead Russian and French artists. There were several paintings of pudgy nude women who seemed, to Dahji, misshapen and very pink, but he was sure that by their sheer ugliness they must have been worth a lot of money. In the far corner was a shining grand piano that sat on a brightly weaved carpet. Mirabelle had once said she'd bought it while in Persia.

"This arrived from England only last week," she said, a return to her proper station and voice as she leaned forward from a white linen couch to pour tea from a flower print ceramic pot.

Dahji shed his coat and threw it on the arm of the couch. "Does the Queen drink it?" he asked as she handed him a cup filled with herbal tea. She smiled appreciatively with his observance.

"I'm sure she does, so count us fortunate," she replied before taking a small sip. "Like?"

Dahji nodded slowly, the tea coursing down his throat and settling in his lap. This was some special tea. "This might cure me."

Her sparkling blue eyes widened. "From what pray tell."

"From a limp joint."

She hooted with subdued laughter as she set her cup down. "I so needed to see you Dahji McBeth. You bring such color to my dreary life."

"Talk to me, beautiful." Dahji urged her. "What has your feathers ruffled?"

"It's bad, Dahji. It's so bad I don't know how I'll survive it. All I need is two more quarters to recover dividends from an overseas market account and ..."

Dahji was shaking his head in confusion.

"You really should watch the Nightly Business Report. How are you going to handle the money you inherit from me?"

This was the first he'd heard of an inheritance.

"Oh. Was I supposed to mention that? Well, you don't think I'll live forever do you?"

Dahji smiled. He didn't want to answer this question.

"I'll be forty-six years old next month. How much longer do you think I have?" she asked frightfully.

"As long as I keep giving you this fountain of youth."

She hooted with laughter again, reaching across to rub her fingers down the length of the snake in his pants. "That's clever," she declared soberly, returning her hand to her lap. The tea cooled in the cup and he set it on the varnished slice of redwood table in front of them.

"Well, you've got a new girlfriend who seems to attract a lot of your time?" she asked, her thin eyebrows raised in speculation.

"I don't know about all that," Dahji hedged.

She tapped him on the leg. "Come on now. Don't be bashful. You should know that I'm not the jealous type. Takes too much energy. But she must be special to have you traipsing through a court room."

"She's good people," Dahji confessed.

"Well, if there's anything I can do to help just let me know. Most of the judges owe me a favor." She said this off-handedly as if it were a simple matter of asking for a pack of Now & Laters.

"That's good to know. But you still haven't expressed why your clouds are dark." She looked to Dahji as if the reason for her sorrow had just occurred to her. After setting her tea on the table casually she folded her legs under her slender body and eased closer to him. Dahji noticed the fine lines around her large, blue eyes and the way her rouged lips turned down at the edges.

"This may be our last, Dahji McBeth" she whispered as she stroked his leg, the tips of her slim fingers brushing across the length of his joint.

Dahji remained silent, inhaling her flowery scent. There was a sliver of fine, black strands that escaped her attempt to pin her hair behind her ear.

She looked up to him as if she were a small girl. "Would you love me if I had no money?" she asked inquisitively.

Dahji's eyes moved across her face quickly, looking for some sign of how serious her question was. Her eyes stared back at him plainly. Her small nostrils flared slightly and he was suddenly aware of her fright.

"You mean more to me than that", he answered. There was an instance when their eyes met, searching for sincerity, before she let a small grin tease her lips.

"Well, that's good to hear, but so much to ask of you."

"Do me a favor, sunshine. Tell me what the problem is and let's see if I can help you."

She exhaled grandly in preparation for what she had to say. "Okay. Here it is. My husband left his twin sisters in charge of my real estate holdings. They invested the equity in subprime mortgages."

Dahji nodded. He'd heard how the economy was in a spiral because people were taking advantage of poor people.

"Well, these bitches hate me and have long been looking for any opportunity to take what belongs to me."

Dahji was trying to figure out how this affected him.

"The interest and revenue from my real estate trust is how I enjoy my big pleasures," she admitted with a rub of his leg. Her hand was warm through the khaki material as it rest just out of reach of his organ.

"So the bank will take the property"? he asked.

"Oh no!" she quipped, snatching her hand from his lap and covering her heaving breast. "I own it outright! They don't care what happens to the Trust as long as I suffer! They refuse to wait for ten days. They've illegally invested my Trust. All I need is ten days," she said with a hint of anger.

"What happens in ten days?"

She'd placed her head on his chest by this point. She turned her eyes up to his face and whispered, "Every six months I get a million dollars from a Trust account. I can satisfy the debt they've incurred and then take those witches to court!" She'd folded her fingers into a pale fist with this announcement.

"You spend two meal tickets a year?" Dahji asked in what he hoped was a calm voice. He realized that he'd been selling himself short. The penthouse, Range Rover and other trinkets were nothing more than a trip to the market for a bag of bananas for her.

"It takes a million dollars to breathe," she confessed breathlessly.

"How much property are we talking about?"

"Among other commercial property, I own your building," she replied without emotion. Suddenly her predicament was close to home. Literally.

Dahji felt sick. It wasn't even about being friends anymore. He needed to save his own ass. Without Mirabelle he would be reduced to an average player that sweat hunger from his pores. His mind was reeling as she stood with his hand in hers. He'd never paid a note on the penthouse, but knew that he couldn't afford it even if it was half of what he thought it should be. As she led him through the carpeted hallway and up a winding staircase, the low keys of a piano became more distinct. Her hand was feather in his palm, the silk gown trailing her like a rose-scented apparition.

Mirabelle's bedroom was a series of sections dedicated to either entertaining (where two over-stuffed chairs faced one another before a fireplace), leisure (a low fluffy couch sat before a stand of books and magazines), and rest (where a large, high bed sat under a beam of light).

The sun washed over these entire sections, but none more so than the bed itself, the benefactor of a sky-light. The decorative colors grew brighter; from powder blue to pink and then finally to white, the closer they got to the bed. It was covered in layers of pure white silk, its pillows shiny and carelessly thrown about. Beside an open window, where a slight breeze blew in stood a small black piano; its keys moved of their own to the tune he'd heard throughout the room.

When Mirabelle finally turned to him, sitting on the edge of the mattress, she had tears in her eyes. She reached silently for his belt buckle and unfastened it. Her movements were slow and meticulous. His pants dropped to his ankles and he was free before her as she pulled his silk boxers over the thick appendage.

Dahji had never seen her like this. He wanted to help her in any way he could, but it seemed that she needed something he didn't have. Money. Money before ten days. He wondered, as she placed his thick meat to her cheek, if it was as serious as she'd made it sound. She now moaned against the bulbous head and tentatively wrapped her lips around it as her fingers delicately held him aloft.

"Please undress and make love to me, Dahji," she whispered, freeing him from her touch and backing up on the mattress. She slowly peeled the nightgown from her slender body, revealing the firm breasts of a much younger woman. Her skin fought tightly against the looseness of age.

Dahji's ten-inch pendulum led the way as he crawled onto the mattress and between her legs. He let the heavy meat rest on the soft mound of her black-haired pussy. He was wrapped in her long limbed embrace. Her lips were wet with tears as she kissed him hungrily. Her hands rubbed along his body and up through his long hair. Her legs wrapped around his waist so that he dipped into her hot opening, the heat wrapping the swollen head of his dick in welcome. Her shoulders shook and her stomach heaved up against him. She cried onto his tongue with small whispers urging him to love her. He slid into her gently, causing her to gasp and scratch at his back. Her legs quivered and her pussy opened like a blooming flower. Their bodies rolled together in a tight embrace as he inched further into her. Tears streamed from her eyes as she tilted her head back, her mouth ajar like an untended hinge. She gasped hotly with each gentle thrust inside of her. She locked her legs around him tightly and held him close to enhance the feeling.

Dahji moved slowly, caressing her with care. Her body was hot beneath him. She wrapped him in her sorrow. Her cheeks were wet with tears as she leaned to his mouth and covered his lips with hers. The salt of her despair reached his tongue, mingling with the damp strands of her loose hair.

Mirabelle grew more excited with each controlled stroke. When she unlocked her legs and spread them wide, she released all control of the moment and surrendered to what Dahji knew she needed. Her body convulsed as she thrashed about under the hard, penetrating strokes between her legs.

The piano serenaded them as the soft breeze soothed their passion. Each of their senses were seduced on the scented silk sheets. They made love as if it were the last time; made passionate by impending loss.

CHAPTER TWELVE

She was doing her part and she felt good about it. There was a certain level of pride she felt with being part of something positive. This feeling was a much needed salve against her earlier doldrums. The horror of the morning's courtroom appearance seemed so far away.

The sun left an orange glow across the horizon with its setting as she turned onto Sherrelle's street. She looked forward to seeing the new shipment of HoodSweet apparel that arrived while she was getting poked in the ass by Dr. Kim.

Because she'd stopped by her apartment to bathe and change clothes, she was later than expected; for this reason she answered her iPhone without checking the caller I.D. If she had, she would have known that it was not Sherrelle calling to find out where she was. If she saw the unrecognizable number she would not have been so surprised to hear Tequan's voice.

"Waddup tho?" he asked with a mixture of torture and surprise. The feeling that Peaches had succeeded in burying with her optimism sprang to the surface.

"What's up," she replied wearily, Sherrelle's Jaguar parked in the driveway, a small comfort.

"How did it go?" he asked.

"How did what go?" Peaches pulled to the curb. She could see two shapely figures moving around behind Sherrelle's living room curtain.

"Court. You thought I was gon' be there, hunh?"

"Yeah," she huffed out, her earlier wonder returning. "What happened?"

"They had me on the TV. You didn't see the TV when you was in there?"

"Okay. So what's next Tequan because I have to go."

"Like that? You just gon' shake a nigga like that after all we been through?" There was a note of anger under his plea.

"NIGGA!" she yelled out in sudden anger. "I got a fucking dope case Tequan! What the hell are you talking about? There is no me and you! I'm tired ... Do you hear me? Tired!"

There was a minute of silence before he said, "Tired of what? So you just gon' fold like an accordion behind some punk ass case. They ain't gon' do nothing but give you probation. You'll still be able to come see me if we work it right."

Peaches held the phone to her ear in shock. She was looking up the street where a new Cadillac was pulling into a driveway.

"Hello?"

"I know, Tequan ..." she began in a calm voice. "I shouldn't be surprised that all you're thinking about is yourself. That was going to be my last time coming to see you. I thought I was doing the right thing by telling you face to face and ..."

"Telling me what?!" he broke in, afraid to let her keep her thoughts straight. The boom in his voice was meant to deter her, but it only made her more sure.

"That we've run our course, Tequan."

"Run our course? ... What kind of shit is that? Nigga take a little ... What ... You got another nigga or something?" A measure of uncertainty was creeping into his voice.

"That don't even matter. I just can't do it anymore ... You didn't even ask me how I was doing or if I need a lawyer or nothing," she said, trying hard to keep the cry in her heart from making it to her voice. She'd let the motor idle, afraid of the sound it would make when she cut it off. Now she didn't care.

"Damn baby, is that your car?"

"Yep."

"So you just gon' let my ride sit in the impound?"

She wanted to say that once again it was all about him, but instead she said, "Have your mother go get it. Don't she have the pink slip?"

"If you woulda followed instructions the ...

"Bo?" she asked of the new familiar voice.

"You know what it is. You shoulda put that in the safe with a string." Bo said in his gruff, threatening manner.

"Well, Tequan ... I gotta go. I'm sorry about your car." Peaches did not want to argue about the right way to do wrong. The last thing she heard was Bo saying something about how his product costing money before she ended the call and stepped from the car. When the phone rang again she turned it off. Before she knocked on the front of Sherrelle's door she worked to shake the effects of the phone call from her watery eyes.

The powerful, sultry voice of Keisha Cole followed Sherrelle as she opened the door, a wide grin on her face as she looked to Peaches. "What happened?" she asked, the smile vanishing. Behind her Ayana danced in a seductive way, her eyes closed and her thin arms raised to the ceiling in swirling motions.

Peaches hurriedly wiped at her eyes, pushing the Versace shades to the crown of her ponytail. "Niggas!" she huffed out as she stepped into the warm house. Ayana turned to her and their eyes met. Peaches could immediately see herself ten years ago in the young, pretty woman with a shape like syrup.

"Hi," Ayana said, smiling wide. "You gotta be Peaches. My aunt says you're the baddest bitch ever!" she added, causing Peaches to burst out in much needed laughter. She accepted Ayana's warm embrace with enthusiasm. She entertained the idea that Sherrelle's niece would be the jealous, ghetto sort, but was happy to see damn near herself in front of her.

"Don't believe her!" Sherrelle countered as she closed the door to the night.

"What y'all got going on?" Peaches asked, shedding her oversized Davoucci leather jacket to reveal the red cashmere sweater. Her legs were shaped by rust colored Request jeans, descending to black leather pumps with pearls across he leather straps.

"Whatever you got going on!" Ayana cheered, her eyes moving down the length of Peaches' body in appreciation. "I wanna do what you do."

Peaches waved her off as she moved to the fresh pile of HoodSweet apparel. "No you don't. My knees and my back hurt."

"I don't care. I want my back to hurt if it means I can dress like you."

Peaches looked to Sherrelle with wide eyes. "Is she serious?" she asked

"Unfortunately," Sherrelle replied.

"Whatever," Ayana gestured with a light wave and stepped to a neat stack of boy-shorts. "These just came today Peaches." She held up a pair.

"See, they're ribbed around the bottom and cut sharper up the sides." She was busy demonstrating while Peaches exchanged a secret glance with Sherrelle.

"She likes the clothes," Sherrelle offered.

"I see."

'Don't you think they're cute?" Ayana asked, placing the boy-shorts to her waist. She'd covered over the mid thigh stretch pants she was wearing. Peaches had noted at the outset how her body was shaped in a perfect Coke bottle. *It should be against the law for an eighteen-year-old girl to have such a body,* Peaches thought, remembering that she didn't fill out until she was old enough to legally buy liquor.

"You talk to Dahji?" Ayana asked quickly, her youth exposing itself. She was in the middle of pulling the boy-shorts up her thighs. Peaches had turned to Sherrelle when she'd shed the stretch pants. Now she was forced back to her, getting a good glimpse of her fine shape with its gentle curves.

"Yeah. Why?" Peaches said, her own sense of ghetto coming forth.

Ayana retreated, fitting the boy-shorts over her waist and occupying herself with the way they fit over her bulging pussy. "I saw him when I got here, that's all," she replied, never looking up to Peaches' inquisitive stare.

Peaches watched the young version of her and saw the same wants and needs. "You like him, hunh?" she asked, forcing Ayana's light-brown gaze to her.

"Naw!" she replied with a screwed up face. "He think he some type of pimp!"

"Bitch, you lying. He got you open like an oyster at midnight. What he say to you?" she asked after smiling mischievously to Sherrelle.

Ayana leaned on one hip, her hand on her waist. "He said I needed new management." She twisted her lips together with the absurdity of the proposal, letting them slide to a smile when Peaches started laughing and slapping hands with Sherrelle.

"He a pimp, hunh?" Ayana wanted to know, feeling left out of the joke.

Peaches let her jeweled fingers land on Ayana's bare arm as she passed. "Naw girl. He ain't no pimp. He just a brother trying to stay out the pen." She laughed with this and shoved off.

"Well, he talk like a pimp," Ayana complained more to Sherrelle because Peaches was on her way into the kitchen.

Sherrelle pointed to the stretch pants at Ayana's feet. "You shouldn't judge people so quickly. You wouldn't want people to think you're for sell just because you dress ..."

"Well his uncle Prince Sweetwater is a pimp for sure! And you can't tell me he ain't," Ayana cut in, waving the stretch pants in the air.

"I don't know his uncle. That was my first time meeting him."

"Meeting who?" Peaches wanted to know as she stepped back in to the living room carrying a miniature bottle of Smirnoff Grand Cosmopolitan.

"Did Dahji tell you about his uncle Prince? Ayana seems to think he's a pimp."

Peaches stopped at the threshold and sipped the drink. "This is good," she said, tilting the bottle up to look at the label again. "I didn't know you like cosmo's, Sherrelle."

"That's mine," Ayana informed her evenly then broke into a wide grin at having introduced something she liked. "They good, hunh?"

Peaches gave Ayana a high five as she passed by. "You did good kid. Real good." She stopped over the couch and peered through the front window. "There go your fantasy husband," she announced. Ayana was the first to join her at the front window, her knees digging into the sofa cushions.

Sherrelle's body grew hot as she moved towards the front door. She peered through a break in the curtain as she glided slowly to the door, telling herself that any good neighbor would appear on their porch to say hello.

"Ain't that the one who plays football?" Ayana asked as Sherrelle stepped through the door.

Yes. He was supposed to be playing football, Sherrelle thought to herself as the cool night air washed over her. There were many nights she'd waited for him to come home. Her view of his truck was too clear. It was then she noticed that his wife Stacy wasn't home yet. How late was it? How early? It was odd to see him. Where was she? Now she was curious, her bare feet guiding her across the porch and down the steps; all the while her mind was struggling to make out the odd instruments Marlin was struggling to place on the ground. She was walking faster now, somehow the beat of her heart registering some as yet unknown tragedy.

Now she was light on her feet as she trotted with baited breath to where he leaned from the door of the Escalade. Her eyes moved rapidly from the heavy brace on his leg to his face. She wanted him to tell her that it wasn't serious. She wanted for him to say that the crutches were just a precaution; that the brace was only for a few days and that his career was not in jeopardy. She'd covered her lips with trembling fingers as a lone tear dropped from her right eye and made its way down her cheek. She wiped it away quickly when his eyes focused on her with the pain of the truth. It was hard for her to breathe and she didn't want her concern to be so apparent; but it was too late for that now.

She moved to him silently, not hearing him say that he was okay. She made a motion to grab the duffel bag from him before he hoisted it onto his shoulder.

"That some of your new stuff?" he asked, looking from the lavender cotton drawstring sweats and pull-over hoodie to her face. He steadied the crutches for his weight.

It is all so absurd, she thought to herself as she mechanically answered that she'd gotten a new shipment that morning. Gone was her excitement. She tried to smile when he said how cool it was that she was doing her thing.

"So how's your niece settling in?" he wanted to know as he stood up, assuring her with his body language and a quick "I got it" that he could manage.

Sherrelle barely heard herself answer. "She's good." A small, brave smile played on her lips as she watched him take a step away from the door. "I'll close it for you," she said, thinking of how she'd been avoiding him all this time and now that they were within arms reach they were separated by this new tragedy. She walked beside him slowly, listening to him say that he would be fine and not to worry. Her eyes were on his as he looked to her with what she knew were words he couldn't ... or didn't want to say. There was too much unsaid between them and if they had the courage to press on there was no telling what might occur. But now this. She felt her heart breaking for him. She knew how much it meant for him to make the team. It was too much for her to take, watching him struggle on metal sticks. She stepped in front of him suddenly and wrapped her arms around his neck. Her lips found his quickly before she stepped back in apology.

"It's cool," Marlin managed, holding in all emotion.

Sherrelle turned away, her fingers brushing along his arm before contact was broken. She trotted across the slim slice of grass that separated their yards, her eyes blurry with new tears. She did not notice Percy approaching in the street. She was through the front door when he finally made it to the driveway.

CHAPTER THIRTEEN

Why would her husband leave control of Mirabelle's property with his twin sisters? This is the question that plagued Dahji. Rich people made no sense to him. Maybe there was something Mirabelle was leaving out. Was this her way of shutting him down? This shit was way too funky. *If that wasn't break-up sex then my name ain't Dahji McBeth,* he mumbled to himself as he pulled onto his parents' street.

He was late. Mirabelle wouldn't let him from her sight until she made sure he understood that she would do everything possible to keep him in her life. It was all so dramatic. Tears. Pleas. Anger. Vows of revenge. All of this from Mirabelle as she raged against her deceased husband and his two sisters, who she referred to as witches. Dahji had formed a mental picture of the twins as hideous creatures who resembled cave dwellers for the way Mirabelle talked about them. She'd only released him when his daughter called to ask if he was coming to dinner. It was the first Mirabelle had heard of him having a daughter. On his way out of her mini-mansion he promised to explain all the details of how he'd come to learn of his daughter only recently.

Coretta was riding in style. Her forest green Volvo wagon was squatted at the curb on 20" rims. Dahji had to give her credit for the way she rode her husband all the way to jail and jumped off with the loot and goods. She'd sold the house and furniture, giving half the proceeds to his lawyer. With that last act and the admission that Aryn wasn't his daughter, she was done with him like a good rally on Wall Street. She made off with the dividends and sold the rest of her shares short. Now she was looking for another rally to climb, Dahji reminded himself.

A black Mercedes SL500 was parked in the driveway. This must belong to the woman his uncle mentioned. Dahji couldn't remember her name, but he did remember Prince telling him how she was at the tail end of a long walk with a million dollar mark. *That was the bidness,* Dahji thought to himself as he checked his profile in the rearview mirror. He'd hardly had the energy to do anything with his hair, so he'd pulled it into a tight ponytail, the loose bang hanging over the collar of his leather coat. With a diamond bezel Rolex watch and chain draping his neck he still felt light. It was true; it had to be in you not on you. He breathed out hard in preparation of meeting the colorful personalities awaiting him. And here was the unpredictability of Coretta. Suddenly he felt weighed down with an uncertain future. His situation was up in the air; but if Marlin made the team ...

Dahji's daughter burst through the screen door. Coretta appeared on the porch as Aryn scampered down the stone steps. She smiled brightly as she navigated the last step and ran to him with her arms wide.

"Hi daddy! Hi daddy!" she screamed through the night air. She succeeded in lifting the cloud that seemed to have descended over him suddenly. She was light in his arms as he raised her to him and accepting her wet kiss on the check. She smelled of a mixture of licorice and collared greens with pork chunks sautéed in cayenne pepper.

"How's my little angel?" Dahji asked, looking into the light brown eyes that looked more like his in the night. During the day they had the darker glimmer of her mother's eyes.

"I'm fine, daddy. Uncle Prince Sweetwater is over," she said in a bubbly voice. Dahji suspected that she enjoyed saying his name. With it was the experience of his presence; this explained the mischievous, excited look in her eyes.

"Really. Who else is here?"

"His friend from Chicago," she replied.

"Hi Roger," Coretta said once they'd reached the porch. She called him this when she was either angry or planning to blackmail him with guilt. Either way she would not return to "Dahji" until she'd been pleased. She had license to do this since his mother refused to call him Dahji McBeth.

"That's how it's going to be tonight?" he wanted to know, sliding Aryn from his arms. She looked to her mother for her answer.

"You said you were going to be here for dinner," she complained. Her legs and ass were her best asset. They served her well as a former cheerleader. Petite and feminine, Coretta learned her subtle ways from a mother who'd been married for nearly fifty years. You don't keep a husband for half a century without knowing something about subtlety. Added to this was the way her shapely legs escaped her mini-skirt. This combination made him smile.

"It's not funny," she huffed with a small hand on her waist. Her palm-sized breasts were hidden under a jean jacket.

Dahji turned his attention to Aryn as he climbed the steps. "What grandma cook?" He could feel Coretta's eyes on him. This is not what he wanted or needed at this moment: Argument. Nor did he want their relationship to be typical of a baby momma drama. It was hard to call up his pimp hand when it was with a woman who had his seed.

"It was a lot daddy! It was ..."

"There was," Coretta corrected her.

Aryn quickly recovered, returning her attention to Dahji. "There was cornbread and cake and kool-aid and ..."

"Where the meat at?" Dahji wanted to know.

Aryn was unaffected by his interruption. "There was ham hocksis ..."

"Hamhocks." This was Coretta, her voice softening with the sight of Dahji interacting with his daughter. He'd made no move towards the front door. His father's deep, graveled voice could be heard. He was telling a story – which Dahji had heard before – about how he'd rescued his uncle Prince from an angry mob of white men in Mississippi. Prince stood accused of White Slavery. The story traversed Reverend Reed's connections with the Southern Baptist Church and the power they exerted to save a pimp's life.

"That sounds good. You think there's some left for me or did you eat it all up?" With this question Dahji bent to rub his fingers across her tight stomach. She squealed out in laughter.

"Come on in here boy." Dahji's mother appeared at the screen, her big eyes wide behind round, black rimmed glasses. She opened the door in invitation. "Y'all gon' get that baby sick out here in this air. Come on inside." With her instruction was the love in her eyes for Dahji. She rubbed her soft hand across his chin as he passed by her into the warm house.

"There he go right there," Prince cheered from the center of the sofa. His long limbs were folded one over the other as he lounged brightly with gold and diamonds glittering like a halo around him. Added to this effect was the smiling woman beside him. Without further inspection – by the sheer blackness of her skin and the shiny softness of her long hair – he knew that her sky blue eyes were real. Prince said that she was born on an island where everyone looked like her. Seeing her now, Dahji could not imagine being around an island full of women who looked like her. She was a rare treat. A rare treat indeed.

"Roger!" his father boomed out. He, too, refused to call him by his adopted name. Prince Sweetwater had escaped this prison because he'd announced himself at an early age before Reverend Reed's church. There had been a concerted effort to get Prince to follow in Reverend Reed's footsteps, but Prince had other plans. He knew early on – after reading PIMP by Iceberg Slim – that he wanted to be a pimp. It didn't matter to him that Iceberg Slim had done time in prison and ended up broke and alone before turning to writing. Prince swore that he would be better. And so far he'd been true to his word. Consequently, not since Prince Sweetwater's ninth birthday was he called Othello Reed.

"You haven't met Emma Jean," Prince said, cupping his hand in her direction as if she were a prize on The Price Is Right.

"Bonjour," she said sweetly with a small wave of her slim, black fingers. Her shiny, black hair was parted in the middle of her high forehead and descended in lustrous curls down the side of her slender face. Her limbs were as long as Prince's and folded over one another in similar fashion. Dahji could only imagine the nature of her intricate seductions. Seeing her solidified in Dahji's mind his conviction that Prince was playing in a higher league than himself. *But there was time,* Dahji said to himself as his mother invited him the table to eat.

"He probably just come from somebody's table," Reverend Reed boomed out around silent laughter, the effect making his slender body adjust in the leather lazy-boy by the fireplace.

"Cleotis! Now you stop that fool talk. I'm sure he's been hard at work." They'd been talking as if Dahji was not in the room until his mother looked to him sideways. "So you still got that man on the football team?" she asked cautiously.

"Yeah!" his father erupted. "That's Marlin Cassidy. Used to play for the Seahawks. He's going to work out just fine! So, Roger you're going to be a big-time agent, hunh?" he finished.

There seemed to be some doubt laced in his father's question, but whatever feeling that threatened his optimism was saved by Emma Jean.

"Tres bien. Very Good. Fait acomplite. It is already done," she sang in her lilting voice, giving Dahji a hint to her secret allure.

"That's good business," Prince echoed with a wide smile, nodding his head subtly. "Spaceships don't come with rear view mirrors," he added cryptically. This amused Emma Jean. Her laughter was a musical note that brought to mind a sandy beach with a colorful drink in hand.

"Yeah. We get the final contract in a week or so," Dahji said as he pulled the vibrating iPhone from his coat pocket. Peaches' smiling screwed up face appeared on the screen. She'd refused to send him a glamour shot. Coretta let out a small gasp when she saw the picture.

"Who's that?" she wanted to know. Dahji was already on his way to the room he was raised in. His mother had never dismantled the attic space.

"Momma, make me a plate. I'ma go wash up," he said with Coretta in tow. They were being followed by Aryn to the stairway in the middle of the hallway that led to the attic when Coretta turned to her and suggested that she go help grandma.

"Go check that out," Dahji instructed Coretta, having already answered the phone and telling Peaches to hold on.

Coretta looked to him sharply. "I'm coming with you," she vowed before repeating her instruction to Aryn.

"What's up," he said into the phone as he climbed the narrow steps, Coretta on his heels.

The top of the stairway opened onto a wide space of childhood memories. There were his football trophies and bowling Plaques. In the far corner, under the pyramid-shaped window was a basket containing every ball for sports imaginable, including Lacrosse. The low twin bed was situated between a tall boudoir and a low end table with a Jim Beam lamp atop it that he'd made in ninth grade electronics class.

Dahji was listening to how Peaches' day went with the manufacturer as he shed his leather coat and sat down on the bed. Coretta busied herself with his model airplane set against the wall, pretending not to listen.

"That's cool," he said plainly. She went on to say that she'd finally met Ayana and that she might be someone to put on the website.

"Yeah. I met her. She's a little rough around the edges though," he replied. When Peaches mentioned that he hadn't told her he'd met Ayana or that he'd been by Marlin's house, he remained silent so that she could hear the control over him she was trying to exert.

"Well, I guess that's not important," she said in apology.

"But she might work though," he assured her, thinking that he would need some face time with the young beauty to initiate her into his lifestyle.

"So, I'm on my way home to rest and change for work. You won't believe the drama Sherrelle is having with her husband and poor Ayana is caught up in the middle ..." Dahji tuned her gossip out as Coretta slid the jean jacket from her arms and sat next to him on the bed. She'd bored herself with fondling things she'd seen before. Now she concentrated her attention on him. She was paying close attention to his Cole Haan shoes. Dahji pointed his toes out unconsciously.

"So you wanna meet at your house before I go to work?"

"No problem," he responded as Coretta stood from the bed and closed the door at the top of the stairs. She smiled seductively as she strolled back in his direction and positioned herself between his legs.

"Okay then ..." Peaches said, her voice halting as she searched for some important news she wanted to tell him. Coretta kneeled to the carpet and reached for his zipper. He slapped her hand away in protest. This only encouraged her.

"Oh yeah," Peaches erupted after mentioning some minor details about the new shipment of clothes Sherrelle had received. "Marlin got hurt!"

Dahji jerked and stiffened. Coretta's playful smile faded as she looked up to him. "What you mean by that?" he asked, the hollow feeling in his stomach growing deeper with each nano second of uncertain news.

"He came home on crutches and he had an ugly brace on his knee."

Dahji let out a long sigh as he ended the call with Peaches without notice. He looked to the ceiling when Coretta asked if everything was alright. His finger had already pressed Marlin's number.

"Marly Marl. Please tell me something good," he said desperately, feeling as if all was lost to him and his next move was doomed from the start.

"Waddup Dah," Marlin replied sleepily on the other end.

"Word is you done got hurt. Come on Marly Marl. I'm your agent. I gotta know these things for damage control reasons."

"It ain't much," Marlin replied unconvincingly. In his voice was surrender. *This can't be happening,* Dahji thought to himself as he leaned back on the bed, away from Coretta's inquiring gaze.

"What the doctor say?" Dahji placed his arm across his eyes. He didn't have the energy to stop Coretta from unzipping his pants.

"Just a minor twist. Tomorrow I gotta go for some x-rays. They say they want the swelling to go down and see how the knee reacts overnight."

Dahji listened with detachment. There was a visual running through his mind of him driving a used Ford Escort and living in an apartment building with no security. "Awright peeps. Check with me tomorrow." Marlin assured him that he would before Dahji let the iPhone bounce to the bed. He groaned out his frustration through clenched teeth. He shot his balled fists into the air, only vaguely aware that Coretta had pulled his organ through his zipper. The cold air met him before she closed her warm mouth over the head.

"Not right now," he said in a low voice, his mind searching for a solution to the growing list of problems in his life.

Coretta continued sucking the limp joint, stroking him lightly in hopes he would react.

Dahji leaned up. "What are you doing?"

She looked up to him and asked, "What's wrong with it?"

"IT ain't in the mood."

"Come on ...Please ..."

He made a move to get up and was met by a gentle shove back onto the bed. "Where are you going?"

"Watch out man. It's a lot on my mind right now."

"I don't care. You owe me!" she railed with his limp dick still in her hand.

"I owe YOU? ... Seriously though. Watch out. He reached for his dick and she gripped it tightly.

"I ain't playing," she said seriously, her eyes gazing into his while he searched her motivations.

"Awright ..." he said at length, deciding on what he would do. She smiled in response, loosening her grip. "Suck it then," he instructed, concealing the well of anger that rose in him. The universe was conspiring against him. Everything was being done right and it still threatened to end up wrong. This is how niggas pick up a dope sac or a pistol to peddle and rob for their pie in the sky.

Coretta choked with his sudden inflation in her mouth. She could only put half of him to her throat with her small mouth stretched wide.

You *want it, right?* Dahji thought to himself as he reached his full length. He rose up and roughly grabbed her up and rolled her to her back. He grabbed her ankles high in the air and reached with one hand to move the light silk panties to the side. He then shoved the bulbous head of his dick past her moist lips.

"Ahhh ..." she moaned, her head rolling abruptly to the side as she gripped at the Batman comforter.

The thin lining of her silk panties rubbed against his shaft as he squeezed further inside of her, more of a nuisance than a hindrance. He snatched at the material until the silk ripped apart, exposing the hairy muff between her legs. Her ass was at the edge of the bed and Dahji sunk into her with renewed zest, watching himself disappear between her puckered lips and come out new and shiny wet.

"Uummmmhh!" she hissed with her eyes shut tight and her tongue rolling across her lips. With her ankles raised to the air, tightly in his grip, he dove into her again.

Her screams became a soft, whimpering melody to mark every thrust and retreat. She'd pulled a section of the comforter to her mouth and bit into the fabric. Her thumping body motion recorded the depth and energy of his thrusts. There was no mercy in his pounding. The bed squeaked rhythmically as Dahji pushed in and out of her wet pussy, her hairs shiny and slick, matted atop her mound.

Where was the reward for the struggle?, he asked himself. *How can a nigga catch a break.*

Her gasps took on an urgent tone and her ankles were hot in his grasp. His dick was bone hard and shot into her like a piston, only to slide out and dive back in with the anger he was feeling about his situation. Somehow one of her breasts had escaped its place and bounced up to her chin like a balloon filled with syrup.

"Damn. All I needed was for Marlin to make the teams and the rest would handle itself," he hissed under his breath. With the last bit of news, Mirabelle's financial crisis proved more urgent. And then there was Peaches. She was showing her insecurity at a time he couldn't summon the patience.

He pounded into Coretta with this on his mind. She completely opened for him without resistance. The swollen head smashed into her bottom and caused a series of jerks and spasms in her body. She accepted the pounding without complaint, her mouth now open and her arms thrown over her head in surrender. The lone cinnamon breast with the small nipple, rocked and rolled this way and that according to the direction Dahji entered and retreated. Her hair was fanned out around her head like a halo of thick, black strands that curled widely at the ends.

But none of this mattered to Dahji. For this moment she was merely a receptacle for his anger at all going wrong in his life. He hardly noticed that she was reaching up for him in a silent plea; either cum or stop. Her expensively manicured nails clawed at the space between them. There was no intimacy; only a primal energy that went past decorum. His name was arrested at her lips with each new, hard motion between her legs. His eyes stared past the triangular window and into the night. A vision of his funeral passed through his mind. *Who would come?* Surely there would be surprises and wonder by family at who the odd attendees were. But death was not an option. He wanted to live. Not just live, but live rich. Death would come soon enough and he would be ready.

When he looked into Coretta's eyes he saw the pain he was inflicting on her and allowed feeling to reach him. With a gentler stroke he let himself release into her with short pulses of energy. Only now did he notice the sweat pulling his shirt to him. The front of his Karl Kani Khaki's were soaked and milky shiny with her sex. In his recovering delirium he hardly heard Coretta accusing him of trying to hurt her.

CHAPTER FOURTEEN

This is getting interesting, Ayana thought to herself just as the first rays of morning light reached her pillow. She lay awake replaying the events of last night. She could hardly believe her eyes when Sherrelle kissed their neighbor. She had no clue that her aunt was secretly in love with the man next door. She had it so good already. She had a man who gave her everything she wanted and she didn't even have to work? This was enough for Ayana.

But it always seemed to be that way. We are never satisfied with what we have, she thought to herself; though she couldn't blame her aunt. After all, Marlin was not only handsome, but a pro football player – or at least he was trying to be. Maybe that was the reason he was with that skinny little model-looking chick, Ayana mused. Maybe she was taking care of him. Maybe they had it good at one time. Maybe he thought he loved her once.

Then Percy came home. Ayana was like an excited child, big eyed and hopeful in anticipation of the drama about to unfold. Yeah, it was the same all over the world and in the ghettos, except here the language was coded. Ayana was catching on quick. All that was left was for her was to find her place in the chaos.

She wasn't mad at Peaches for leaving when Percy walked in the door. Apparently, she'd seen it all before and would no doubt get an update from Sherrelle later. Besides this, Percy nearly killed her with his look when he stepped into the living room. He'd swept his glance across Ayana, who was standing by this time, and lost some of his anger at the sight of her long legs erupting from the extra revealing boy-shorts that cut higher up the hip. She smiled in recognition of his attraction, watching as he broke away from her to address the concern that had been momentarily interrupted by her sex appeal.

With Peaches making a hasty exit, Ayana was free to eavesdrop. Sherrelle had come into the house with fresh tears coating her face, and dashed into her bedroom. She didn't answer Peaches' question as to how she was feeling, so Ayana knew it was going to be good.

It quickly became obvious that Percy wasn't sure if he saw the kiss or not. With this uncertainty, he argued, at first, about why she was outside with Marlin in the first place. There was not much he could say to her response of him being their neighbor and needing help because he'd hurt himself. Percy was undaunted by her play of sympathy for the football player. He next questioned why she'd run into the house when he approached. He did see her touch him.

Ayana had kneeled to the door, their voices rising and fading with their movement in the room. She imagine Percy following Sherrelle into the bathroom and out again. She'd jumped away several times, ducking into the hallway bathroom when it seemed that Sherrelle would open the door at any moment.

Then she turned the tables on Percy, questioning him about his sudden bouts with nightmares. Sherrelle didn't care to hear his explanation about how things at work were really tough. This was nothing new to Sherrelle and she let him know it. This is what kept him out of her bed and away from the house. She hinted that it sounded like he was having an affair.

There was a few beats of silence. Ayana's heart pounded in her chest. She wanted to hear what Percy had to say to this. She wondered what kind of woman he would cheat with. *Probably a white woman,* she thought to herself.

Oh, that was it! Percy had been talking in a low voice. Apparently Sherrelle's accusation cut him to the quick. He'd pretended to be hurt by this and ran off a list of duties he'd fulfilled as a show of his love to Sherrelle and now she had the nerve to accuse him of having an affair. He was disgusted.

Sherrelle was not done, though. She'd reminded him of how he'd come into the house and questioned her. The tenor of her voice grew more urgent as it neared the space where his came from (probably by the dresser) as she told him that she had not once cheated on him and that she would never disrespect him that way or disrespect their marriage vows.

Ayana believed her, but that didn't mean she didn't secretly love her next door neighbor. Still, he was dispatched to the couch. Ayana couldn't be sure whose idea it was, but when she'd gotten up in the early morning to get a drink of lemonade, there he was sprawled out on the sofa.

Ayana stretched under the sheets and thought about what drama this day would bring. She didn't smell any breakfast and wondered if Sherrelle was still in the bed or had left already. There were no sounds in the house. She swung her legs from the bed hoping that she hadn't been left home alone. The thought reminded her that she had to get her some sort of transportation or meet somebody (a man) so she could get around. The only part of Indianapolis she'd seen was the path from the airport to this street. Sherrelle had mentioned something about going to Dahji's house to take pictures for the website. This she looked forward to.

Ayana had a sudden urge to pee. She wrapped her naked body in a pink silk robe and stepped from the spare bedroom. She listened for some signs of life. There was the sound of running water becoming more distinct as she neared the bathroom.

"Good morning Uncle Percy," she greeted him as she opened the bathroom door suddenly and sat down on the toilet. She held back her recognition of his startled expression. She also saw the smooth criss-crossed scars on his back before he pulled up his shirt. He'd been examining the damage Carrie inflicted on him.

Percy was unsure of how to respond. He had been caught at something he wasn't sure was enough to warrant suspicion. Added to this was the assault on his ears of her pee streaming into the bowl. He turned nervously in a full circle, at first thinking that he would leave the bathroom, but it wasn't only her legs that partially blocked his escape as she sat on the toilet; he could have easily squeezed past her, but what held him in place, observing her curious expression, was his own need to know if she'd seen the scars on his back and her new impression of him based on this and last night's arguing. Maybe she could be his eyes and ears when he was away from home. Maybe they could become allies. Added to this catch in his escape was her obvious nakedness under the loose silk robe. Her breasts hung heavily to the fabric, the nipples pressing forth softly. She had yet to put in her contact lenses and her dark eyes gave off a fresh take on her innocence.

"Where's auntie?" she wanted to know, seemingly unaware of his awkwardness.

"Oh. Well ... she's probably making breakfast," he replied unconvincingly. "Couldn't you have waited for me to come out?"

"I had to go real bad." Though the stream had stopped, she made no move to clean herself. She studied Percy with elbow on knee and chin in palm, her eyes steady.

Percy's fingers moved absently over the buttons of his white shirt, fastening them upwards. He was dressed for work and had apparently stopped to study his scars. He was struck by how comfortable she seemed sitting on the toilet in front of him. He turned away from her and worked at the tie around his neck.

"Do you like your job?" she asked, watching him through the mirror as she rolled toilet paper around her hand.

He shrugged, answering, "It's a job."

The sound of the flushing toilet made their meeting even more intimate. Percy privately thought how unpredictable this young girl was. And the thought moved some hidden lever inside of him, making his eyes shift to her in the mirror. She smiled.

"How did you get the scars?" she whispered in a conspiratorial manner. That something that she'd moved inside of him was now opening a flood gate of what he now recognized as fear. He was afraid and attracted to her unpredictability.

He turned to her slowly. There was no answer that would dispel the knowing look in her eyes. She'd stood and leaned against the frame of the door, blocking any escape he thought to make.

"Does it hurt?" A small smile played across her full lips. Her dark eyes sparkled with mischief.

"No."

"Does my aunt know about it?"

Percy was struck by her assumption that Sherrelle had not made the scars. He briefly thought to lie and say that she had, but knew that this would only be exposed and the repercussions would come swiftly.

"No," he answered in what he hoped was not a vulnerable voice.

Ayana brought the tip of her finger to her lips and grinned sadistically. She knew she was right. She could see straight through Percy and his conservative front. She observed him curiously.

He could see her mind working at how she could benefit. The only question was how devoted she was to exposing him. "So ... You tell Sherrelle about the scars and there is no way to deny what she might think."

He shrugged nonchalantly before he narrowed his eyes at her. "Are you here to cause trouble between me and my wife?" he asked suddenly.

"You're doing that just fine all by yourself."

"So, you're not going to tell her?"

Ayana slowly shook her head from side to side.

"What do you want?" he asked, assuming a manner of control that he knew could be unraveled at any moment. Everyone had a price and this young girl couldn't want much. But the way she smiled made him feel like a fresh wound open to whatever the wind blew into the sensitive space. He couldn't be sure if she purposely let her robe fall open or what. He'd shifted his gaze over her shoulder for an instant. When he returned to her, there was more of the gentle curve of her breasts visible. The part in her robe stopped just after the diamond heart pendant in her navel. His breath caught in his throat.

"I need a car," she stated, enjoying the effect she had on him.

"A car?"

"Yep. I need to get around."

A car, he thought to himself. Is that all? He'd seen a used Altima for sale in the parking lot at work. "We might be able to get you something to ride around in. Let me talk to Sherrelle about it."

"Talk? ..."

"I can't just up and buy you a car without making her think it's her idea."

Ayana nodded, nearly forgetting that he was smart in that kind of way. "Okay. You talk to her. And in the meantime I'll think of what else I want."

"More?" he asked, stopping her roll from the door.

She turned to him. "Oh. You're ready to say no already? Maybe we can just forget about it and I'll just be the good niece and tell my aunt what I think about the kinky sex she has with her husband. I want to see the whip and ask her to show me how she whipped you." She smiled with this.

Percy could see the fangs developing between her smirking lips. "I'll talk to Sherrelle about the car," he readily agreed.

"I've always wanted a convertible Mustang," she said as she peeled away and stepped with swaying hips down the hallway. She closed the door behind her and leaned against it with an exhalation of exhilaration. She covered her mouth to stifle the laughter of audacity from escaping. She worked to bring her excitement under control and hissed out, with a fist pump, a silent shout of victory. She could barely believe her manipulation. *It can't be this easy,* she thought to herself as she sat slowly on the bed and stared at the brightly weaved area rug beneath her feet.

Ayana lay on her back with a devilish smile splayed across her lips. She thought of how incredible it was that her aunt was in a marriage that resembled regular ghetto hood drama. And *where is she anyway?* she wondered as she finally decided to rise. No doubt enough time had passed for Percy to have left for work. She didn't want to see him again until he had time to replay their meeting in his mind over and over again. She was sure that she would be on his mind throughout the day.

"Wassup late riser?" Sherrelle inquired, looking up from the freshly picked roses she held, when Ayana strolled sleepily into the kitchen.

"I started to pick some roses yesterday," Ayana responded, reminded of what she'd seen through the neighbor's window as Sherrelle arranged her collection in a glass vase.

"Don't mess up my flowers," Sherrelle warned playfully before adding, "This is my therapy."

"What do you need therapy for? You have everything." With this Ayana paid careful attention to her aunt. Between last night's arguing and the secret she possessed about both her and her husband's secret love interests, she saw this entire living arrangement in a new light. There was now room for her to get something from it before everything came crashing down around them. She knew from personal experience that this kind of drama couldn't go on for long.

"Therapy ..." Ayana said around soft laughter before turning intimately to her aunt. "Do you two argue like that all the time?" she asked, her eyes moving over Sherrelle's brown face; the way her eyelids sloped thickly over big, pretty eyes; the way her thick, dark hair cascaded carelessly to her shoulders. Women paid good money to have hair like that.

"Not really. There's something going on with him though," she responded.

"Is it work?" Ayana asked, keeping her eyes on Sherrelle when she'd looked to her.

"Were you listening?" Ayana nodded slowly, her eyes big in expectation of some juicy detail. "Well, that's what he says," Sherrelle went on. "But it's always something with him."

"He don't like your business or Peaches, hunh?"

Sherrelle smiled as she turned on the faucet. Water crashed over her hands as she arranged the roses just so. "He acts like he's cool with it, but ..." she trailed off, shrugging her shoulders.

"You think he's having an affair?" Ayana ventured, her eyes bouncing across Sherrelle's contorted expression of doubt.

"I hope he is!" she said at last. "I feel sorry for her," she added as she pulled the water-filled vase from the sink and stepped past Ayana into the dining room.

Ayana followed. "So you wouldn't care if he had an affair?"

"Him having an affair is the last thing on my mind."

Ayana heard her clearly, but doubted that she seriously was so nonchalant about the affair unless ... "Oh, I see. That's because you're in love with the neighbor dude."

Sherrelle made a final adjustment of the vase on the dining room table as if she didn't hear a word Ayana said. She then turned slowly and folded her arms under her breasts. She looked to her niece thoughtfully. "The neighbor dude, as you call him, is a good friend. Besides that, he's married." This last she said as verification of the first.

Ayana was done with her questioning. "He is fine though," she swooned.

"Isn't he? I just hope he's okay and makes the team. Dahji needs for this to happen, too." Sherrelle jumped as if she'd only just now remembered something important. "I have to go to Circuit City!" she announced and stopped to look at Ayana as if for the first time. "I can't wait for you to get dressed. I'll be right back."

"What do you have to get?" Ayana asked, following her into the bedroom.

"We're going by Dahji's house Saturday. I need to pick up a digital camcorder so we can take some film around here in the clothes." As she talked she shed the boy-shorts and wife-beater and stood naked before Ayana. "Are you a secret lesbian?" she asked with amusement?

"If I was, then I would want a woman just like you," she replied seductively. "You don't even know how perfectly sexy you are."

Sherrelle grabbed up the sky-blue, cotton HoodSweet jogging suit. "I don't have time to know. As long as he recognizes." With this she dipped past Ayana and swayed her hips into the bathroom.

"I know who HE is," Ayana called after her. She was stepping from the room when she yelled, "You could have at least made breakfast!"

One thing she could say about Sherrelle was that she kept food in the refrigerator. Ayana lifted a box of Entenmann's Strawberry Cake from the top shelf. After pouring herself a glass of milk she grabbed a fork and strolled leisurely to the living room. Passing the roses Sherrelle picked made her think of the old man she'd seen through the neighbor's window the day before.

"I'll be right back. If Peaches gets here before me then tell her to wait,"

Sherrelle instructed as she stepped into the living room with her purse. Ayana was standing at the open door. The sun streamed in around her as if welcoming her to a new opportunity.

"It might be too hot for that," she suggested, nodding at the cotton sweatsuit hugging her aunt's curves.

Sherrelle joined her on the porch. She tried not to make it seem so obvious that she was checking for Marlin's Escalade parked at the curb. "It's not that heavy," she noted casually as she turned back to Ayana. "And why do you have the whole cake?" she wanted to know.

"I didn't feel like cutting a piece. Besides why dirty up a dish?"

"Don't eat up my cake."

"Neighbor dude is out early. Where do you think he went since he ain't gotta practice?" Ayana asked before slipping a fresh morsel of cake between her lips.

Sherrelle thought to respond, but instead she grabbed the fork from Ayana's fingers and cut a thin slice of cake from the box.

"You need to mind your own business," she said around a small bite of cake. She held the remainder daintily as she turned down the porch with an exaggerated dip of her hips.

"Don't break'em," Ayana joked as she followed her down the steps. The sun felt good through the silk robe, warming her breasts and coating her stomach. She knocked her hips lazily from side to side, peering to the neighbors' porch as she slipped another piece of cake between her lips. She wondered what the old man was doing.

Sherrelle was watching her when she turned back. "You leave our neighbor alone," she warned, tossing the Coach purse onto the passenger seat. She slipped the key into the ignition and dropped the convertible top on the Jaguar.

"He's still alone. They don't have nobody to look after him?" Ayana asked with sincerity. She couldn't help but feel sorry for the man who must be lonely in that house all day by himself.

"Stacy's hiring somebody to look after ... A professional," she quickly added when Ayana looked hopeful.

"How hard can it be? Wipe him up and bathe him right? Make sure he takes his medications and don't hurt himself." She shrugged to show how simple the task would be.

Sherrelle pretended not to hear her plea. She looked to Ayana with her Chanel shades poised to cover her eyes. "How come Percy got it in his head to get you a car?"

Ayana nearly choked on the piece of cake she'd just deposited onto her tongue. She transformed this into genuine surprise while trying to calculate Sherrelle's curiosity. "I have no idea," she said with wide, helpless eyes. "I might have ... mentioned something about how I want to see the city." She tried to see how this answer affected Sherrelle, but she'd already slid the shades over her eyes and was checking her reflection in the mirror. "You gon' let me drive the Jag?" she asked, knowing the answer before Sherrelle gave her a shocked look.

"The only woman that's going to be charging him is me," Sherrelle said. "But I have no problem matching what you earn working for me."

"I ain't afraid of work, but so far all you got me doing is cataloguing clothes. When are we going to sell some? And when am I going to get paid?"

"Damn, speedy! You just got here. Be patient. I'll pay you this weekend."

"How much?"

"However much people get paid for cataloguing clothes," Sherrelle assured her with a wide smile as she began backing out of the driveway.

"That's what I'm afraid of?!" Ayana called after her.

Ayana waited until the Jaguar turned the corner before she turned back up the driveway. Her curiosity moved her feet across the slim slice of grass into the neighbor's driveway. She approached the porch as if she were invited.

Once on the porch she tried to peek through a crease of open space in the curtain. Her angle was bad. There was no sign of the old man, but they had nice furniture. She imagined that he was in the lazy-boy chair against the wall. She did not see the flickering of light from the television in the dim living room. There was no turning back after she opened the screen door and knocked on the hard wood.

There was no answer. A sliver of doubt crept into her mind. *Maybe this isn't a good idea,* she thought to herself. But her curiosity got the better of her. She knocked again. There was a faint sound that resembled a moving chair on the other side of the door.

"Hello ... Is anyone home?" she called out.

"Yes!" came a faint voice. "Who is it?"

Ayana's heart pounded for no other reason than the thrill of meeting new people and the opportunity this presented. "My name is ..."

The door opened with a wide berth. The old man stood before her in a pair of linen pajamas. His slim body was covered over except for the noticeable bulge in his crotch. He looked blindly to a spot above her forehead.

"Hi," she said much too loudly. Grump frowned.

"Hello," he replied, straightening his posture and running a dark, thickly veined hand down the length of his abdomen.

"My name is Ms. Ayana Cherry and ..."

"You that one from next door," he stated. "I recognize your voice. You're a nice young woman, aren't you?" he asked, a crooked smile revealing a half row of gums.

Ayana smiled. "Yes. I'm very nice." She became aware that he could not see the way her breasts pressed against the silk fabric of her robe or the way she'd dipped her hip out. None of this mattered and these were her sure-fire tricks.

"Well, that's right nice of you to come by. You know my daughter Stacy and her husband?"

"I've seen them, but I don't know them that well."

"Just the same. They're fine people."

"Well, I brought you some cake. You like strawberries?" she asked. Behind him on the plasma screen played a porno movie. The sounds of the woman slurping on a thick dick resonated throughout the living room. *Freaky old man,* she thought to herself.

"That's a fine stroke of luck. I was born on national strawberry day." He smiled widely with this, showing his full range of pink gums.

Ayana giggled softly. "Well, here you go. I hope you don't mind that I ate some of it. I'm in love with strawberries and everything associated with them." As she handed the box to him she let her fingers brush across his cool hands gently.

"Okey dokey," he whispered. "Thank you."

"No problem. Enjoy."

"I will. And you feel free to come by any time. Any woman who loves strawberries is a friend of mine." He held his palm out as he said this. Ayana placed her hand in his and let her fingers gently massage his palm. The effect and meaning was unmistakable to Grump. He breathed in hard and softened his expression even more so. He could have been asleep and dreaming of heaven for the way his face glowed.

"Anytime, right?" she asked as she slipped her hand from his.

"Anytime."

"Okay. I'll see you soon then," she assured him and turned away. There was no need for her to look back. She had yet to hear the door close as she bounded down the steps and crossed into her yard. She had no way of knowing that he was inhaling her scent and bathing in her presence long after she'd gone.

CHAPTER FIFTEEN

Peaches didn't exactly know how upset she should be with Dahji. He was doing everything he could to help her. No one but him had stepped forward to hire a lawyer for her. And he did bail her out of jail. But he was sending her mixed signals. She'd assumed they'd developed a special bond and were moving forward in a meaningful relationship. But last night the desk guard said that he wasn't at home when he'd agreed to meet her there. She tried to call him, but her call went unanswered. This was her dilemma. She didn't know if she should be upset or worried. She was nearly afraid of what this new day would bring, and more afraid of calling him and not being able to reach him. Or worse, she would begin to argue and complain about not being able to contact him. She didn't want to have this kind of relationship with him. She was committed to being a better woman and this called for not jumping to conclusions. *He could have had an emergency,* she thought to herself as she lay beneath the sheets, getting mentally prepared for what she had to do today.

When her iPhone rang she leaned over the side of the bed and fished it from the depths of her Fendi bag on the floor. Only thirty minutes before she'd foolishly answered the house phone without checking caller I.D. and was made frustrated by having to deny Tequan's collect call. After this he'd called no less than three times until she turned off her ringer.

"Hey girlfriend," she answered with a shadow of sleep in her voice.

"Are you at home?" Sherrelle wanted to know. "I couldn't get an answer at your house."

"The ringer is off. Tequan keeps calling. Where are you on your way to?" she asked through the sounds of traffic seeping through the phone.

"To get a video camera. You need to come by so we can do some filming. I'm about to get my Spike Lee on."

"That sounds like fun, but you know I have to meet the manufacturer today," Peaches reminded her.

Sherrelle moaned in appreciation. "In case I haven't said so lately ... I really appreciate what you're doing," she said sincerely.

Peaches smiled. "Shit. This ain't just for you, bitch. We both gon' be rich." She stretched and rose up in the bed. "Bitch ain't trying to be broke forever and stuck with a nigga just because he got the loot. Speaking of which ... How did hubby feel about you kissing Marlin?"

"He realizes it was all a figment of his imagination." Sherrelle replied with a giggle.

"How's that ... You give him some pussy?"

"No."

"Some of that gold throat?"

"No girl!" Sherrelle insisted. "You know he didn't really want to believe that."

"Did he sleep on the couch?"

"Yep. And I ain't mad at him either. Me and Buford are just fine without him," she insisted, referring to her trusty hand-held companion.

"You are truly touched. I be glad when Marlin comes to his senses and snatch your crazy ass up."

"You ain't the only one. Okay girl, let me get in here and spend some money. Stop by if you get a chance. Did you give Dahji my message?"

Peaches let out a low sigh. "Don't get me started on him."

"What's wrong?" Sherrelle asked. Peaches could see her face frowned up with concern.

"Oh ... nothing but the usual, me chasing him and he being who he is. I just need to chill out for a minute."

"Listen girl, I shouldn't have to be the one to tell you this, but you need to approach this from a business standpoint. You messed up by getting your feelings involved. He got you out of jail and paid for your lawy ..."

"He fucked her!" Peaches hissed quickly in correction.

"There you go," Sherrelle complained.

"I know. I know. But I can't help it. I just love HARD!"

"Listen. Come by after you see the manufacturer. And in the meantime freeze your heart, girl. We'll thaw it out over some cheese and red wine later on."

Peaches attempted a smile. "Okay, but you're so bourgeois."

"Somebody gotta be," Sherrelle responded enthusiastically. "See you later girlfriend. Call me," she sang.

Peaches assured her that she would before she ended the call. She rolled onto her back and contemplated calling Dahji. She wondered if he was still in bed. She missed him. She missed lying next to him. There was a moment right after he'd bailed her out of jail that she thought she would be moving in with him. She'd already dismissed this dingy excuse for an apartment. The kitchen faucet still leaked because she refused to give the leering, obese manager permission to enter her space again.

Her skin tingled with anticipation before she realized that she'd dialed Dahji's number. The small window high over her headboard let in the little light that made it over the high roof of the apartment building only a few feet from her room; it stopped rising at the middle of her mattress. No matter that it was nearly noon outside, the sun would never rise past early morning by the standard of the illumination along her bedcovers.

"Speak on it," Dahji drawled into the phone. The smooth sound of a blender chased his voice to the phone.

Peaches smiled with his energy. "Good morning. I have a bone to pick with you," she said with a mixture of giddiness and residual frustration. The mixing sound came to a halt and she wished she were there with him.

"Is it a big bone?" Dahji wanted to know.

"Well, it can be ..."

"I got caught up last night and got in kinda late," he confessed. Peaches knew better to expect an apology. He wasn't that sort of man. It was what it was.

"Oh. I tried to call you." As soon as she said this she wanted to take the tone of it back. It didn't come out as soft as she would have liked. Her emotions were betraying her attempt at restraint as evidenced by Dahji's thoughtful silence.

"Ran into a little situation and had to kill the com," he replied easily. His words sounded as if they were coated with his famous protein shake.

"I miss you."

"Miss you, too. We getting together today?" he asked and Peaches was elated.

"I have to meet the manufacturer for the clothing line today. How long will you be home?" She didn't want to meet him in traffic. She needed to know that he still felt good about her. She needed to see him in his environment and know that she was welcomed in a way that separated her from the other women she knew to visit; this last she struggled not to be jealous about.

"We good. Got some traps to check here so holla when the leash is off."

"Okay," she agreed, feeling tightness in her chest. He was so cool. How can he be? "Do you miss me?" she wanted to know. She held her breath waiting for his reply. His lips smacked loudly, followed by a healthy burp.

"Like a zoo without animals," he assured her, glad to hear the laughter in her voice. She almost succeeded in dissolving his resolution to turn his situation around. Dragging around a clinging woman wouldn't help matters.

"Okay then. I'll call you when I'm on my way."

"I got a better idea. Call me when you're on your way."

"Bye funny man," she shouted cheerfully before ending the call. Peaches was happy again and re-energized for the day before her.

***

It was a struggle understanding Sun Yi. He had to repeat himself several times before Peaches understood the specific directions he gave her to his manufacturing warehouse. She had a suspicious feeling that the cousin of Dr. Kim would not be as attractive or so charming.

Still, she'd dressed in a sexy, thigh length Gucci leopard print silk dress. Her long legs stood polished and toned from white leather shallow heeled espadrilles. Because of the sound of machinery in the background she decided to tie her hair in a silk Hermes scarf. She carried a small leather purse for compact convenience. She had no idea what Sun Yi would expect from her for his generosity, but she was charged with the determination to make HoodSweet a success.

The large white, nondescript building was situated at the end of a block of similar buildings. The commercial area included a Metro Bus depot, welding school, and railroad car cemetery. The effect was a metallic taste that floated through the air on a plume of dry, gunpowder scented smoke that gripped her lungs tightly. The noise of screeching metal assaulted her senses.

The front of the building had no obvious entry. Its walls held high, open windows that were obscured by a thick film of white dust. She'd pulled around to the back where more dilapidated cars were parked. After grabbing up the large Coach duffel bag with samples of HoodSweet apparel in it, she stood from the car, the engine still muttering its death. She breathed the harsh air with shallow breaths.

Standing outside the rust rimmed white door was a short man smoking a cigar. *It has to be a cigar by the way the plumes of smoke swirled from its end,* Peaches thought to herself as she crossed the pavement. There were two black S500 Benzes framing this man. He had the nonchalant attitude of someone in charge. In one hand the cigar was stuffed between fat lips while the other fat hand held a phone to his ear. He laughed, grinned, talked, and puffed with eager mischief. Peaches could not tell if his eyes were open for how tight they were.

She slowed up as she approached the space between the two Benzes. Now she could smell the tartness of the cigar. The man's eyes widened to mere slits, the dark, oily orbs shining at her in new recognition as he puffed away at his cigar. Smoke escaped through his puffy lips as he responded into the phone. A slight nod of his fat head said for Peaches to wait.

She studied him closely, a sinking feeling telling her that this was Sun Yi. His skin was the color of brown egg shells; it was darkly tanned and cracked. His hair, a shade of black that only a box could provide, was pulled into a tight ponytail. She cringed at the sight of the trail of auburn colored hair escaping the top of his wrinkled silk trousers and disappearing again into a flower print silk shirt that sat high on a pregnant stomach. No less than three fingers of each hand supported large gold rings, their wide bands pinching into his skin. She wondered if he could remove the gaudy jewelry.

"Ho," the fat man said, clapping the phone shut and shooting his chin up to her.

"Hi. My name is ..." She approached with a brave smile with her hand extended while her mind located the wet-wipes in her purse.

"Peach," he responded quickly, taking her hand in his sweaty palm. "Ho. I am Sun Yi," he announced with a smile of a perfect row of square white teeth.

Damn, she thought to herself in complaint. "It's good to meet you," she said. He extended his beefy hand to the Coach bag she held and gestured with the roll of his fingers for her to hand it over.

"I carry," he chirped briskly. His phone rang again and it was back to his ear. Though she could not tell what he was saying, she could sense that whoever he was talking to was taking orders or being berated. He alternated between a quick eruption of words to what she assumed was his way of saying, "okay," then he would begin anew with his rapid speech, all the while directing Peaches towards the door of chipped white paint. His tight, smiling eyes moved along her body as if cataloguing the style and fabric of her dress for future counterfeiting.

Peaches clutched her small purse in front of her as she allowed him to open the door. She'd expected a neat room of partitioned sewing and cutting tables where serious women were at work; but this is not the environment she walked into. She was simultaneously assaulted by the noise and the stench. Otherwise, docile looking oriental women shouted across the room with urgency, making demands and flailing their arms over their small, unevenly cut tables; some of which were topped with large, black sewing machines. Behind their screaming was the sound of loud music; here a woman sang amidst the backdrop of blaring horns and violins.

She may have been able to control her reaction if it were not for the smell. She involuntary brought her purse to her nose to guard against the foul odor of what smelled like a mixture of rubbing alcohol, cheap perfume warmed over, and spicy noodles that must be what was in the large pot in the far corner; here there was a line of women carrying small rice bowls; they accepted the hot stew with short nods before retreating to a long wooden table behind a sheer curtain hanging from an overhead steel beam.

Sun Yi chuckled beside her. Peaches at first thought that he was laughing at her painful reaction, but when she looked his way he seemed to be absorbed in the conversation he was having on the phone. He appeared oblivious to the chaos around him. The large warehouse was divided into two sections. One half was for the measuring and cutting of fabric and leathers, while the second half was devoted to sewing. These two halves were book ended on one side by the eating area with its hanging sheer fabric, and on the other end by a wall-to-wall mirror; it was in this direction that Sun Yi began walking with short steps, gesturing for Peaches to follow.

Peaches followed along the row nearest the wall as harried, dull women looked up from their sewing stations. Their eyes never rose above her waist before returning to their task. Sun Yi stopped briefly at infrequent intervals to examine a strip of cloth before moving on with a slow nod of approval.

It wasn't until they disappeared through a mirrored doorway at the end of the wall that the noise and funk dissipated. This area served as his office. It was a thickly carpeted width of space cut off from the chaos on the other side. Through the one-way mirror she had a view of the entire building, noting that this old man must get some pleasure from being able to observe his workers at all times.

Sun Yi barked a quick order into his phone before laying it on the wooden round table that sat low in the center of the room. Beyond this wooden island was a sleek metal desk against the far wall. A low, brown leather couch bridged the space, its back to the wall between the two odd pieces of furniture. The walls were undecorated white washed brick.

"Come," Sun Yi gestured as he placed the Chanel duffel bag onto the wooden platform.

"I like your office," Peaches said with a weak smile as she stood on the other side of the round table.

"Hoyt," he responded, stabbing his stubby finger, the cigar smoldering over his distended stomach, at the Chanel bag.

"Oh, yes," Peaches said, nearly forgetting her mission with the oddness of the situation. She could very well see someone murdered here and sewn up in a swath of fake Louis Vuitton leather she'd seen on a wide, wall-mounted spool.

"What you need favor for?" he asked before placing the cigar between his thick, purple-tinted lips.

Peaches proceeded to pull a sample of boy-shorts, half-t's, full-t's, hoodies, sweat pants, and scarves from the duffel. She spread them out onto the wood and explained in slow English that she wanted one thousand of each item in small, medium, and large or four through twelve sizes. He nodded in concentration only when she mentioned the amount and the sizes. When she was done she looked up to him for what he would say next. She was tempted to repeat herself when it appeared that he didn't understand her. He was simply looking to the clothing in a confused state. The ringing of his cell phone broke him from his eerie-looking thoughts as cigar smoke billowed from his mouth.

Peaches was unsure of what Sun Yi thought about what she'd just said. She had no idea if he even understood what it was that she wanted. She wanted to have a conversation about the graphics and cut of the materials, but his odd nature made her wonder how he was even in business. She was even more confused when he suddenly stopped his rapid speech and shoved the phone across the table at her. It was wrapped in a weathered, leather case.

"For me?" she asked with wide eyes, reaching her hand to the phone with hesitation.

"Ho." Sun Yi nodded shortly.

She held the phone lightly with two fingers, barely bringing the soiled device to her ear. "Hello?"

"Hewwo!" Dr. Kim shouted happily, his voice less formal. She was relieved at the familiarity of him.

"Oh, Dr. Kim. How are you? This is such a surprise!" she said, genuinely happy and smiling broadly as the effect of her interaction washed over Sun Yi.

"So, I see that you have found my cousin."

"Yes," she exhaled, her eyes moving to Sun Yi, who was bowed to the garments upon the table. He didn't appear to be scrutinizing the clothing, but in deep thought.

"Well, that is good. He will help you. He says that he will give you the one thousand of each piece in every size," Dr. Kim explained. "This for ten percent of profits and special favor."

Peaches wanted to shout her joy, but was held in check by the unknown special favor. "Okay," she replied, casting a quick glance to Sun Yi. He'd moved to the couch and sat with his short, thick legs spread wide. He seemed bored without his phone.

"Not to worry," Dr. Kim began. "He is a very simple man with peculiar taste.

"Okay."

"He enjoys feet. He asked me if you had pretty feet and I assured him that you did."

Peaches wanted to smile with relief. She could let him have her feet. "That sounds good. Thank you, Dr. Kim."

"Well, good. Then I will see you perhaps Monday?" There was anticipation in his voice for the appreciation she would show him.

"I look forward to it," she responded. "Thank you again."

"Great. I will see you next week."

Peaches strolled around the table to where Sun Yi was sitting. She understood him better now and smiled with pleasure as she handed the phone back to him. She did not move from before him as he spoke rapidly into the phone. His voice had calmed after listening to what Dr. Kim must have explained to him.

"Hoyt," Sun Yi finally said. He seemed reluctant to take the phone from his ear. He nervously held it as he slowly lowered it to the sofa cushion. Peaches had seen his type before so she decided to be proactive, buoyed by the fact that since the deal was done she was ready to leave.

"Thank you," she said in a sexy voice as she simultaneously untied her Hermes scarf and stepped from her shoes. Her dark red hair fell in big curls across her shoulders as she lifted one foot to his knee. She smiled as his eyes jerked to the fatness between her legs and back to the pale foot on his leg.

He squirmed in his seat, his tongue darting out across his fat lips. "Ho," he said, holding up one finger. He reached across the edge of the sofa and picked up a small Chinese food bucket. He flipped it open quickly and pulled a small tub of rust colored sauce from its depths. He looked up to her then with a wry smile. He stood and motioned her to the couch.

Peaches looked up at him now as he flipped the plastic top from the container and dipped his pudgy finger into the sauce. He licked it from his skin with delight as he kneeled before her. His attention was concentrated on her feet as if they were not attached to any part of who she was. He rested on his heels and placed one of her feet on each of his thighs. He began to hum to himself as he dipped his now wet finger back into the sauce. He then devoted his attention to covering first one foot, then the other, in the sweet smelling sauce. Her feet were tinted orange and sticky. He was careful to slide his sauced finger between her toes with care; the thick liquid pooled around the rim of the platinum ring on her long second toe.

Peaches was not surprised that this odd man would treat her feet as a delicacy. She cocked her head to the side, looking down the length of her body as he hummed in quiet devotion. He rose one foot to the air, cupping her heel in his palm, and licked slowly along the base of her foot.

Peaches jerked with the sensation. This seemed to please him, for a crooked smile teased his wet lips. Over his head, through the one-way mirror, his employees were still at work with a fervor set on automatic in his absence.

"Hoyt," Sun Yi muttered as he gently brought her other foot into the air. He puckered his lips and wedged her big toe snugly between them. He sucked at the sauce with smacking sounds until she was wet only with his saliva. He then played across her toes with his lips like a piano, the tune of his own making from deep within his throat throttling against her toes.

This strange sensation made Peaches squint in pleasure. Never had anyone paid so much attention to her feet in this way. She could not help that her eyes shuttered together in slow stages of recline. His attentive tongue and fat lips expertly massaged her instep and the pads of her feet. She was soothed by the way he carefully placed each toe into his mouth and dragged it out smoothly between pursed lips. A low moan escaped her as he spread her toes and licked the sweet smelling sauce from the crevices. Her nerve endings fired up as he dragged the slick meat of his tongue along the bones atop her feet and back down to roll across the polished nails on her toes. He'd stopped to suck gently on her big toe as if expecting cream to emerge. With this Peaches cummed quietly, surprised at her own arousal.

Then there was a lull in his attention, her toes being met with air and growing dry. Her eyes opened slowly only to find him standing before her with his pants around his ankles. The rose colored joint between his legs jutted out uncircumcised. His milky white thighs were coated with a shallow marsh of fine amber colored hair. The hairy balls hung from his organ like two oversized albino prunes. Her quivers were only just subsiding when he wedged his penis between her cool feet, the loose foreskin rolling between her insteps. His balls swung against the heels of her feet with growing rapidity. With her legs in the air and her heels in the palms of his hands, he treated the curve of her feet as an orifice.

The humming became more intense as he found a comfortable space between her feet. His lips trembled and his palms grew sweaty. Peaches closed her eyes to the peek-a-boo show of his slick head as it drove towards her and then away, disappearing behind the excited folds of foreskin. She was now uncomfortable, her panties soaked with her earlier excitement. The back of her thighs ached. He was now gripping her heels hard in an attempt to keep them from slipping away as he pumped between her feet rapidly.

"HOYT ... HO ... HOYT!" he hissed out as he squirted forth his pleasure. The hot stream fell across her legs like snot. Peaches felt as if she would vomit, closing her eyes to the disgust of his heaving, hairy stomach. She could not escape the raspy panting of his labored breath. There was no escape from the cooling, drying feeling of sticky cum splashed across her legs and now rolling across her feet. Added to this trauma was the tight curling of her thigh muscles.

She cramped up in agony, snatching her feet from his palms and stretching out on the couch. She yelped out in pain as she massaged the back of her thighs to ease the knot that developed.

This was an oddly welcomed respite from the disgust that had suddenly plagued her. She vaguely heard him speak in his rapid foreign tongue as he made florid movements in his dance away from her. She was thankful for his return with a warm towel. He rubbed it along her thighs and on down to her feet, erasing the evidence of his pleasure. Peaches could only look forward to soaking in a tub of scented oil as she tried to erase this experience from her judgmental conscience, as she had so many others.

CHAPTER SIXTEEN

Coretta had succeeded in keeping Dahji in his room until his mother demanded that they both come downstairs. She reminded Dahji that his Uncle Prince and his lady friend Emma Jean were waiting for him. She also included his daughter Aryn, more for Coretta's sake, in her chastisement for their absence. Dahji could not deny Coretta's success in lifting him from his doldrums. With the news of Mirabelle's pending financial collapse and Marlin's injury, he was in no mood for what Coretta had in mind.

He didn't mean to hurt her. And he shouldn't have been surprised that she'd been turned on by the pounding. She welcomed more. She took all that he had and sucked their juices from his spent organ. Though he knew how manipulative she could be, there was no denying the effect she had on him. Something changed between them that night. Dahji had the suspicion that she was making a power move. This both intrigued and angered him in some way...intrigued him because the power that attracted them together in the first place still existed. There was anger because she'd cheated him out of a daughter for seven years and this was hard to forgive.

Coretta had been heavy on his mind until Peaches called. He'd awakened with a renewed zest to get his reward. He realized that he was giving Mirabelle too much room to play him out. Though he enjoyed her largesse, he committed himself anew to the world he knew best: Women.

His first call was to Ebony. He confirmed that she would be stopping by for a photo session. She was the most popular woman inmates wanted. They spent hundreds at a time for photos of her. And now that he had the HoodSweet thing going with Sherrelle, he would take her to new levels of exposure with a video shoot. She would become famous on You Tube. He believed this with all his heart.

Then there was Marlin. He didn't care if the running back was in a wheelchair, he was determined to get him on the team. To be a real live sports agent meant everything. This would legitimize him in his father's eyes. And as much as he hated to admit it, he wanted his father's approval; Marlin was the key to getting this done.

Dahji was in the midst of making his special protein shake of avocados and bananas with ginseng root when Peaches called. He was thinking of how he would get at Gloria Richards, the assistant coach's wife of the Indianapolis Colts. She was his key to getting Marlin on the field. He was prepared to lay pipe to anyone she needed him to in order to get Marlin Cassidy on the roster.

Now he had to get his mind focused again. He realized Peaches didn't mean to be clingy, but damn! she was starting to make him avoid her. He didn't realize that he needed some alone time until she'd called last night. He was home, but needed to get his head right. He needed to get prepared for the new day and BOSS PIMPIN' state of mind that had temporarily lapsed with last night's bad news. And he thought he was ready to hear from her this morning but there was that residual anger in her voice; and it wasn't attractive. But he still had to pimp because she was the key to getting the manufacturing and distributing deal for the apparel line. This whole situation was going to come together like sweaty butt cheeks. He was determined to make it so.

He leaned against the black marble counter and looked out across the penthouse to the morning sky. He sipped on the protein shake and shivered with its potency. He would need every ounce of it. There was about to be some major fucking going on.

He dialed Gloria's number and strolled across the hardwood living room floor in Calvin Klein house shoes. The blue silk Perry Ellis robe dragged across the heels. He stood before the floor to ceiling window and looked down to the city below. It was coming to life. He was taking another sip of shake when Gloria answered the phone. It was time to pimp.

"Glo Glo. How's my favorite coach wife?" he cheered. He lifted one foot to the low ledge in front of the window and leaned an elbow on his knee so that the heavy Rolex chain swung fabulously. His long hair swung forward across his shoulders.

"Good morning Dahji," she replied around the sound of jazz music.

"He got hurt." This came out with the pain that Dahji felt when he'd heard about it, but he wasn't trying to live with that pain.

"Thas what I need to holla at you about." He took another sip of elixir. "I don't know if there's much I can do, but I will say that Edith has asked about you."

"Really," he replied as he looked down at a group of sharply dressed business men walking along the street. They were made small by the distance from the ground to his penthouse. He wasn't surprised by Edith's interest. She'd passed out after he served her up with his ten-inch slab of steak.

"Yes. Really. She wants to meet you privately. Away from her husband."

"Really." He wasn't surprised by this either. Tom liked to watch. Maybe she wanted to be more free, but Dahji couldn't see how more free a woman could get than fucking herself unconscious.

"Don't get cocky. Do you want to meet with her or not?" Gloria asked in her nasally, pampered wife way. Dahji imagined that this voice was used to subduing her husband in an argument.

"Thas not gon' help me get Marlin on the team."

"Dahji," she began helplessly. "He was barely on the team in the first place. It's stated clearly in his medical contract that he has to stay healthy through training camp."

"What about putting him on injured reserve?" The man got skills. He just need a few weeks."

"He's only just now arriving at the sports medicine clinic for an examination."

Dahji was unbowed by her pessimism. "Look Glo. Let's have lunch and talk about this. I'm sure we can work something out. We don't get this far to cancel the show." There was a pause before he added. "I need this Glo Glo. You gotta come through for me."

Gloria exhaled with her contemplation. "Will you see Edith for me?" she asked.

"What is it about her that makes you press me like this?"

"Did you like her?" she asked coyly.

He did. "She was awright," he answered, thinking back to how shocked he was at how beautiful she was. To take a look at her husband no one would expect to find her hidden in that mansion.

"She wants to see you again and is prepared to reward you handsomely. She said for me to say that to you."

Now she had Dahji's attention. "Where are we having lunch?"

"Um ... Not lunch ..." The sound of turning pages filled the void. "Let's make it the afternoon ... Say around three?"

Dahji did the quick math. Ebony would be arriving soon and he had to see Peaches' lawyer before the day was up. Maybe he could swing by there for lunch. Below him a trio of beautiful, long-limbed women laughed gaily as they passed a trio of equally yoked, sharply dressed men on the sidewalk. The morning sun was having a nice effect on people. "Sounds good," he replied as he swung from the window.

"Chin Chin's okay?"

"That's perfect." He was headed back into the kitchen for another glass of protein shake when the phone beeped.

"You're getting started early I see. I'll let you go. Call me after lunch. Tootles," Gloria sang before she disconnected.

"Mr. McBeth. There is a Ms. Coretta here to see you," came the gruff voice of the lobby desk guard.

Dahji checked his watch. No doubt she was coming from the daycare center and decided to make a surprise visit. He was mixed about how to feel about this. She was taking advantage of her status as the mother of his daughter. "Its' cool," he responded into the phone.

Maybe I sent the wrong message last night, he thought to himself as he dialed the number of Viola Sparks. Maybe he was over thinking this situation. It could be simply that she was in the neighborhood and wanted to say hello, but he doubted this. Coretta rarely did anything without an angle. "Viola Sparks, please. This is Dahji McBeth," he said when her secretary answered.

"Hi Dahji," replied the syrup laced cutie he'd met on his last visit. Everything about her was petite and properly coifed.

"What's good?" He could feel her smile through the phone.

"Hold on. She just left the office for court. I'll transfer you to her cell phone," she said cheerfully.

"Thank you, Angel."

"You're welcome." There was no doubt that she was feeling him and he liked her, too. It was against the pimp code to turn down a woman who was choice.

Viola came onto the line just as Dahji's doorbell rang. "Good morning," she answered in her proper voice. "I was expecting to hear from you last night." There was traffic noise breaking in between her sex-laced innuendo.

"Yeah. I got a little busy," he replied as he opened the door for Coretta. She stood before him in a white rose print sun dress. It dropped along her petite, yet ample curves and rest on sandaled, pedicured feet. Seeing her moved something in him.

"I bet," Viola was saying as Coretta said, "Hey Mr. Man." Her brown eyes sparkled as she moved into him for a hug. Her hair smelled of fresh rain and he liked the way she'd parted it at the top of her smooth forehead to let the rest fall to her soft shoulders in a sheet of black, bone-straight strands.

"My, aren't we busy?" Viola was saying as Coretta released him and strolled into the penthouse.

"So where we at?" he asked, watching Coretta move into the kitchen and sample his protein shake. Her face screwed up as she smacked her small, heart-shaped lips together.

"Well, we have a court date ... Arraignment ... In the Superior Court in two weeks. We'll move from there. How is your lady friend holding up? She seemed pretty out of it."

"She's tough," Dahji assured her as he strolled casually across the open space to the kitchen.

"So here it is ... I'm a successful attorney who's been in love with you since high school and you chase a woman who's ..."

"Hold on. Stop the drama. That ain't you." At this Coretta furrowed her brow in question. Who was he talking to?

"Okay. That wasn't fair. But you owe me a payment. We're still on for lunch, right?"

"Yeah." Coretta was distracting him with her movements around the kitchen. She was now leaning into the refrigerator, her ass swaying from side to side.

"I'll see you at my office Dahji," Viola sang before ending the call.

"Who was that?" Coretta wanted to know from deep inside the kitchen. She held a banana in her hand.

"Remember Viola Sparks?"

She thought carefully, her mind echoing her lips as she whispered the name. "Viola. Viola. Sparks."

"She was the chubby girl that spilled strawberry milk on you that time."

"OH!!" Coretta shrieked with recognition. "HER!" Then she grew curious. "How she ..."

"She's a lawyer now."

Coretta quickly ran the high school movie in her head. Viola was jealous of her and wanted Dahji for herself. Now she remembered and decided calmly that she was no more a threat now than she was then. She calmly peeled her banana as Dahji explained that she was representing a friend of his.

"That Peaches girl who tried to take dope into the prison?" she asked.

"One and the same."

She bit into the banana tenderly, using her teeth. "So y'all getting serious now?"

"She's good people," he replied, moving back into the living room.

Coretta followed. "I know good people, but that doesn't mean that I'll hire them as an attorney."

Dahji was busy adjusting the focus on a digital camera as he said, "Let me get this straight. You drop our daughter off and slide through here to help me run my situation, right?"

She smiled with his lazy drawl of accusation. "Nope. You seem to be handling it just fine, but we both know that I'm the right woman for you." She was seated on the couch now, watching as he lay a burgundy silk sheet over the half-backed chaise lounge next to the window.

"What are you doing?" she asked after it became apparent he wouldn't respond.

"Handling my business," he answered as he moved to a tripod stand and placed it in the center of the room. He thought of telling her that she should leave, but decided it may do her good to see how fine Ebony was.

"Well, don't let me stop you," she said as she wiggled further into the leather cushions. "Aryn really had fun last night. She couldn't stop talking about your uncle." She giggled in remembrance of the funny story he told about getting stuck in a Chicago snow blizzard because he'd forced a whore to walk home from the track. He admitted that he grew soft and tried to rescue her. His Cadillac got stuck and he had to foot it home. Waiting for him was the whore. She'd copped a ride from a police officer.

"What time does she get out of school?" Dahji wanted to know, busy positioning the digital recorder onto the tri-pod.

"Three o'clock."

"So, what brings you by?"

Coretta grinned behind his back. "Well, I wanted to come by to tell you that I had a great time last night."

"And?" he asked, turning to her now just as his phone rang. She smiled with the rescue.

Dahji pointed an accusatory finger at her as he strolled to grab the phone.

"Mr. McBeth. There is Ms. Ebony here to see you," said the lobby desk guard.

"Send her up."

"Oh, you're about to do your film thing for the clothes?" Coretta asked when he stepped back into the living room.

"Just handling business, baby."

"I ain't mad at you. So, why you never ask me to model?"

Dahji observed her with a cool glance. "This might not be the right situation for you," he said finally.

"Why?"

"You want our daughter to see you damn near naked on the internet?"

"Oh. So, you're protecting my honor now?"

"I'm protecting the honor of our daughter," he replied as a soft knock came at the door.

"I could still do something classy and appro ..." she was saying as Dahji opened the door. What she saw left her mouth open.

Ebony stepped through wearing a sheer white cotton dress that sculpted her voluptuous figure from the deep cleavage of her full breasts to the sharp drop off of her ass. Her hair hung long and thick, draping in slinky-like curls to her shoulders. She turned to whisper something to Dahji, showing Coretta the true largeness of her ass. It resembled two basketballs sitting side by side under her slim waist. Creasing the tight mounds was a pink thong that only heightened the spectacular effect.

Dahji broke away from her slight touch with a grin, gesturing to Coretta who'd managed to compose herself. "Ebony, meet Coretta."

"Hi. We have a daughter together," Coretta informed the statuesque woman with slanted eyes and a wide mouth.

"Is your daughter here?" Ebony asked with a mixture of hidden desire and pure wonder.

"Naw. She's at the daycare place."

Ebony nodded with understanding before she dropped her large leather purse to the floor carelessly. She then strolled towards the window, her high heels clacking softly against the hardwood floor as she passed Coretta. "I absolutely love this view. Remember the last time I was here?" she asked, suddenly turning around to find her audience entranced by her sultry stride.

Dahji did remember. The photo shoot was an out-of-this-world experience. She had transformed herself into another person. And afterwards she'd sucked him off with raw emotion. She'd left upset because he wouldn't sex her, promising that their time would come. She had to feel some kind of way to find Coretta here.

"How have those photos been selling?" she asked, taking in the tripod and silk sheet over the low half-back lounge seat.

"Best sellers," Dahji informed her as he lifted his camera from the couch beside Coretta. She looked as if she had snuck into a movie theatre and was waiting for the usher to escort her out with a warning not to sneak in again.

"Coretta," Ebony began, making her dark brown eyes sparkle. "Are you modeling, too?"

Coretta looked to Dahji sharply. "He won't let me."

"I don't see why not. You're pretty enough."

"Well, thank you," Coretta replied with mock cheer. She'd made up her mind not to like Ebony.

"You feelin good doll?" Dahji asked as he lifted the camera to his eye.

Ebony smiled in reply, lifting her gold bangled wrists to the ceiling, the backdrop of the city showing through the window behind her. Dahji moved to the video camera and peered through the site to make sure the entire scene was captured.

"When are we going to do the HoodSweet shoot?" she asked as she turned away and looked back to the camera.

"Thas Saturday," he responded, moving across the room to capture each new pose. "Good. Good. Go to the window," he instructed.

In three long strides she was placing her palms onto the window and thrusting her ass out. She threw her hair from side to side and adjusted her body slightly with each movement.

Dahji clicked away as she turned in a full circle, posing at every angle. There were no words for the effect she had on Coretta. There was a switch she'd turned on that magnified the roundness of her breasts and the tone of her shapely thighs. With a smooth glide she was on the chaise lounge.

"You got it baby," Dahji urged, following her with the lens.

She lay down with one knee up, turning her head this way and that with an electric smile. Then she was on her stomach, her creased mounds raised seductively. One foot on the floor, and she was split open for a convict's imagination. Then she sat up and pulled the dress between her long legs. She squeezed her breasts to inflated wet cinnamon hills, looking up with head bowed to effect a sinister pose. She was a different person once again.

"Thas the bidness right there," Dahji called out as he clicked away.

Without instruction Ebony shed the sheer tube dress and was topless.

Her breasts stood perfectly away from her body. There was not one mark, blemish, or scar on her. She shined under the sunlight. She repeated her same poses before the window and upon the chaise lounge, but the effect was entirely new and more erotic.

A light sheen coated Ebony's dark skin. She stood before the sunlit window like an apparition. Sex appeal exuded from her every pore. Coretta's eyes were on Dahji as he circled her with his camera. She wanted the session to be over. Her pussy throbbed with wanting. She'd crossed her legs at the ankles and bathed in a glow that she felt emanating from herself.

To her eyes Ebony's movements became fluid as if in a dream. The clicking of the camera was like a timer and the sunlight streaming in through the window was heaven's blessing. Her nipples flexed beneath her bra as she marveled at the beauty of Ebony's titties; the nipples were raised thickly at the center of a milky dark patch.

Then Dahji announced that she had done well. Coretta was broken from her spell. It was over. She blinked from her delirium as Dahji moved into the kitchen and returned with an envelope. He handed it to Ebony just as she slipped back inside of her dress.

"Thank you Dahji" she said softly. She bounced the envelope of money against her leg as she asked if Dahji remembered her telling him about wanting to be in SMOOTH magazine.

"No doubt," he replied.

"Well, I might be moving to L.A. to pursue that."

"You ain't gotta move to L.A. to get into SMOOTH magazine. We got product to send to 'em."

She made her lips move to one side of her face so that a deep dimple formed on her dark cheek. "I know ... But I met somebody that can help me get some acting experience," she explained.

"What kind of acting experience?" he wanted to know.

"Just some light weight stuff," she hedged.

"Porn. Just last month you couldn't understand how a woman stripped and now you off to get plugged by ten niggas a day?" He couldn't understand her logic. "It ain't that. He's talking about getting me some roles on sitcoms and some spokesmodel training." She'd grabbed up her purse and stood near the door.

"Well, I still don't think you gotta go out there to do that. Before you make your final decision, come back through Saturday and meet Sherrelle. Maybe you'll listen to her."

"Okay. I'll see you then,' she assured him before waving over to Coretta. "It was nice meeting you."

"You too," she responded quickly, eager for the sexy woman to leave.

Dahji stood in the opened door, obscured from Coretta's view as Ebony stepped into the hallway. She leaned in close and whispered in his ear, "You got away this time." She reached for the thick meat between his legs and squeezed it softly.

"I'm scared of you," he responded with a grin.

"You should be," she hissed as she turned away from him and sashayed to the elevator that would take her to the ground floor. He stayed in the doorway, nodding at her backwards glance, until she disappeared behind the closing doors with a sexy wave and wide smile.

When Dahji closed the door he was startled to find Coretta standing before him naked. She looked to him with dreamy eyes.

"What you get away from?" she asked hoarsely.

He was awestruck at her boldness. He wanted to ask why she was naked, but it didn't take a scientist to deduce that she wanted to get fucked. He had to admit that Ebony had made him grow on a few occasions during the shoot. He'd been faced away from her, giving Ebony a full view of his arousal. It made for a great photo session.

"Never mind that," she quickly added. "You are going to fuck me right now!" she demanded, grabbing at his joint and leading him into the living room.

"I got a busy day Coco," he complained with futile resistance.

Coretta smiled with her progress. He hadn't called her Coco since their first date in high school. She reached into his robe and pulled his half erect organ through his silk boxers. The tip of his head was wet with his earlier arousal.

"You did like it," she observed with panting breath before placing him onto her tongue. She sucked on the head powerfully, making Dahji's knees grow weak and buckle.

This only encouraged her as he grew large in her mouth. She stroked the length of him as she rolled her lips around the swollen, meaty head. Feeling him tense up under her attentive tongue, she popped off of him and strolled to the window. With his pole leading the way, bouncing heavily in the air, he followed her. She placed her hands across the city, palms flat against the floor-to-ceiling window. She pushed her ass out to him seductively as she watched his approach eagerly.

"I like the view too," she whispered as he came up behind her.

Dahji parted her wet pussy and slid into her with a tight embrace. The city was coming to life below them as he inched further into her waiting hotness. She moaned before him, turning her head up to meet his tongue. High above the landscape they made love with an urgency spurred on by Ebony's foreplay. Her skin was hot against his chest as he eased slow, long strokes into her.

Coretta spread her legs to receive him better, nearly bent over entirely against the window. She swayed and gripped him to near orgasm before turning abruptly away, making him slip from her, and running to the chaise lounge.

Dahji followed; amused that she would retrace Ebony's steps. She lay on her stomach and he kneeled to her, directing the shiny missile into her silo. She put one foot to the ground and received him with a soft moan, allowing her pussy to breathe around his thickness. She gripped the lone tube pillow and squirmed beneath him in an effort to ease the length of him from penetrating too deeply.

"Turn me over," she panted in pleasurable pain.

With a swift turn she was on her back, Dahji's pendulum swung mightily; it was slick and shining with her sex. She reached up for him and brought him down to her. She lifted one leg over the low, sloping back of the chaise lounge and opened for his entry.

Dahji long stroked her deeply as she gripped his straining back with tense emotion. Her hot, panting breath hissed into his ear with a rhythmic wash to match each slow rolling thrust inside of her steaming pussy.

This was what she wanted: To make love in a real way; like how they used to make love. This was the way Aryn was conceived. This was not like the night before. This lovemaking was energized by a longing for a family.

CHAPTER SEVENTEEN

Her early morning trip to the neighbor's house was still on her mind. Just knowing that the old man was so close and still so alone made her want to see him again. The giddiness she felt with her secret knowledge of seeing him masturbating raised goose bumps on her bare arms. As she moved about in the kitchen, frying hamburger meat, she stole glances through the window to the neighbor's house. There was nothing she could see from this angle, but her curiosity would not let this fact keep her from checking for any movement across the curtained windows.

She was liking this new city more every day. It was all too easy. Men were making themselves available to her wishes at every turn. In her mind she was placing them in categories that suited her various needs and excitements. Dahji represented a certain level of intrigue and excitement. She felt he would be someone cool to know. The challenge of resisting his charm was appealing to her. Percy was a no-brainer. He would do as she wanted. There was a sinister part of her that was excited at the prospect of turning him out. The scars on his back was proof that he craved for something more than what her aunt was providing. Her aunt's indifference to Percy's existence was all the license she needed to play him for the fool she knew him to be. And then there was her next door neighbor. The old man had to have some money stashed away. Her interest in him was financial. How much could she bleed him for while the opportunity presented itself?

She moved about the kitchen, the afternoon sun washing in through the open window like a caress of privilege. The world was open to her. There were three men in her orbit that contained fruit ripe for the picking. She couldn't have planned it better than this.

"What are you cooking?" Sherrelle called from the living room.

Ayana leaned into the kitchen archway with the top of a hamburger bun in one hand and a spoonful of mayonnaise in the other. She still had not unwrapped her hair or changed from the silk robe. On her feet were a pair of large, furry rabbit slippers. "Hamburgers. Want one?" she asked as Sherrelle dropped the Circuit City bag onto the dining room table.

"I see I'm going to have to find you something to do so you can get dressed for a change," Sherrelle commented as she reached the kitchen archway.

Ayana spinned away from her. "Don't rush on my account," she replied, returning to the stove-side counter where a pile of lettuce, tomatoes, and pickles were neatly stacked to continue with her burger preparations.

"Who are you cooking for?" Sherrelle asked, moving to her side. There were no less than five thick hamburger patties on a plate and three more frying in the pan.

Ayana turned to her with a simple expression. "You don't cook the whole pack when you open it?" she asked innocently.

"Hell naw, girl! Are you on some type of drug?" Sherrelle looked to her with an incredulous stare, having to remind herself that her niece had just turned eighteen years old.

Ayana grinned. "You have some weed?"

Sherrelle giggled in a fit as she pointed a finger to Ayana's face.

"See, you gon' make me send you back to your momma. No wonder she was so eager to see you go." She was immediately sorry for this when a sad pall washed over Ayana's face. "I didn't mean to say that."

It was a few beats before Ayana recovered. During this time she'd made a complete sandwich and now lifted it for Sherrelle. "So, do you want one?" she asked with an odd smile spreading her full lips. She'd returned to her giddy state. She'd grown used to being criticized and found it much easier to forget the insult as soon as it occurred. This worked especially well with men who didn't want to upset her interest in them, thus depriving them of her carefully laid plan to offer elusive attention and seduction.

Sherrelle took the hamburger, unable to resist Ayana's youthful charm.

"I went to see the neighbor today," Ayana confessed.

Sherrelle was prevented from talking due to the mouth full of hamburger, but the look on her face said what she couldn't.

"I just wanted to say hello and take him some strawberry cake." Here she turned from the counter with a freshly made hamburger in her hand.

She bit into it slowly, her lips trapping the loose meat and lettuce as she chewed.

"Did you have a boyfriend in L.A.?" Sherrelle asked suddenly, realizing in that instant that she barely knew her niece.

"He was a piece of a boyfriend."

"What does that mean?"

Ayana smiled as if remembering a fond time. "You like my cooking?" she wanted to know, the same smile on her lips.

"It's okay, but don't change the subject. What do you mean by him being a piece of a boyfriend?"

"He was good for some things."

"Some things like what ... Money?"

"Not really."

"Sex?"

Ayana grinned with that earlier memory. "Something like that," she confessed, not wanting to reveal that she enjoyed his thug appeal. It was this love that her mother hated and for this hatred she seduced her mother's boyfriend. It was an appropriate get-back according to Ayana.

Simple girl, Sherrelle thought to herself. "Are you interested in going to college?" she asked as Ayana turned to flip the remaining three hamburgers in the frying pan.

"I was thinking about it."

"Well, that's good to know. I have some information here for you about some junior colleges in the area." Ayana was silent. In truth, going to school was the last thing on her mind. "If this clothing company goes like I plan then we can't have you be a dummy and ..."

"I ain't stupid," Ayana interjected.

Sherrelle rolled her head on her neck at the sharp rebuke. "Oh, did I say that? I don't think I did. What I am saying is that you can't rely on your looks forever."

"What about you and the neighbor dude?" Ayana asked suddenly.

"Oh, you are really growing your ass today, hunh?" Ayana was smiling mischievously. "It ain't funny," she added as a lightness began to fill her. Sherrelle could not help but to feel Ayana's charm and join in the laughter. With that one question Ayana had succeeded in showing her aunt that they were two sides of the same coin.

"All those muscles ... Mmmm," Ayana moaned, swaying her body sensuously. "Just rub him down with some hot oil and watch his muscles glisten. Oooohhh!" she added as Sherrelle slapped her across the shoulder.

"Stay away from him!" she warned playfully.

"Stop hitting me. I don't want your man!"

"Well, you better act like it. Now hurry up and finish so we can film you in some of these clothes." With this, Sherrelle bit into her hamburger and turned to leave the kitchen. "And you better be careful with that old man, too!" she added just before walking through the kitchen archway.

"Don't worry. I will!" Ayana called after her cheerfully.

"That's what I'm scared of!" Sherrelle answered from somewhere in the dining room.

Ayana smiled to herself, nodding her head to the music that Sherrelle turned on. R. Kelly's powerful voice filled the house. He sang of doing it all for love.

Ayana had become well practiced in going from homely to exotic. Even without her hair let free from its wrapping she had a special allure, but with a few touches of eyeliner and a tangerine lip gloss she was transformed into the woman who made traffic stop on Sunday along Crenshaw Boulevard.

When she stepped from the hallway bathroom dressed in nothing more than the pink high-cut boy-shorts and the nearly transparent half-t Sherrelle had advised her to wear, she was brand new and exotic. Seeing how beautiful she was made Sherrelle shake her head in dismay. She didn't want to voice her feelings because the smile on Ayana's face told her that her niece knew well enough the effect she was capable of having on people.

"You ready?" Ayana asked with one hand on her hip as if her appearance was nothing special. She'd tied her hair in two long braids that descended along the side of her face and met at the deep cleavage of her breasts. Her caramel colored skin was oiled and her light-brown eyes sparkled inside a thin rim of black eyeliner.

"You're going to make me a millionaire," Sherrelle commented before adding, "Let's start by the fireplace." She'd set a small log alight so that the living room was cast in a deep orange glow.

Sherrelle took up position in the center of the room as Ayana began posing in front of the fireplace. The flames illuminated her body and gave the scene an ephemeral effect.

"Like that?" Ayana asked, turning away from Sherrelle and leaning to the fireplace with her legs spread.

"Yeah. That's good."

Ayana made graceful moves across the glow of embers, posing

provocatively and turning this way and that, dipping and rising as if attached to a stripper's pole. The warmth of the fire made her skin glow with a light sheen. And with every move she was further absorbed in her role as seductress. Her breasts heaved, nipples straining forward, inside the thin cotton shirt.

"Over to the couch now," Sherrelle instructed while holding the camcorder steady on her.

Ayana smiled for the camera as she made the transition from the fireplace to the cool couch. She lay down and raised her arms above her head. Her shining, taut stomach undulated suggestively as she lay on her back with one leg out and one knee up. She rubbed her legs together like scissors seductively, making her breasts pulse with life. Then she turned on her stomach, creating a deep arch in her back so that her ass popped into the air like twin hills on a smoky horizon.

She is a natural, Sherrelle was thinking to herself as a shaft of light broke into the room. The effect broke the spell, but not before Percy walked into the house and saw Ayana half naked upon the couch. He looked to Sherrelle and cocked his head sideways in confusion, his heart pounding with Ayana's ass in his mind, as he realized that it was a camcorder in his wife's hand.

"We're filming for the website," Sherrelle explained, though she wondered why he was home so early.

Percy's eyes traveled back to Ayana, who was still on her stomach. She was swinging her legs so that her feet knocked against her butt. He was nearly hypnotized by the soft movements before Sherrelle asked him if he was okay. He blinked Ayana's evil grin away. *Why won't she get up?*, he vaguely wondered as he looked to his wife.

"Yeah … Yeah …" he stammered, trying to shake the effects of being told by his boss to take the rest of the day off. A swarm of FBI auditors had descended on the office to collect his computer files and accounting records. They'd asked Carrie to stay behind to answer some questions. Percy wanted to tell her that she should have a lawyer present, but what was the need for one if she didn't do anything wrong?

"You don't look good" Ayana noted, now sitting up with her hands jabbed between her knees. This pose forced already artificially enhanced breasts to two sumptuous mounds of toffee-colored delight. If it weren't for the way her ass dipped into the couch and the sexual appeal shooting from her eyes, Percy could have mistaken her for a teenager. *Well, she is eighteen,* he thought to himself.

These sexual thoughts seemed to ease some of the tension he was currently afflicted with. His mind was going a mile a minute as he contemplated over and over again his situation. He barely knew where he was headed as he drove home from the office. Fear gripped him momentarily at the prospect of being indicted, only to be covered over with some hidden pleasure that beckoned to him. The stress he was suffering made this feeling ever more present. And as soon as he walked in the door he knew that he couldn't stay.

"Oh yeah ... Yeah ..." he began as he moved in small steps towards the dining room. "I forgot an important file this morning," he added.

"You left your Halliburton case. It might be in there," Sherrelle suggested.

"Yeah. That's it," he replied unconvincingly as he disappeared into the hallway.

"Your husband is strange," Ayana whispered as Sherrelle stared in wonder at the hall space Percy had only a second before occupied.

"He's having a tough time at work," she replied. "Let me go see what's going on with my baby." With this she dropped the video camcorder into lounge chair and followed her husband to the bedroom.

Ayana crept from the couch slowly. She waited at the hallway entrance until Sherrelle closed the door behind her. She walked on tip toe along the edge of the wall until she was just outside of their bedroom. She listened at the door.

"Are you sure you're okay?" Sherrelle was saying.

"Yeah. I told you I just forgot some paperwork," Percy responded from near the bathroom. His voice faded and echoed as he entered the bathroom. "And why do you have all the lights out. Do you really mean to have your niece posing like that for the world to see?" he asked, his voice losing its echo as he walked back into the bedroom.

"Why are you so concerned about her and what I do with my business? You didn't think I could get this far?"

"How far have you gotten? Hunh ... How far? All I see is a bunch of skimpy clothes all over my house and you ..."

"Is that all this is to you?" Sherrelle demanded to know. "Why can't you just support me on this ... Is that too hard for you to do?"

Percy hissed loudly. "I don't have time for this. There's too much going on right now." There sounded like a light tussle before Percy added, "I told you I don't have time for this right now, Sherrelle."

"You don't sleep with me. You don't talk to me. You don't spend time with me. You don't take me out anymore ..."

"Geeesh, Sherrelle! Must we have this conversation now?" he asked, his voice closer to the door. Ayana sprang from her crouching position and was immediately assaulted by a sharp pain in her calf muscle. She limped through the hallway and hobbled over to the couch. She barely made it by the time she heard Sherrelle's voice in the hallway.

"No, we don't have to talk about it. You don't have to talk to me about anything." She was behind him as he made a bee-line for the front door without his briefcase.

"Bye Percy," Ayana said painfully as she held her calf to her lap, massaging the muscle with attentive fingers.

Percy glanced at her with menace; as if she were responsible for his troubles.

There was a pause at the door. Percy mumbled incoherently before Sherrelle stepped back into the house, followed by Peaches.

"What's wrong with him?" Peaches wanted to know.

"The usual," Sherrelle replied.

"Does this mean I can't get my Mustang?" Ayana asked as she tended to the cramp in her leg.

"Oooh! I want to be adopted," Peaches began. "Y'all giving away Mustangs!"

Sherrelle was closing the door as Peaches commented on how sexy Ayana was looking.

"We're shooting for the website," Ayana informed her with pride.

"Oh! Speaking of which," Peaches began as she walked to the lounge chair and sat down, picking the camcorder up and pointing it at Sherrelle. "What do you have to say about your girl coming through for you on that manufacturing contract?" she asked excitedly. Sherrelle jumped with excitement in the view finder.

"Really!? That's huge!" she shrieked.

"That's how we do and you know this. And what do you have to say about me meeting with a distributor who will negotiate putting us in popular stores across the country?"

Sherrelle had no more words. Her image grew large in the screen as she quickly skipped and hopped to the leather lounger and squeezed in next to Peaches. She hugged her friend closely to her and shrieked with joy, "I can't believe it!"

"I can because you're hurting my neck," Peaches complained, her cream colored skin blushing red.

Sherrelle exhaled excitedly as she released her. "So, the manufacturer agreed to a thousand of each garment and size?"

"Of course."

"When will it all be ready?"

"I have to check back next week. Oh!" she said, remembering something. "I have the contracts for you to sign in my car." She turned to Sherrelle then. "When do I get my business cards?"

"Tomorrow we have to go apply for a franchise license and form our corporation. You want to be the president or something?" Sherrelle asked, her words giddy with excitement and punctuated with peels of laughter.

"I don't know ..." Peaches hedged.

Ayana stood up and tested her cramped leg. "How about Executive Boss Bitch," she suggested.

"I like that," Peaches agreed with more laughter. She'd been feeling downcast after her meeting with Sun Yi and was thankful that she didn't have to rehash the experience with an explanation as to how she accomplished the deal.

"I don't think so," Sherrelle began as she jumped from the seat. She strolled over to Ayana and hugged her around the neck, squeezing her tightly for good measure; she enjoyed the short gasp of complaint that escaped her lips. "How about Director of Regional Sales? You'll be responsible for making sure we are in every strip club in the country."

"I'm in love with a stripper," Ayana sang under Sherrelle's loose choke hold.

"I don't care what you call me as long as I get paid. I need to buy me a house with two lemon trees in the front yard." She'd stood up and walked over to where Ayana and Sherrelle stood as she said this. They ended up in a group hug to celebrate their achievement.

"What's my title going to be?" Ayana asked in the midst of their girlish excitement. She was the only one not laughing.

"You act right and we might ... We just might LET you be a sales rep."

"Oh that's great. Thanks a lot auntie," she replied dejectedly.

Peaches broke away from their embrace. "Come on girl. We have to get to Applebottoms so we can show these clothes off. Everyone has been waiting for the new shipment."

Sherrelle was already on her way to her bedroom when Ayana asked if she could go.

"You have to be twenty-one," Peaches replied shortly on her way to the kitchen.

"I can be twenty-one if I need to be!" Ayana called after her.

"Who made the hamburgers? I'm starving!" Peaches called out.

"You have to be twenty-one!" Ayana teased as she eased to the couch to rub her calf some more. She was no longer excited at the prospect of going to a strip club. She'd been in enough of them to know that it wasn't a place she would fight for to be inside.

She waited patiently, checking the time for Peaches to emerge from the kitchen with a fat hamburger in her hands and Sherrelle to emerge from the bedroom. She was constantly surprised at how her aunt could make a pair of jeans look like a sweet dish of dessert. She'd tied her hair into a ponytail and dropped a Phat Farm hat over her head. There was no hiding her full breasts under the University of Arkansas sweater she'd put on.

"You have kitchen clean up duty today, Ayana. And the hallway bathroom is a disaster."

"I was just in a hurry ..." Ayana was saying when Peaches entered the room chewing on a big bite of hamburger.

"This is a good ass ... Damn! Who made this?" Peaches groaned, walking up beside Sherrelle.

"That would be chef boyar pippie long stocking." With this, Sherrelle picked up the large canvas Nike bag of HoodSweet apparel.

Peaches took another small bite. "I didn't realize how hungry I was."

"Dahji didn't feed you?" Sherrelle asked with a furrowed brow under her lowered cotton hat.

"He ain't got time for me no more," she replied with a shrug.

"I don't believe that," Ayana offered. "Not the way y'all be talking about him."

Peaches exhaled sweetly. "That's my boo. We were supposed to hook up earlier, but I was running late ..." She swooned with rolling eyes. "And he had to go see my lawyer and ... Just too much to do and too little time."

"Well, at least he's still handling business. He goin' to see your lawyer and all that," Ayana said, her eyes looking to Peaches sympathetically.

"Who is this girl?" Peaches asked, looking to Sherrelle. "Is she trying to give me comfort when she don't know that he could have his ten-inch dick inside her right this very minute?" With this she matched her mock-shocked look with Ayana's wide-eyed stare.

"There you go again," Sherrelle warned her friend. "Let's go before you break all the way down."

"Naw. I'm cool. I know it's just business and he's looking out for me."

Peaches was moving behind Sherrelle towards the door. She looked back to Ayana and said, "You need to open a hamburger stand, girlfriend."

"What I need is a man who owns a chain of Burger King's," she countered as she jumped from the couch. Peaches raised her palm for a high five.

"I like the way you think. You remind me of me when I was young and hopeful," Peaches sang as they walked out onto the porch. The sun was making its descending arc from the sky.

"Don't worry, she's about to check in school," Sherrelle informed Peaches as she led the way down the driveway.

Peaches turned to Ayana. "Be smart. Stay in school. Don't do drugs. Don't have pre-marital sex." She said all this with beady gray eyes and a mocking tone.

"Laugh all you want," Sherrelle said to Ayana before looking over the roof of the car to Peaches. "Don't make me hurt you."

Peaches shivered in mock fear as she looked to Ayana, whose laughter was renewed with Peaches' antics. The laughter aside, Ayana could see the pain just below the surface of Peaches' smiling face. She privately faulted Peaches for letting her feelings get involved when it came to Dahji. She reminded herself not to make that mistake.

Ayana waved, standing in the driveway in her furry white rabbit house shoes, as Sherrelle backed out of the driveway. When she turned to walk back into the house she looked into the neighbor's front door. Her heart heaved with mischievous excitement at the shadow of the old man behind the screen door. He stood still and silent as if feeling the night descend.

"Hi neighbor friend," she called out, waving despite the fact that he couldn't see her.

Grump opened the screen door and lifted his head to the sky. "Hello pretty cotton tail," he responded. This was enough to draw Ayana across the slim slice of grass and onto the neighbor's porch.

"How was your day?" she asked as she stepped near. He smiled with her question, opening the screen door further.

"Mind if I say you have been on my mind since morning?"

"No, I don't mind at all. What are you doing?"

"Same ol same ol," he answered.

"Oh," she giggled sexily. "Watching those nasty movies, hunh?"

Grump smiled his toothless, bashful grin. "That's all I got," he confessed. "Old man like me all alone."

"You don't have to be. I'll keep you company when I can." With this she'd reached out and rubbed down the length of his ribs hidden beneath the baggy plaid shirt he wore.

"Well, that sounds mighty nice."

"Maybe I can give you a fresh shave and haircut?"

"Sounds mighty fine with me." He was giddy with amusement.

"Well, are you going to let me in?" she wanted to know.

Grump backed up slowly so that Ayana could come into the house. She did a quick scan of the finely appointed house and could see that the old man was left alone far too often. It was a shame that there was no one to tidy up and keep the place smelling fresh. All the curtains had been drawn and he was left to sit in the dark. The air was stuffy and smelled of musty linen. As she suspected there was a porno movie playing on the large plasma screen. A dark, thick woman was paying special attention to the large white dick in her mouth while she was being pounded from behind. Her body shook with the motions as they sandwiched her.

"This stuff ain't healthy for you. Aren't you blind?" she asked as she moved about to lift a window and let some fresh air inside.

"That's what they say, but I see jess fine," he replied as he stepped slowly to the leather lay-z-boy across the room.

"Has your daughter found someone to look after you?"

"NO, she's too busy with the white folk." His face was pressed forward, following her movements around the house; to the fireplace where she was looking at wedding photos of Marlin and Stacy; then to the crystal spiral case that held Stacy's collection of glass figurines.

She stepped to him now. "So what am I going to do with you?" He could not see the way she spread her legs before him or the way her pussy was creased fat by the boy-shorts.

"Let's start with a shave," he suggested. "There's a razor in the bathroom in the hallway," he added, gesturing with a lazy hand.

Ayana stepped away. "I'm going to hook you up," she promised with a bouncing step into the hallway. She took quick steps to the master bedroom and noticed the bed was unmade and there were clothes strewn about. *Damn, homegirl ain't taking care of her business. White folks can't have her that busy,* she thought to herself. She grabbed the electric shaver from below the sink and pranced back into the living room.

"Your daughter must be pretty important," she said as the clippers came to life in her hand.

"Dem white folks keep her gone. I worry about her. It just ain't natural."

"You don't have much hair on your face. You want me to trim this fuzz from your chin?" she asked, stepping between his legs, not surprised that he licked his lips and jutted his chin to her waist. He inhaled the air before him.

"Make me happy pop," he responded as she gently lay her fingers across his face.

"So how do you know I'm a pretty cotton tail?" she asked as she moved the clippers across the stubble on his chin.

"I see jess fine," he mumbled.

"Oh. Like you can see what's on the television?"

"Blarney right."

Ayana giggled softly, her leg rubbing against his inner thigh. She moved the clippers to his head and slowly sheared the stray strands from his scalp. "I might lose my balance so help me stay up," she suggested, moving further between his thighs.

"Is that okay?" she asked, looking down into his shining face.

"Fine stroke of luck. Feels bloody well," he replied, stopping on her rounded hips and flexing his long fingers around her ass.

"I'm glad you like that. It ain't right that you have to be alone all the time."

"It ain't right at all. You alone, too?" he asked.

"For right now. But I'm trying to go to school and buy a car, but ..." she trailed off.

"Shame that a pretty cotton tail like you should have to worry about stuff like that."

"That's life."

"Shouldn't be so hard. You got good family in Ms. Sherrelle and her husband. I 'spect they look after you right nuff."

"They are good, but they have their own lives to live." She leaned over him so that her breasts pressed gently against his forehead.

"Fine stroke of luck," he mumbled.

"Just a minute. I almost got it," she said as if she were a burden upon him, taking extra care to move softly along his body. She could feel his breath rush gently to her stomach. His hands grew hot through the sheer boy-shorts. When she rose up she took a look into his lap and was proud to see the straining bulge in his khakis.

"That feel better?" she asked, rubbing her hand across his clean scalp and down his face to his chin. The attention spread his lips into a grand smile.

"Easy peezy lemon squeezy," he sang, looking to a spot just above her head.

Her laughter was genuine as she backed away from his embrace. *That's enough touching for one day. The seeds have been planted well,* she thought to herself.

When the front door opened Ayana briefly thought to dash through the house and out the back door. She was glad that she'd stayed put when she saw that it was Marlin. He smiled when he saw her with the barber clippers in her hand. His eyes scanned her body and shifted to the smiling face of his father-in-law.

"Hey. What a surprise. See he finally got you over here," Marlin said as he closed the door behind him.

"Hi, Marlin. My aunt said to tell you hello. How's your knee?"

"It's cool," he responded, slightly shocked at her nakedness.

"Well, we're ALL rooting for you," she gushed. Grump was smiling wider than ever now.

"Hey pop. Stacy call?" Marlin asked the smiling man. He let the sports bag drop to the floor. Ayana could see why Sherrelle was attracted to this tall, muscular, handsome man with dark features. He exuded a calm sense of manly confidence and strength.

"White folk got her!" he replied cheerfully. Marlin let out an exasperated breath.

"She's probably out with her dyke boss again," he complained.

"Sho smell like her. White folk smell funny," Grump added.

This was all so very interesting to Ayana, but she felt it was time to leave. "Well, I have to go. It was nice spending time with you, Grump. Bye Marlin. I'll tell Sherrelle that you said hello." She moved towards the door after handing him the clippers.

"Awright now. Take it easy and don't get sick," Marlin said with a small smile as he scanned her shapely figure.

"I promise," she replied, returning a generous smile as she passed through the door.

"You eat yet, pop?" Marlin was asking just as Ayana was stepping onto the porch.

"I made some hamburgers earlier," Ayana was happy to inform them as she stepped back into the house.

"I'm starving!" Grump called out.

"What can I say except that's right on time. I just hope you can cook."

Ayana hooted with laughter. She couldn't have planned this any better.

I'll let you be the judge of that, but you should know that my hamburgers won the Crenshaw High School award for fattest most delicious patty."

"I can taste 'em already!" Grump shouted, his slim frame jerking in the seat with excitement.

Ayana followed Marlin's instruction to go get dinner. The air had chilled during her time in the neighbor's house and the sun had disappeared from the sky. She could still feel Grump's palms on her hips as she trotted onto her porch, thinking how much she wanted to see him react to being inside of her.

CHAPTER EIGHTEEN

Dahji knew that she had an angle. Coretta made no move without some purpose. And her purpose this morning had been to make love to him in a way that reminded him of the power that still existed between them. He had to admit to himself that she still moved through him.

Fortunately for him, he had a busy schedule to attend to. He couldn't afford to lay up with her and reminisce on old times and speculate about how good it would be to have their daughter grow up with both parents in the house. This was her angle and he couldn't be mad at her for that. The thought of seeing his daughter every morning sent a good feeling through him. And if he could get Marlin on the squad and square up his hand just a little, he might be able to do something like that.

Just as this thought settled in, a reminder of his personal obligation called him on the phone. He was suddenly torn between two loves. A new love that meant something good and an old love that represented family. It was hard to choose and he felt that maybe Peaches was growing suspicious. He hated to lead her on, which was why he was committed to seeing his word through, evidenced by making sure her dope case was handled properly. He didn't want to see her go to jail.

"Waddup angel," he answered, prepared for her disappointment at hearing that he wasn't at home.

"Hi. What's up?" Peaches asked, the sound of her car throttling beneath her.

"Just left the house to go see your lawyer."

"Dahji!" she called out slowly in complaint. "I thought we were going to come together like sweaty butt cheeks. You promised. I miss you!"

"I know, baby girl. But some thangs got mixed up so we gon' have to get together later on. Right now I gotta check on your lawyer to make sure you don't sleep in a four-man cell with three manly bitches who like snatch."

Peaches smiled despite her frustration. "Later tonight?"

"Tonight."

"I'm going to camp outside. You need to be giving me a key," she insisted.

"Yeah. Yeah. We gon' have to work on that after a minute."

"How long is a minute?" she asked.

"Sixty seconds," he answered quickly before asking, "How did the meet with the machine man go?"

"The manufacturer ... It went well. Tomorrow is when I meet with a distributor."

"That's good bizness right there."

"Yeah," she said, reminded of how disgusting the short, fat man was. She'd wanted to go straight to Dahji's house and take a shower and relax; but now she would have to go to her raggedy apartment and make do with some candles and a tub that was too narrow after being in Dahji's Jacuzzi-sized tub and closet-sized shower. She'd hoped to maybe take a few laps in his swimming pool and lounge with a view of the city below.

"So holla back. I'm right here bout to handle this lawyer bizness. Cool?"

"Okay. Thank you," she said in what she hoped was a cheerful voice.

"When Dahji say he got you then leave your parachute at home. If Dahji say there's cheese on the moon ..."

"I know," Peaches cut in. "Then grab your spoon."

"That's right. Holla back later. You goin' to work tonight?" he asked as he stepped from the Range Rover. His voice was losing its clarity in the underground parking garage.

"Yes. Me and Sherrelle are going to take some of the new clothes for the girls to see."

"Sounds like a plan. Let me go."

"Love you," she whispered.

"You feel me then," he responded before disconnecting the call. "Love," he whispered to himself. What was it with that word?, he wanted to know as he stood in front of the elevator. A woman will have a nigga dick in her pussy with a knife behind her back. The last thing a nigga hear is how much she love him before she stab the sucker in the heart. *Love me by giving me money,* he hissed as the doors opened on a sharp-suited white couple with soft leather briefcases. They observed him casually with tight smiles, obviously moved by his tailored navy- blue suit and the way his shiny hair hung past the lapels. Soft bottom gators and the customary diamond Rolex chain and watch sent them a signal they weren't prepared to receive. Added to this was his gold trimmed grin.

"Pimp or die," he said genially as he stepped past them into the silver plated elevator. He took special delight in the way the white woman's eyes were glued to him until the doors closed. Her associate/ companion/ coworker had to grab at her elbow gently to get her attention.

Dahji was still smiling when the elevator doors opened onto the ninth floor of the Citicorp Financial building. Viola Sparks had an entire floor of offices dedicated to her private law practice. Her personal domain rest at the edge of a thickly carpeted oval that was conservatively decorated with impressionist paintings and abstract charcoal drawings. At the center of the oval was the smiling cutie pie he'd spoken to earlier. She had a small microphone at the tip of full, dark lips; it was attached to a thin black plastic wire that ran to her ear. She watched Dahji as he approached; speaking into the mic and smiling pearly white teeth for his benefit.

He leaned against the waist-high, redwood desk while she finished her message taking. She simultaneously looked to the computer monitor where she typed in whatever was being said through her small ear piece.

"Hello Mr. Dahji McBeth," she breathed out sweetly as she typed in some final words. With delicate features and her Anita Baker hair cut, she was the total opposite of the woman who signed her paychecks.

"What it do working woman ... Your man ain't got you off this roll yet?"

She worked to control her laughter, but not before her small body bounced back in her chair and dipped forward with her hand cupped to her mouth. "I enjoy my job," she gushed out.

"That's a good thing. Viola ain't as bad as the prosecutor wants people to believe."

"No, she's not. We need more women like her in the courtroom."

"You just saying that because she pays you."

"You're crazy Dahji," she giggled out before tapping on the console of her computer. "You can go right in. She's waiting for you."

He tapped the counter one time before pushing off. "Don't work too hard," he said as his hair swung into place.

Soft jazz bounced off the suede walls as he stepped along the darkening section that fronted the large office. The closer he got to Viola Sparks' office the more personal the art work became. War masks from Africa shared space with intricate tapestries of Kente cloth art; this was situated inside of square glass cases that extended from the wall. On the smoked glass door her name was stenciled in gold leaf lettering. He knocked softly before opening the door slowly.

This area felt nothing like a lawyer's office at all. It was a world away from the receptionist's desk.

Viola looked up from behind her desk. Her pink blouse was unbuttoned to the bottom of her white satin-covered bra. She'd been absorbed in a file on her desk. "You're late," she announced as she stood up and walked around the desk. "And you're lucky I don't have to be back in court until two."

She was walking on bare feet. She met Dahji at the front of her desk and wrapped her arms around his neck.

"Dahji always on time though," he responded, looking into her hazel eyes, noting how small freckles marched across her red tinted skin like little ants. She'd been to the salon. Her hair was freshly permed and curled. It hung in bouncing auburn tresses, with blonde highlights, to her shoulders.

"Your hair is lookin' right," Dahji said as she pulled him between her legs. She leaned against the edge of the desk while looking into his eyes.

"It's about time, right?"

"When did you find the time?"

She smiled. "I had a beautician come to my house early this morning. Cost me a fortune."

"You can afford it," he replied as he looked around her redecorated office. On her desk was a Marie Cristophe Hibou lamp. Dahji had seen the wirey frame – made to look like an owl – in a Vanity Fair magazine he'd peeked through while at Mirabelle's house. He remembered that it cost $1,400. Mirabelle had her head in his lap at the time, telling him more about the odd relationship she had with her late husband's twin sisters.

"Yeah. I made a few changes. Got a couple good clients and I might have found somebody to love me," she hinted.

Dahji raised his eyebrows. He'd long ago told her to get out more often after she complained of being lonely.

"But he's not really the kind of man I would go for," she added.

"What's wrong with 'im? He got a wood leg or something?"

"NO ..." she answered. "He's white." Her face taking on an embarrassed look.

"What's wrong with that? Ain't nothing wrong with jungle fever."

"I don't know ... He's nice though. And I think he might have a little thing."

Dahji smiled with this. "What you mean by that?" he asked, though he suspected he already knew. His answer came quickly as she dropped an arm from around his neck and grabbed his organ.

"He ain't strapped like that," she hissed. "So, if I can get my fresh cut of beef then it might work out." She smiled mischievously.

"Already you planning on cheating. Now that ain't very church-folk like."

Her thick body shook with soft laughter. "Why can't I find a man like you?" she wanted to know, raising her arms around his neck again.

"I ain't fit like that. You gon' want me to cut my hair and give up all my women."

"I'll be all the woman you need and I'll only make you cut your hair a little. You might get away with your gold teeth if you let me dress you."

Dahji grinned. "That don't sound like a bad deal, but my women do some crazy stuff for me. I couldn't ask you to get down like that."

"Stuff like what?"

"You don't really want to know that," he assured her.

"Like anal sex ... Head ... Sex in the morning?"

"That's square. If you can name it we'll get down."

Viola gave this some thought as she looked into his brown eyes. "Should I be scared?" she asked finally.

"Very."

"Does your felony chick do all those unmentionables?" she wanted to know, her breasts bubbling from her satin bra seductively.

"Only cause she ain't got no options. You, on the other hand, got options and that beats a grind any time."

"I like it when you talk to me like that," she said in a sexy voice, running her fingers up the back of his scalp.

"That's because you feel me."

She dropped her hands to his zipper. "I want to feel you more," she hissed.

"What's the name of the judge that will hear my girl's case in superior court?" He'd looked off to the illuminated portrait of a beautiful Viola against the far wall; she was dressed in a lavender floral print dress. He wondered how long she had it.

Viola cocked her head to the side. "Why ... You got something up?"

"Something like that."

"He's a hard ass. I was going to get a change of venue. Judge Stein is trying to get appointed to the Federal Court so ..."

"Stein, you say?" he asked as she unzipped his pants.

"Yeah," she confirmed absently as his pants dropped to the carpet. "Who do you know .... Should I know them, too?" She held his meat in her palm as her eyes sparkled, looking to him with this question.

"Ever see a rabbit disappear in a top-hat?" Dahji asked with a sly grin.

Viola smiled. "I'll show you a disappearing act," she said before kneeling before him and taking him into her mouth. She lay the head between her lips and sucked off him slowly as if savoring the taste.

Dahji spread his legs to help keep his balance. Viola grinned wickedly with her small accomplishment. "White boy don't deserve that," he hissed as she licked across the base of his shaft.

There was no reply from Viola. Instead, she slid down the length of him as far as her mouth would allow before pulling off him again. The slow, tight stride made Dahji wince in pleasure.

"Damn, V. You bin practicing?" Dahji wanted to know.

In reply she slid her lips down the side of his organ like an ear of corn. She held him aloft with both hands as she moved up one side of him, kissed the head, and moved down the other side. She sucked at the thick tube sideways and dragged her tongue across his meat with a tension to make his thighs tense.

"I really wish you ..." he began as she rounded the tip of his joint with puckered lips. "Would let me pay ..." As she moved down the other side of his dick her hair brushed across the sensitive head. He inhaled a slice of air with the sensation.

"Were you saying something?" Viola asked, looking up to him.

He let out a deep breath as he shook his head from side to side. "I thought only white girls gave throat like that," he confessed.

Viola raised up with a gentle finger wipe across her lips. "So, you're going to do something slick to ... A backdoor deal to get your chick off?"

"You killing my buzz V," Dahji complained.

She grabbed his swollen pendulum. "Answer my question."

"Something like that," he replied under her gentle stroking.

"Will you still visit me?"

"Do a dog need a hole to bury his bone?"

Viola's breasts bounced with her laughter. She hiked up her skirt and slid onto her desk. "Bury that bone," she demanded, spreading her thick, toffee-colored legs to reveal the sandy brown hair of her muff topping off a tight, pink pair of vertical lips.

Dahji barked as he stepped from the slacks around his ankles. He quickly shed his suit jacket and unbuttoned his shirt; this he flung to a nearby leather studded chair. The space between her thighs was warm. His slim frame was absorbed by her girth as his meat met the sweet lips snugly. With rare service, her box was tight and smooth.

"Come on baby," she moaned as he parted her lips. She leaned back to observe the action. He held her legs apart as he rotated his hips, feeling her grow wet along the length of him as more of him slid into her.

Viola eased from her blouse and snapped her bra loose. Her breasts hung full and soft, bouncing subtly with Dahji's slow entrance. She opened to him gradually hissing and moaning with every inch of tight penetration.

"Oh god!" she whispered as he reached her nexus. Her soft, thick thighs shivered as he found an easy groove and slid from her warmth. Back in again as she watched, he braced himself between her legs.

"Yeah ... That's it ... Come on ... Bury that bone ..." she instructed, leaning back onto the desk as he grabbed her around the bottom of her thighs. Her ass nearly hung off the desk as he slipped in and out of her with growing rhythms. With each thrust her breasts jumped and she let out a low shriek of pleasure.

Viola was tight from inactivity and long hours of work. She spread snugly around him like a glove. Her creamy sex coated him with a transparent sheen that lubricated his slide inside of her wet pussy. His thighs slapped against her with each motion. She knocked files from the desk as her body vibrated under his pounding.

Dahji pulled her legs together and lifted them to the air. In front of him was nothing but the back of her thighs and the flushed flesh of her love box. He slid inside of her like a missile, and long stroked her at varying angles. Her panting hot breath told of how she felt about this position. Her eyes were closed and her breasts had fallen to her sides, bouncing and rolling with his powerful thrusts.

She was sopping wet and the smacking sounds grew louder as he stroked her. The cream soaked his balls and ran down his inner thighs. Her skin glistened and her pubic hairs were matted and soggy. Her skin was flushed red and bruised.

"Ahhhummmm," she groaned and shook, releasing yet more of her excitement over his shaft. The slickness of his meat allowed even further penetration. When he hit her bottom she raised up in protest.

"That's it," she hissed as she moved her disheveled hair from her face. She ran her hands down the length of her body as if to cool it off. Her breathing was shallow as she struggled to catch her breath. She squeezed her pussy over the immobile dick inside her pussy.

"You still in the minors?" Dahji asked, observing her exhaustion.

She flipped her eyes to him, acknowledging the challenge. "Oh, I'm not done with you." She pushed him from her and guided him to the pair of suede- covered floor blocks in front of a leather couch by the wall. She pushed him to his back and straddled him. She grabbed his glowing shaft and gently inserted him inside of her.

"You wanna ride, hunh? I can go all day like this," he teased.

"We'll see," she taunted as she braced her feet on the carpeted floor. With her breasts hanging to his face she bucked back onto him. Dahji jerked beneath her as the tip of his dick hit a bone.

She frowned in concentration as she worked herself up to a frenzy of rapid bucking, bending his meat crooked and relaxing to let him slide inside of her again. Dahji gripped her waist tightly in an effort to control her rapid movements and calm the growing boil of passion at the head of his organ. Her breasts swung over him as if of their own volition while she chased an elusive goal.

Dahji hit her bottom with growing frequency, the effect making him squirm in rebellion until he could do nothing but yield to what she commanded of him.

"Give it to me," she demanded hotly as she bucked on top of him. Her hair swung madly in spite of being fresh from the salon. She'd sweat her perm out. He pumped into her with finality just as her body shook and trembled.

Viola's skin was hot and flushed when she collapsed onto Dahji. She milked him snugly while he deflated inside of her.

"Damn, V. You tried to put it on me," Dahji hissed, liking the feeling of her large breasts pressed against his chest. She kissed along the ridge of his ear.

"You made me sweat my hair out," she whispered hotly in complaint between nibbles of his ear lobe.

"You gon' make that white boy insecure," he replied. Her body vibrated with her soft giggle on top of him.

"Ready for more?" she asked, squeezing around his dick as it lay inside her walls.

"You only made one appearance."

"We've been past what you owe me. We're working on pure lust."

"You lucky I like you," he replied, making his dick pulse inside of her. He knew it was a bad idea. There was a full day ahead of him and he still had no idea what Gloria would ask him to do to get Marlin on the team. But when Viola slid down the length of his body and began sucking their combined juices from his organ there was no turning back.

***

Viola Sparks was a thoughtful and remarkable woman. She'd planned their meeting to the very end. And with her BOSS status she was afforded a private bathroom complete with a Kohn shower. She'd produced a small designer gift bag that contained Calvin Klein cologne, body wash, lotion, and moisturizer.

So, now his body was fragranced differently from the morning, which he wasn't mad at, at all. Their shower together was more intimate than he thought possible. He was completely aware that Viola had been in love with him all along, but was unaware of the depth of her womanhood. It amazed him that she found it hard to find a suitable man. She'd joked, under the spray of water that she refused to dumb herself down just to keep a man and warm dick in her bed.

It was interesting to Dahji how they shared such powerfully sexual energy. When he mentioned this to her she confessed that she was motivated by the fact that he might not need her anymore since he had something going on to get Peaches out of her case. As her hands rubbed along his tightly muscled torso he assured her that she was a very special treat and would always be a good friend with benefits for her.

He resisted answering her inquiries as to what things his other women did for him. He felt she was better off not knowing about these things. His only reply was that he likes her the way she is. To make her into someone else would make her less special. She'd smiled graciously with this, happy to offer him another sexual session in the shower before they departed.

Dahji felt completely drained and incapable of anything more in the way of sexual favors for the rest of the day. On his way to meet Gloria at Chin Chin's (the seafood would do him good) he sipped on ginseng and chewed the root. His dick hung lazily and tender in his trousers from the sexual activity. With that business out the way and approaching the restaurant where Gloria was waiting for him he dialed Mirabelle's number. The pieces for a grand reward were showing themselves; the only thing left to do was put them together.

"I was just thinking about you," Mirabelle said when she answered the phone. Her voice chimed like proper musical notes.

"Clearly you know that I got you like a baseball mitt."

She smiled into the phone as a piano play in the background. He pictured her in that large bedroom with the piano that no one had to play for the keys to roll.

"You know a cat name Stein?" Dahji asked.

"Judge Stein ... He's the one hearing your friend's case?"

"One and the same."

"Well, that shouldn't be a problem. Isn't it great how I'm able to help out?" she asked with a soft treble in her voice.

"Yeah. It's absolutely great."

"Now now, Dahji. Don't be sardonic."

"I don't even know what that means," he confessed.

"I'm going to speak with the evil twins about my situation. I don't know what it is that you can say to them that will get them to release me from their treacherously greedy, vindictive claws."

"They can't be all that bad. Maybe I can meet them and feel them out. Everybody has a price and they don't have you over a barrel because they need the money."

Mirabelle gasped with the irony of it all. "They certainly do have me over a cracker barrel and they certainly do not need the money. He left them as much as he left me. I would dig that man from his grave if he could tell me why he placed me in their pointed beaks!"

Dahji was smiling with her rant. "Well, let's see what they look like."

"Not much!" she interjected, though he didn't mean in the looks department. Now he truly wondered what they looked like.

"Awright. Call me in the morning. Let's see if we can put this to bed."

"Can I see you tonight?" she asked in her sexy way. Dahji knew that she would want to see him and he knew that this could not be. The issue of her impending bankruptcy wouldn't allow his dick to get hard for her. Their sex would be passionless and disappointing. *Whether getting laid or getting paid, when I did one I missed the other,* he thought to himself.

"I miss you like a bacon sandwich, but things kinda tragic right now. Call me in the morning."

"Okay love," she said sadly. He'd never heard this tone in her voice before and it moved something inside of him. He felt as if she were trying to press him and he didn't like it.

"Awright sunshine. Daddy gotta roll," he finished while pulling into the parking lot of Chin Chin's.

Chin Chin's was located on famed restaurant row. Here was where the fashionable and high minded dined to see and be seen. Mixed in with the popular and trendy restaurants were specialty boutiques that catered to those who needed to feel privileged for being in a position to exercise their peculiar taste.

Dahji strolled into the cool, dimly lit reception area. To his left was a wall tank that housed live crab and lobster. On the other side of an invisible barrier were squid and octopus. Diners had the option of choosing their own crustacean or squid variety in which to dine on.

Before him, illuminated by a dim yellow light, was a tall brunette. The black-rimmed glasses she wore gave her a sexy bookish appearance. She looked up as Dahji approached the waist high podium where she'd been making a notation in a leather bound reservation book.

"Welcome to Chin Chin's," she greeted him. Her smile was electric in the dim light.

Dahji was struck by how she resembled Mirabelle. She could have easily been a younger twin sister. With a wide full mouth and sky blue eyes she was a darker version of Julia Roberts.

"Good afternoon," Dahji began, moving with purpose while she noted his fine appointments and took in his freshly scrubbed scent. His recent sexual escapade seemed to wash over her with some allure for her smile broadened as he approached. He looked to the ledger with his diamond bezeled Rolex twinkling over the pages of the appointment book. He saw Gloria Richards' name scrawled in this beautiful woman's handwriting and planted a finger on top of it.

"That's my party," he announced, letting his eyes rise from the page with a smile of his own.

She looked to where his finger stabbed the page. "Oh, Mrs. Richards. I'll take you to your table," she announced genially.

On a Thursday afternoon in the fashionable district of boutiques and restaurants, Chin Chin's played host to power luncheons and shady deals by power brokers. Dahji felt like he was in the right spot and good things were on the horizon for him.

As they strolled side by side through the dimly lit restaurant, polite laughter, satisfied smiles, and congratulatory laughter met them with every step. He returned the hostess' compliment for a finely tailored suit with one of his own; he was really feeling the way she cut into that skirt. This made her blue eyes shine and her chin dip to the sheen of his aqua-colored soft bottom gators. She pretended at being bashful, but Dahji knew better than this.

"Have you lived long in Indy?" she asked as they stepped into a brightly lit room of glass walls. Here the sun was allowed to stream in through shallow yellow tint.

Dahji knew that she was choosing before the question. "Long enough to see the true meaning of beauty," he replied, giving her a once over with a knowing glance. Her friendly smile was his reward.

"What do you do?" she wanted to know as they turned down the middle aisle. Dahji could see the complicated coifed hair of Gloria bobbing at the end of the row. Beside her was a raven-haired woman with deeply slanted eyes. She had her head leaned back in slow laughter, exposing a long milky neck.

"Management," he responded, meeting her questioning gaze as she worked to find what that actually meant.

"Sounds interesting," she replied with a slight nod. Gloria was looking their way as they approached.

"You gotta be a part of it to really know the feeling," he hinted.

Her eyes sparkled with this invitation. "Be sure to leave a card with me," she said just before they were within ear shot of the round table Gloria and the glamorous, slant-eyed woman occupied. "Here you go Mr." ... she hesitated.

"Dahji McBeth," he said, extending his hand to her.

"Annabelle Dixon," she returned with a wide smile, her hand sliding in and out of his smoothly before she looked to the table. "Ladies. Is everything okay here?" she wanted to know.

"Absolutely. Thank you," Gloria answered, her eyes flowing to Dahji as he took the seat placed conspicuously close to the woman she was introducing as May Ling.

They were seated at a round table at the back row of a sunlit space. A silver bucket of champagne was in the center, surrounded by silver platters of shelled oysters, clams, and shrimp. A quick glance revealed May Ling to be the object of any jacker's dream. She was draped and dipped in large diamond baubles. Her thin frame was sheathed in a vibrant dragon-decorated kimono. There was no shape to her that he could see except that she had the most remarkably rich demeanor. She intrigued him right away. She had to be as rich - if not more rich – than Mirabelle.

"Gloria speaks of you often and I can see why," May Ling said, finding humor with Dahji's subtle reaction to her British accent as he poured himself a glass of champagne.

"Not as much as you imagine," Gloria joined in with a small smile. She was in tight competition with her oriental friend as far as poise and privilege went.

Dahji took a healthy sip of champagne before he turned to May Ling. "You ever see an elephant have sex with a rhino?" he asked, holding her coal black eyes to his. She reminded him of Lucy Liu of Charlie's Angels for the way her small, dark freckles littered her narrow face. She had hair like a sheet of black silk that trailed shiny and dense to a loose knot at the bottom of her long neck; shooting from the knot, tied with intricately designed black lacquer chopsticks, were uneven shafts of hair in all directions. He wondered how she achieved this effect and exactly how long her hair was.

May Ling grinned with one side of her mouth as she turned her shoulders to him. Her dark, small eyes sparkled with his question. "How big is the elephant?" she wanted to know.

Dahji liked her already. "Oh, it's a very big elephant," he replied with an arching of one eyebrow.

"Well, in that case ... I must ask if the rhino agreed with this arrangement."

Dahji could not look away from this enigmatic woman. He could feel Gloria's proper gaze upon him. She was enjoying the show and he wondered who exactly was this woman sitting next to him?" "It was the rhino's idea," he answered, touched by the spreading of her crooked smile.

"Well, now that you two have been properly introduced," Gloria began, "what I'd like to know is how long this lovemaking lasted ... Everyone knows that elephant's are notoriously short winded."

May Ling smiled with this comment, adjusting herself in her seat. Dahji speared the meat from the center of an oyster and doused it with hot sauce before slipping it into his mouth.

"Is this elephant you speak of short winded?" May Ling asked. The large pink diamond on her index finger captured the sunlight like a prism as she lifted her champagne flute to her lightly glossed lips.

"By no means. This here is bull elephants we talking about," he assured them.

Gloria shot up in her seat and took on an exaggerated expression. "Well, that settles it. Everyone knows that bull elephants are very picky. How can we be sure this love affair even took place?"

"I believe him," May Ling chimed in with a gentle stroke of his hand.

"On my last safari I do believe witnessing a bull elephant making love to a rhino. It was quite a sight to behold."

Dahji looked to Gloria and was perplexed to see how satisfied she was at the attraction May Ling showed for him.

"You must be something special because ain't many that can stand to watch that," Dahji noted, spearing another shelled oyster. The steamed elixir felt good going down. He envisioned the oysters going straight to his balls and replenishing his spent supply of jism. Their combined laughter settled over the table like morning dew. Dahji felt as if he'd been handed a surprise exam and passed with flying colors. All that was left was to see what his reward would be.

"Have you spoken with Marlin today?" Gloria asked, her bosom still shaking from her laughter. She was unremarkable to look at, but this lack was made up for by wit and intelligence. She was the sort of woman that every church needed and every husband could succeed with. She was both presentable, articulate, and intuitive; this was a rare trifecta that she worked to her advantage.

"Next time we talk I wanna let him know that the ducks are indeed flying in the right direction," Dahji replied.

Gloria and May Ling exchanged a quick glance, which prompted Dahji to ask May Ling if she was simply beautiful or functional as well."

"Very functional," she replied with a large shrimp on the end of her fork. She held Dahji's gaze while she wrapped her lips around the fat end of the shrimp and bit into it. Her smile was laced with unmistakable sexual innuendo.

"Edith is looking forward to seeing you," Gloria announced as if warding off some unintended interaction. Edith's name gathered his attention. He had to admit that he'd been pleasantly surprised with her sex appeal and now she wanted to meet with him privately for a handsome price. He couldn't imagine what would transpire between them this time.

"You know Edith?" May Ling asked. Dahji couldn't be sure if she was as surprised as she sounded. She'd let her hand rest on his arm as she looked to him with bright eyes.

"Dahji knows everyone," Gloria cut in.

"Oh, that's great! Such a small world. She's very beautiful, don't you think?" May Ling asked, her hand still on his arm. He looked her over more closely this time. The black silk kimono ran flat down her slim body. Her chin was delicately rounded and her forehead was high and flat. The twinkle in her eyes hid some secret he felt he should know.

"No doubt. Inside and out," he replied in barely a whisper so that Gloria had to lean up to catch the last of what he said.

"May Ling and Edith used to work together at the Ford Modeling Agency."

"Oh, you're a model," Dahji confirmed, not at all surprised and glad to know this part of who she was.

"Sometimes," she responded vaguely.

"She's more famous in Europe," Gloria began. "She's been spending more time in the states as of late."

"They shoot all the bull elephants in the brit world?" Dahji asked, beginning to enjoy her musical giggles. May Ling looked to Gloria with appreciation.

"He's wonderful," she cheered.

"Well, glad to be wonderful. Now tell me what keeps you away from your fans in queen land?"

"She's highly connected to the Colts organization," Gloria chimed in, exerting her control over the progress of this meeting. She produced a powder blue card from the flat billfold on the table and passed it to Dahji. "This is where Edith is staying."

"And Marlin?" he asked, noticing May Ling's conspicuous silence.

"This will go a long way to getting him on the team," she answered him with a slight nod.

There was more here than met the eye. Dahji noted the secret glances she exchanged with May Ling. Who was she really? And how connected was she to the organization? Dahji had a feeling that he would find out. Gloria never left a desire untended when she had the upper hand.

CHAPTER NINETEEN

It only took a few minutes to make hamburgers for Marlin and his father-in-law. She'd heated up a couple patties and placed them between toasted buns; the lettuce, tomatoes, pickles, and onions spilled from the innards invitingly. She'd thrown on a silk robe for the return trip.

She'd only been back inside the house for a few minutes, looking at herself in the bathroom mirror to see how she'd looked to Marlin, when the front door slammed shut. She rushed into the living room and found Percy standing there in a daze, his tie loosened, looking to the stacks of HoodSweet apparel placed atop the coffee table. She stood still, at the edge of the hallway, as he swiped at the clothes, knocking them to the floor.

"Shiiiit!" he mumbled, staggering backwards and lifting his head. He peered towards Ayana with an unfocused gaze. He lifted a lazy finger to her and attempted to speak, but instead lurched backwards and twirled towards the door.

Ayana rushed through the living room and caught him as he knocked the back of his head into the door. "Percy, are you okay?" she asked, wrinkling her nose to the stench of alcohol on his breath. He slumped his forehead into her breasts and breathed out a slobbering indictment of some person unknown to her. She could not associate the "boot licking nigga" with the woman he referred to as "Carrie" and her "lies."

"Come on ... Sit down on the couch, she suggested as she struggled to help him to the sofa.

Percy sat down hard into the cushions as he reached out for Ayana's retreating arms. He caught her by the hands and held her between his legs.

His clouded eyes at first went to the long braids coursing from her head and then to the deep cleavage where the bowed ends had come to rest.

"Let me get you some bread," she offered, thinking it would help absorb the alcohol in his stomach, but his grip tightened around the ends of her fingers before she could turn away.

"No ... No ... No ..." he stammered, a wicked grin spreading across his thin lips. His light eyes sparkled with some hidden thought as he focused on the diamond pendant piercing her navel. He leaned forward slowly with his tongue extended and sloppily licked across her stomach, just missing her navel. He retracted his head and stared at the mark he was trying to hit.

"You're drunk, Percy. Come on ... Let me help you to the shower," Ayana suggested, feeling both fearful that Sherrelle would find him this way and anxious that he was vulnerable.

"I 'ont need no da .. no damn ... shower,' he slobbered out, his eyes peering to her stomach as if in a daze. He then moved across the rim of her boy-shorts and fixed on the fat imprint her pussy lips made against the thin cotton. The silk robe framed her sex like a present.

Ayana felt the heat reach her pussy from his eyes as he moved slowly to lift the waistband from her skin. She knew that she should stop him, but his movements were so slow she thought he would stop at any moment. The house was quiet except for the occasional crackle of slow-burning wood in the fireplace.

"So pretty," he muttered, pressing the lace band between his fingers. Ayana lay her fingers on the top of his head; and if someone were to ask her later she would deny that she nudged him towards her center. She would deny that she thrust her hips into his mouth ever so gently as he blew hot breath towards her navel. She would never admit that the feeling made her shiver as she directed this hot spray of breath towards her pussy.

Percy buried his face in her muff and hummed alternately with short bursts of hot air. Ayana ground her pussy against his face.

Then his tongue slid against the thin material of her boy-shorts. He licked her in a wide circle while he continued his drunk hum. With Ayana's slow rub through his low-cropped hair he closed his eyes to massage her. He lost himself in her sweet scent, his nose pressed against her as he inhaled her through the thin material.

Ayana slowly placed her hands atop his and moved them from her ass to the rim of her boy-shorts. She assisted him with the rocking slide of the material down her thighs. She released him to complete the task of dragging the flimsy cloth down her legs.

"It never adds ..." he grumbled with his face inches from the dark, coarse, heart-trimmed hair fronting her pussy.

Ayana lifted one leg to the couch and positioned herself just above his extended tongue. He licked up into her snatch as if to taste a new dish; and decided that it was good and moaned softly before lapping at her again.

As if reunited with his earlier pain he groaned loudly while slipping sideways to the sofa. He lay on his back while his feet were still planted on the carpet. His arms were heavy as they moved to cover his eyes. "Never adds up ... Boot ... Licker ... Bitch!" he groaned beneath his arms.

"It's okay Percy," Ayana whispered as she lifted his legs to the sofa. "Let me help you," she added, moving to straddle his body at the chest. She then gently removed his arms from over his face and lay them to the side. She held his cloudy gaze as she scooted to his chin and positioned herself over his mouth.

Percy kissed her muff as she pressed down on him. She tasted like cucumbers. It was good. He slipped his tongue through her wet lips and probed this good taste.

"That's right Percy," she encouraged him as she braced herself on the armrest. She gently swayed over his lips as his tongue darted in and out of her tender lovebox. Up and down over his mouth she gyrated, enjoying the pure luxury of his tongue inside of her. It was fat with unbridled exploration. His tongue licked the wetness from her and rubbed along her sensitive areas.

"That feels so good Percy," she whispered as she peeked out the window for signs of Sherrelle.

Percy was trapped beneath her, his tongue working around the pubic hair that lodged between his lips. Ayana shivered, her thighs tightening around him as a flood of cream squirted from her. He heard the pleasure stream from her mouth and her pussy like an echo as if he were under water. Her cream dribbled down the side of his face and into his nose. He appreciated her warbled compliments just before she raised from him, cooling air washing over his face with her departure. Her cream felt good drying on his skin. He closed his eyes to the feeling and thought how wonderful it was to be appreciated.

Ayana looked to him one time before kneeling to retrieve her discarded clothing. She made a mental note to wash her cum from his face and cover him with a sheet after she washed herself. Her heart beat wildly as she hurriedly rushed to the bathroom.

***

Thursday night at Applebottoms was like the pre-game show that announced what everyone should expect for Friday night. This night showcased featured talent and introduced a new woman whose reputation preceded her.

Applebottoms Gentlemen's Lounge was electrified with a hypnotic beat behind Trina rapping about how she could drop it down low and look back while her ass rolled. The rhythm made everyone sway as a cocoa- colored, thickly proportioned woman swung around the silver pole on center stage. This raised wooden platform dominated the large space, surrounded by tables. Along the far right wall was a semi-private alcove where nearly naked women traipsed up and down the three stairs with drinks from the bar or carrying money from sex-fueled transactions. A bar ran along the left wall; here strippers congregated to meet and greet patrons in an effort to lure them to the back pit where they could receive a private show. Along the entrance were dining tables along a raised platform; this space was an innocent space for those who wanted a more wholesome entertainment experience.

"I'm surprised at how busy it is already," Sherrelle commented as she followed Peaches through the entrance. She scanned the darkness as her eyes adjusted, hoisting the duffel bag onto her shoulder. "I hope no one thinks I have my stripper clothes in here," she added as a familiar man approached. He was dressed flamboyantly in a shiny alligator skin suit with a large diamond 'live rich die ready' emblem covering his forest green silk shirt. Next to him was the similarly dark and mysterious man she remembered as Talib; he was dressed in an all black suit of fine silk with red trimming, the same emblem emblazoned across his chest. Sherrelle wondered if these two slight of frame men were scared someone would take their jewelry.

"Hello Jon Ansar," Peaches said with a wide grin before accepting a gentle kiss on the cheek. Jon Ansar smiled with gold and diamond teeth, his slim, dark hand extended to Sherrelle.

"Hello Ms. Entrepreneur," he said with Sherrelle's palm in his. "Y'all remember my bru, Talib."

Sherrelle exchanged a smile to Talib's serious nod before they were approached by Prince Sweetwater.

"Pimp!" he called out, smiling around the small circle.

"Bru!" Jon Ansar replied with a show of dap. "Nobody told me you was out here ... And is this Emma Jean?" he sang with true delight, gesturing the voluptuous, blue-eyed amazon into his arms. He moaned over her shoulder, ignoring Prince's playful warning to be careful because she bites.

Prince accepted Emma Jean back to his side. "It's a fine night, pimp! I'm surprised Dimp didn't tell you I was out this way."

"Dimp is busy helping Milo open up another Haitian Jack's in Seattle. Bru, it's like the eighties. Bru is international. Hutch in Vancouver, Canada talking about another Applebottoms. Milo is in Europe speaking on something grandfantabulous ... Bru's eating good right now," Jon Ansar informed him with excited dark eyes. He shared the short, wavy hair style as Talib.

"Healthy egos?" Prince asked.

"Live rich die ready," Jon Ansar responded.

"Gators fitting right?"

"Like good snatch."

"How's your stable?" Prince wanted to know.

John Ansar grinned brightly. "Never get friendly or confide in 'em," he replied.

Prince exchanged a knowing look with Emma Jean before he retorted, "Nails long?"

"I cut my nails if I pull her hair." Jon Ansar's reply tickled Emma Jean, her breasts bubbling over her silk tube dress.

"If she good to you she good for you," Prince replied. Sherrelle was enjoying this game of pimpology. She tried to decipher the meaning of each quip as they spilled forth.

"Realize I'm the truth and not a fable," Jon Ansar countered. Two strippers hovered near to listen to the private conversation. Peaches smiled proudly in their direction, feeling privileged to be included. She wished Dahji were here to hear what he would have to say. Her heart ached anew with having not seen him in what felt like weeks.

Prince Sweetwater proffered his jeweled hand. "A good pimp is always really alone," he noted sardonically as Jon Ansar slipped slim, dark fingers into his palm.

"You're not alone Sweet," Emma Jean inserted gently, rolling her sexy blue eyes to him with hidden meaning.

"So what do we have here," Jon Ansar began, his eyes scanning Sherrelle's shapely figure. "You planning a sleep-over?" he asked.

"Oh, this is my girlfriend Sherrelle," Peaches began.

"She's working with my nephew on that HoodSweet thang," Prince finished.

Jon Ansar's fine eyebrows lifted in recognition. "That's good business right there. That's my bru Isiko." He turned to Talib and said in a low voice, "Remind me to give our girl Renee his location."

Talib nodded shortly before Sherrelle asked, "You know him?"

"Do I know him?" Jon Ansar beamed as he looked around the room. "He started all this," he said, throwing his arms in the air.

"From jail?" Sherrelle asked in wonder.

"Started with that book HoodSweet," Jon Ansar replied. "He is the BRU CAPO. He's the reason we eat." This was said as a matter of fact.

Sherrelle suddenly felt both small and large. Small in the way that the man she'd come to know on MySpace was larger than she gave him credit for; large because she felt closer to success, knowing that she was a part of something international. She wanted to read the novel that started it all.

"Tell Isiko I said hello even though he doesn't know me," Peaches said to Jon Ansar.

"He knows everyone who works here," Jon Ansar replied. "He probably got you in his photo album," he added with a grin.

Peaches smiled brightly with such recognition. "That's cool."

Prince Sweetwater clapped his hands together and announced that they should move to his table in the raised alcove. As Jon Ansar and Talib moved in his direction he pointed to Peaches with a slender finger and said, "I got my eyes on you."

"As long as you tip I don't mind," she replied.

"Spoken like a true pro," was his retort before leading the procession to the dimly lit stairs.

"Damn, them niggas is paid!" Peaches announced as she linked her arm with Sherrelle. They rushed through the narrow aisle along the stage, a thick redbone now prancing across the hard wood on their way to the dressing room.

"I had no idea that Isiko was connected like that," Sherrelle replied after smiling politely to a man who gestured towards her from his seat.

"Dahji need to get his shit together!"

"You mean you, right?" Sherrelle asked as they slipped through a beaded curtain at the rear of the stage.

"Hell yeah," Peaches replied huskily. There was hunger in her voice. The dressing room represented a cosmopolitan array of body types, skin tones, and natural beauty. Women skirted about dramatically, speaking on who was currently in the club and who was expected to arrive. They primped before the floor-to-ceiling mirrors and lifted their breasts as a sort of training mechanism. They teased natural and weaved hair to make sure it lay just right across scented shoulders. Though Sherrelle had seen this scene before, she still marveled at the sheer desperation of it. She was silently thankful for Percy. He was not a lot of things, but at least he paid the bills and afforded her a nice lifestyle.

Peaches greeted some of the girls on the way to her locker, smiling for those she knew to be back-stabbing bitches and directing those who hated her to Sherrelle, mentioning that she had a new shipment of HoodSweet apparel in her duffel bag.

There was a frenzy of activity behind her as she dressed for her stage performance. While the women pawed over the HoodSweet selection she dressed in a sheer red negligee and black thong. Her dark, red hair hung loose and curly over her shoulders. After slipping on a pair of red stockings with black garter belts she checked the little makeup she wore (eyeliner and lipstick) and closed her locker.

"I'll be back in a minute," she said to Sherrelle who was pocketing a fifty-dollar bill from a recent sale, as she passed by.

"Okay," Sherrelle replied, paying attention to the business deals being completed before her.

Snoop Dogg's lazy drawl coated the room as Peaches heard her name being introduced to the stage. She was thankful for this because she was being hailed by an obese white man who liked for her to sit on his lap. This night she didn't feel much like making other people feel good. She looked forward to losing herself on the stage and dancing some of her pain away.

What pain? On her way to work she kept getting phone calls from a number she recognized as Bo's. She knew what he wanted. Why should she have to pay for the impounded car? She'd went to jail. She wasn't asking Tequan to pay for her bail ... So why is he sending Bo her way to harass her? Why should she have to pay for the drugs that were found on her by the prison guard?

The music moved through her as the audience cheered her arrival. Though she waved politely and smiled glamorously, she saw no one and heard nothing. Her moves were languid around the silver pole, the smooth beat washing over her. It was a pleasant escape as she strolled around the edges of the stage to tease the front row. She stopped here and there to accept money into her garter belt, spreading her legs as a reward before moving on. There was no room for the hard bumping and grinding this night. She moved with fluid emotion across the hard-wood stage, bending over seductively as she rubbed slowly down the length of her legs.

... And Dahji ... Was he really trying to avoid her? She'd let herself open up to him, thinking that he was different than the many men who wanted to possess her. Maybe that was it ... Maybe it was because he made no move to possess her that allowed her guard to fall. All he did was be there for her in her time of need. Why should she expect anything more after he bailed her out of jail and made sure she had a lawyer? Maybe she was expecting too much. Maybe it was the way he made love to her that opened her to this heartache. She searched for the remedy. She wanted to make him love her the way she knew he could.

She'd made a full circuit of the stage, her garter belts feathered with crisp notes for her smooth delivery. She returned to the pole and swung around it, her hair trailing her like a flame. She landed softly and reached her hands up the pole as she slid to the floor. She backed up on the hard wood on hands and knees, dipping her back and swaying her ass. She was lost in her thoughts, her eyes wet with tears.

She'd never felt as dirty as she felt when leaving Sun Yi's warehouse. It seemed that all the women who sat at their stations knew, upon her walk down the narrow aisle to the door, that she had done something very disgusting. It had to be disgusting if it involved their nasty boss. She had to remind herself that there was a reason for her sacrifice: HoodSweet. This represented a better opportunity. Sometimes she lost sight of this reward against the backdrop of a love being held away from her, a love that refused to depart, and a court case that could send her to jail. It all seemed so much to overcome to claim something so beautiful. *No struggle no reward,* she thought to herself. She was trying to remember where she'd heard this when through the haze of her half-opened eyes she saw a sinister grin directed at her from the front row.

It was not only the evil grin that sent a hollow stake through her stomach, nor was it the surprise of finding Bo just feet from her. Not even the leering stares of Drew and Bam, who flanked Bo, meant much to her except that they were scrubs who welcomed any opportunity to cause pain. Perhaps it was the fact that she now felt vulnerable and trapped at having been found at a time of deep reflection. She'd sought to escape her real life drama through dance. And now he was infringing on her private moment of retreat.

Bo rubbed his fingers together to indicate that she owed him money. Drew and Bam echoed this threatening sentiment as Peaches turned and ran from the stage, new tears springing from her eyes.

***

The lunch of oysters, clams, and shrimp was what his body called for. All that was needed next was a short nap and a tall protein shake upon waking. He was refreshed and ready to give Edith what she wanted.

May Ling was still a mystery to him. He'd learned nothing more from her during the time they spent together, though he was sure that she felt him in some way. But she would have to wait. There was more urgent business to tend to in his pursuit to get Marlin on the squad. He still had not gotten Gloria's final answer as to his status, but he was confident she would come through for him. How? Now this remained to be seen. He just hoped the mission wasn't too extreme.

The address on the card Gloria handed to him named the Regency Inn as the place Edith would be waiting for him. It was nearly nine in the evening when he pulled into the quiet courtyard of small bungalows. The Regency Inn was located in a rich suburb on the outskirts of the city. It could have easily been mistaken for the adjacent houses of either of the mansions that flanked the shaded Inn. Tall trees obscured the bungalows. The cobble stone entrance was framed by low hedges. The effect of the greenery gave this place a quaint and discreet appeal. There were no cars visible from the road. Dahji worked to discard his feelings that her husband would show up at any moment to find him sexing his wife. Edith didn't seem like the type to compromise what made her feel so good.

He pulled to a stop at the end of the long driveway. The BMW Roadster he'd seen at the Tom & Edith Warrington mansion was parked in front of a log cabin-style bungalow. A yellow porch light illuminated the narrow space that led to the low wooden stair steps.

Dahji drank a small vial of ginseng for good measure. It was always a challenge to repeat a magnificent performance. If he fucked her unconscious, as before, this would be a repeat performance. He suspected that she had something special in store for him as her way of retaliation. Maybe she wanted to prove to him that she was stronger than their last meeting. *But why did she want to meet me alone?*, he reminded himself to ask her as he stepped from the Range Rover.

The gravel crunched beneath his leather Tod's loafers. He'd dressed conservatively in a Perry Ellis linen suit. There was no denying the full body of his hair as it hung in large curls across his shoulders. His only jewelry were a pair of diamond earrings and a gold, black-face Longines watch; this had been a gift from Mirabelle, as was most of his jewelry.

The door slipped ajar as he reached the porch. A swirling powder blue form passed across the narrow opening. Dahji approached slowly, cautiously putting his hand on the knob and whispering her name.

"Please," Edith whispered. "Come inside."

The inside of the bungalow matched the outer appearance that promised a rustic experience. A large canopied bed with huge mahogany bedposts dominated the room. On the walls, illuminated by small wall lamps, were landscape paintings of colorful flowers standing in expansive fields.

"Hello Mr. McBeth," Edith said as she sat perched on the arm of a flower print, overstuffed chair placed against the far wall. She smiled mischievously in his direction under the dim glow of light.

"This is nice," he replied, stepping further into the room. To his right there was an open door that revealed a porcelain sink.

"This is no set-up," she said as she stood and strolled to the closet door. She opened it and displayed its empty contents as if presenting a prize on *The Price Is Right*.

Dahji smiled with her antics as he walked to her and lightly kissed her on the cheek. "It's good to see you again. Kind of a shock when Gloria said you needed to see me privately, though."

Edith moved to the bed and sat down on its edge. Tall and slender, she moved with effortless grace. Her long, blonde hair flowed out behind her as if air were blowing from some hidden port. The effect, coupled with the way the blue silk gown swirled around her soft limbs, gave her an angelic resemblance. It could have been her soft, pale features; or maybe it was the clearness of her blue eyes that gave Dahji this impression. Either way he was drawn to her as he had been during that first meeting.

"Forgive me for my secrecy," she began, her long legs crossed at the ankles. Her hands lay lightly in her lap. "But I am selfish in this way and would rather have you to myself... That is unless you enjoy being observed?" There was a smile that play at the corners of her wide, full mouth.

"Yeah, that was a bit strange," he remarked, momentarily reliving the way her husband urged him on as he fucked his wife. "Watching don't bother me, but the cowboy chaps was kinda strange," he added, standing before her just out of reach. She'd let the teasing smile fully form into a soft chuckle. The way her head tilted subtly reminded him that she was a model and May Ling was a friend of hers.

"Do you mind that I am selfish in this way?" she asked.

"Not at all."

"What is it exactly that you think?" she wanted to know.

"I think you're a special sort of woman who deserves a special sort of man," Dahji responded.

She cocked her head slightly in thought. "Do you judge me?"

"Don't I need a license for that?"

Her smile returned as she motioned him forward with the curling of her pale fingers. "I was so embarrassed," she confessed when he stopped at her knees. "It's just that ... Just that I wasn't prepared for you," she added, her eyes lowering to his waist before rising again to his eyes.

So this was it in a nutshell. She wanted to be free of her husband's presence and redeem herself. Still, Dahji wondered at their union. "When Tom told me he wanted me to meet his wife I was surprised ..."

"That she would look like me?" she asked, knowing this would be coming. Dahji nodded. "He's good to me ... He's really nice."

"You want your cake and eat it too," he stated.

"Is that bad?"

This was becoming more common with women, Dahji noted to himself. They wanted to live nice and have the dick to go with it. "So you call and I come?"

She smiled with this. "I hope so ... Do you want to come?"

Dahji spread his legs and placed his hands on his waist. He stared down at her, examining her demure pose and seemingly innocent demeanor. *She is hardly innocent,* he thought to himself. This was a dangerous situation this white woman was asking him to be in. If her husband came bursting through the door then it would be nobody's fault but his for being with his wife.

"What is it that you want from me?" Edith wanted to know, unsure of what to make of his silent inspection of her.

"There's a simple answer for that, but first you need to tell me what it is exactly that you need from me and for how long?"

She seemed confused by that question. "I hadn't really thought that far ahead," she replied.

Dahji thought as much. If he was going to take a chance with her then it was going to have to be cloaked to allay any suspicion. Might as well put her to work while they were at it.

"I brought ten-thousand dollars with me. All cash," she whispered like a little girl.

Choosing fee. He was right about her. She wasn't as innocent as she appeared. Dahji pretended that the money was nothing. He moved to her side and sat next to her on the bed. He asked her to tell him her story. "Start wherever you want," he added.

Edith seemed relieved with this request. No one had ever shown interest in anything except her body and face. She relaxed with a slow exhalation. She began with her graduation from the College of William & Mary. Her parents were from Sweden and now lived in New York. She'd met Tom at a fashion show. He was a self made multi-millionaire from imports & exports, among other things such as real estate and tech stocks.

Dahji undressed slowly as she spoke on feeling lost and afraid even though she had everything in life. She admitted that she'd never been with a black man and Tom was willing to please her in this way. This is how Dahji had entered their lives. She also confessed that Tom had shown himself to be more sexually liberal than she'd imagined. This eroded her respect for him. She at first thought she would be okay with him watching her have sex, but afterwards all he did was ask how Dahji made her feel. He wanted to relive every moment and dissect every emotion. He questioned how sexing Dahji was different from making love to him. She was forced to lie to him and in doing so she realized that she needed to see Dahji again.

She looked to him with this revelation with a small smile, her eyes wet with emotion.

With her story it was apparent that she needed him more than he needed her. She placed no value on money except that it provided her security, not in the monetary sense, but with privilege as it was associated to a respectable man. Models were hoes, too, only they were more skilled at the long con in the guise of romance and career advancement. In the end all women wanted was to be loved and provided with a hard dick. It was a bonus to have both in one man.

"Can you get your hands on a hundred grand?" he asked without emotion as he leaned back onto the bed. He was completely naked, having undressed casually while she committed herself to telling her story.

The tears that had been threatening to roll from her eyes suddenly dropped with a big smile that spread her face.

"Of course I can," she answered happily, as if this solidified their arrangement. She restrained herself as he lay naked alongside her, his arms folded behind his head. She looked up and down the length of him, stopping at the thick meat laying between his legs, before meeting his eyes. She was waiting for his instruction.

"Welcome home, baby. Dahji McBeth is your friend for life. How can I help you?"

Edith jumped up suddenly and lay along the length of his body. Her laughter was mixed with tears as she alternately confessed her love for him and kissed across his eyes, ears, forehead, nose, and mouth. She then leaned up on one elbow and peered into his brown eyes.

"Thank you for coming," she said.

"Thank you for having me."

"CAN I have you?" There was a twinkle of mischief in her light-blue eyes.

"Like a lollipop," Dahji replied as his organ jumped into the air. She whooped with delight as it popped warmly against her waist.

"And lick you all over," she whispered as she began to kiss him down the center of his chest, her blonde hair trailing her as her mouth found the swollen head pulsing over his stomach. She wrapped the helmet-shaped dome in her lips and taste him slowly. Her fingers trailed back up the length of his body as she suspended his joint into the air between her tight lips.

The combination of her soft palms massaging his abdomen and her control of his penis with her mouth alone sent hot waves of pleasure through his body. Her long hair pooled around his shaft and settled between his legs, massaging and tingling his scrotum. Her mouth was warm and tender as she slid down half his length. She teased him further by letting her tongue reach further along before retracing her exploration back to his throbbing head.

In the dim light his dick stood from his body under a shadow of blonde light, appearing in shadow only after she'd dove down onto him hungrily. He swelled over her tongue as she kept him pulled tightly in the air with her attentive sucking. Her hair folded against his thighs and poured between his legs with each downward motion, only to lift and separate when she rose up again. The combined effect of his dick in her mouth and her hair brushing against his sensitive skin forced a low growl from his throat. He felt her smile over his slick meat, encouraged by his reaction.

When he thought he could take no more she suddenly popped off of him and straddled his body. She grabbed hold of his straining joint and placed him at her moist entrance. She rose on tip toe and lowered herself over the head slowly. She braced herself against his chest as she allowed only the tip of him inside of her. She moaned with the sensation, her hair falling to his face as she bowed.

"You see that?" she asked huskily, looking down at how he stood from her whiteness. "Isn't that beautiful?"

Dahji grit his teeth. She would not go past his head. She dipped him inside of her as if it were a toe testing a warm pool. Her pussy lips were tight around his helmet, the feeling of his ridge crossing her soft boundary proving to be a form of pleasurable torture. She was like a long-legged spider spread over him as her hair swung to his face with gentle strokes.

"Thank you," she hissed as she leaned to his mouth and took his tongue between her lips. She sucked on him softly while continuing the partial coating of his joint between her walls.

Damn, she's limber, Dahji thought to himself as he gave himself over to her seduction. She'd let him free from her grasp and pushed his hardness to his stomach, trapping him there between her hot lips. She was like a pair of soft tracks around his thick meat. With her knees lowered to the bed she slid from the base of his ten inches to the very tip, her hot flesh warming his stomach.

"Oh my goodness," she breathed out as he was caught in the groove of her sex, rubbing snugly against all sensitive parts of her. Her motion increased as if she were grinding to some hidden beat; her hair began to thrash about wildly and her breathing came out in increasingly loud gasps. With her eyes closed she slid up and down the length of him, her pussy hot and wet with excitement. He had yet to enter her fully. She was forestalling his aggression, preferring to control the action until she was given more than she could handle.

"Oh ...Oh ... Oh ..." she panted hotly, her head dropping to his ear. She wrapped her lips around his ear lobe, her tongue catching at the back of his diamond. She then folded his entire ear inside her mouth and moaned against him as she shuddered violently. Her rowing motion stuttered as if prepared to die out before catching up to the sensation which produced the cream that washed over his meaty organ and onto his stomach. Her body shook with this accomplishment as she released his ear from her mouth.

"Oh my ... My goodness," she whispered as she raised her hand through her hair to show him her flushed face. Her eyes were bright and daring. "That was hot," she said with a wan smile.

Dahji raised himself and positioned her on her side. With her back to him, he lifted one leg into the air and inserted the heavy pendulum into her waiting pink snatch. Her body rolled with the intrusion, absorbing his weighty entrance. Slowly he slid inside of her as she reached back to push against his hip. He was having none of it though. He slowly began to pull out of her, letting her space fall in on itself before he filled her up again. The slow traction lulled her to a pleasurable anticipation. She abandoned her protests and brought her thumb to her mouth. She sucked on this while he slowly increased his motion into her cream-coated center. Her soft, pink lips parted around him as he pulled from her in the dim light. It was a gentle stride as he knocked against her body with a soft thrust, forcing a rhythmic gasp from her mouth. In the quiet were the sounds of their sex: Her low moans, punctuated with a sharp gasp and the squash squash of his meat entering and retreating her creamy snatch.

Edith slowly turned to her stomach and rose to her hands and knees. She looked to him over her shoulder with hooded eyes as he came up behind her. As he parted the creamy center again, his hands on her hips, she closed her eyes to him in pleasure. She took him with bravery as he gently moved from side to side while inside of her. Her pale butt cheeks were hot beneath his hands. Her back was long and narrow, the skin glowing translucent in the dim light. His dick was swollen large and contrasted darkly against her white skin. He disappeared beneath her paleness and came back glistening with cream.

Edith lowered her shoulders to the bed and Dahji followed. With her ass in the air he entered her at a new angle. She'd grabbed a pillow to muffle her cries. At ten-second intervals her body shook and she grew quiet and limp in his grip. After he changed strides she would come to life again and push back onto him.

"I can't ..." she stammered in barely a whisper. She huffed with panting breath as Dahji slid all the way into her and let his dick rest at her bottom.

"You got it baby," he assured her, rubbing her along the length of her back. "That feel good to you?"

"Yes," she replied at length. "Okay. I'm ready," she added with a determined glance up at him.

He turned her to her back and slid in between her thighs gently. She wrapped her arms around his neck and held him tightly to her breasts as he moved in and out of her slowly. She was creamy and slick around him. She wrapped her long legs around his waist forcing him to stroke shortly inside of her. She moved under him in rhythm with his grinding. Her breasts were hot and sticky against his chest.

"You make me feel like a flower," she hissed past his ear, her nails running along his spine.

"You are a flower," Dahji responded, brushing the darkened, damp hair from her forehead. She was hot as if she had a fever. Her blue eyes blazed passionately and her face was flushed magenta red. Her soft pubic hairs met his coarseness and blended their scents as one.

Dahji was grinding into her with smooth strokes, finding room to maneuver inside of her loosening embrace. She opened for him as he repeatedly tapped her center. Her arms grew slack around his neck and her legs dropped to the bed. He then rose up and lifted her legs high into the air. Her pink snatch was exposed and vulnerable. He rose to his knees and sunk into her with a powerful thrust. Her entire body shifted towards the headboard. She let out a shriek as he hit bottom and ground into her quickly before retreating.

He wedged his hands into the back of her knees and dove into her again, her pussy swollen and bruised with the deep penetration. Her shrieks grew more hoarse as she thrashed her head from side to side. Her lips were parted in ecstasy, her tongue trapped between her teeth. He slid into her with another stroke and retreated from a different angle. A light sheen coated her body and he smacked into her again. Her pubic hairs were damp and soft as he slid into her again and again.

She accepted his deep thrusts with a loud shriek, her body offering no resistance. She coated him with more cream as if saving herself from the torment of his large organ. He grew hot at his head and grit his teeth as he buried his meat inside of her again and again. She arched her head back into the pillows so that her face was no longer visible. Her creamy neck was exposed and tender. He slapped into her, feeling himself boil to completion. Her moans turned to a low gurgling sound as she gripped the bed covers with whitened knuckles.

Just as Dahji exploded into her, jerking violently between her legs and smashing to her center, she went limp with a hissing sound escaping her lips. Her arms and legs fell to the mattress and her eyes rolled into her skull. *Damn, I done killed her,* Dahji thought to himself as he placed his ear to her mouth. She was breathing. He was thinking of how weird this was when his cell phone rang inside the pocket of his linen coat. He reached over the side of the bed and wasn't surprised to see Peaches' sarcastic smirk on the screen.

"Dahji, where are you? I just called you at home," she said with a hint of frustration.

"What's up?" he replied in a low voice as he peered to an unconscious Edith. He had one foot on the floor as his organ hung half erect between his legs, weighed down by the bulbous head at the end of a gleaming, thick shaft.

"I need you. I thought we were going to get together? Bo came into the club with Drew and Bam tonight." Behind her the excited laughter of women could be heard against the backdrop of Ludacris rapping about a woman being too much to handle.

"Yeah ... What? He responded absently. Edith stirred.

"They talking about I owe them money for Tequan's car being impounded and the stuff I got caught with." There were tears in her throat.

"Where you at now?"

"I'm leaving work. I can't stay here. Will you be home?" she wanted to know.

Edith rolled to her side and let out a moan. She was curling into a fetal position, rubbing her slick thighs together. "Naw. Um ... I'm a little ways away ... Handling something right now. Let me get with you in the morning."

Peaches huffed with disappointment. "Man. This shit is gettin old."

"Awright. Don't get wrinkled up like that. I got you. Let me ..." Edith mumbled incoherently. "Call me in the morning," he whispered before ending the call.

Dahji threw the phone to the floor as he crawled over Edith to reach her front. He caressed her damp hair away from her face and whispered her name. She opened her eyes to him barely and stretched her arms out.

"That was amazing!" she gushed with a slim, quivering smile. Dahji folded her into his embrace. She collapsed into his body and twined her limbs with his. Her scent was that of butterscotch pudding and her skin was warm like a summer breeze. She exhaled softly as she melted into him further.

Dahji had not expected this level of intimacy. He welcomed this new kind of woman into his life and knew that she would be a benefit. For the moment he was lost in her passion, far away from the drama, fears, and pressures that existed outside of this rustic inn.

PART THREE

Sherrelle
Ayana
Dahji
& Peaches

"If no great prizes can be won unless some heavy labor's done you must suffer the exhaustion of many toils to be able to attain the favors you seek, since what you ask for is a greater prize."

- Andreas Capellanus
ON LOVE

CHAPTER TWENTY

This was therapeutic. The water was as hot as she could stand it. She let it course over her shapely body, her head arched back and eyes closed to the ceiling. She couldn't help but to think that there was always a personal price to pay for success. She shouldn't have been surprised to see Percy sprawled out on the couch, stinking of liquor, when she'd come home last night. The women at Applebottoms had bought every piece of clothing she'd brought with her. This only added to her enthusiasm.

Sherrelle breathed out heavily under the spray of water. She didn't want to think about him, but he was her husband and there was a part of her that hated to see him disintegrate the way he was doing. At first she thought it was just the pressures of work, but lately it seemed something more deep and sinister.

The first time he had a nightmare and proved to be a danger to her, she didn't mind that he chose to sleep on the couch. But this, too, had turned into a permanent situation and she struggled to remain focused on getting her money. She constantly had to remind herself that she deserved better. She was sexy and desirable. She deserved a man who could appreciate this.

There was no denying her attraction to Marlin. And she knew that he felt the same way. It was a devil's trick to deny them both a love just because they'd made vows in the church to someone else. And he'd been right about her avoiding him. She could not stand to be next to him and not express what she felt inside.

There was no more peeking into his window. She suspected that his wife put a stop to that. And she was done masturbating with thoughts of him.

She vowed to never have sex again until she felt some love in her bones. And lately Percy seemed beyond reach, not to mention the fact that he'd never satisfied her in the first place.

She stayed in the shower to avoid another confrontation with Percy. She didn't want to argue and fight. She didn't want to hear about how she'll never be successful at business. She didn't want to hear how everything at work for him was not adding up. She didn't care to hear how he promised to make everything right; that he just needed a little time. She laughed to herself with the thought that he actually tried to make it her fault when she pointed out the stench on his breath this morning.

Sherrelle stepped from the shower when she was sure Percy had gone to work. She released her long, luxurious hair from its cover and stood in front of the mirror on the back of the door. The smell of strawberry waffles wafted through the air along with the powerful voice of Mary J. Blige, signaling Ayana's rise from her bed. Her niece was a small comfort. She was glad to have her and amused at how fresh she was in her attempt to be a woman.

The water glistened on her dark chocolate body, running along the curves and dipping into her recesses. Her breasts stood firm and erect over her flat stomach. Her hips rounded out tightly and gave way to shapely thighs. There was very little mileage on her and it showed. She had Percy to thank for this.

It's a shame to let such a beautiful body go unexplored, she thought to herself as she rubbed baby oil onto her damp skin. Her hands rubbed across her smooth stomach with purpose. Her dream was just around the corner. She would be free of this turmoil. She prayed for God to deliver her a reward that was consistent with her faith and belief. She silently asked to be protected from the evilness around her and asked that Peaches be included in this protection. As she rubbed around her inner thighs, her thumbs crossing the fine hairs of her muff, she prayed that God grant Marlin a position on the football team. She hoped her prayers weren't perceived as being selfish simply because she wanted to be happy.

After oiling her body she slipped a long flower- print sun dress over her shapely figure. She felt proud to be wearing what would be her private collection of HoodSweet lingerie under the peach dress. She grabbed the phone as she stepped from the room, guided by the smell of what she hoped were properly cooked waffles.

"Hey girl. You okay?" she asked when Peaches answered the phone. There was an exhalation of breath on the other end.

"Yeah, I'm cool. A good night's sleep does a body good," she replied.

Ayana had cleaned up the living room and erased all traces of Percy's drunken stupor. The living room curtains were opened. Percy's car was not in the driveway. She felt a hint of regret that she had not seen him leave. Maybe she should have answered his plea to talk at the bathroom door.

"So, what are you going to do?" Sherrelle asked as she walked into the kitchen.

Ayana turned to her with a big smile and her hair flowing down past her shoulders. Sherrelle wanted to comment on the transparent Nike body suit that sculpted her shapely body from neck to ankle. It was easy to see that she was naked underneath by the way her nipples contrasted darkly against the white material and the outline of her peach-colored thong showed through. The spatula in her hand did nothing to ease her sex appeal.

"Well, what we're going to do is lock down this distribution deal so we can be about our money. Wasn't it cool meeting Jon Ansar last night?" Peaches asked. It was obvious to Sherrelle that her girlfriend was avoiding the most dangerous aspects about last night. A small red flag raised in her conscience.

"Well, that's good to hear, but I want to know what you're going to do about Tequan's thug homies."

"They punks. I ain't payin them niggas nothing!" Peaches hissed in rebellion.

"Peaches. It can't be that much. It ain't like you ain't got the money. Did you talk to Dahji this morning?" Sherrelle was concerned for her friend. She knew what it was like to love a man who was not readily available. But added to this heartache was the issue of her court case and the ex-boyfriend who refused to accept responsibility for putting her in this position in the first place.

"Please. Don't even mention Dahji. He act like he didn't have time for me last night when I called."

Sherrelle didn't want to remind her that she knew what type of man Dahji was when she met him. "That's secondary. We'll be at his house tomorrow to handle business. And if I know anything about Dahji, it's that business ain't never second." Ayana was looking to her proudly, as if to say that her aunt was more hip than she realized.

"That's true," Peaches noted.

"But seriously P. We need to give them wanna-be thugs whatever it is the car cost or whatever. It can't be that much. I'll even put in half if it means they'll leave you alone." In Sherrelle's plea was her desire to see her friend benefit from this new business venture. She wanted Peaches to be free from her past.

"Can we not talk about this right now? I'm getting ready to go see the distributor."

Sherrelle inhaled to calm herself. "Okay girlfriend," she agreed as she turned to the kitchen window. Her heart leaped as she saw Marlin walking along the edge of his fence. He was raking up stray leaves and debris.

"What?" Ayana asked from behind her when she noticed her aunt slowly following something outside the window.

"Don't cook so many waffles," Sherrelle said as she shot a look at the stack on the counter. She then stepped into the service porch past the washing and drying machines. Behind her Ayana was looking out the kitchen window, straining to catch a glimpse of Marlin as he passed by.

Sherrelle stopped at the back screen door and ran her hands down her body as if to check that she was still intact. She started to step through the screen door and remembered that she still held the phone in her hand.

"Hurry up before he go in the house!" Ayana whispered loudly, gesturing her along before leaning over the sink to the window.

Sherrelle waved her off before taking a deep breath and stepping through the screen door. The sun washed over her brilliantly, making her shield her eyes to see across the yard. "Hey homeboy," she called out after he came into view. She was glad to see that he was not on crutches. He looked to her with a grin.

"What's up homegirl?" he replied, standing at the edge of the low picket fence with the rake standing under his palm.

Sherrelle took the stairs slowly, bouncing her hips sexily with each step. "So, you're doing better I see," she said as she approached the fence, her hand shielding her eyes as she looked up to him. She could still feel his lips against hers. It seemed like so long ago that she helped him from his Escalade, but the feeling of being personally wounded at seeing him on crutches was fresh. She so much wanted to reach across the fence and touch him. This game of don't touch was getting hard to play.

"Yeah," he began, looking at her with a cool gaze. There was the hint of amusement playing at his wide lips. "Should be awright though."

"Well, that's good." She felt like a girl in grade school. "How's everything going at home?" she asked, and wanted to take it back.

His lips spread into a crooked smile as he nodded shortly. "I know Grump is good. Your niece hooked him up with a shave and a burger. She can cook."

Sherrelle pretended to be angry as she said, "I told her to leave him alone."

Marlin shook this off with a smile. "It's cool. He needs the company. Stacy is off trying to be the super career woman and …" he trailed off as he directed his attention to a brown leaf stuck in the bottom of the fence.

"Well, as long as you say it's okay," she replied as he looked back up to her after having speared the dead leaf with the rake.

"So, what about you … Everything cool with you? I saw your husband stumble in last night. Is he okay?"

Sherrelle tried to keep from rolling her eyes, but it was no use. "To be honest with you, I don't know what's going on with him."

"When you gon' shake that situation … You deserve better than that," he said, holding the rake with both hands in front of his chest.

Sherrelle looked at him sharply. Was he playing with me … Did he not feel what I felt? … "You make it sound like I have a choice," she replied.

"We all got a choice."

"Then who do you choose Marlin?" she asked seriously.

He smiled with this. "My mom told me when I was a little boy that women do the choosing."

"Really … Did she tell you about how women changed their minds when their choice didn't have the heart to choose in return?" This conversation had suddenly taken on the tenor of a lover's quarrel. This wasn't the first time this had occurred between them. They'd shared no more than two kisses on that first day when they were surprised to find each other at Dahji's penthouse, and now they were acting as if they'd been in love for years. Marlin's eyes raised from her even stare just as the screen door opened.

"Auntie! Peaches said you hung up on her," Ayana complained as she pranced down the stairs and over the grass with the phone in her hand. Her eyes were on Marlin, a knowing smile on her face. She held the phone out for Sherrelle as she stopped to her side. "Hi Marlin," she said sweetly with a gentle wave. Her body swayed softly and naked beneath the transparent body glove.

Sherrelle was watching Marlin's eyes as she apologized to Peaches for leaving her hanging; she was inwardly ecstatic that Marlin's eyes never left Ayana's face as he returned her greeting. This made her smile as he looked back to her. *Maybe he would think that I'm smiling at something Peaches is saying,* she thought.

"Standing outside talking to my neighbor," Sherrelle answered into the phone.

"Tell Grump that I made waffles," Ayana was saying as Peaches screamed in Sherrelle's ear, urging her to jump over the fence and claim her man.

"That's thoughtful of you, but we just ate."

"What y'all eat?" Ayana wanted to know, folding her arms under her large breasts in protest. Marlin kept his eyes raised despite her near naked sex appeal. Sherrelle was proud of him, gathering his attention as she assured Peaches that, "he's looking good," with a sexy appraisal of his muscular frame.

"Just some chicken omeletes," Marlin replied with a mischievous smirk to Sherrelle before returning his attention to Ayana.

"Well, he's going to have to make room for my strawberry waffles. He loves everything that has to do with strawberries," Ayana sulked.

"He's allergic to strawberry. You might be thinking about cherries. He likes cherries."

"Yeah. She call herself making breakfast for our neighbor and he's allergic to it," Sherrelle was saying into the phone as Marlin poked at a pile of leaves with the rake.

"What she say?" Ayana asked, wanting to know the reason for Sherrelle's hushed laughter through her raised hand over mouth.

"She said he's allergic to YOU," she replied with a giggle.

"FORGET YOU PEACHES!" Ayana yelled towards the phone before turning and stomping off. Her ass jumped like gorillas fighting in a pillow case as she took the steps and disappeared into the house.

"Okay. See you in a minute. Cheesecake Factory sounds good ... Okay ... Bye ..." Sherrelle's laughter bubbled to a low chorus as she breathed out, dropping the phone to her side.

"Your niece is a real piece of work," Marlin observed.

"That she is ... So, what's on your program for today?"

"My day consists of rubdowns, massages, and a hot tub," he responded.

"I'm jealous."

"Don't be. On the other side of that is some underwater exercises and isometrics ... Boring."

"Any word on the status of your contract?" They had returned to civility and it felt good. She could see herself talking to him until the wee hours of the morning after a night of passionate lovemaking.

"It's up in the air right now. You know Dahji ... He says not to worry." His face became animated, mimicking the vibrant personality of Dahji as he said, "Marly Marl! If I tell you there's cheese on the moon, then grab your spoon."

He has such a beautiful smile, Sherrelle thought to herself as they shared this moment of laughter. "That's him right there," she giggled out. "If I tell you a flea can pull a car, then grab a rope," she offered in return.

"Yeah ..." he sighed. "That's my boy, though. I don't know how he pull off some of things he do, but ..."

"Like he say, it gotta be in you not on you," Sherrelle suggested.

Marlin nodded his agreement. "No doubt," he replied, then looked to her seriously. "What was up with that kiss?"

"I'm sorry."

"Naw ... Don't be sorry. You coulda warned a brotha, though. My lips was all crusty."

Sherrelle ran a finger across her bottom lip. "You WUZZ kinda salty."

Marlin nodded, grinning over the fence at her. "That's good ... Real good ... So what's up ... Can I get a good morning kiss?" He licked his full lips suggestively as he cocked his head to the side. "All of a sudden you scared?" he asked when she hesitated to answer.

Sherrelle felt like she was in a powerful storm. There was nothing more she wanted to do than to kiss him, but not like this. She was backing away from him as if on a cloud. He grinned to her knowingly and lifted his hand to say goodbye just before she turned silently to the porch.

"See you later Marlin," she choked out before disappearing through the door. She leaned against the washing machine and slammed her palm to her forehead. Stupid! Stupid!

"What happened?" Ayana asked, ducking her head around the corner, her mouth full of strawberry waffles. She'd dimmed her glow now that no one was watching. "What's wrong?"

"Nothing," Sherrelle gushed out, regaining her composure. She had to get away from here. There was business to handle downtown.

"What he do to you?" Ayana asked as Sherrelle walked past her into the living room.

"You need to change clothes if you're going with me," Sherrelle stated over her shoulder.

Ayana followed her into the bedroom. "Where you going?"

"Downtown to get some paperwork," she responded. In Ayana's eyes this represented a day of sterile buildings and long lines.

"No thank you," she said, thinking that she'd much rather watch

Lifetime on the big screen. "What he say?" She wanted to know the details of how Sherrelle became flushed and so determined to leave all of a sudden.

Sherrelle's mind was swimming in desire. He'd actually done the thing she privately dared him to do and she had no response. She felt like a fool. He must think she was daft. Her body swelled with emotion as she changed into a sky-blue linen pants suit and grabbed a pair of Dior shades and Fendi purse from the tall bureau of accessories.

"He said what I wanted him to say," she finally replied as she walked from the bedroom.

"What was that?" Ayana wanted to know. She followed her aunt through the house to the front door.

"I should be back in a few hours," Sherrelle said as she stepped onto the porch and slipped the black shades over her eyes.

"If y'all downtown is like any other downtown, then I doubt if you're back in a few hours," Ayana said as she walked slowly behind her down the driveway, taking a peek to the neighbor's porch; *maybe Grump is in the doorway*. The thought pleased her.

"Maybe a little later than that ... Me and Peaches are meeting for lunch. Too bad you didn't want to come." This was said as she slid behind the wheel of the Jaguar.

"Tell her I said hi ... And bring me back a doggy bag," Ayana called out as the pink Jag backed out the driveway. Sherrelle waved her jeweled fingers in response.

Ayana was absorbed in a Lifetime program about an interracial marriage that produced albino children when she heard the familiar thump thump of Marlin's Escalade come to life. Too Short yelled out, "BITCH!"

Ayana glided to the couch and peered through the front window. Sherrelle had left only sixty minutes before. Ayana thought that they could easily meet somewhere secret and get their freak on. She couldn't understand how her aunt could be so stubborn when it came to satisfying herself. To bring this up felt hypocritical to Ayana, being that she'd let her aunt's husband suck her pussy. She wanted to tell Sherrelle that she should go ahead and fuck Marlin and get it over with. *She can be so square*, she thought to herself as the Escalade pulled away from the curb and turned in the other direction, the beat thumping down the block.

Ayana was up and strolling to the bathroom to freshen up, her body tingling with thoughts of how she would make the old man smile today.

She observed herself in the mirror, liking what she saw, and felt that there was some way for the old man to experience her in a better way. Maybe she would let him feel all over her body. *But this would not do,* she thought to herself as she made one final survey of her curves before her short trip next door.

This is too easy, old man at home alone and fine ass chick turning him out, she thought to herself. It was like something in a porno film. Maybe she was fulfilling this drama for herself.

The front door was open as if he were expecting her arrival. The customary sounds of porno wafted through the screen door, the woman's moans lay over the corny soundtrack like grits over sausage. The sun spread through the house in a haze of horizontal shafts of light, showing the fine appointments of a successful career woman and her pro football player husband. Grump was like a grown child they could leave at home without supervision.

"Hello ... Is anyone home?" she called out, leaning to the edge of the screen to see more of the house. Maybe he was sitting in the leather lounge chair. She then looked out to the street, not sure if she should disturb the old man.

"Imagine that," Grump called out cheerfully from the depths of the house. Ayana was glad to hear his voice. He slowly came into view, walking slowly with his head cocked oddly to the corner of the ceiling. He walked with a rickety gait. Elbows and knees akimbo with each stride.

"Hi ... How are you?" she asked as he neared, smiling though he could not see. She wished that he could see the way she was sheathed in her body suit.

"Is that my pretty cotton tail?" Grump reached for the screen and pushed it open. "Pretty hottentot make happy pop." He smiled his toothless grin while turning sideways.

"It's your one and only Ms. Ayana Cherry," she said, moving past him while letting her fingers drag along his mid-section. He wore a fresh wife-beater and Ayana could see how his daughter might have fitted him with it, along with fresh socks and boxer-briefs.

"Can't help but to admit that you make a fine play ..." His serpent-like tongue slipped between his thin lips as he ambled to the chair. Ayana held her hand out to guide him, catching at his angled elbow.

"Cotton tail," he breathed out as he settled into the leather cushions. "So, you want to go to school, hunh?" he asked, staring blindly towards the plasma screen where a woman's bouncing breasts filled the screen. Up and down they dribbled as she rode the pole between a thin pair of white, hairy legs. The camera panned down to reveal how the pale organ penetrated her dark muff, the juices making it shiny and the tightness making it bend and bulge at the large vein running along the shaft.

"Do you see what he's doing to that woman?" Ayana asked with alarm. The high definition plasma made it all so graphic.

"Of course I do ... Now ..." When she looked back in his direction there was a small stack of crisp notes in his weathered hand. "Here's a little something to help with your books." He held his hand at the front of his stomach. He still had not taken off his new plaid pajama bottoms. There was a slight movement under the cloth between his legs.

Ayana's eyes brightened with the surprise. "You didn't have to ..."

He waved this off and said, "Eezy peezy lemon squeezy. Maybe I'll have my daughter bury it with me then." He shrugged his narrow shoulders with this suggestion.

"Thank you." As she moved between his legs to retrieve the money he moved it lower to his lap. This did not deter Ayana. She stepped between his thighs and reached for the money slowly, letting her fingers drag along the length of his joint as it lay thick in his lap. He motioned his head from side to side like Stevie Wonder and grabbed the arms of the chair. Ayana had not moved from between his legs. She smiled with his reaction, the moans of the woman getting boned dancing in her ears.

"Okey dokey hottentot happy pop," he cheered with muted excitement while his joint jumped in his lap.

"I knew that's what you wanted." Ayana held the money against her waist as she stood over him.

"Bloody well you know," he replied, smiling happily.

"Want me to do it again?"

"That would be a fine stroke of luck. I'm just a lonely old man." His voice dipped to a sad plea at the end of this.

Ayana reached down and stroked him one good time. She stretched him along the length of his thigh and was pleased to find him strapped like a cowboy. She then stood to watch his reaction. His head swayed from side to side in slow motion while his hips rolled, his joint jerking as if it were being resuscitated.

Ayana peeked to the money in her hand. They were all twenty dollar bills, some new and some weathered. The amount had to be at least four-hundred dollars. "When was the last time you went to a strip club? ... And don't lie." She felt they'd crossed some boundary with the exchange of money and a small favor. *And Sherrelle had the nerve to think I would miss being at a strip club,* she thought to herself. Strip clubs in L.A. didn't ask for identification. A cool handle and a banging body was all that was needed. She imagined that Sherrelle would think differently of her if she knew her niece had worked the pole for a two-month summer stretch. It was just enough time to meet a rich man who would pay for what she wanted without the hard work. He liked to take her out to dinner and show her off to his friends. But she had to admit to herself that she was young and didn't really know what to do with him. Besides that she had to return to school for her senior year. Him finding out she was still in high school would have ended the relationship anyway.

"Strip club ..." Grump repeated as if trying to remember exactly when the last time was that he'd been to one.

"A long time, hunh?" Ayana whispered as she knocked her leg against his thigh. He grinned with pink gums before her as she trailed her fingers along his scalp.

"Happy pop," he mumbled as she continued down his chest and gripped his thighs.

Ayana leaned forward and placed her pursed lips on his cool forehead. She kissed him with a loud smacking sound, her breasts hanging in front of him invitingly. His palms found their way to her thighs. She swayed beneath his gentle touch, moving her hips in soft circles. She watched as he rose in his pajamas, the thick meat rising as if coiled like a snake.

"Is that how you remember it?" she asked, her lips brushing against his warm cheek, which pressed back with his smile. "You're growing up," she added as she leaned away from him, leaning to stroke him one time.

"Wanker," he sighed, tilting his head back, a tight grin spreading his lips. He could have been in heaven for the way his face glowed.

Ayana turned from him and backed her ass into his lap. She trapped his thick meat between her firm mounds and moved over him with a smooth, rhythmic motion. He grew larger in her grasp as she pressed onto him, stroking him with the fatness of her ass. She watched the porno as she gave him a lap dance.

On the screen there was a muscular man who looked to be about fifty years old. He sat at the edge of a swimming pool. He waited for a slim, feminine figure to reach him swimming through the crystal blue water. The young brunette rose from the water's edge between his legs, her hair trailing down her slim back. She smiled before pulling him from his swim shorts and taking him into her mouth. She sucked him with long, sensuous strokes, her wet cheeks sucked in tight while her lips pulled at his muscle. The man rubbed his hand over her shiny, black hair before raising her from the pool.

"Baldergash," Grump whispered behind her, lurching forward into her narrow back and gripping her rounded hips. He absorbed her motions against him, breathing against her hoarsely.

"You like that?" she asked in a sexy whisper.

In reply he grew even stiffer between her massaging mounds, letting a low growl escape from deep within himself.

The fifty-year-old looking white man had taken the young, naked brunette to a plastic lounge chair and spread her legs wide into the air while he hung long and thick before her. She smiled up at him and closed her eyes as he sunk into her slowly. The screen filled with his hairy ass squeezing and flexing as he dove into her.

Ayana squeezed hard against Grump's thick meat between her ass cheeks. Up and down she stroked and round and round she ground, using his bony knees like a pilot. He'd leaned back and frowned his face up in sexual agony. He looked as if he'd eaten an extra sour piece of candy for the way his lips reached to the tip of his wrinkled nose and his eyes shut tight.

Ayana enjoyed the effect that she was having on him, and had to admit to herself that she enjoyed this form of pleasure; she enjoyed the mischief and the excitement of it. She enjoyed the feeling of his hardness between her center. His low grunts and moans excited her. She liked the way he gripped her ass and hips firmly as a gauge to how much he was enjoying himself. The occasional pain of this pressure only encouraged her movements. She felt him tensing beneath her and knew that it would not be long before he creamed in his pajamas.

On the screen the young brunette had now switched places with the fifty-year-old man. She was now straddling him wide legged over the plastic lounge chair. Her small breasts bounced with her as she slammed down onto his meaty shaft. The screen slowly filled with her pussy being parted by his slick meat. It was apparent by their joint moans that they were both ready to explode.

Ayana trapped Grump's straining meat against his stomach and rode him like a train over a single track. She bounced her ass high on his chest and dropped down to the base of his thick organ. He gasped behind her, making her wonder if he was okay. She looked back quickly to make sure he was okay, eager to get to her own orgasm. Her pussy swelled with pleasure. She caught him between her damp folds and stroked him tightly. His fingers dug into her waist as she squeezed along his joint and let her ass bounce to his stomach.

With another gasp, his grip tightening around her, she felt him jerk under her assault. She continued to ride him with urgency, chasing the burning cream threatening to spill from her. He was softening with quick spasms. She worked to keep him trapped between her crease until she finally creamed with a sweet exhalation. She let her ass rest in his lap, feeling him pulse beneath her wet snatch. *He will need to change his clothes,* she thought to herself before suddenly rising up.

She turned to him just as he was lifting his eyelids. She kissed him on the lips and said how much she appreciated the money. He waved lazily, his head rolling to the side, as she strode victoriously towards the door. She peeked both ways down the street before turning to him to say that she would see him later. She closed the door gently behind her and skipped across the yard excitedly, gripping the warm money in her palm.

CHAPTER TWENTY ONE

It was nearly six in the morning by the time Dahji walked into his penthouse. He was truly exhausted from his night with Edith. They'd cuddled for the rest of the evening as Dahji explored her mind and motivations. He'd been right about her; no one had ever taken the time to hear what she had to say. She'd learned to use her beauty to speak for her, but yearned to express her intelligence.

As Dahji rose to leave in the early morning she'd confessed her lifetime commitment to him and wanted to see him succeed. She vowed to help him in any way she could. Before he stepped through the door into the early morning dawn he suggested that she, "Be about it, don't talk about it." This left her in a fit of frustration, just the way he wanted her after a night of pleasure.

Slumber claimed him during the morning. He willed his body to recuperate from yesterday's sexual marathon because today would be more of the same. It was time to tie the knot on his future. He stretched out like a cat in silk boxers as he looked out the floor-to-ceiling window past the swimming pool that looked like it spilled directly onto the city below to the tall buildings in the distance. He contemplated his meeting with Mirabelle's sisters. How could he get them to release his sunshine from their collective grip? He grimaced with satisfaction at the fact that he'd copped a new runner; Edith would no doubt give him room to move. He liked Mirabelle true enough, but not enough to be broke.

Yeah, it was all coming together. All that was left was to see what Gloria had in mind to get Marlin on the team. He lay back with his arms folded behind his head, amused at Gloria's strategy. She probably already had Marlin a spot on the roster, but was using his injury as a ploy to pimp him out. He couldn't be mad at her though. She'd come through for him in more ways than one. He was in her debt, no matter how much pipe he lay to her friends; but he did wonder at what price her friends exacted this favor from her. Gloria was a shrewd woman.

And only now did he realize that Peaches had not called him yet. No doubt she was upset with him for not being able to connect with her in a real way lately. Maybe she thought he was feeling differently about her, which was not entirely true. There were some things that just had to be tended to. He still liked her style, but had to admit that he'd expected a little more understanding on her part for how he had to move. He understood perfectly well that she had to do whatever she had to do to get where she needed to be. He felt her on this because he was involved in HoodSweet, too. He realized that she was letting her heart get in the way of her money; their money. And this went against everything he believed in. Until now he thought she believed this way, too. He resolved that next time he spoke with her he would put everything on hold and get into her mind. *All she needed was some attention,* he reasoned.

He thought this opportunity would be sooner than he thought when the phone rang. *Was she here?,* he asked himself when he noticed the small blue light blinking to indicate that it was the security desk calling. He reached across the bed for the phone and lifted it from its cradle.

"Mr. McBeth, there is a Ms. Ebony who wishes to visit with you."

"What?" Dahji asked absently. The desk clerk was repeating what he'd said before as he reached for his Rolex. Ten o'clock. He thought quickly of what it was she might have wanted. She'd last said that she was moving to Los Angeles to pursue modeling and acting. He'd warned her against this. Maybe he could persuade her to stay and be a top money getter with this HoodSweet thing that was about to pop.

"Send her up," he instructed the desk guard.

Dahji rolled from the bed and stretched before the full-length window overlooking the city. It was going to be a good day. He felt this in his bones. The sun was shining brightly. It was Friday and the end of the week was always good. He grabbed a silk robe from the suede footstool at the end of a momosan bamboo chair.

By the time the doorbell rang he'd brushed his teeth and washed his face. He was applying Victoria's Secret Citrus Cream to his skin (a gift from Coretta) when he opened the door. Ebony stood before him like a shining chocolate-covered angel. She was dressed in a cocaine white linen dress that dropped from her shoulders as if needing to be near her curves. She smiled, knowing she was beautiful for the way his eyes caressed her shapely figure. She didn't have to be in a net tube dress to be sexy.

This was the woman Dahji fell in love with the first time he saw her. She was as she is now. Conservatively dressed with minimal jewelry; gold bangles wrapped her wrists and a thin gold herringbone necklace shimmied against her gleaming cocoa complexion. Her hair was pulled to a curling tail atop her head, accentuating her slanted eyes.

"Good morning," she gushed out with a pearly white smile, her sumptuous breasts heaving and hidden beneath the soft fabric.

"Good morning yourself. You look delicious. If I wasn't a vegetarian I would eat you."

"But you're not a vegetarian," she retorted as she slid past him into the penthouse. In her hand was a shiny gold wrapped book-sized gift.

"When you leave I go back to eating meat," he joked, closing the door behind her.

Ebony frowned sexily. "That's no fun."

Dahji pointed to her hand. "What you got there?"

She thrust the gift to him. "Open it and find out."

Dahji raised the gift to his ear and shook it. "Will it blow up?"

"Not with me standing here," she responded as she backed up.

"Where you going?"

She smiled mischievously before replying that she was going to turn on some music. "Are you just getting out of bed? ... Everybody ain't able."

The Isley Brothers sprang to life as she stepped away from the Technic sound system. They sang of the pleasure of loving a beautiful woman and wanting to buy them expensive furs and travel to exotic places. They would do what other men were unable or unwilling to do. Ebony looked to the loft, his bed still unmade, as she walked back to where he held the book of poems in his hand. In gold lettering, on a purple cover, read the title: *Live Rich Die Ready.*

"I thought you might like it. Turn to the page I marked," she suggested. "Her name is Crystal Franklin. She's the hottest."

Dahji flipped to the page she'd marked with a purple silk ribbon. He'd walked into the black ceramic kitchen and leaned onto the stainless steel range. "Completion vs. Compliment," he said aloud as Ebony walked past him to the refrigerator.

"Yep. That's the one. What do you want for breakfast?" she asked, opening the refrigerator and looking back to him with a small grin.

He met her eyes, considering her comfort in his home. "You slide through to give me a gift and make me breakfast?"

"Well, I thought since I was here ..."

"That's how you get your feelings hurt. Stopping by a pimp's house without warning.

"You didn't have to let me up. That's the whole point of the security desk, right? ... Now, can I make you breakfast before I make love to you?"

Dahji grinned with recognition. "Oh ... That's what this is about," he said, the book still open in his palm.

"You know you want me," she stated as she casually looked into the refrigerator. "How about some scrambled eggs and ... You got bell peppers and onions."

"That's cool," he said as she was already moving about the kitchen. He bowed to the book, the first line of the poem gathering his attention.

A ½ + ½ equals a whole -

but only in the mathematical world.

He looked up to Ebony as she reached for an overhead frying pan. "What made you mark this?" he asked.

"Keep reading," she suggested.

He bowed his head silently to read further.

In the relationship world a ½ + ½ =

a relationship unequally yoked.

We are inundated with the thought

that our mate is to complete us as if

we are the donut and they are the donut hole.

How unappealing is that?

Dahji looked up now as Ebony sliced bell peppers on a cutting board.

"That's deep, hunh?" she asked, meeting his cool gaze.

"The half and half part don't add up."

"Go on," she instructed.

I'd like to present the following argument:

We should spend our alone time

completing ourselves mentally,

spiritually, and physically so that

when our true mate arrives, what we have

are two people who compliment one another

in every aspect.

Dahji nodded as he said, "I can feel that." Ebony smiled, the knife held in mid strike over a ball of onion. Her eyes threatened to water as she stepped next to him and pointed the blade of the knife to the end of the poem.

"Completion keeps you constantly on the move looking for the plug for your emptiness," she began, the silver edge of the blade marking her progress. Dahji inhaled her scent and noticed that she had fine strands of midnight-colored hair growing along her forearms. "But compliment is as still as a puzzle. You surround yourself with the right accenting parts and you can simply wait for the rest of the pieces to compliment your position."

Dahji was watching her peach glossed lips move; the soft ridges pressing with each word so tenderly. Her collar bone lay just under her dark skin, sturdy and inviting. She smelled like expensive perfume. "What is that?" he asked suddenly.

"What?" She looked to him and seemed only now to recognize how close she was to him. Her dark brown eyes moved over his face and settled on his lips.

"That perfume."

"Oh," she smiled, her fine eyebrows arching with the sudden question. "Um ... I think it's Golden Amber."

Dahji nodded. "That smells good," he said.

"Thank you," she replied with a sexy smile before returning to the poem. "No matter how your position changes, your compliment is a perfect fit and simply changes with you." She looked up to him now with serious eyes. "So I pose the question. Do you want someone to complete you or compliment you?"

"Is that part of the poem?" Dahji wanted to know, looking down to the page.

Ebony leaned away from him. "It is ... And I want you to answer the question. Compliment or complete?" She moved back to the cutting board and began slicing thin arcs of onion.

"Ice T said it best when he said that two people should be able to see the same thing when they look at their future."

"That could be a compliment," Ebony hedged, her head bowed to the sliced onions. "You have been a compliment to me," she added as she slid the onions into a bowl with the sliced bell peppers.

"You're easy to compliment," Dahji responded slowly. "If I'm so good for you then why you shaking me for a clown in L.A.?"

The frying pan sizzled with eggs as she stirred freshly cut onions and bell peppers into the mix. "I already told you."

"Yeah. You said something about acting and modeling but that don't add up. You ain't got to do that to be famous."

She looked to him with a plain stare. "I have to go and see what might happen Dahji."

"Well, do what you have to do, but you gon' miss out. Tomorrow I got my girl Sherrelle coming through. She runs the HoodSweet thing. It's about to blow up and I believe it's the right move for you."

"Can't I represent the clothes in L.A.?" she asked, and suddenly Dahji saw the genius in it.

He pressed his lips together and nodded. "That might work. Like a West coast representative ..."

"Exactly," she echoed with an excited gleam in her eyes.

"You serious about this? You know ... All it takes is your commitment to bubble with us."

"I'm as serious as a bad hair day," she giggled out.

"I guess that's serious enough," Dahji responded as the wall phone rang. He reached for it as a cloud passed over Ebony's face. Her private time was being interrupted.

"Mr. Dahji McBeth," Mirabelle breathed out the familiar sound of the vacant piano playing in the background.

"Good morning sunshine. Did you kiss the clouds this morning?" he asked as he walked into the living room and sat down on the leather sofa. He grabbed up the remote and turned to CNN.

"Just for you," she responded breathlessly. "And you are well this morning? ... It sounds romantic there."

"Can't really say right now. Any day now I might be homeless and broke." On the muted screen Barack Obama was before a large crowd of voters. Along the bottom of the plasma screen scrolled numbers listing him as ahead in the polls.

Mirabelle clucked. "This will not be so," she assured him. "My late husband's sisters are very interested in meeting with you. They will be at my home later this evening. Are you free?"

"As government cheese."

Mirabelle's laughter reached high and settled low before she quipped, "Well, I don't know if you're as free as that, but your presence would be greatly appreciated.

"Sounds good," Dahji answered.

Ebony approached silently with a large plate of scrambled eggs and a tall glass of orange juice. *This is something I could get used to,* he thought to himself as she smiled to him while placing the breakfast on the glass table before him. She sat next to him without a word or ill expression of jealousy. Obviously she'd recovered from her earlier bout of shadow face.

"We'll be waiting," Mirabelle cheered, her voice dripping with sexual mischief.

"Is she a compliment?" Ebony asked as he placed the phone in his lap. On the plasma screen there was a mob of men in military uniform chasing down what appeared to be a civilian population. Wisps of smoke rose from the ends of rifles as the military gave chase down a dusty road framed by cardboard shacks. The caption at the bottom of the melee read: Nairobi, Kenya: Opposition flee government forces on second day of protests of election.

Dahji nodded as a man fell under gunfire. He was trying to squeeze through a fence along with what looked to be at least one hundred other men. "Most definitely," he answered.

"Am I a benefit?"

"No doubt," he replied, absorbed in the political violence on the screen. An elderly woman was being chased from her home by government forces.

Dahji answered the ringing phone just as Ebony mentioned that she wanted to be more of a benefit. "Speak on it."

"Well, hello. How are you?" Gloria wanted to know, some secret knowledge lacing her words.

He accepted the eggs piled onto a fork into his mouth. Ebony fed him slowly. "Breakfast," he mumbled around the peppered eggs. He nodded his agreement and gave a thumbs up signal for how delicious the eggs were.

"How's Edith?"

"Can't say. She was alive when I left her," he replied, opening his mouth for another helping of eggs.

"Ha ha ... That's funny," Gloria mocked. "Especially since I spoke with her this morning. I don't know what you did ... Well, maybe I do, but you should know that she's in love with you. So be good to her."

"She's married."

A sharp hiss escaped her lips. "She's nothing more than a status symbol for Tom. He rarely knows she exists. So, my other news is that May Ling wants to meet with you."

"Why?" he asked as Ebony slowly guided the fork of eggs between his lips. She held a palm under the silver to catch any spillage. She was enjoying her enterprise.

"Do you not remember me informing you that she's highly placed in the Colts organization?"

"That don't mean nothing to me. Is she or ain't she got the power?" CNN was now showing the recent plunge in the stock market. The nation was headed for a recession.

"She has the power. Trust me."

"You pimpin kinda hard, Glo Glo." He pointed to the glass of orange juice. Ebony followed his suggestion and handed the cold juice to his waiting palm.

"That's hardly the case, Dahji. Have I led you wrong to date? ... I didn't think so. Now, give her a call. She'll be available for lunch."

"I got something to do for lunch," he said, nearly upset that Gloria was so confident that he would believe May Ling was the answer to his problem.

"Really," she sulked.

"Really. Tell her I'll call after lunch."

There was silence. Dahji avoided this moment of uncertainty by focusing on the plasma screen where a talking head was no doubt explaining the scene behind him where O.J. Simpson was being led into a courtroom. "Dumb ass nigga," Dahji said in barely a whisper.

"Excuse me?" Gloria asked, her voice shooting through the phone.

"Not you ... O.J."

"Him again," she replied with a tired sigh. "Okay. I'll let her know, but you owe me so long as you know," she added. It was her ploy to keep him in her debt.

"You got a crooked calculator," Dahji stated in a lazy drawl, making Ebony giggle beside him. She rose to take the plate into the kitchen, sliding by him and knocking against his knees suggestively.

"You'd like to think so," Gloria taunted, laughing out loud. "Goodbye Dahji. Tell Marlin that I said hello."

"You ever suck on a chicken foot?" he asked, a smile on his face.

"Bye bye." She was gone. Dahji let the phone drop to his lap and smirked towards the screen with his accomplishment. He knew that May Ling wanted pipe. He'd never sexed a ... He wondered if she was Japanese, Chinese, or Vietnamese. Maybe she was Cambodian. He couldn't tell the difference. What was Lucy Liu? Whatever she was, then May Ling was probably that. In any case he looked forward to seeing her naked.

"So, this is the lifestyle of Dahji McBeth ... And here it was I thought you were just the picture man," Ebony said as she returned to the living room and sat next to him on the couch.

He looked over to her. "Good looking out on that breakfast."

"No problem. I'll stay if I can stay here," she suggested with a sexy smirk.

Dahji shook his head towards the plasma. "You say that now, but then you start catching feelings and try to dictate my situation."

"I promise to keep my feelings in check." There was a playful note in her voice.

Dahji tapped her leg as if she were a small girl. "Yeah, that's what you say now ... " he sighed, standing up and strolling to the spiral staircase.

She followed him silently to the loft. "You might be the one who catches feelings. That's why you running from me ..." She passed him as he turned to her and stepped quickly to the window that exposed the city beyond. "I didn't know you had a swimming pool," she gushed, her palms on the window.

"That's cuz you ain't bin past the living room." The sun was rising to its zenith, making the glass and chrome of the city sparkle and blaze. The infinity pool shimmered beneath its rays.

"That is beautiful," she whispered in muted excitement.

"Naw. Go on to L.A. and breathe that bus smoke. I wouldn't be surprised if you come back with plastic titties."

She turned to him in rebellion as he dropped a pair of Rocawear jeans and Polo Rugby shirt to the rumpled bed sheets.

"Not those," she advised, pointing to the mustard oxfords in his hand. "Wear the blue Waller B's. They go better with the thin lines in the shirt and the stitching in the jeans," she advised as she sat in the bamboo mamosan. She watched him select a thick gold rope from his jewelry carousel along with a diamond bezeled Cartier Tank watch.

"And ain't nobody scared of you," he said casually as he dropped a pair of socks to the bed.

Ebony smiled. "Yes you are."

"Okay. I'm scared," he mocked.

"Then why do you act like I'm not sexy? I see the effect I have on you when I take pictures." She'd crossed her legs and looked to him with a mischievous grin.

"This ain't no party treat," he commented, pointing to his lap.

"Well, somebody's getting that dick and I just want to know how I can be down."

Dahji turned from his bureau. He held a pair of silk boxers in his hand. He observed her for a second before nodding with understanding. "You want to be on the team, is that it?"

Ebony nodded.

"You don't know what you want, but I'ma tell you what. Go to L.A. like you plan to do and represent HoodSweet. Get the money and bring it back to the locker. Follow the play book I provide and you guaranteed to carry the balls." He smiled with this.

She stood from the chair and walked across the hard floor to where he stood counting a roll of hundred dollar bills. "So, in other words you're saying that the money comes first." He could feel the heat from her body. It was too easy to lay pipe to her, but he had cock lined up for the day that would need his full mojo.

"Bartholomew don't even wink if ain't no cheddar involved."

"I can respect that, but what I'm proposing is a new level in our relationship." She turned with him as he inserted a slim stack of money into a gold money clip.

He grabbed her by the shoulders and trapped her in his gaze. "Check it out baby girl. You green right now, but I'ma season you up like Lawry's. I already know you gon' catch feelings and I ain't resisting that, but right now ain't the time. Come back tomorrow and meet with Sherrelle. Let's get this money, get your mission statement tight, and then we can party like a rock star. Feel me?" Her eyes danced across the bridge of his nose as he gave his instruction.

Ebony smiled bravely. "You're tough to crack."

"Like an oyster in the day time."

"Okay. I'm in. What time tomorrow?"

"Same time as right now," he replied before leaning in to kiss her on the forehead.

She pouted. "That's the last time for that. Next time you're going to give me what I want."

"See, that's where you got it wrong. Start thinking in terms of earned income. Life don't give us nothing but the opportunity to earn our reward." He was following her to the staircase as he said this.

She turned to him when they reached the bottom, squinting her eyes for effect as she said, "When I get you ... " Her finger pointed into his heart. "It's over for you."

"You got action," he responded sincerely before falling in stride beside her to the door.

Ebony turned to him suddenly and leaned in close. Her lips pressed against his tightly, her tongue slipping into his mouth. Dahji allowed her sweet probe as he rest his palms on the high section of her ass. She released herself from him with a soft series of light kisses.

"See you tomorrow Dahji," she promised, dropping her Roberto Cavalli shades to her eyes.

"Sounds good," he responded. He watched her sexy stride to the elevator, waving in return before she disappeared. He let out a deep breath with his effort to avoid her advances. He didn't know how much longer he could have stayed true. Now it was time to pursue his immediate reward.

***

Corporate Pointe stood high to the sky, gleaming glass and chrome under the noon-day sky. She'd been by this section of downtown, but never had reason to stop.

For some reason she thought that her meeting with Max Strong would be a repeat of visiting some out-of- the-way dusty commercial warehouse district. This was exactly the opposite, making her car stand out like a man in a pork suit at a Masjid. Here, there were upright men and women of purpose striding along clean walkways between glimmering buildings of commerce. They were suited to effect change and smiled their accomplishment and joy of duty.

Peaches did not feel totally comfortable until she'd parked in a far corner of the multi-level parking structure. For this occasion she wore a thigh length Vera Wang dress and Jimmy Choo heels. A thin gold necklace with Tiffany heart pendant raced around her slender neck. A gold Dior watch hugged her slim wrists, the dial diamonds classy and sparkling. With her dark red hair tied to a bun at the back of her head she could easily be mistaken for an urban model or mid-level executive at any one of the shining offices in Corporate Pointe.

At the center of this conflagration of glass buildings was a grass area fronted by a multi-colored directory to guide visitors to their destination. Peaches searched for Strong Distribution. A thin blue dot next to his name was traced by a line to the building on the other side of the grassy area. In the middle of the small park was a large concrete dolphin, blue water spilling from its mouth as it stood on its rear fins. Around this aqua blue cement structure were low wooden benches; these were sparsely populated by solo professionals either absorbed between the pages of newspapers or their laptops. It is here that Peaches felt good about her mission and the fashionable black Tod's Pashmy Bauletto bag she carried.

Her sparkling gray eyes adjusted behind her gold rimmed DKNY Lenses as she stepped into the cool foyer of the Strong Distribution building. It stood four stories high and as a centerpiece to two higher (one architectural, the other a marketing firm) buildings.

The foyer was artfully decorated with silver suede sofas and three dimensional metal art work adorning the walls. Behind a high arching black lacquer wall the blonde top of a receptionist's head could be seen.

"Welcome to Strong Distribution. How may I help you?" the brown-eyed blonde asked, looking from a monitor as Peaches approached. Her hair hung in straight lines to her padded shoulders, framing a young, narrow face of ceramic whiteness.

"Mr. Strong is expecting me. Ms. Adebenro," Peaches responded, feeling a certain sense of pride at pronouncing her given name. She was becoming official in a world of progress.

"Yes ..." the receptionist said as she peered towards her monitor. She looked back to Peaches with a certifying smile. "Mr. Strong is on floor number four. To the left. I'll announce your arrival," she added as she picked up a phone.

Peaches heard her name mentioned as she walked away, feeling the white woman's curious eyes on her as she approached the elevator situated to the side of the desk, partly obscured by a large green potted plant.

Walking amongst business professionals had a special allure. There was the sense of purpose. The smiles exchanged with the sharply dressed men and women exiting, riding, and boarding at floors two and three felt good. She was alone in the mirrored elevator when she reached the fourth floor.

A floor-to-ceiling shark tank was the first thing she saw when she stepped from the elevator. To the right, behind a glass wall was a basketball court, and beyond this was a swimming pool. She imagined that somewhere outside of view was a sauna or steam room, maybe even a juice bar.

"Hello," called a deep base voice from the other end. Peaches turned and was met by the handsome white man she'd seen at Dr. Kim's office. *What is he doing here today?* she asked herself as he extended his hand to her. She worked to conceal her surprise.

"It's a small world," he said with a wide smile, his dark eyes pleased at seeing her. Here was the man she'd planned on giving some special attention to the next time he visited Applebottoms. She would have never guessed that this man who sat in the front row during her performances was the owner of a multi-million dollar distribution firm. Even better for her was the fact that he was very attractive.

"Hello, Mr. Strong. I feel like we know each other from another galaxy," she confessed.

"I suppose you could call Applebottoms another galaxy," he replied, his dark eyes crinkling at the corners with his smile. "It's great to see you pursuing what I think is a great business move."

"Thank you, but the brainchild is my friend Sherrelle."

He nodded with understanding. "Let's get to my office and hammer this thing out," he suggested, holding his arm out to lead the way down the thickly carpeted corridor.

"I've never seen a tank this big," she admitted as they walked along, followed by a shark on the other side of the glass.

"It was specially built by the people who did the L.A. Aquarium."

"Impressive," she replied, meaning both the layout of his office and his taste in design. He was both minimal and tasteful. To the far left of the open space was a lounge area lit by dim light. She could easily see him reclining here with a cigar and cognac as he devised his next business opportunity.

"My wife picked all of this out," he said as he strolled to the stainless steel desk. She shouldn't have been surprised to hear that he was married.

"She has nice taste." The sharks reached into the office. Now she wanted to see the basketball court. It had to be a remarkable feeling to play ball before such a magnificent aquarium.

Peaches sauntered to his desk and reclined in the sleek leather chair at its side. The gold golf club cufflinks caught her attention. As he pulled a leather-bound note book from the desk's edge her eyes followed up his striped sleeve to his neat hair cut. Everything about him was carefully measured and accounted for. His desk was sparse. At her elbow were Roost's Scrimshaw desk accessories: flat bone-handle magnifying glass, sundial with compass that looked to be chipped from elephant tusk and enumerated with feathered ink, and a bronze-edged bone ruler that folded at the six-inch marking.

"Okay," he began as he opened the folder between them. He produced a sheaf of papers and placed them in her hands. He leaned close to explain each page.

Peaches tried to comprehend him as his long finger traced the paragraphs. He explained that he could place her in both an upscale chain and budget stores across the country. As soon as the manufacturing process was complete he would arrange meetings with the product placement managers of major stores. They would then bid on how much stock to place and at what price.

"I should have brought Sherrelle," Peaches said as they shuffled the pages.

"There's plenty of time to meet with her," Max Strong said, his eyes looking deeply into her before returning to the page, a shadow of a smile across his wide lips. "Here is where we place the numbers for our rate. We can charge your company an upfront fee based on size and lot of the eventual placement or we can agree on a percentage of eventual sales." He looked up to her then. "The latter is what I would prefer because I want to get rich with you."

Peaches returned his smile, feeling heat rush through her. It was really about to happen. She was about to be in a position to chart her own course. He was talking about placing HoodSweet in stores nationwide.

He leaned up now, his face losing some of its mirth. "Usually by the time I get to meet with a company they've already secured their necessary franchisee, trademark, and manufacturing commitments. I'm willing to hold your hand on this as a favor to my good friend Dr. Kim. By virtue of your meeting with me your company is already in my debt."

"I appreciate you meeting with me," Peaches cut in.

He smiled graciously. "It's my pleasure. I love helping young entrepreneurs. Besides that ..." his voice trailed off as his fingers drummed the steel of his desk. "When I realized that you were attached to this ... It was a no brainer for me."

Peaches was no fool. Brainer or no brainer, nothing was for free. She awaited his punch line.

"So we can officially begin the process when we produce the required paperwork then?" she asked.

Max Strong nodded and then shrugged. "Well, we can agree to work together and I will defer your consulting costs until we are placed and stocked." He leaned across the desk now and narrowed his eyes. His lips trembled as he said, "You must know that there's no one else that interests me when I make my trips to Applebottoms. You invade my dreams."

"How so?" she asked carefully, letting her eyes slide in sexual seduction.

He inhaled before confessing, "I think you have the most wonderful ass. I've never seen such a perfect ass as yours." His tongue flicked across his lips before he continued with, "And the way you move on the stage is mesmerizing."

"Thank you."

"Would you mind?" he asked, nodding his head to the center of the floor. There it was. He'd let the cat out of the bag. He was an ass man, but what sort ... Licking ... Fucking ... Fondling?

"You would like a private show?" she asked.

"That would be the most wonderful thing."

"And for this we are signing on the dotted line with deferred payment?"

He nodded slowly, his eyes eager. "This is a private floor. No one comes up here without my consent," he assured her. A shark returned to turn the corner at the edge of the tank against the far wall; it's eye shined dark and menacing as if waiting for some forbidden opportunity.

Peaches let her purse drop as she rose from her seat. The rest of Corporate Pointe appeared in slices through the horizontal blinds behind the desk. She stepped to the center of the room and transformed her expression to the one he was used to seeing at Appplebottoms. It was laced with sexual appeal and dripping with seduction. Without a pole she raised her slender arms above her head and twirled her body sensuously.

Max Strong leaned back in his chair and pushed a hidden button to dim the lights. What replaced the bright glow were a slow series of strobing red and blue lights. Peaches was illuminated in a soft glow as her body moved with the elegance of a feline.

Peaches pulled her gold frames from her eyes and let her flowing hair fall across her shoulders. Next the dress crumpled to her feet and she was naked save for a pair of pink lace HoodSweet boy-shorts and lace bra. She swayed her hips wide as she kneeled to the floor and up again, her body snakelike and inviting. She then pranced towards the desk and rolled her curvaceous figure in a complete circle, pleased at the glow emanating from Max Strong's face on her return.

"Absolutely beautiful," he hissed as he rose from the leather chair.

Peaches watched him with smiling eyes as he came round the desk and stood behind her.

His palms were warm on her hips as she moved like a rattler under his touch. She could feel him growing stiff against the top of her ass, his breathing rushing past her with growing excitement.

"Will you be my special friend?" he asked against her ear. Peaches recognized the fragrance he wore. Michael Kors. She'd wanted to get it for Dahji.

"What kind of special friend?" she wanted to know, placing her hands atop his as she moved against him, rubbing her ass over his stiffness. She was pleased with its growth; still, it was nothing compared to Dahji.

"Very special. Theatre plays. Movies. Dinner. Parks. Shopping." He mentioned this last as if it were a magic word.

"Well, I would be a fool to deny you as a special friend." She turned to look into his eyes, her arms around his neck. "But I doubt that either of us can afford the time."

He grinned a crooked slice of a smile. "When I mean special ... I mean situating you in a penthouse apartment and making sure that you don't have to lift a finger if you don't want to. That's what I mean by special." His tone had started with a note of desire, but ended with the surety of a man who was never denied and got what he wanted. Peaches' silver eyes stared long into this dark orbs, her hips swaying as if to a silent song, his touch gentle on her curvy hips.

What a steep climb this was, she thought to herself. She'd wanted love and thought she had it with Dahji; though she still was not prepared to give up on this. At the same time she did not want to throw this opportunity away. He said a penthouse. She envisioned open spaces and tall windows; this was a world away from her apartment where the kitchen sink still dripped and the security gate was nothing more than a slab of metal on a hinge.

"Tell me more about this penthouse," she gushed, moving her body into his and looking into his face.

His arms wrapped around her waist in sure possession. The shark had returned for a turn at the edge of the tank. Max Strong still had a crooked grin on his thin, wide lips. "Well, I'll let you decide where to set up house. How does that sound?"

"I've always dreamed of owning a small house with two lemon trees in the front yard."

"It's yours."

"Why?" she asked, her eyes turning serious.

"Because I can ... And you're the most beautiful woman in the world."

She wanted to mention his wife. And did he have children? Her body tingled with the promise in his eyes, but there was also a warning that signaled caution. She silenced this bell immediately with this question. "Will it be in my name?"

He nodded proudly at her thoroughness. "The house would be the property of Stone Distribution. Let's say ... After five years we can transfer the title to your name."

"And my part in this?"

"Just be beautiful. No pressure. Should you not like me any longer," he said lifting his hands from her waist in surrender, "We part ways. No harm. No foul."

This was business and Peaches could appreciate his candor. *Will this be my life ... A business arrangement?* she asked herself. "I love dancing," she informed him.

"And I love to watch. So, will you be my special friend and let me take care of you?" he asked, returning to his voice of desire.

"Only if you promise that you will always be nice to me," she replied.

"Scouts honor," he said, placing three fingers over his heart, happy to see her smile. "Allow me to show you my appreciation," he added, slowly backing her to the desk.

Peaches followed his gentle nudges and turned around. She looked back to him as he unclipped his gold cufflinks and unbuttoned his shirt.

"You have the most beautiful skin tone" he marveled, his eyes traveling over her body. His pants dropped around his ankles.

"You're not so bad yourself," Peaches replied at the sight of his flaccid organ dropping from his body. It jumped under her gaze, the pale head lifting like a sleepy child.

"But my most favorite is ..." He stepped to her and leaned her over the desk. With one motion he pulled the boy-shorts from her hips and down her legs. He inhaled strongly at the sight of her puffy pussy lips. Her ass cheeks met softly, covering the spot he wanted to get inside of. He rubbed a finger up the back of her leg, making her shudder as he passed the fat part of her knee, and up to her inner thigh. He creased her pussy lips and brought his finger to his lips. He smacked loudly after dipping her nectar to his tongue.

"Beautiful," he whispered behind her.

Peaches was exposed before him. She'd been bought and paid for and had only now begun to contemplate the price of this purchase. He'd said no harm, no foul. This was her veto card. No harm. No foul.

He gently spread her ass cheeks apart, the pink knot tight and clean before him. This was a thing of beauty. It was as he'd remembered in the dim light of Applebottoms. He licked his lips hungrily now that he had her to himself. He kneeled to her ass and inhaled. He rubbed his face across the soft mounds and moaned softly of how beautiful she was.

This is okay so far. Not a bad price; a little kinky, but not so bad, she thought to herself.

He dragged his tongue across her tender flesh and let it dip into her crease, dabbing at her tight center. Her ass cheeks flexed under the gentle licking. The bone magnifying glass fell to the carpet with his next tongue probe of her ass hole. Here he became energized, lapping at the soft hairs and licking at her hole. With long, hard strokes he dragged his tongue up her center while dipping his finger into her warm pussy.

"Mmmmm," Peaches moaned softly now. It was as if nothing else existed on her body except this concentration of nerve endings. She reached for some leverage on the stainless steel desk as he rubbed the pad of his thumb along the wetness rim of her hole while his tongue dipped into her tightness. The matching compass fell to the carpet, knocked over by her thrusting gasp.

"Magnificent," he hissed over her gleaming ass hole. The sensitive, pink knot breathed and pulsed with a short blow of breath. His thumb was snug between her ridged ring. He moved it in and out slowly while licking across her sensitive sounds.

Peaches was not prepared for the spreading of her ass and the slow shove of his penis into her. She winced under the saliva lubed entry. She could feel his hot breath on her back as he leaned to her. He shoved himself past her resistance and pumped eagerly, encouraged by her soft moans and straining fingertips. The shark had stopped in the tank and hovered to watch this primal act.

This is what his wife wouldn't let him do, Peaches knew for certain. She opened for him and allowed him a few strokes before squeezing shut again. The effect brought him to a quick orgasm. He jerked inside of her and gasped out her name as his slick chest fell to her back. He breathed heavily past her ear as he regained his composure, wilting and slipping from her ass hole with the tightening of her muscles.

She struggled to hold back her tears. There was this trap that she was constantly being forced into that only served to humiliate her. The salve for this lowness was the pursuit of a better situation; a situation that was meant to shield her from this degradation. No harm; no foul, he'd said. She was ready to call him on it if it meant that she would feel this way again. This feeling mixed with the other uncertainties in her life. Maybe this was not a good time to be accepting new responsibilities. Maybe she should be herself for awhile to help heal her soul from this constant self-inflicted pain. The reward seemed so far off and the struggle always so near and painfully raw.

CHAPTER TWENTY TWO

The Sports Medicine Clinic represented the beginning of it all for Dahji McBeth. This was the place where he met Marlin Cassidy and saw his opportunity to get his weight up. After their first conversation he knew that he had the connections to get Marlin a spot on the Indianapolis Colts football team. Up to this point he'd been slanging dick for bread. When he'd first approached Gloria about getting him an interview she'd put Dahji through his paces with some of her most dick-hungry friends.

He wasn't mad though. Some people had a wicked jump shot, while others slang crack rocks; he had a ten-inch dick with stamina to match. This was his blessing and his curse. A blessing in the fact that his organ was like a scholarship that paid the bills; a curse because it seemed to matter most of all to everyone else besides him. He had to admit to himself that sometimes he wanted to be with a woman and not be expected to lay pipe to her. This thought had resided in the back of his mind since the early morning, which was one of the reasons he did not want to sex Ebony. She was a rare woman in that she was nearly pure and innocent. But he knew that she would be ruined in L.A. and didn't want to be the first to put the pipe in her mouth and get her addicted; at least without making her a part of his team. Farewell dick that's free was bad for business.

Dahji finally found Marlin in the sauna. His muscular frame was slouched against the far wall, the result of an early morning of deep tissue massages and underwater leg work; all this after rehabilitation therapy that included limb stretches that no person should have to perform.

Dahji's heavy gold rope dangled above the thick cotton towel draped around his slim waist. "Marly Marl!" he called through the hot haze. He dapped the big man before taking a seat on the side wall.

"Waddup Dah?" Marlin barely looked in Dahji's direction, his eyes mere slits as he inhaled the eucalyptus mist.

"You. You. That's what's up. What I tell you in the begin Marly Marl? I told you that I was gon' get you a spot on the team and I was gon' be a bonafied super agent. Now, didn't this come out of my gold mouth?"

"That's what you said."

"Now if I say there's cheese on the moon ..." Dahji began, stopped by Marlin's sudden outburst of laughter. "What ... What's so funny? Share so I can laugh. I need laughter in my life."

Marlin was shaking his head, remembering his conversation with Sherrelle. She'd mocked this very phrase with her pretty face screwed up. There was no making her unpretty. "Nothin man. I was just ..." He waved the thought away. "Nothing."

"Nothing that funny, hunh? ... Well, try this nothing for size." Dahji leaned across the space between them and jabbed his finger through the hot mist. "You gon' be a professional football player Marly Marl!" He leaned back to let this sink in...

Marlin nodded. He wasn't skeptical. He was just being patient. He knew the little man with big hands, head, and feet would come through for him; at least he had the belief ... The hope that he would.

"My hair can't take too much of this Marly Marl," Dahji announced as he stepped down the ceramic seat. "Let's get in the Jacuzzi, he instructed, opening the door to the cool, chlorinated air. The Jacuzzi was a mere twenty steps along a tiled walkway. Further along was a shimmering blue lap pool. A pale, lithe woman languidly stroked across the water, feet kicking slowly.

"So, how's the HoodSweet thing going?" Marlin asked, falling in step beside Dahji on the cool tiles.

"I can show you better than I can tell you. Be at my spot in the morning and be a part of history." Dahji said this as he slid into the Jacuzzi. "Now this is more my speed," he hissed as the bubbling water licked at the diamond bezel clenched fist ornament weighing down his gold rope.

"Sherrelle said she supposed to slide through."

Dahji nodded. "It's gon' be live Marly Marl. History in the making."

"That's cool. So, what's up with Peaches? You ain't bin speaking on her lately." Marlin observed the uncertain expression cross Dahji's face.

"She's like ..." He snapped his wet fingers. "She's like a ... She's fine as cat hair ..." He searched for the words to describe the enigma of her total being.

"She's a woman with issues and you thought they would just go away like Casper the ghost," Marlin suggested.

"Usually I can see straight through to it, but she got something that held me tight," Dahji confessed, his fist grabbing at his imaginary heart.

Marlin leaned back on the rim of the Jacuzzi. He knew exactly what Dahji was talking about. Sherrelle had invaded his thoughts and his dreams. She was like the something that he wasn't supposed to have, but knew that it was going to be good for him. She was no longer appearing at his window in the early mornings. Stacy had put a stop to that with her vigilante watch over the window covering.

"Your neighbor ... Now, she's official," Dahji said as if reading his mind. The bubbling water had relaxed him so that he peered beneath lowered eyelids across the frothy water to Marlin, his arms flanked above the tiled rim.

"I figured as much."

"She really cares about you. But it's always that way ain't it? The one we want ain't the one we with."

Marlin nodded in agreement, his body fatigued and relaxed.

"Marly Marl," Dahji began in a lazy drawl. "I envy you sometimes."

"I don't see why."

"You got the kind of loyalty that I need. Me ... When I get bored with a woman or she's run her course ... She gets rotated like worn tires. But not you Marly Marl ... You gon' ride until you catch a flat in the desert in two hundred degree heat with no water or air conditioner."

Marlin grinned without opening his eyes.

"You got a fresh tire in the trunk. Is it true or ain't it true that wifey got a girlfriend."

Marlin opened his eyes then. He'd spoken about Stacy spending more time at the office; and he'd admitted, at Dahji's prompting, that her boss was a woman. He'd also spoke on his father-in-law's uncanny ability to notice the way Stacy had taken on the smell and gestures of a white woman. But he'd never suggested to Dahji that Stacy was having a lesbian affair.

"When you in people management like I am, you get to feel these things," Dahji added.

"You mean like how you figured Peaches out."

Dahji waved this off. "That's different. All lawyers gotta get they pro-bono work in. It's good for the soul. But don't sleep on her. She's a bonafied star. Just gotta get that sea dirt off her shoulders because it's weighing her down. But back to you ..."

"Don't trip on me, Dah. You get me on the squad and I'll handle the rest."

Dahji jabbed his arm into the air, flinging water towards Marlin. "Good point Marly Marl. As a matter of fact I have an appointment in a few to address just that." He smiled triumphantly with this announcement as Marlin gave him lazy thumbs up. But first thing was to chill right here and get the mojo right, Dahji thought to himself as the frothy bubbles caught his attention with their incessant rumbling.

Thoughts of May Ling visited his mind. He wondered what it was she had to offer. This would be a new experience. He'd heard once that Asians had slanted love boxes, but a quick perusal of an Asian adult magazine had dispelled this notion. One thing he did like was that they were so tiny. He doubted that May Ling could take his full ten inches, but it was going to be a pleasure to see if she could. Maybe she didn't want sex. Maybe she had some other eastern way of making love to him without taking her clothes off. This was intriguing. Maybe all she wanted to do was talk. Maybe.

Whatever she wanted to do it was going to get done if it meant that Marlin would be on the roster.

That Gloria is a shrewd pro, he thought to himself as he let a fart loose in the Jacuzzi. Marlin opened his eyes slightly in that instant. Dahji grinned, wondering if he could feel the vibrations from the other side of the bubbling water.

***

Strawberry cheesecake. Blueberry cheesecake. Cherry cheesecake. Lemon cheesecake. It was so hard to decide. They all looked delicious. And the celebratory Dom Perignon was not making the process of choosing any easier.

Sherrelle and Peaches were presented with no less than four different cheesecakes to choose from. The waitresses were becoming impatient, though their smiles remained professionally intact.

"Well, I'ma take the strawberry cheesecake," Peaches announced. "You get the cherry and we'll switch and get real fat," she added with a gleam in her eyes. She'd arrived later after having to go home and bathe. The water was becoming less useful in shedding the feeling of worthlessness that washed over her with her sexual escapades. There was a time when she felt nothing after trading on her body; now it seemed that her conscience was her constant companion. There was a voice calling her to a better situation, shaming her when she used her body to get there. "There is no other way," she'd said aloud on her way home from Max Strong's office.

"Okay. Give me the cherry," Sherrelle agreed. She looked to Peaches then. "If I get fat it's your fault. And you're going to the gym with me."

"You gon' be more worried about Percy leaving your fat ass. Besides, the gym makes me sweat."

Sherrelle brightened with an idea. "I'm going on a cheesecake diet. Give me two more!" she yelled to the backs of the retreating waitresses. Peaches joined in her soft laughter.

"Then you can claim your real man. That skinny bitch ain't gon' put up a fight," Peaches observed, the champagne fluke held over the strawberry cheesecake. "Marlin won't care if you're a fat whale. That's real love."

"I think she knows I've been peeking in their window," Sherrelle replied soberly. "And I miss seeing him."

"You are such a pervert. That should let you know right there that she can't fade you. A real bitch woulda stomped on your front porch and called you out," Peaches said, her neck rolling.

"I ain't thinking about her." With this Sherrelle looked across the blue water. They were seated over the Marina. On the bay were small boats, their bright sails blowing in the noon breeze.

"Is love a business?" Peaches wanted to know. The question made Sherrelle look back to her slowly. She'd been thinking of Marlin and threatened to indulge in one of her sexual fantasies. Marlin had taken her out on a boat and she already knew that she wanted to make love in the middle of the bay. They would be in view of any suspecting patron seated on this very patio. This was a thrilling thought.

"What ... Is love a business?" she asked, turning to Peaches with a remnant of the warmth her fantasy created ebbing between her legs.

Peaches nodded. "Yeah. Is it a trade-off like in business?" she asked. There was no mistaking the seriousness of her question.

Sherrelle gave this some thought, her lips pressing to the side so that a deep dimple formed in her cheek. She lifted the clear plastic cover from the cheesecake and dipped her finger into the sweet cherry confection.

"Don't get me started on what love is," Sherrelle suggested before dipping her cream topped finger into her mouth.

"Seriously though ... Think about it. You with Percy ..."

"I love Percy," Sherrelle cut in.

"NO, you LEARNED to love Percy. I was there so I know. Your first requirements were that he have a good job and was decent with no drugs."

Sherrelle nodded as she broke off a small piece of cake with her fingers.

"You didn't even care that he had a little dick. Remember that conversation?"

"Uhm Mmmm." Sherrelle agreed.

"Now, tell me ... Is that business?"

Sherrelle looked to her friend soberly. She hated to be called out in this way. Her love for Percy was real and she didn't like the way it had been diluted with the obvious. She'd had a hard enough time dealing with this reality when it had finally occurred to her.

"So, today when I was at the distribution company," Peaches began, stopping to avert her gaze to the strawberry cheesecake. She didn't want Sherrelle to see the tears which threatened to spill over. "Max Strong offered to let me live in a house if I became his mistress. And it just made me think of how here he is married and he wants to set me up so he can freak ..." Her voice trailed off as she bowed her head and shook away her tears.

Sherrelle was silent across the table. Her friend was in rare emotional form and this frightened her a bit. She'd never seen Peaches so raw and exposed to what Sherrelle felt should have no effect on her friend's tough will. Apparently, with the combination of all that she was going through, life was becoming heavier on her shoulders.

"I don't know ..." Peaches said before slowly slipping a piece of cheesecake into her mouth. "I miss Dahji." Her voice was small as she confessed this.

"Why haven't you called him?"

Peaches looked out to the water. *It was business,* she thought to herself. "Why do I have to chase him? ..." She looked to Sherrelle with her question, her eyes wet and imploring. "It's just bullshit," she added with a quick shake of her head.

"Don't go there, girlfriend. You act like you don't know what type of person he is. Your problem is that you got sprung on the dick and now you want love. You shoulda never gave him the pussy if you wanted love."

A slow tear escaped from her eye. It trailed to the corner of her mouth as she stared at Sherrelle. This was a hard truth. She breathed in heavily and deflated with the exhale.

"We'll see him tomorrow. Just step to him and tell him how you feel. I guarantee he still cares for you."

Peaches smiled in stages at this advice. "So, now you're giving me man advice, hunh?"

Sherrelle reached across the table and waited for Peaches to lay her hand in her open palm. "It ain't as big as you're making it. You got a lot of stuff going on right now, so just step back and stop putting everything in one bucket like they are all related." Sherrelle's voice was low and sincere.

"But ain't it all related ... Don't it all got to do with me being raggedy with my shit?" she asked, unafraid to let her tears drop now.

Sherrelle squeezed her hand. "No. Your shit ain't raggedy. You got good love for bad men. That ain't got nothin to do with you."

"Maybe you're right," Peaches began as she reclaimed her hand. "Maybe I oughta just chill for a minute. I got enough money saved up until the clothing line takes off, right?"

Sherrelle nodded her agreement.

"Just stop dancing and ..."

"And do not let Max Strong keep you as a concubine. We will both be in a position to buy our own houses in a minute, right next door to each other."

Peaches grinned with this vision. She let out a quick breath and cleared the air before her with a wave of her hands before wiping the tears from her face. "So, that's it. I'm going to take a step back and get myself together. And if Dahji feeling me like that ... Then ..."

"Just let him know that for right now it's best that y'all keep it professional," Sherrelle inserted.

The sense of this was filling Peaches with a new calm. She could see the benefit of her friend's suggestion.

"Is Bo still calling you for Tequan's money?" Sherrelle wanted to know.

"Hell yeah. I don't even answer the phone. But you know what ... I might just pay them that little change to get them outta my life."

"I ain't even gon' say how I told you to do that already."

"I know. Blame my hard head on my crack momma." Peaches laughed with this indictment. She felt light and airy as this pronouncement seemed to tie the bow on her immediate future, freeing her from some dark blanket cast over her life. Suddenly the sun felt good and the light breeze was a welcomed feeling. The cheesecake melted on her tongue and it was absolutely delicious.

"My niece has been creeping next door," Sherrelle said into the silence. Peaches was nodding her head with a knowing air.

"I can see the future," Peaches commented, pointing her fork across the table to Sherrelle. "She's going to end up in a strip club ... If she ain't already bin in one."

"She's only eighteen!"

"So was I," Peaches replied. "But who am I to talk. She might be smarter than me. Besides, she has you to look after her," she added with an innocent grin as she reached for her champagne.

"You should have seen her face when I showed her the college brochures. She tried to play it off, but I know she thought she was just going to come out here and be free to do whatever."

"That'll be good for her. Why didn't you bring her with you today? Show her around," Peaches said.

"She wasn't ready. Plus, I had some business to handle and let her tell it she'd rather watch Lifetime ... But all that's going to end when she starts school."

"Are you going to let her come to Dahji's house tomorrow? She might be good as a model."

"I was thinking about it, but haven't made up my mind yet. Dahji might be a bad influence on her." Sherrelle said this last with a bit of humor, noting the amused smirk on her friend's face.

"Girl, you tripping. You better put that heffa in front of the camera."

Sherrelle had already made up her mind about allowing Ayana to pose in lingerie and have her image blasted on the web. This wasn't something she wanted to promote with her eighteen-year-old niece. She was thinking of how to relay this to Peaches when she saw her neighbor walk onto the patio swaying softly against a white woman in a tailored business suit. They laughed gaily together at some private joke.

"Is that my neighbor?" Sherrelle asked in a low voice, her attention focused across the patio. Peaches had to nearly turn fully around in her seat to see Stacy being seated at a table along with a tall brunette.

"Stacy?" Peaches asked to no one in particular.

"That's her boss, I bet. Marlin said she's spending a lot of time at the office." This was said as an innuendo, causing Peaches to turn her way to get the rest of the message written across Sherrelle's face.

"Look!" Sherrelle whispered. Peaches turned around just in time to see the white woman lean away from Stacy.

"Did they kiss?" she wanted to know, turning back to Sherrelle.

"Yeah," she answered her breathlessly. "And look ... They're holding hands across the table ... Look at the way they're looking into each other's eyes.

"That's how I look at you," Peaches joked with a quick look away from the public display of affection.

"Damn ... I would have never guessed," Sherrelle said in awe as Stacy smiled and grinned like an enamored pupil; Rebecca reached to a stray lope of hair and curled it behind Stacy's ear.

Peaches turned to Sherrelle, her face bright with excitement. "I'ma tell Marlin," she gushed. "That way he can leave her stank ass and then you can swoop in!" Peaches illustrated this plan with a slice of her hand through the air.

"Stay out of their business. I'm sure he knows already," Sherrelle insisted.

"He told you that?!"

"That ain't none of our business!" Sherrelle said protectively. Peaches leaned back in her seat and observed her friend with a cool gaze.

"So, that's how it's gon' be?" she asked finally. "You finna hold back on your girl?"

Sherrelle was suddenly interested in stabbing another piece of cheesecake onto her fork. She did not want to engage in this conversation. She felt that this was personal in some way.

When she looked up she pretended not to see the way Stacy rubbed her hand down the arm of the white woman. All this time Marlin worked hard to be faithful to his wife, and here she was with another woman. Sherrelle felt her heart break for him. It wasn't a simple matter of claiming him for herself. He obviously loved his wife. And Sherrelle loved him for his faithfulness. With the void in her own marriage she could appreciate the way he tried to uphold his vows.

No. She wasn't happy at all. Maybe she should have been. She was sad and mad at the same time. Sad for Marlin and mad because she knew that Marlin was a good husband. The world had conspired to give them both spouses that deserved each other. This thought made her smile, imagining Percy with Stacy.

"Are we laughing with ourselves now?" Peaches asked with wide eyes.

Sherrelle only laughed more. Louder this time. Everything about this scene was funny all of a sudden. The tears fell down her cheeks for more than this very day. They'd been at the back of her eyes for the past week. Only now did they have the courage to spring forth. They were probably tears of pain when they first formed, but now they were tears of irony. An ironic joy. She didn't mind that Peaches probably thought she was losing her mind. Maybe that is what it took; to lose your mind and get a new and better one. If this was the case she hoped never to find the old one.

CHAPTER TWENTY THREE

Tupac was encouraging women to keep their heads up as Dahji coached the Range Rover down quiet streets with tall trees. The beat knocked and he bobbed his head as he looked up an occasional driveway to see what kind of car was parked behind the black wrought-iron fences. He passed a thin white woman, her muscular legs pale and straining, thinking how amusing it would be if she could hear what he was listening to. She had an iPod strapped to her bare arm. He could not imagine what it was she might have been listening to; maybe Clint Black; or maybe she was listening to Norah Jones.

As Dahji passed by the stately mansions and the occasional dog-walker, he thought of how close he was to living in a neighborhood like this. This was the kind of neighborhood where people did not hang out or congregate on the corners. This neighborhood was one where the police responded within seconds; and if you got hurt then you were sure to be taken to the best hospital. It would automatically be assumed that you were someone important and required the most urgent care.

Cherokee Lane. This was the street May Ling said that he should make a right on off of Daniels Road. He waited until the gleaming royal blue Rolls passed from the opposite direction before he made his turn. The distinguished looking, silver-haired white man sat perfectly erect behind the wheel. Dahji had the thought that this was where white folk differed from black people. Though white people were filthy rich, they did not wear flashy jewelry or get tattoos and fancy clothes to advertise their wealth. Here it was, this man was anonymous. He was unrecognizable behind the wheel of his Rolls Royce and he probably had more money than those rappers who professed to be paid. Dahji chuckled, thinking of a recent article he'd read where a young rapper went out and bought ten Dodge Chargers. Stupid.

These thoughts invariably turned on himself. How far could he actually get with a perm and gold teeth? Sure, his persona had served him well, but riding in this neighborhood gave him a look to his future. How much respect could he command as a sports agent when he looked like an Oakland pimp? Maybe his father was right. Maybe he should cut his hair and invest in a few finely tailored conservative suits that spoke of business. Shit, when Marlin make the roster then ...

39 Cherokee Lane. Here it was in a quiet cul-de-sac. Before him was a high, black fence that made the small white booth off to the left seem vulnerable. Through the fence all that was visible was a large wooden structure that resembled a gazebo. It was draped in colorful foliage and surrounded by green grass.

Dahji pulled to a stop beside the small wooden booth. The pink-faced, obese white man that leaned from the stool looked constipated. The 9.mm Glock attached to his side was made to look like a toy against his bulk. His eyes were gray slits and his lips were nothing more than two lines pressed together. The blue security guard suit fit him snugly, highlighting the rolls of fat bulging over his waistline.

"How can I help you?" he asked, his tone inferring that maybe Dahji made a wrong turn.

"Dahji McBeth for Ms. May Ling."

Fat boy stared into Dahji's brown eyes as if to ask where he'd heard the name from. Maybe this was some ruse to get into the complex and commit a crime. Maybe the Range Rover was stolen. Maybe the diamond bezeled Rolex was a fake. And the large diamond earrings had to be fake. Niggers.

"Yeah. Right." He nodded before shifting his bulk back onto the stool and lifting a phone. It was a small toy inside of his bear-sized palm.

Dahji flipped the CD changer and found Biggie Smalls. He rapped about playing monopoly with real cash. The beat knocked as Diddy flew across the country racking up frequent flyer miles. Biggie was letting you know that he made the best CD's and the best tapes. He had rocks in his beard and mustache. He couldn't understand why niggas looked at him the way they did. He hated them too and wished he was in the Caribbean sands with Rachel.

Dahji was feeling this. The groove moved through him like kool-aid; sweet and feeling good for the soul. They were buying homes in familiar places. Yeah, that was it right there. *I love the dough more than you know. Gotta let it show,* Dahji sang as his head bobbed.

Suddenly the high, black iron gate swung open. Dahji looked to the fat white man. "Last house to the left on the second street," he instructed with a renewed sense of qualified respect.

"Good man. Give to the Salvation Army," Dahji responded before leaving the man to ponder the riddle.

He was not surprised that the beautiful May Ling lived in a gated community. Each mini-mansion had its own architectural character. It was nearly easy to tell which houses were those of pro athletes and corporate types; the former had the obligatory whip on 20"+ chrome discs in the driveway; while the latter homes were more conservative with an Audi or stock Lexus in the driveway. *It's a habit to floss,* Diddy rapped as Dahji made the left on the second street.

He expected something special, but not the house that stood facing him at the end of the street. In the driveway was parked a champagne-colored Range Rover next to a white Lincoln Mark VIII. The house itself was long and flat, its window covered with bamboo shutters. In the center of the lawn was a black jockey, its large pink lips smiling and his huge white eyes bulging with excitement. *What the hell type of shit is this?* Dahji asked himself as he pulled into the long driveway and parked behind the Range Rover.

Dahji drank a vial of ginseng and made one final check of his hair, nails, and breath before stepping onto the graveled driveway. Because he was looking at the smiling jockey on the lawn he didn't see May Ling in the arched doorway. She smiled to him as he climbed the short stairway slowly. Her lithe body was sheathed in a shining burgundy kimono, the dragon tail laying over her shoulder and ending in gold brilliance at the spot where her breast should have been. Even in this sheer gown there was no evidence of her womanhood; the small protrusions bending the fabric at her hips and chest were hardly proof that she was a full-grown woman. If not for her womanly gaze he could have easily mistaken her for a teenager.

"You have good taste in automobiles," she said as he stood before her. Her eyes twinkled before settling on him. She seemed to be calculating some hidden desire she wanted to pursue.

Dahji grinned, suspecting that his choice of automobile hardly meant anything to her; not for the way her eyes had settled briefly on his zipper. "You've got a secret?" he asked for no other reason than to see her give her answer some thought. Whether or not she decided to answer the question meant nothing to him.

"Sure, why don't you come inside and I'll share it with you," she replied with a slight bounce on her bare toes. The carpet beneath her was a full six inches thick and cocaine white. Dahji felt that he was walking in sand and was happy to take the blue Waller B's off that Ebony had suggested he wear.

To the right of the carpeted foyer was a small alcove with several shoe racks stocked with an assortment of intricately designed heels and silk loafers. He let the suede Waller B's drop to the floor, noting the rainbow colored array of silk kimonos that hung against the rear wall of the alcove.

"Tea?" May Ling asked as she turned from him with a crooked finger gesturing him to follow.

The foyer opened onto an open space separated by brightly decorated bamboo dividers; the dragons and serpents crawled over the teaked wood as if they were alive. The outside design of the house gave no indication of the space or originality of the inside. On the walls were large tapestries of Chinese characters stroked boldly in bright red ink. A life-size mural of Buddha stood above the fireplace along the opposite wall of Chinese characters. Between these two distinct points of orientation were low pillows and padded couches that rose no more than four feet from the carpet. In the circle of large pillows surrounding a ceramic bowl atop a low table were transparent tubes extending from its swollen belly.

May Ling kneeled to a low end table and poured him a cup of warm tea. The seductive aroma filled the room of colorful flowers and bold script designs. She smiled to him with mischief before sliding back towards the foyer and disappearing behind a tall red silk divider with bright blue Chinese characters stabbed across the shiny material.

Dahji was left alone to peruse the large, partitioned space. Between large gaps of dividers he could see to the rest of the house. Solid walls were absent. The rest of the home seemed to be dedicated to less leisurely activity. He caught sight of a transparent blue laptop sitting on the carpeted floor before a low stack of pillows further into what he thought should be a den. He peered to the black cotton-looking substance in the center of the ceramic bowl which served as a center piece to this lounge area. If it was marijuana then it was unlike any he'd seen before. There were glistening crystals winking throughout the mash of blackness. He leaned over to get a whiff of its flavor. Minty.

Light streamed in through high windows, adding to the already mystic feel of this space.

"It's meditative," May Ling whispered as she stepped back into the room carrying a silver tray, carefully balancing the ceramic flower pot and small tea cups. She nodded when Dahji pointed to the contraption with opaque tubes shooting from its fat middle.

"Some type of drug?" he asked, taking the proffered cup from her fingers.

"Hardly. It's an eastern plant the elders use for relaxation." Her response came as she sat the tea tray on a low pillow and poured herself a warm stream of amber-colored elixir. "And this is an aphrodisiac," she added, folding her legs beneath her.

Dahji nodded before he took a sip. He could feel the smooth liquid coursing through his body. It seemed to reach his finger tips and toes, making them flare with feeling. "Don't tell me ... This is some eastern medicine for having children," he joked as he attempted to sit low on the cushions.

"Your visit here will be much more comfortable if you change into one of the dressings in the closet there," she advised, pointing a lazy finger towards the alcove.

This might be a good idea, Dahji thought to himself as he took another sip of the tangy sweet tea.

"Grab the blue one with gold trim. That suits you splendidly," May Ling suggested as Dahji set the half empty cup on the silver tray.

This is a serious chick, he thought to himself as he sank into the thick carpet on his way to the alcove closet. He debated whether he should shed his underwear as he grabbed the preferred kimono from a shelf. *Is she wearing underwear?* he wondered. The only way either one of them could be sure about the other was if they allowed a peek.

"Feels better, right?" May Ling asked after he'd stepped back into her orbit. She'd lit the black mash of what she referred to as medicinal potion. The thick smoke curled between them and reached the ceiling dispersing against the multi-colored chandelier hanging over their heads.

"This is something I could get used to," he replied as he folded his legs under him. May Ling twirled the plastic cylinder between her dainty finger tips and gestured for him to grab the one nearest him.

"Please, join me," she urged him.

"I'm already crazy and don't need more help."

May Ling smiled generously as if scalding a small child. "This will not make you crazy. It is nothing more than an ancient tribal ritual. The herbs are very natural and healthy for you."

Dahji watched as she proceeded without him, her eyes closing to the smoke that entered her lungs. He could not help but to think had he not seen her in person, and her voice was his only indication of who she was. He would think she was a white woman from London. She smiled to him as wisps of smoke escaped her small nose.

"Oh don't be a wanker," she complained. This was the first time he glimpsed the aggressive adult in her. It struck him as the tip of what lay underneath her passive demeanor. She was obviously rich and cultured. To live his life drug free and then be turned out by a Chinese woman with a British accent seemed surreal. It would be just his luck if he found his way back to her house just to get some more of this stuff she assured him was harmless.

She grinned happily when he put the tube between his lips and sucked in the dank smoke. Its sweetness taste good on his tongue and floated into his skull. His lungs opened up and an involuntary smile spread his lips.

"Now, a sip of tea," she whispered as if he'd joined a secret club.

The tea coated his throat and amped the effect of the smoke swirling through his lungs. His body relaxed of its own volition, forcing him back onto the cushions.

"Feels good, right?" she asked from a far-off place.

Dahji held his grin tight. He felt powerful as he followed May Ling's lead and sucked on the tube again. This new inhalation was smoother, accentuating the feeling of being light. This lightness concentrated itself along the pendulum hanging between his legs.

"Gloria speaks very highly of you," May Ling began, staring with dark eyes through the wisps of smoke at him.

"Yeah. We go way back," he replied with what felt like a thick tongue.

"She's been very helpful for you. This Marlin Cassidy is a special friend of yours?"

"No doubt. He's a good friend."

"Good friends are rare and should be cherished," she said around the edge of the tube. She inhaled softly, allowing the smoke to escape through gaps at the corner of her mouth. "Gloria says that you have a magnificent sex drive."

All inhibition and ego was gone from Dahji. This was not a discussion to advance his agenda. He was merely the object of her questions. Who knew what his answers meant to her.

"No more rare than you," he replied just before taking another toke of the tribal herbs.

"That's special." She eyed him with a wicked grin. The herbs and tea had taken their effect on Dahji. He was completely relaxed. "How long would you say it is?" she asked.

Dahji looked towards the red silk divider near the foyer. The gold dragon seemed to change positions, its wings spreading across the fabric. He looked back to May Ling to match her expression against the strangeness of what he'd just witnessed. He cocked his head to the side and peered to the tube he held between his fingers. *This is some powerful shit,* he thought to himself while her question ebbed in his thoughts. He slowly opened the kimono to show her the snake coiled between his legs.

"Gloria says that you can get Marlin a spot on the roster," he said, letting the slick satin fall over his joint.

"This is true."

"How high are you placed in the organization?" he wanted to know.

"Will you be acting as his agent?" she replied. Dahji nodded in the affirmative. "My family owns a majority stake," she admitted.

"A majority stake," Dahji repeated more for his own ears. The words slid through his ears like syrup. Every fiber of his body was alive to motion and sound. May Ling's slow head nod was followed by a colorful, shuddering shadow. He thought back to his lunch date with Gloria. He knew that there was some purpose for May Ling being present. It had been an interview. And now he was in her home. He was close. He could feel it.

May Ling slid from her pillow and moved across the thick carpet with a languid motion. Along the way her kimono moved to expose a creamy white shoulder. She was next to him now, her body feeling like so much energy. He wanted to reach out and grab her; to contain the colors shooting from her pores.

"Mind if I see it again?" she asked with fascination. When Dahji opened the satin up she reached for the heavy organ that lay between his legs. She placed her fingers under the bulbous head and lifted it into the air as if it were a delicate flower. She curled her fingers so that he rose and fell over her light touch. "You are absolutely beautiful," she whispered in wonderment.

Dahji was used to this reaction, but her warm touch and innocent adulation made him jump in her soft grasp. Her eyes blazed with the sudden movement. She looked to his face and back to the thick meat still weighing down her fingers like a promise.

"Make it grow," she said as he lay in her palm.

"He needs motivation."

She looked to his eyes in amazement. "Does he have a name?" she asked. With her question he became aware of a string instrument being played lightly in the distance. He couldn't be sure if this was in his head or if she'd turned on music in her absence.

"Bartholomew," he answered.

May Ling smiled. "Bartholomew." She said it with a musical note on her tongue. "Perhaps he needs a little blow," she suggested before leaning close with pursed lips. She blew a gentle breath across the sensitive head as if removing an offending eye lash from an eye socket. His joint jerked under her attention, producing a generous wonderment in her eyes. She blew across the expanding head again, this time paying close attention to the way he stretched forth and grew heavy in her palm. She gripped him tightly and relaxed, marveling at the way his skin moved as if it were alive as a separate organ.

"What you want with that?" Dahji asked, leaning back on the pillows as his dick stood straight up. Her hand was small around the width of him.

In response May Ling leaned over him and kissed the midsection of his joint. She nibbled along the length of him like a cob of corn. When she reached the tip she sucked on him like a jaw-breaker. He was like some gigantic mystery to her. She could go around him and not reach all of his space. There was more to see and taste with each rotation. He strained long and thick in her palm. She stroked him lightly for effect. He only grew harder in her hand. She was amazed at the strength of this hardness. This commitment to hardness was foreign to her and completely captivated her senses. He was perfectly shaped; like a missile. The ridge around the head was lighter than the rest of him. Along the base was a thick, dark tube that pressed in with her touch.

She breathed out excitedly as she stood up before him. The kimono dropped to her feet, revealing her petite frame. Her breasts were nothing more than a low mound with a cherry nipple on top. Her hips rounded out with an abrupt slide back to her thighs. Her pussy was shaved, the small lips fit tightly to her body.

"I want to try it," she whispered excitedly before turning away from him. She lowered herself over the missile and planted her palms on his knees. When the swollen head met her warm center she exhaled softly. He fit snug at her opening. She rotated slowly over the knob, wetting him with her excitement.

Dahji looked down the length of his body at his rigged pole standing straight up, stopped only by her creamy ass. Her hair had been loosened so that it hung long and thick down her pale back. It reached to the middle of her ass, nearly burying the show before him behind a shiny curtain of black strands.

May Ling shuddered when she succeeded in allowing the fat head past her tight lips. She breathed out slowly and worked to allow more of him inside of her. She eased onto him slowly, taking his thickness carefully. She was stretched around him, her lips flipped outward.

"That's right," Dahji encouraged her as he held her small waist. She gasped as more of him slid inside of her. He was nearly halfway inside when it felt like he'd hit bottom. She rose up slowly and let herself down with ease, while finding a slow groove and gasping sweetly with every slide up and down. Her hands shook on his knees as if she were in a blistering snowstorm with wet clothes on. Dahji was sure that he would split her in half.

Suddenly she jumped from him and dashed to the floor and landed on all fours. Dahji raised himself up, his head spinning from the sudden movement. His organ stood straight out before him, leading the way to the creamy slice of pink flesh bending over for him. He nudged his head inside of her slowly, his knees sinking into the thick carpet.

"Let go," she moaned as her shoulders fell to the floor. Dahji was sure that she was fainting. *Not again,* he thought to himself.

Then she was up again, pulling herself away from him and dashing around a silk coated divider, her hair a long black sheet behind her. The dragons were alive and blowing fire as he gave chase. Around one divider and into a seeming fantasy world of white clouds and waiting serpents, he caught a glimpse of her as she turned another corner, her hair trailing after her in a long wave. She held her hands to her breasts, her laughter a guide for him to chase her naked through the house.

Past a velvet bar with sparkling crystal decanters and through a sliding glass door, he was suddenly in the waning sun. Darkness was just over the horizon and May Ling was stretched out on a wicker chair, her legs splayed open for him. Dahji slipped between her knees and sunk into her. She trashed about as he eased into her. She creamed over him quickly, bucking under him, providing the lubrication that allowed more of him inside of her. She reached up urgently and gripped his back, digging her nails into his muscle as she pulled him to her. He was barely aware that they were in some type of sunroom. Outside was a glimmering swimming pool and sloping lawn beyond this. The tall, leafy trees in the far distance appeared to be watching them as they groped hungrily for each other. They were at once in nature and alone, separated by the invisible glass partition, protected from the elements that might disrupt their business of communion. They were enthralled within the midst of hypnotic tangy sweet tea poured over a smoky intoxication of tribal herbs, their bodies moving over and into each other with intense heat and desire.

CHAPTER TWENTY FOUR

Fear. Anxiety. Betrayal. Worthlessness. Emptiness. Uncertainty. This last emotion was the most prevalent. He could not be sure what would happen next. He'd been told that Carrie was given a leave of absence for a family emergency. It was then that he realized he knew next to nothing about the woman he let whip him with a leather strap. It was strange that she'd all of a sudden had a family emergency. This was made more perplexing by the polite smiles he received throughout the office. No one seemed to be saying anything of any significance. It was as if they had discovered something about him that was both untrue and scandalous. He felt like he should be able to defend himself against the vicious rumor if only he knew what it was.

He could take the stony silence no more; the tedious accounting of numbers that didn't seem to add up; yet he could not find the error that would bring the disparate bottom lines into one accord. It was no use being in the office. His phone was not ringing and incoming calls were being routed to a less senior accountant. *Maybe they're trying to force me to resign,* he'd thought to himself. Maybe it was because it was time for him to be promoted and this was their way of getting around recognizing his brilliance. Yes, that was it. That had to be it! How else to explain the sudden change in fortune? He'd been the poster man for expediency and accurate accounting. He'd successfully erased the color of his skin through hard work and perfect diction. He prided himself on the effect people had when seeing him for the first time after having spoken with him on the phone. They tried to hide the fact that they'd assumed he was a white man.

This is why the pain ... The betrayal was so acute. He would show them. He would take an extended vacation on Monday. Let them miss his expertise. They would miss the way he double checked his numbers and exacted a maximum profit from all of their accounts. This talk of fraud was a ruse to cheat him of his true reward. It had to be. This bogus investigation would come to naught. It must, because he'd done nothing wrong.

These thoughts swam through his mind as he pulled into his driveway. A strong sense of anger shot through him because Sherrelle was apparently not at home. He was in no mood to be alone. *She probably took her niece to the strip club to sell clothes,* he thought to himself. His neighbors weren't at home either. He felt alone. He felt as if he were out of sync with the natural order of things. There was a time when everything seemed to fall into place with the least amount of effort. He was the most successful one of his family. He had a beautiful wife and owned his own home. He drove a BMW and his wife drove a Jaguar. He prided himself on the fact that his wife didn't have to work. He only pretended to dislike her exorbitant spending habits because she was most sexy when her pretty dark skin was flushed with the absurdity of his critique. This was their private foreplay.

Percy walked into the house as the sun began its descent from the sky behind him. The strong aroma of peach wafted through the air. It was a strong contrast against the loud, hard bass pounding through the house; Scarface was speaking on being the realest nigga alive and refused to leave the neighborhood because the youngsters needed to see a successful role model.

There was something familiar that moved inside of him. It was something that he'd only felt a few times in his life. One of them was when he'd seen Sherrelle for the first time. She was on the campus of the University of Arkansas. Her hair was long and thick, tied into a dark ponytail. Her campus sweater dropped long over her curvaceous figure. Her arms were laden with text books as she laughed gaily amongst her friends. Percy did not approach her this day, but he would always remember that feeling of being alive and lustful that she inspired in him. The other time he'd felt this way was when they'd finally married after a long courtship. She was a virgin and they were on their honeymoon in Hawaii. Her skin was tight and perfectly rounded. She had not a blemish, pimple, or scar on her entire single toned body.

He tried to shake this feeling from him because he realized that it had nothing to do with Sherrelle. This rap music was associated with Ayana and he vaguely remembered some transgression that he'd enjoyed. His lips tingled with the memory as he turned down the sound on the Pioneer sound system. It was then that he heard Ayana rapping along with Scarface and then suddenly stop when she noticed the sound had been reduced.

Ayana walked through the hallway archway holding a red cotton towel to her breasts. She was wet from a recent shower, her skin gleaming a soft light bronze. She smelled of the peach shower gel that filled the air. Her eyes were a dark brown absent the contact lenses and her face was scrubbed with no make-up. Her breasts bubbled over the rim of the towel, the cleavage dipping sharply and invitingly.

Percy's eyes scanned her wet body as she stood looking at him with a placid expression. He wanted to say something about her being surely naked under that towel, but his breath caught in his throat at the sight of her. It was as if she knew the silent power she exerted and he was tempted mightily to surrender.

"Where's Sherrelle?" he managed, taking a step in her direction. He stopped in mid stride when he realized that she had not moved from the space at the hallway entrance.

"She WAS at the Cheesecake Factory," Ayana answered in a way that said nothing about where she was at present.

"When was this?" he was forced to ask. The Halliburton briefcase felt heavy in his hand even though it was nearly empty. He'd had no need to transport any files because the ones left to him had no relevance.

"Oh, that was earlier." Her hand waved carelessly through the air as if she had trouble understanding that he wanted to speak in the present.

Percy stared at her wide eyed. "Do you know where she is now?" he asked with a note of frustration. This annoyance was not merely because it took far too much conversation to get a simple answer, but he was being tested by a woman who'd made him fail once already. *But this shouldn't count,* he insisted to himself because he was drunk. He could argue that she took advantage of him. Maybe Sherrelle would believe this about her. But this paled in comparison to the way she made him feel when she adjusted her towel. She nearly exposed one of her firm breasts. It happened as she answered his last question. She had her eyes on him so she was able to see how he shifted his gaze to the nipple that threatened to make an appearance.

"Why are you looking at me like that?" she asked suddenly, shaking him from his descent into sexual intoxication.

"Like what?"

"Like that ... Like you scared of something," she teased.

His eyes flashed with a mixture of disbelief and uncertainty. Was he afraid ... Of what?

Ayana pressed her lips together doubtfully as she looked him from toe to head. She was enjoying the way he stood on the verge of brushing by her in to the hallway. "Why you home so early anyway ... You get fired?" she asked, leaning on one hip. Her body shifted as she folded her arms under her breasts. *How could she just stand here this way?* he asked himself.

"No, I did not get fired."

"Then why are you home so early?"

"Excuse me ..." He smiled nervously as he looked to the ceiling and into the living room. "Last I checked this was MY house," he replied.

"For how long?"

"What?" Percy asked, leaning his chin in her direction. What was this she just said?

"Are you still cheating on my aunt?" Ayana asked slowly as she made a slow motion to adjust her towel. She'd pulled the tucked cloth from the side of her breast, exposing herself full frontal before re-wrapping herself snugly. The towel was lower on her breasts this time making them bulge dangerously close to spilling over.

Percy forced his gaze from her damp cleavage. There was amusement in her eyes. This young temptress had invaded his very being without so much as a second thought. "No," he answered shortly.

"Was she a white woman?"

Percy did not want to have this conversation, but he could not bring himself to move from this spot. He wanted to lay the briefcase down, but his now sweaty fingers were seemingly glued to the metal handle. Why would she assume that his infidelity was with a white woman ... And why did she have that silly grin on her face? *Sherrelle should be coming home shortly,* he was thinking to himself as Ayana shifted in a way that made her breasts change position over the towel. They seemed to have a life of their own. He had an overwhelming desire to bury his face between her soft mounds.

"Well, was she white?" she repeated a little more directly, losing some of the sex from her tongue.

"Yes ... If you must know. May I pass now?"

"I ain't stopping you from moving around in your own house," she replied with a roll of her neck.

Percy moved forward, but Ayana did not move. She shoved her breasts into his shoulder as he tried to go around her, the softness making him stop more than the force. He looked into her deep brown eyes and was caught in the message of their secret written across the surface of her glittering dark-brown orbs.

Ayana leaned in close, her full lips brushing against his ear as she whispered, "Did you enjoy yourself?"

Percy swallowed hard as she leaned back to look into his wary eyes. She smiled knowingly.

"I was ..." he stammered, already knowing that his drunkenness was no excuse.

"But you enjoyed it didn't you?" she asked quickly. "And you know you want me," she hissed as she pulled the knot loose and let the towel drop to the floor. She stood naked before him, her soft curves rounded at smooth turns along her lean body.

"This ain't right," he said with as much sincerity as he could muster. There was the small matter of overriding the rapid beat of his heart and the shallow breath that threatened to make him collapse at her feet.

"No. What ain't right is you cheating on my aunt with a white woman. What ain't right is you sleeping on the couch and coming home drunk." She'd stepped in front of him with her chastisement. Her nakedness did nothing to take the venom from her voice. "What ain't right is how you sucked my pussy and think that it's over between me and you." With this she'd reached down and grabbed what was left of his erection.

Percy was shaking his head. "No. No. No."

"Yes. Yes. Yes." Ayana's response worked to wear down what little resistance he'd gathered. She reached to the back of his head and pulled him into her breasts, burying his nose in her cleavage. "You know you want this," she whispered as he inhaled her fresh peach scent.

His hands seemed to move of their own will around her waist and rest on her ample ass. Her breasts pressed against the sides of his face like the space on a massage bench. He caressed her tight hips as he raised his head from her bosom and looked to her eyes with a hazy clarity.

"When are you going to get my Mustang?" she asked with a sex-laced tongue. She'd reached into his blazer and rubbed along his ribs, the soft cotton of his Hugo Boss shirt filling the space between their connection.

"Soon," he promised helplessly. He wanted to tell her aunt, his wife. He wanted to warn her that they would regret this secret passion. He wanted to say how wrong this was.

But he didn't. He let Ayana pull him by his tie to the living room couch. The Halliburton case dropped to the floor as he followed the slow sway of her naked ass. *This is very wrong and too close to home. This IS home! Sherrelle could walk in at any minute,* he thought to himself as he kneeled between her spread knees.

Ayana sat on the couch and opened her pussy for him. "Now do it right. You know you want it," she insisted with a bit of authority. Ayana's heart raced with the sheer madness of her actions. She couldn't help herself. The thrill was more than what she could resist.

The clean muff was open for him. The peach scent glistened on her pink flesh. He swallowed hard at the sweet meat before him. They could get caught! This made him as hard as penitentiary steel. Her thighs were soft and warm beneath his palms as he leaned in with his tongue extended.

Ayana's ass dug into the cushion as he licked at her center. She raised her hips so that he could get better access. Her head turned to the driveway for any sign of Sherrelle as Percy became more involved in his task. He'd loosened his tie and situated himself in a way so that he could drape her long legs over his shoulders.

Percy placed his hands high on her inner thighs and used his thumbs to peel her pink lips apart. She was open like an oyster to him; her pink and shiny, pearl nestled between soft folds. This is where he headed. He sucked on this softly before nibbling and licking to soothe. She writhed over him, her body weight shifting on his shoulders.

Ayana opened her eyes after a powerful shudder moved through her. All she could see was the top of Percy's head, but she could feel his tongue darting around her love box with attention to detail. She peered through the small opening in the sheer lace curtains. Marlin was pulling to a stop at the curb in front of his house. He was excited about something. He must have been getting good news because he had a cell phone to his ear. He pumped his fist into the air and then opened the door. Ayana jerked when he looked in her direction. The feeling that he might have seen her was mixed with the sudden sensation of Percy sucking on her swollen clitoris. But then Marlin reached back into the Escalade for a duffel bag. He sat in the driver's seat with his feet on the sidewalk.

Percy had his eyes closed. This way he could better feel the way her body convulsed and shuddered over him. He gently placed her pussy lips between his fingers and blew into her snatch. She eased away with this sensation and then jerked suddenly as if he'd bitten her. He then softly licked the rim of her pussy, tasting her thoroughly and enjoying her tight womb.

Ayana hiked her legs more securely onto his shoulders. She'd never had anyone pay so much attention to eating pussy before. He was not sucking her clit as a form of foreplay. This was the main event. He blew inside of her, making her flesh vibrate with the treble of his groaning. She lolled her head back to the street. Marlin was stepping from the truck. The way he was looking up the block, his body language changing to something familiar and exciting, made Ayana want to see what he saw. Sherrelle!

She was almost there. He could feel it in the way her legs tensed up over his shoulders. He stuck his tongue deep into her recess and probed her thoroughly before licking his way back out. He wanted to taste her cream. He wanted to feel her body convulse with abandon. He wanted to make her curl up into a fetal position. He wanted some respect!

Ayana briefly thought of telling Percy that Sherrelle had driven into the driveway, but he was so involved, and it felt so good, she decided to let him keep going. Besides this, she could feel herself opening to a climax. Her thrill was magnified by the fact that Sherrelle was just outside. She didn't look towards the house before she hugged Marlin! *She is being brash,* Ayana thought to herself. Sherrelle was congratulating him about something. Maybe he made the football team. That's cool.

"Ahhh!" Ayana gasped suddenly as a hot spasm shot through her pussy. She was almost there.

Almost, Percy thought to himself as he backed off his signature maneuver. He licked around her clitoris, enjoying the way her hips moved in a way like flower to sunlight. She wanted him directly on the swollen bulb, but this was the treat that would make her scream out his name. Her pubic hairs were wet and rubbing roughly against his face. Her juices coated his thin mustache and made his chin slick. Her inner thighs were hot and sticky against his face. He was between her ass as if bobbing for an orgasmic apple with no thought to how wet his head would become or if he drowned in the process.

Oh shit! Here comes Marlin's wife. She's home early, Ayana thought to herself. It was exciting watching how Sherrelle had to make space for this man's wife as she pulled into the driveway. Marlin stepped further towards Sherrelle so that Stacy could pass behind him into their driveway. Ayana's body was on fire. She could feel the heat concentrating itself into a tight ball between her hips. Her concentration was torn between this searing heat and the way Stacy smiled to Sherrelle. *There was a lot that was unsaid between them,* Ayana thought to herself. They were being so bourgeois. Stacy was making a demonstration by sidling up to Marlin and leaning up for a spousal peck on the lips. It was interesting to watch how Sherrelle braved this show of affection. *Stacy HAD to see how dry Marlin was acting. She HAD to sense that she was interrupting something,* Ayana thought to herself.

Percy was oblivious to what was going on above him. The thighs that began to quiver against his face motivated him to make this young girl crumple into a messy heap of creamy ecstasy. He was almost there when Ayana announced that Sherrelle was coming. WHAT??!!

"Here she comes!" she repeated with urgency as she lifted a long limb over his shoulder and was off the couch and running into her room before Percy could regain his balance. He was wiping his mouth in near disbelief as Sherrelle passed the window, stepping on to the front porch. Her silhouette was outsized with what he knew were shopping bags. He rolled his tongue across his teeth and tasted Ayana's sex on him. *Shit!* He suddenly bolted from the living room and was barely into the hallway by the time the front door opened.

***

Sherrelle's heart skipped with joy when she turned onto her street and saw Marlin emerging from his Escalade. This feeling quickly swept over her worry for Peaches. Their lunch date was an emotional roller coaster of doubt, fear, and determination. Sherrelle was emotionally drained by the time she'd convinced her best friend to go home and rest. She would see her tomorrow after she cleared that last obstacle in her life of drama; she must pay Bo that chump change that Tequan was sweating her about. Be rid of them tired niggas so you can get on with your life, she'd advised.

And here was the man who moved through her with the rush of a mighty river. She decided that she would not tell him of seeing his wife with another woman. This moment was not about to be ruined with drama that could be avoided. The truth would come to the light soon enough. Plus, she didn't want to be the one to confirm her adultery and have to beat the skinny bitch up in the middle of the street.

DAMN! He's so handsome, she thought to herself as she pulled in behind her husband's BMW. He was home early, she noticed; but even this did not matter. *He could be watching me from the front window,* she thought as she resisted taking a quick glance to the porch. She didn't care. He could fuss all he wanted to about her talking with their neighbor. She was nearly tired of defending herself and exhausting her energy and patience trying to keep their marriage intact.

"What's up homeboy?" she called as she opened the door. Marlin held a cell phone in one hand, dangling loosely at the side of his leg. The duffel bag hung heavy across his shoulder, the bulk of the bag itself nearly hidden behind him.

"Waddup homegirl," he responded, feeling like they were in a community park in the projects. The sexual tension between them was palpable. Even in the waning light her personality was as bright as the sun. He bubbled with the good news Dahji had just relayed to him. It made him that much happier to know that she would be genuinely ecstatic with his triumph.

"What's up?" she asked, stopping just before the slice of grass that separated their driveways. She looked to him with wonder at the brightness in his eyes. A grin teased at the corner of his wide mouth.

"Just finished talking to Dahji."

"And ..." Sherrelle leaned hopefully towards him.

"I made the squad," he informed her. She stared at him with her hand over her mouth.

"Really?"

"Yeah. Apparently Dahji just finished meeting with a minority owner of the team. He sealed the deal," he finished, not telling her that he would be at Dahji's house tomorrow morning to sign the final paperwork.

Sherrelle leaped across the grass and into his arms. "I'm so happy for you!" she whispered loudly against his shoulder. "How did he do it?" she asked as she stepped from his embrace.

Marlin shrugged. "You know Dahji ... How does he do anything?"

"I'm not surprised at anything. He could probably become mayor if he set his talents to it."

Marlin enjoyed seeing her smile. He wanted to touch her again, to feel her in his arms. Her warmth was still floating around him as a result of their brief embrace.

"Here comes the wife," Sherrelle said, looking to the street where a Lexus Coupe was making a turn into the driveway. Sherrelle returned Stacy's fake smile, thinking to how she was hugged up with a white woman earlier in the day. She was pleasantly aware of how Marlin had stepped further than necessary in her direction so that his wife could pull into the driveway behind him.

Marlin seemed to be pitched between two points. He wanted to greet his wife, but felt oddly attached to Sherrelle.

"She's dressed nice today," Sherrelle commented, sensing his slight discomfort. When he looked to her to gauge her sincerity she smiled to him with a wink.

"Hello, Sherrelle ... How are you?" Stacy called over the roof of the Lexus as she lifted a leather briefcase to her padded shoulder.

It was only then did Marlin take a step away from Sherrelle towards his wife as she rounded the back end of the car. Sherrelle felt some sense of loss with his minimal departure of only a step. The motion of his arm to accept her into his wing sent a jealous jolt through her. The smile on her face felt like hot plastic to see them kiss, no matter that it was a sterile peck on the lips. Sherrelle thought to herself that if Marlin was her husband she would kiss him fully and thoroughly at every reunion after any absence of more than half a day. *This is a cold marriage,* she noted with a light giddiness.

"How is Ayana?" Stacy wanted to know. "Apparently she's been spending time with my father," she added before Sherrelle could answer.

"Yeah, I heard," she replied, her eyes darting quickly to Marlin so that Stacy looked to him for some confirmation.

"You knew about this?" she asked.

It was apparent from his expression that he didn't want her to make a big deal about this, which she was so capable of doing. "Yeah. She made us some burgers."

"Oh, really?"

"You were working late," Marlin said with a mixture of some earlier resentment and hidden threat.

"It's okay isn't it?" Sherrelle asked. "I mean ... We all need someone to keep us company, right?" she added with a mischievous grin to Stacy. She'd locked her in some private communication that Stacy was afraid to bring into the open. Marlin stood patiently watching this subtle confrontation unfold. The last time he'd witnessed this type of jealousy was when he was playing college football. It was the same dynamic. There was this beautiful dark-skinned sophomore who tutored him. Stacy was s little more hood then and handled the situation better than she did now. She seemed timid and afraid of something Sherrelle hinted at.

Stacy blinked. "Yeah. Sure, I suppose so," she replied with a careful appraisal of her neighbor.

"That's what I thought," Sherrelle responded with a little more emotion than she'd intended. She could feel the surprised look of Marlin on her, but she had to keep her attention focused on Stacy, who'd bristled at what she'd said.

Sherrelle knew she was half wrong and half stunting for Marlin, but she couldn't help herself. She'd come this far and couldn't punk out now. A quick vision of her throwing Stacy to the ground and socking her in the face two or three times before Marlin could hoist her off flashed through her mind.

Stacy must have seen this same vision written in Sherrelle's stare because she softened, breaking into a small grin. She linked her arm into Marlin's with a show of possession, obviously recognizing her neighbor's stunt.

"Yeah," Stacy said with a light chuckle, "We get it the best way we can, Hunh?" she added as she peeled Marlin away.

Sherrelle smiled with a tap of her finger into the air. "You should know it better than me," she said to Stacy's back.

"It was great seeing you again. Have a nice evening," she responded, ignoring her husband's angry gaze.

Sherrelle turned to the designer bags in the trunk of her car. *Bitch*, she muttered to herself as she lifted the totes to her arms. *That's why your husband loves me*, she added as she slammed the trunk and strolled towards her front door.

Sherrelle was both excited and upset. Stacy had interrupted a special moment. She took solace in the fact that she was the first to hear Marlin's good news. Not even his wife could take that from her.

The house smelled of peach and a tangy spray of cologne. There was a hint of Ayana in the air as well. Scarface was rapping low through the living room. She was too absorbed in her thoughts to entertain the fact that no one was in the living room or appeared after she closed the door.

"Ayana," she called, dropping her bags to the sofa.

There was no answer.

"Percy?"

Still no answer. As she reached the hallway Percy emerged from the bathroom in a huff. His face drenched with water. He was making a special effort to smile. Sherrelle noted with some fatigue that he looked nervous. She didn't even want to question him about why he looked like he'd been doing something he wasn't supposed to be doing. Truthfully, she didn't care.

"Hey babe," Percy said, standing between her and Ayana's room. Sherrelle looked past him to Ayana's door.

"Where's Ayana?" she asked, wondering why the door was closed. "Is she sick? Has she eaten dinner?"

Percy looked behind him as if he'd never noticed there was a spare room in the house. "Oh ... Yeah, I guess so. I just got in a few minutes ago." He looked to her for her next move.

Sherrelle was already done with this strange conversation. "You have a good day?" she asked as she made a motion to move past him.

"Yeah ... Numbers ... Crazy numbers ..." he whispered nervously as he took a step back into the bathroom. It was almost as if he were afraid to let Sherrelle get too close to him. She looked to him oddly before opening Ayana's door.

Ayana was under the covers. She raised her head and opened her eyes as if a bright light was being shined into her face. "Hi auntie," she said in a sleepy voice. "You just getting home?"

"Yeah ... You okay?"

"I'm cramping," Ayana moaned out.

"You want some tea?"

Ayana cringed. "No .. That's okay. I'm just going to rest. Did everything go okay today? ... How's Peaches?"

Sherrelle looked back to Percy, who was watching her suspiciously at the door of the bathroom. "Yeah. Everything's okay," she replied, turning back to her niece. "Let me know if you need anything. I'll be in my room," she added before closing the door on Ayana's forced smile.

"She okay?" Percy wanted to know, looking to Sherrelle's face for any sign that he'd been found out.

"I guess so ..." She brushed past him, aware of his need to be in her presence. This was not going to happen. All she wanted to do was take a long shower and get in the bed with thoughts of Marlin. She'd sworn off masturbating. She hoped to have a dream that was just as rewarding. She closed the door on Percy as he walked slowly to the entrance of the hallway.

CHAPTER TWENTY FIVE

The smile left Stacy's face as soon as she stepped into her house. She was both nervous at Marlin's anger and suspicious at what Sherrelle mentioned. What did she know?

"Hey there," Grump called out from his seat. "That's going to be sunflower seeds," he added with his head cocked towards the plasma screen. He was no longer watching porn movies. Ayana had supplanted this with her presence. He was now watching Wheel Of Fortune.

"Hi daddy," Stacy said with a new sense of mock cheer as she leaned to kiss him on the cheek.

Grump pointed to the screen. "Watch," he insisted.

Stacy and Marlin stood side by side, their respective carry totes weighted on their shoulders, as they watched a conservatively dressed blonde woman solve the puzzle.

"See what I say? Eezy peezy lemon squeezy," Grump sang out, his head rowing from side to side.

"That's great dad. Are you hungry?"

"Should Barack Obama be our President?" he responded.

"I'll take that as a yes then. How about some chicken tacos?" Stacy asked as she passed by him on her way to her room.

"And negroes had the nerve to say that Bill Clinton was the first black President. Kill me please when I get that desperate that I made a white man black. You ask me ... He ain't never done nothing for blacks. And the way he ... I have to give it to slick willy though ..." Grump wagged a long finger into the air. "He was one slick crook and loved him some white women. We oughta be a shame to say he was our black President. Can't dance or nothing ... I ain't even see him eat fried chicken ... Have you? ..."

Marlin closed the door on his father-in-law's tirade. He watched Stacy drop her briefcase to the bed, wondering if she was going to voluntarily explain herself.

"How was your day?" she asked as she began to unbutton her blouse. She looked to him as if what had just happened between her and Sherrelle was in fact a dream long past forgotten.

"What was that about?" he asked, not moving from his spot. He followed her with his eyes as she removed her earrings by the mirrored dresser.

"What's that?" she replied with raised eyebrows.

"You know what I'm talking about. Don't play stupid."

"Stupid? You mean with the neighbor who likes to peak in our windows?" she asked.

"There was no need to be rude to her."

Stacy narrowed her eyes. "Am I missing something here? ... You feeling her in some kind of way?"

"This ain't about me. This is about you and the way you've been bouncing around here like you got your nose in the air."

She laughed nervously. "Me ... My nose in the air? ... Sure Marlin. Go ahead. Criticize the fact that I work hard everyday just so you can go to practice and make a football team ..." There it was. She'd let her true feelings expose themselves.

"You don't think I can do it, hunh?" he asked, withholding his recent accomplishment. "Or maybe you really like the fact that you got me for right now." This last had long been his suspicion.

Stacy grinned wickedly as she walked into the bathroom, waving her finger at him. "Maybe you should focus on something else ..." She looked to Marlin in the mirror as he appeared at the bathroom door. "Do you really think that a fake pimp can get you on a professional football team?" Oh, she was feeling herself. Maybe she thought this would pierce the audacity he showed to bring the untended feeling of the shift in power to the light.

Marlin still did not want to tell her that he made the team. He stood watching her for a few beats, finally deciding that it was over for them, before he threw the bomb into the air. "See your boss today?"

The look that this question forced from her told him that Dahji's suspicions were correct. A shadow of recognition passed over Stacy's face. He could see her searching for some way to respond that was equally revealing.

"Of course ..." she answered directly, peeling her stockings from her legs. "Rebecca's my boss so I have to see her."

"Do you have to fuck her, too? ... I mean ..." he began, making a casual gesture as he leaned against the doorframe. "All you had to say was that you wanted to bring somebody into our relationship and ..."

"And what Marlin?" Stacy jerked, her arm flailing towards him. "You mean like how you should have told me that you dream about Sherrelle every night? ...Oh, you thought I didn't hear you whispering her name in the middle of the night ... And you pretended to know nothing about her peeking through our window. I was a fool to think that maybe I could be enough for you since I was the one taking care of you!" Her chest heaved with emotion when she ended her demonstrative tirade. She refused to wipe the tears from her hot face.

That's it, Marlin thought to himself. There was nothing more to say. He peeled slowly from the doorframe. "I made the team," he called over his shoulder before closing the bedroom door behind him. He ignored Stacy as she called his name, asking what he meant by, "I made the team." How? She wanted to know.

Stacy wasn't ready for him to leave. She regret everything that spilled from her lips. She wanted to talk to him about what he'd just said. She wanted to hear his response to what she said. Maybe he would deny it and she could believe him and they could go back to the way things were. They could be a football couple again and he would love having her as a wife.

Marlin knew all that he cared to know and didn't want to hear any more. He didn't want to hear her apologize. He couldn't deny that he'd dreamed of Sherrelle nearly every night since he'd first seen her. Finally, it was all in the open and he felt good about this.

Stacy couldn't bring herself to open the door and follow him into the living room. Her heart was breaking into a million pieces. The aching started from the center of her heart and radiated outwards, paralyzing her as she stood at the bedroom door. First her knees felt weak, and then it was her arms that could no longer support themselves. She crumpled to the hardwood floor as she wailed in grief. Suddenly there was a flood of tears and snot dribbling down her face. She could not get up and was oddly relieved that the charade was over, though her body felt empty with grief and uncertainty. She'd been found out.

Grump looked in Marlin's direction with a knowing, blind gaze as he walked into the living room.

"These things must happen," he whispered as he motioned to the leather chair on the other side of the Tiffany lamp. "Come solve this next puzzle with me. My daughter's a strong cookie. She'll be all right. These things must happen," he added cheerfully.

Marlin sat down in the leather chair. He could hear Stacy's faint cry from the bedroom. Grump was making an educated guess as to what the phrase was that Vanna White hinted at. Marlin knew before Grump guessed that it was a popular phrase that was popularized by a series of novels and associated with a popular clothing line.

"A Neighborly Affair," Grump cheered a second before a middle-aged black woman answered. She won $25,000 for her knowledge of contemporary erotic fiction.

***

It was still a surprise to him that she'd called. Her voice was as sweet and heavenly as that night in the Rustic Inn; only now there was a more intimate quality washing over her tongue. It was rare that Dahji was able to knock a million dollar chick. She was like a younger version of Mirabelle for the way she wanted to see him do well.

Dahji was feeling himself as he ended his call with Edith. She was still on point and hinted that she had a special surprise for him. He'd played it cool, suspecting that she would show up in the morning at his penthouse with an expensive gift. She was Mirabelle all over again and if he calculated right she would make the seed he'd planted grow with that $100,000 fruit. This was her first test. She could blow kisses and testify to her loyalty a hundred times over, but this didn't deposit at the bank of commerce. So, he'd played it cool while giving her the aloof impression that it remained to be seen if her feelings for him were true.

These streets smelled of damp forest. The night time in this rich neighborhood gave the sense of privilege and relaxation. He could feel the reward of his struggle coursing through his bones. As he neared Mirabelle's mini-mansion he dialed Marlin's cell phone, thinking it should be just about time for him to be getting home from therapy.

"Speak on it," Marlin answered, Too Short rapping "BITCH" in the background. His voice was muted so that the beat was an echo floating through the Escalade.

"Marly Marl," Dahji cheered as he rode silently down the tree lined street of mansions and mile-long driveways. "Should I even tell you that my name is Dahji McBeth and what I say is like a check you can cash?"

Marlin knew that there was good news to follow. He felt himself be set free from the grips of his wife's infidelity and newfound control in their relationship.

"That's right. You have the right to remain silent," Dahji continued. "In some parts I am known as the law. Call me the law giver."

Marlin was laughing now as he pulled to the curb in front of his house. "So, tell me what the charges are then," he said in his gruff voice.

"You are being charged with a shared running back position for the Indianapolis Colts ... With some special teams work," Dahji explained. "I just met with a minority owner of the squad. Remind me to tell you about this little piece of China."

"Maybe not, but thanks man. You really came through for me." The last couple of words were a mere whisper.

"Who got your attention? Is wifey taking charge of this situation?" Dahji asked as he pulled through the cleanly cut shrubbery of Mirabelle's driveway. He was leaning out to press in the code at the waist-high call box when Marlin replied that Sherrelle was pulling into her driveway.

"So, we good for tomorrow?" Marlin asked as he opened his door. He was trying to pretend that he wasn't excited to see Sherrelle. He wanted to tell her his good news.

"No doubt. In the meantime don't hurt yourself celebrating. I would come and scoop you up, but I got some last-minute details to iron out before I can lay down and sleep like that white girl in the fairy tales."

"Snow White," Marlin answered, waving to Sherrelle as she stood from her Jaguar. She was absolutely gorgeous. There was never an off day for her.

"Is that the one that was sleeping good?" Mirabelle was standing in the tall doorway as he pulled into the circular driveway behind her convertible Bentley Azzure. At the far edge of the driveway were a pair of identical Lexus Sedans. Mirabelle had company. He suspected that the sisters were already here.

"Yeah, a white boy had to kiss her to wake her up." Marlin stood from the truck and hoisted his duffel bag to his shoulder.

"Well, maybe that's the one. Manana ball player. It's going to be good eating from here on out. Buffet like at a million dollar spread," Dahji said excitedly as he stepped onto the graveled driveway. In Mirabelle's stance was an eager awaiting; she stared with a passive expression, otherwise her large blue eyes watching him steadily as he made his way up the stairs.

"In the morning," Marlin replied before ending the call. Sherrelle was before him and everything in the world was perfect. He didn't care that her husband's BMW was in the driveway. It was all on her.

Dahji had to admit to himself that Mirabelle was a striking woman. The way her limbs were sheathed in the long, black silk gown gave him the impression of a woman who had too much money to be truly happy. The Harry Winston diamond necklace sparkled brightly around her slender neck. There was a glow in her bright blue eyes that danced more vibrantly with each step closer. She couldn't know that his fortunes had changed dramatically and he was in a position to tell her no. He would play it cool until he heard her out on what she'd told her late husband's sisters about him and how he could possibly be of assistance.

"You are quite the busy man," she whispered sexily as her pale hand brushed across his arm.

"Do the work and earn the perks," he replied before leaning in close to kiss her lovingly on her cool cheek.

"Well, I do hope you'll allow me to earn the perks as well," she said as she led the way inside to the marble-floored foyer with its high, arched ceiling. "This way please." She gestured to the sitting room where a fireplace was sparkling. Dahji expected to see the women who held the purse strings sitting coyly on the cream-colored linen sofa, but they were suspiciously absent.

Dahji turned to her as he neared the sofa. There was an uncertain look in her eyes; they shined brightly with impending tears.

"What's wrong, sunshine?" Dahji asked, concern wrinkling his otherwise smooth forehead.

"I don't want to share you, but ..." she stammered with a slow head shake of disappointment.

Dahji remained silent. He had no clue as to what was making her break down this way, but assumed it had something to do with the Lexus Sedans parked out front. Mirabelle slowly recovered and looked to him with reddened eyes.

"They want you for themselves, Dahji. I can't bare the thought of them having you in this way. They want everything that I enjoy so terribly, but it's the only way!" she shrieked at the end of this. There was a plea in her voice that threatened an unbalance should he decide not to share himself with them.

"Share how?" he asked.

"I told them," Mirabelle confessed, her body convulsing with some hidden sob. "When I said that you wanted to speak with them ... What was

I to suspect?" she asked suddenly, searching his eyes for the answer, Dahji had never seen her this way.

"Just slow down and give it to me straight," he said calmly, taking a step away from her harried grasp and sitting on the couch. Mirabelle followed and sat next to him, inhaling slowly to calm herself.

"I apologize," she said in barely a whisper before lifting her head with her accustomed composure. "They wanted to know who you are to me ... What you meant to me. Of course you are everything to me, but they are shrewd women, Dahji. They got it out of me as if they knew ..."

"Got what, Mirabelle? You make as much sense as one of them crossword puzzles." Dahji's complaint made her smile, restoring youth to her strained expression.

"Again, I apologize. You must understand how difficult this is for me." She looked to him now with probing blue eyes. Her long, dark hair fanned down around her narrow, pale face giving her an exotic appeal. Dahji could have easily made love to her – as he had on so many occasions on this very couch – and get caught up in soothing her worry.

"It's okay, sunshine. Just give it to me raw."

She exhaled before she locked her eyes onto his. "They know that you're my special friend. They want to have sex with you," she confessed.

Is that all? Dahji thought to ask, but instead said, "So, what do you get out the deal?"

"Oh," she replied as if this had not occurred to her. "They will give me control of my fund. "They want to meet with you first." She looked to him hopefully.

Dahji allowed a crooked grin to shape his lips. "Are they pretty?"

"Hardly," she scoffed. "But I suppose they're presentable," she added to assuage Dahji's questioning look.

He settled into the couch. It was time to get this started. If all it took was for him to fuck them then this would be a piece of cake. "Send them in," he instructed. Mirabelle looked at him skeptically, which made Dahji suspect that it would not be so easy as that.

"Okay," she began, tapping her fingers along his leg. She was hesitating as if there was something else on her mind.

"It's cool sunshine. Me and you straight like a dyke who hate dick."

Mirabelle smiled for the second time. It was the only time she didn't look preoccupied with worry. She stood with some effort and made her mind up to fetch the evil twins.

Dahji shed his camel-hair blazer and bent his neck from side to side. *This is it*, he thought to himself. Finally, he would be a success in his father's eyes. Marlin made the team, which was no small feat. May Ling was dynamite in a small package. She was not satisfied with running around so that he could chase her; she was more enamored with the whole business of being caught and subdued. No sooner than he'd pierced her snug love box with his swollen head would she beg to be let up again. It became a continual struggle to keep her in place until Dahji caught on to her game. She wanted to be denied and forced to take the dick. This was when she howled like a wounded animal and spoke in her native tongue. The effect was one that at first startled Dahji, only to turn into an eery turn on, boosting his resolve to split her in two. She fought against him with a fierce mock-struggle to free herself from his impaling until she shook violently with an orgasm that made her head thrash about as if she were speeding into a deep delirium.

Dahji smiled now with thoughts of her. He could still feel the effects of the herbs and tea ebbing in his loins like smoke after a blazing fire. His entire body felt as if it were a parked-performance car, ready with a press of a pedal to show its power. He could still feel her spent energy in his grasp. Her hair lay damp and matted to her long neck and forehead as she gasped for breath. Her body was burning hot in his hands as she shuddered and moaned. She'd nearly taken him to his limits of sexual performance. The satisfied look in her dreamy, black eyes was reward enough for their sexual marathon that came to an end in the kitchen before an open refrigerator of exotic fruits and juices. They'd shared a pitcher of grapefruit juice while she lay between his legs. She was definitely a special piece of Chinese import.

Mirabelle was the first to enter the room. Behind her were two brightly colored balls of pink flesh and white linen. Dahji's heart skipped a beat at the sight of the two obese women who emerged as Mirabelle stepped to the side with a grand gesture. She looked nervously from Dahji to the women who resembled something out of a macabre film about magicians and circus animals.

"Dahji McBeth, please meet Erva and Ensa."

Dahji nodded, deciding that he would remain seated. He wasn't feeling this situation at all. It was the first time he was truly considering walking away from this whole outfit. Leaving Mirabelle behind would be a loss, but not so much since his situation had turned for the better.

The twins were a testimony of the way white people could look when they had children inside the family tree. They were as pale as ghosts. The large diamonds and fine white fabric did nothing to lift his spirits from the sight of the white hair that ran in thin sheets down the sides of their round heads. Their chins were a series of doughy rolls, partly disguised by matching Tiffany necklaces with large diamond hearts at the ends. Their fingers were squeezed like raw bread tubes by diamond rings; their fat wrists were covered over with a series of gold and platinum bracelets.

The one that Mirabelle said was Erva stepped forward. She was distinctive from her twin by the eraser-colored mole standing up on the side of her chin. It gave her the impression of being in constant thought. Her pale-blue eyes sparkled at him as she opened her pink, fleshy lips.

"So very good to meet you Mr. McBeth," Erva said, her voice surprisingly lilting. Dahji immediately thought that she would make a fine phone sex operator.

"So very nice," Ensa echoed. She looked to be the more wicked one. Dahji suspected that it was this one, with the serious eyes, that did most of the bullying.

"My pleasure," Dahji replied from his reclined position. He could see why Mirabelle's late husband gave them control over the finances. It was impossible that they would ever become married and be provided for in a customary fashion.

"Mirabelle has shared with us so many wonderful things about you," Erva went on with her pulpy hands clasped together in front of her bulging stomach. The fine white linen dress she wore was intricately designed with snow flakes. A silk sash wrapped around her invisible waist, giving her the appearance of being a present at Easter time.

"That's always good to hear," Dahji responded after listening for Ensa to echo her sister's sentiments. They both looked to Mirabelle hopefully, exchanging some private communication.

"I'll be with you shortly," Mirabelle said with a jerking smile. The twins seemed only too relieved to hear this command. They were not the women Dahji had expected to meet. They rolled from the sitting room with small steps on pink cylinder cankles.

When they'd gone Mirabelle rushed to Dahji's side. Her hands were clasped together tightly in some form of agony.

"Are they okay?" Dahji asked, looking into Mirabelle's pleading eyes. He hated to see her in such a state.

She looked towards the doorway before she said, "They are absolutely wicked. Don't believe their docility."

Dahji studied Mirabelle's expression. She was seriously unnerved by the ghostly pig women. Having only been in a room with them for an instant,

Dahji was thrown also; so he could imagine Mirabelle's conundrum. Her husband had to be an evil man to leave her in their grip.

"What did you tell them about me?" he wanted to know, sensing from Erva that it was something quite delicious.

"They do everything together," she began before looking nervously to the doorway again. "And have never been with a black man ... or any man before. They've led very sheltered lives.

"Virgins? They got to be at least forty, right?"

"Thirty three."

"Virgins?" he asked with incredulity. This was unheard of, but seeing them now he could believe how they could go without dick for so long. No man in his right mind would lay with them. "Do they do everything together?" he asked, figuring that because of their obvious handicap, they rarely ventured out alone.

"EVERYTHING," Mirabelle assured him.

"Why do they drive separate cars?"

"Erva likes bluegrass and Ensa likes opera."

"What do they want exactly?" Dahji asked with a slight cringe. He couldn't imagine rolling around the bed between the two of them.

Mirabelle threw her hands up and huffed. "Oh! It's too much to bear. How can I even ask this of you?" she said, her eyes darting across his face for some solace.

"Because they got your money," he reminded her plainly. The corners of her pressed lips turned up slightly.

"How can I ever repay you?"

Dahji was becoming tired of her emotional outbursts. It took all of his pimp skills to remain calm and detached. His mind worked to answer how she could repay him when he said, "First, tell me what they want and we'll go from there." He no longer cared what she'd told them about him.

"Okay," she breathed out. "Ensa was the one who suggested that they lose their virginity together. And you can see their size ... When I told them that you were at least ten inches long ... Well, they absolutely shrieked with joy."

"Really," Dahji whispered, unable to imagine how they'd managed to get on the subject of his dick. *White people are freaks,* he thought to himself as Mirabelle prepared to tell him more.

"Yes. They made me tell them about you. I didn't want to do it, but they insisted," she breathed out. "So, Ensa had this divine idea that they would be side by side while you ... while you ..." Mirabelle teared up.

Dahji waited, letting his eyes float throughout the room. He knew what he wanted now. He wanted to be free from this bondage. This is what it was. He didn't have to be here, but due to the fact that he lived in a penthouse and drove a Range Rover provided by Mirabelle, he was obligated to indulge her various moods this night.

"They feel that you have the talents to satisfy them both at the same time," Mirabelle whispered.

Dahji nodded with understanding before looking to the narrow, pale faced woman slowly. "I want the deed and the pink slip to a new Bentley GT."

Her eyes brightened with calculation. "Are you done with me?" she wanted to know, her voice full of alarm.

"Naw sunshine ... But you've been playing me cheap. Free me up so I can love you better. You about to be freed up and I want the same thing."

She watched him passively for a few beats before breaking into a mischievous grin. "You are such a devil," she gushed as she leaned to kiss him wetly on the cheek. She tapped at his arm excitedly. "It's a deal," she added as she stood and pointed towards the doorway. "They're in the guest room. Second door on the right."

"Well, let's get free," he said as he stood from the sofa.

Mirabelle grabbed his arm as he was about to walk through the door. Her eyes searched his as her lips trembled with some unspoken declaration. They stared into one another's eyes with some private communication: It was only business.

Dahji could still feel the warmth of her fingers as they dragged across his arm when he walked into the hallway. The familiar piano concerto wafted through the finely decorated hallway as he stepped along the marble floor. He took a deep breath before knocking softly on the door.

"Please come in," came a faint voice from the other side. Dahji looked back to the sitting room. Mirabelle stood with her fingers intertwined beneath her bowed chin as Dahji disappeared through the door of the second room on the right.

The twins sat together at the foot of a canopied bed, its thick white wood bedposts hemming them in like pigs in a stall. They giggled together and turned to their stomachs shyly. Both raised their dresses to reveal what looked like four halves of two moons; their pink thighs, with their tiny red pimples and purple abrasions where they rubbed together, were spread as far as the small bed would allow.

Dahji was oddly thankful that they could not see his pained expression.

The deed to the penthouse and a brand new Bentley GT Sports Coupe moved him forward as he let his pants fall to the floor. He stepped from them and stroked himself, thinking of Edith. He let a fog cover his eyes as he stepped to the first moon halves and slapped the flaccid meat across its backside. Ensa, beside her, reached back to slap her ass as an instruction for him to share.

So, this is what it was to be like a hot dog inside a bun, Dahji thought to himself as he stepped over to slap her smooth ass with the head of his dick. The soft thud sounded like a gentle smacking of the lips.

Meanwhile, Erva had reached behind her and spread her hefty ass cheeks open, exposing the fleshy meat at her center. Her pussy was as fat as a Whopper with extra lettuce and tomato. The shiny innards awaited him eagerly.

He'd grown to a considerable length by this time. He directed himself to her spread-open snatch and dipped into her center. A low gurgling sound emanated from her as she moved away from him. She panted without having ever been penetrated properly and then suddenly backed onto him so that he was slipped snugly inside of her warmth. He felt like a vice had gripped him and his knees became weak with her combination of tightness and full warmth.

Ensa was slapping her smooth ass eagerly, wanting to feel the same way as her sister. Dahji moved to the side and sunk himself past her tight folds. She accepted him with a loud, suppressed moan. He imagined that she was biting her tongue and had her eyes shut. She opened for him with each tight stroke. He didn't imagine that this would feel so good. His length extended inside of her fat pussy. Now, Erva was slapping her pimpled ass with a jealous urgency.

In this way he went from one to the other, sliding inside of them for a few strokes before going to the other. Throughout, he forced from them a series of choking sounds that soon turned to syncopated moaning. Their only relief was when he eased from one to the other. In his absence they swayed their asses in anticipation of his return while moaning low and guttural into the bed sheets.

Soon enough their combined scent filled the room. It's coarse acidity made Dahji frown up his nose as he went about the duty of sliding between their wet flesh. They'd become slick and thoroughly abandoned any form of conservative decency. They openly vied for his attention; their asses red from the slapping. Dahji suspected that they enjoyed the slapping of their own asses more than the pounding. Though he disappeared inside of them with deep thrusts, he took it upon himself to slap their asses in rhythm. They groveled in unison at this, no matter which of them he was dicking down at the moment.

With every thrust the pasty skin shuddered and rolled. He long-stroked both of them, coming to enjoy the sexual abandon they exhibited. It was a strange scene sure enough, but the joy in seeing their reaction to being deflowered together was an experience worth having.

Dahji slapped one ass while he was inside of the other's pussy. The effect was that they both fed off of each other's excitement. He became like a DJ, slipping into one while smacking the other, and then reversing course. The hot air hitting his dick between shifts made him sensitive. And with each reentry his bulbous head flexed and jerked through their slickened holes. He slid through to their bottom; his waist smacking into the moist flesh before him.

Behind Ensa, to get deeper, he spread her ass up and away, feeling a new level of warm pussy with this stroke. The sudden outburst instantly made her sister jealous. He repeated this on Erva with the same result.

Their bodies were equally hot and open. He was soon drawing thick white cream from their wells as if it were oil. They squirted their treasures out in unison as true twins. Dahji went from one to the other to cap the geysers with his thick meat.

When they were spent and murmuring into the bed sheets, he stepped away from them with heaving breath. He could feel the cool drip of perspiration running down the center of his back. Before him were two pair of thighs shining and glistening with sexual passion. They had been deflowered and had gushed forth their treasure with abandon.

That was the business, he thought to himself. He'd backed away from them, his dick hanging long and thick, dripping with their hot oil between his legs. He observed them with hooded eyes as they writhed on the bed in a frenzy of after-sex pleasure. Now, he was free.

CHAPTER TWENTY SIX

That was close. And exciting. Ayana could hardly believe that her aunt didn't suspect something. *She probably doesn't even care,* she thought to herself as she stretched under the covers. Still, there was the chance that Sherrelle had done her math overnight and reached the sum of sins committed by her husband and her niece. It was for this reason that Ayana was reluctant to get up from bed. The sun had long since breached the middle of the comforter to alert her that it was just past nine o'clock.

She could hear them speaking – well, mostly Percy – in hushed tones. He wanted to spend the day with her. *Maybe he was trying to make up,* Ayana thought to herself as she strained to hear. Sherrelle must have been about to leave because Percy was complaining that they didn't spend time together like they used to; he wanted to get back to that.

Sherrelle's voice grew strong and then faint as she entered the hallway and walked into the living room. She was asking Percy how all of a sudden he had time for her on the weekends. She suggested that he go play golf. "Isn't that the Saturday thing for you?" she asked.

Ayana was at the bedroom door. She pressed her ear to the wood slowly. She could tell by the high pitch of Percy's voice that he was afraid of something. He didn't want to go play golf. He wanted to spend time with his wife. He wanted to know how long Ayana would be living with them.

This question forced a furrow across her brow. *He wants me to leave?* Ayana asked herself as the anger welled up in her. *Who the fuck he think he fucking with? Ain't no way this nigga gon' get away with trying to kick me out after he don' did what he did to me!* she hissed. She was determined to put an end to this line of rebuke.

"For however long I need her to," Sherrelle was saying as Ayana stepped from her bedroom in a pair of sheer HoodSweet boy-shorts and a cocaine white wife- beater. Her breasts filled out the ridges and pressed the cotton tight. She walked slowly, listening as Percy asked how long this would be. *Is he scared of me?* she wondered as she stood at the door of the bathroom.

Sherrelle startled her when she suddenly appeared at the hallway entrance. She was headed to her room, giving Ayana time to recover before looking back in her direction. "Hey sleepy head," she said quickly with Percy on her heels.

"Good morning," Ayana answered with a genial smile. She waited until Sherrelle turned her back before she shot a murderous glare at Percy, who hurried along with a new emphasis on his mission. He closed the bedroom door behind him and asked how long Sherrelle thought that would be.

"WHY!?" Sherrelle shouted to Ayana's surprise and glee. Though the power of her voice was muted by the door, there was no mistaking her anger. *Good,* Ayana thought. She held the toothbrush in her hand, preparing to squeeze toothpaste onto the bristles, as Sherrelle asked him if he had a problem with a member of her family staying with them or if it was his way of trying to stop her from succeeding with her business. She went on to say that Ayana was here to help, and if he didn't like it then that was just TOO DAMN BAD.

Damn! Auntie is really mad, Ayana thought to herself as Sherrelle's angry voice spilled from the room. Ayana closed the bathroom door and slipped the toothbrush through her lips and stroked her gums slowly as Percy followed with his questions about why Sherrelle was dressed like that. He accused her of looking like a prostitute. Then he was apologizing, asking her to stop so he could talk to her. He confessed that he was in a lot of trouble and needed her right now. His voice grew fainter and urgent right before the front door slammed shut.

Silence followed and Ayana could not be sure if they both left. It was then that Ayana remembered that the day was Saturday. This was the big day for everyone to meet up at Dahji's house for the photo shoot. She'd looked forward to this day all week long and now Sherrelle had left without her. *Damn.*

Percy was stepping through the front door when she ran into the living room. "She left already?" she asked urgently, peering around him through the front window. She caught the tail end of the pink Jaguar as it swerved in the street and sped up the block.

Percy passed her up with a frustrated looked. Ayana was suddenly angry, feeling that it was Percy's fault that she was left behind. Added to this was his desire for her to leave. "Who the fuck do he think he is?" she huffed as she turned to follow him through the hallway. *Square ass nigga don't know who he fuckin' with,* she thought as his petite frame disappeared around the corner of the master bedroom.

"You don't want me here?" she asked as she stepped into the room. Percy was standing over the bed as if he missed laying in it.

He looked up with unfocused eyes and waved her away.

Ayana stepped to him quickly and knocked his arm down. The toothbrush she was holding flew to the other side of the room with the contact. "Don't be waving me away like I'm some piece of lint. Who the fuck are you? Nobody!" she railed.

"Please. Just leave me alone. I'm not in the mood," he replied, making a move to walk past her.

Ayana shoved him hard in the chest, making him stumble backwards and fall onto the bed. He looked to her with widened eyes, his mouth agape in disbelief. "Answer my question. You want me to leave? Be a man about it and tell it to my face." She stood over him with her arms akimbo.

"I don't have to answer you," he began, his courage growing. "This is my house!" he added, trying to get up. He was caught with another shove onto the bed. "What the hell is your problem?" he asked with a startled expression.

"You a muthafuckin lie. This is my auntie's house! You keep fuckin with me and I'ma let her know the real with you," she huffed with anger, her breasts heaving.

"Go ahead and tell her. I don't care."

"You think I won't do it? You really don't know me, do you? And what you think she's gon' do when I tell her that you sucked my pussy? Yo shit gon' be all fucked up. So, you better get your shit right before your shit *is* all fucked up." Her voice was a loud whisper. She'd positioned herself between his legs and forced him to lean back on his elbows. She'd surprised him with her aggression.

"I don't believe you'd tell her. What will you do then?" he asked with narrowed eyes.

"What I always do. Survive. But whatever I do it ain't got nothing to do with what my auntie will do to you. And she was a white girl ..." Ayana frowned with disgust as she waved her finger down at him. "That's a no no. You might get your little dick cut off," she added, grabbing at the lump in his pants.

"Move out the way," Percy squealed as he tried to rise from his elbows. Ayana pushed him back to the bed.

"I ain't done with you yet."

"I knew you would be trouble," he whispered in defeat. Ayana smiled crookedly with this acknowledgement.

"And you like this trouble, don't you?" she quizzed as she lifted the wife-beater from her breasts. His eyes were riveted to her thick brown nipples. "Yeah, I know you like it. You can't help yourself."

Percy breathed out in exasperation. It was going to end very badly for him. He knew this to be true. There had to be some way to unwind the grip she had on him. There was no explaining why he didn't stop her from stepping from her boy-shorts. He could feel his breathing come short and the tightness in his groin. She was like a drug that he couldn't rehab from. She was pure evil and there was some sick pleasure he felt about this. She made him feel irresistible. The scent of her grew more intense the closer she climbed up his chest. She was on her way to sitting on his face, looking down to him with a look of seduction.

He was her prey and was properly bound by a web of wily seduction. He groaned with relief and protest as she fit her pussy over his mouth. She cooed and soothed him as she moved across his lips. It was all over for him when he felt her firm ass beneath the palms of his hands. His tongue recognized his submission and flipped from his lips for a taste of her nectar. And it was good and tangy. Yeah, it was all over for him and he wanted to taste her cream now more than at any other time. This would calm his nerves like a needle full of heroin.

***

Marlin was up early. He was in the kitchen making a large breakfast of chicken omelets when Stacy walked in wearing a thick cotton robe. She'd wanted to pick up where they left off the night before. She complained that she missed him in bed last night. Before she could get properly started, he held his hand up to stop her. He couldn't rely on being able to control the anger that he felt as a result of her infidelity.

He didn't want to argue with Stacy or hear her apologies or explanations. He was off to Dahji's house; the man she thought couldn't make it happen for him. She'd finally admitted her pessimism and it was like lancing a boil; the poisonous puss of control finally spilled from her curled lips. He'd felt a certain sense of freedom. All this time he'd played nice out of respect for the fact that she was being cool about paying the bills and basically supporting his rehabilitation. He had a goal of playing pro ball again and he at least thought she shared this with him.

But it had all come to the light. The jealousy and the adultery. Marlin chuckled to himself, remembering her reaction to his statement of them having run their course. He had to give it to her, she could be funny when she least wanted to be. She'd responded, "Run our course? ... This ain't no race track!" The funny part was how some hood had edged into her voice and mannerisms. It was what he'd fell in love with; but this flavor to her personality had been lost with her corporate merging.

Marlin allowed the valet to park his Escalade before he stepped into the cool, carpeted lobby of the glass and shining steel building. This was the second time Marlin had come to Dahji's house and he still felt a sense of power when he stepped through the expensively decorated lobby. This is what Stacy didn't know about Dahji. She didn't know that he lived like a rock star and had connections like a mob figure.

The lobby desk was manned by a tall, muscular, clean-shaven man with piercing black eyes. His black uniform only accented the darkness of his skin. He was hanging up the phone behind the black marble counter as Marlin walked up.

"Marlin Cassidy?" the deep voiced man asked before Marlin could announce himself.

"Yeah," he replied. The white lettered, black nameplate identified this bulk of man as Gerald Little. He extended his bear palm across the high table.

"Dahji is expecting you. Congratulations on making the team. The City is counting on you," Gerald said, smiling a big row of pearly white teeth. It was Marlin's first introduction to the City's fan base and their excitement with him joining the Colts football team.

"Thanks a lot man. I'ma give it my all," Marlin responded. Gerald gestured to the gold-plated elevator framed by two tall, potted plants. "That's all we can ask. Right this way, sir."

"Thanks man," Marlin replied before stepping to the elevator. The doors hissed open just as he reached them. Gerald was already on the phone again, enjoying his leisurely station, when Marlin turned to press the button that would take him to the penthouse. He was buoyed by the exchange with Gerald. He wondered how he'd come to find out about him making the team. Maybe there was some news announcement that he didn't know about.

The elevator opened onto a thickly carpeted lobby. Dahji's door was at the end of a long hallway. The hallway itself could serve as a kind of reception area for the way it was furnished with an elegant leather sofa with matching foot stool. Further along was a low glass table complete with two wicker chairs opposite one another. On the walls were landscape portraits and wooden carvings of ornate, swirling designs that seemed to have no function or cultural history.

The door opened as he prepared to ring the bell. A beautiful dark-skinned woman stood before him. She could have easily been Sherrelle's sister for the way her skin shined darkly and her hair flowed long and lustrous past her shoulders. Her soft curves were sheathed in a magenta body suit. The sexy look made Marlin shiver.

"Hi Marlin," this beaming starlet said as she stepped aside to allow him in. "My name is Ebony. Dahji is by the pool," she added.

"Y'all up early, hunh?" he asked, feeling the celebratory vibe as Mac Dre rapped through hidden speakers. He was speaking on how he was an all-star quarterback for a super bowl team. He had a million dollar gift and kept a billion dollar chick.

Ebony led the way through the penthouse, past the downstairs bedroom, under the loft. Through the glass windows he could see a trio of men lounging in silk slacks and shirts. They were all smiling, looking to the pool area, their gold Gucci chains and diamond pendants shining brightly in the sun. Though Marlin didn't have a clear glimpse of their faces, he recognized their general style.

"Who else is here?" he asked Ebony just before she slid open the glass partition. She turned to him with a large grin. She was obviously happy to be amongst such company.

"The two really black guys are Jon Ansar and Talib. They're visiting from California. I think they have something to do with that strip club ... Applebottoms. And the light-skinned one with the long hair is Prince Sweetwater. He's Dahji's uncle. I forget where he's visiting from. Chicago ... I think." Her face frowned up in thought. This made her look even more beautiful.

The Infiniti pool spilled right off the roof. Two lithe figures with long, black hair swam slowly across the blue waters. On the other side Dahji was standing with his back turned to a bar-b-que grill. The air was thick with the sweet smell of charred beef and honey. Standing with him was a tall midnight black woman with blue eyes and long, shining black hair. She tapped Dahji on the arm and he looked around with a grand smile of achievement.

"Marly Marl!" Dahji called out with a wave of the silver fork in his hand. The trio of sharply dressed men waved two fingers (peace) in the air from their places by the pool before returning to some intimate discussion. Marlin remembered seeing the two dark men in the Applebottoms parking lot almost three weeks ago. He remembered that they knew who he was and had won big money on him when he was playing football at Alabama. He felt like he was amongst a private group that moved with peace, power, and position.

"Meet Emma Jean," Dahji said when Marlin approached. Emma Jean was more beautiful up close. She was like some rare bird that had been imported from some far off place. Her limbs were draped up and dripped with bright diamonds set in rose gold.

"Bonjour Monsieur Marlin," Emma Jean said while placing her jeweled fingers softly in his palm. "Comment allez-vous?" Her blue eyes sparkled naturally. From the roots her hair was straight and fine. *Where is she from?* he wondered.

"That's how are you," Dahji translated with a wicked grin before turning back to the grill of meaty ribs and toasted chicken wings and legs.

"I'm good. Real good. Thank you," Marlin assured her.

"Tres bien. Congratulations is in order," she offered with a smile.

"Thank you," he responded and then took a deep breath. He felt slightly intoxicated with his surroundings. He didn't expect to see two naked women swimming laps in the pool that seemed to go on forever. Dahji was in rare form in a pair of Gucci loafers, silk shorts and nothing but a Rolex chain hanging across his chest. His flowing mane of soft curls seemed to drink in the morning sunlight. And this woman standing before him in a lavender silk dress emanated some type of sexual energy that he'd never felt before. There was a communication with her every glance and gesture. He felt he was too square to decode it, but oddly felt that whatever was in her was only controllable by the caliber of men sitting on the lounge chairs across the pool.

"Go meet my uncle Prince. Grab a seat. We eat in a minute Marly Marl. Oh, that's Maria and Sophia in the pool. Today is the day we get filthy rich Marly Marl!" Dahji said excitedly. There was profound energy in his eyes. He hadn't known before that there was hunger deep within him. Now it had seemed to be sated. He appeared settled after having won some important battle. This made him feel good. For the first time he gave no thought to how the uncertainty with his injury might have affected Dahji. But now everything seemed to have worked out fine.

"Got some beer?" Marlin asked.

"Let me show you," Emma Jean volunteered, taking his hand in hers and leading him towards the pool house. *This is the business,* he thought to himself. His heart beat cooly in anticipation of seeing Sherrelle arrive. Her Jaguar was still in the driveway when he left.

***

No matter how many stairs she climbed there was no reaching the sunlight above. This brightness spilling in through the door at the top of the stairway represented escape and freedom. There was darkness all around and the rotted wood threatened to crumble beneath her feet. The dark walls breathed with a life of their own, swelling in on her every step, only to retreat and begin anew with an eerie cry. Below her was a howling unrecognizable figure, its limbs cloaked in a dense black smoke. The red eyes peered up to her from the blackness, willing her to give up her climb and succumb to being swallowed up by the abyss.

Peaches struggled, her hands gripping the rickety banisters for support. Her escape from the menacing figure began at what seemed like forty floors below. With every turn on a small landing, seemingly closer to the top, there was a new landing and new set of stairs added. There was no escape and she was losing hope that she would even reach the light.

Her legs were becoming heavy and she couldn't run as fast as she wanted to. Her body felt as if it were filled with wet sand. Sweat poured from her and made her sluggish. The shadowy figure was now on the same set of stairs. It no longer looked to her from the last set below. There was no room now for her occasional stumble. A low ringing sound of doom emanated from the dark, dense smoke.

Peaches struggled to maintain her balance. She barely escaped capture as she turned at another landing. Above her the sun shined brightly. She'd expected that a new staircase would be added. She was almost there. Then there was a tight grip on her ankle.

"Ahhhhh!" Peaches screamed, jerking awake. She was drenched in sweat and her heart beat wildly. The phone was ringing on her night stand. Her eyes were wide as she stared around the small room. The dream was quickly evaporating from memory like a rolling fog out to sea, but the sense of dread remained.

The room was bathed in the minimal sunlight that the tall apartment building next door would allow into her space. This gave the room an abbreviated feeling of openness. There still existed the shadow across half her room that spoke to the cramped apartment buildings which rose to the sky in an effort to house as many renters as possible.

The ringing phone shook her from the pall that followed her from sleep.

Her mouth was sticky and her stomach felt hollow. She'd gone to bed feeling as though this would be a good day. She would pay for the dope she'd been busted with and pay to get Tequan's car out of impound. That would clear her to concentrate on her criminal case which Dahji assured her would go away. And thinking of him reminded her of the fact that she hadn't spoken with him. She made a mental note to call him to say good morning after she answered this phone. She needed to hear his voice. She needed reassurance.

"Hey girlfriend," she answered, trying to clear her throat from the dryness that plagued her. She looked through the partially opened bedroom door into the hazy living room. This day her apartment looked more like a trap than any other day.

"You okay?" Sherrelle asked, frowning with concern as she turned off of her street.

"Yeah. I'm cool," Peaches replied as she swung her feet to the floor. The bedside clock read ten o'clock. *How could I have slept so late?*" she thought to herself.

"Well, come on girl. Get up. I'm on my way to Dahji's house. Why aren't you up yet?"

"Chill out drill sergeant," Peaches instructed as she rubbed the edge of her palm over her eyes. "Get your panties out of your ass."

Sherrelle breathed out to relax herself. "I'm sorry. I just had a fight with Percy."

"Do I have to guess what it was about?" Peaches stood and slipped her feet into a pair of pink bunny slippers.

"It don't even matter. Really, it don't," she sighed.

"I feel you. Okay ... Let me get ready." She was in the bathroom, lifting her t-shirt to sit on the toilet. The stream of pee echoed through the small bathroom.

"Are you on the toilet?" Sherrelle asked with alarm.

"Yep."

"Well, thanks for the warning. So, what time are you going to be at the penthouse?"

"Right after I drop off this money to Bo."

"You be careful," Sherrelle said.

"Girl, I ain't worried about ..." Peaches began, but was stopped by someone banging on her front door. She cringed with the feeling that if they knocked any harder the door might fall off its thin hinges. That was another thing about this ghetto apartment; everything was cheap. It was probably the manager coming to fix her leaking faucet.

"Peaches ..." Sherrelle called into the silence.

Peaches waited for the sound of the flushing toilet to ask, "Is Ayana with you?" There were two bodies silhouetted against the living room curtains. They were leaning against the banister. Slim men. *Who is this?* she asked herself as she walked through the living room, leaning slightly to get a glimpse of who might be in front of the door.

"Not this time. Maybe next time."

"You bring your camcorder?"

"Oh shit!" Sherrelle cried, remembering that she'd forgotten it in her haste to get away from Percy's whining voice. "I'ma call you back. There's a police car next to me and I need to hurry up and get in the left lane." Then she was gone.

A pang of abandonment shot through Peaches when she realized that Sherrelle had hung up. The line went dead just as she realized it was Bo who stood at her door. His wide frame filled the peep hole. The two shadowy figures must be Bam and Drew. They were like his personal hood assistants.

"Yeah!" she yelled through the closed door, trying to make her voice sound more forceful and assured than she felt. It was a strange feeling having them right outside her door. She'd stopped answering their calls. Now she regret that she didn't call him last night to say that she would come by to pay them in the morning. Tequan must have given them her address.

Peaches felt naked. It was as if the illusion she'd created with her persona had been shattered. They now saw her for who she was, a struggling stripper who lived in a run-down apartment that didn't even have a working security gate. She imagined that they laughed at the way they could just walk up to her apartment.

"What's up Peaches. Open up. We here to get that bread," Bo barked.

"Okay. Hold on." Peaches backed away from the door, watching how the slim figures lifted from the banister and seemed to turn around to look into the empty pool with its broken furniture, spare bike parts, and broken dolls strewn along its muddied bottom.

In the far corner of her bedroom closet was a large Louis Vuitton bag. It was filled with the items she needed in case she had to leave in a hurry. There were a pair of sweats, toiletries, a disposable pre-paid cell phone, jewelry and an envelope containing five thousand dollars in cash. She grabbed this and quickly counted it. She was halfway out of the bedroom when she realized that the impound charges were probably five thousand dollars alone. She raced back to the closet and peeled up a corner of the rug under the Louis Vuitton and lifted one of five manila envelopes from the floor. She emptied the bag onto the bed and out tumbled ten bound stacks of five thousand dollar bundles. She grabbed one up quickly as the door rattled with renewed banging.

"Here I come?" she called out, assembling the money in her hands. *Ten thousand dollars should easily be enough,* she thought to herself. Finally, she would be rid of these hungry niggas.

CHAPTER TWENTY SEVEN

Where did Marlin go that quick? Sherrelle asked herself as she pulled into her driveway. Stacy's Lexus was still in the driveway. *Maybe he made a quick run to the store,* she thought to herself as a warm feeling ran through her with the notion that she would've been able to see him this morning if she'd remembered her camcorder a little earlier. *He must have left right after me,* she thought as she hopped out the Jag and skipped up the stairs and onto the porch.

The front door was rarely locked. The only crime that was committed in this neighborhood was someone not setting their trash cans out on time or parking on the street on trash pick-up day. This neighborhood took anything related to trash very seriously.

She was through the living room with a few long strides. The house was quiet. She could see the camcorder in her mind, sitting on the flower print mamosan in the corner of her bedroom, next to the mahogany boudoir.

The scene before her did not register at first. She could see the slim, bare back and the squatting legs above the neck of ... She was shocked. Was that Percy ...? Was she sitting on his face ...?

The gasp that escaped Sherrelle's mouth, as her hand shot to her lips in surprise, made Ayana turn around. With one fluid motion the young seductress peeled herself from Percy's lips and hopped from the bed. She stood naked, looking to Percy with wide eyes, her mind quickly formulating her strategy.

Percy raised himself up and looked to Sherrelle as if she were a ghost. He expected her to vanish at any moment.

"It wasn't me!" Ayana called out, her arm flinging out to Percy with a silent indictment. "It was him!"

Sherrelle looked slowly from her to Percy. This was all so surreal. She had a mind to laugh out loud. It was all too perfect. *My niece is fucking my husband!* she thought out loud.

"No no no honey," Percy said suddenly, waving his arms criss crossed before him. "She made me do it, Sherrelle."

"I didn't make him do nothing! He said that he would send me back to L.A. if I didn't let him do that!"

Sherrelle felt as if she was floating on a cloud as she moved across the floor towards Ayana. Her open palm came up from her side and whipped across her niece's face in slow motion. She barely noticed how Percy jumped from the bed and moved out of range.

"You don't care anyway!" Ayana called out, holding her stinging face. "You just using him anyway!"

Sherrelle opened her mouth, but no words came out.

"Baby," Percy said, taking her silence for an invitation to move in her direction.

"Don't be calling my auntie baby" Ayana cried as if she and Sherrelle were a team. "Show her the marks on your back! Show her the marks that white bitch bin making on your back! That's why he bin sleeping on the couch, auntie!"

"WHAT!" Sherrelle finally uttered out. Percy lifted his hands in a plea. "She doesn't know what she's talking about, baby. Look, let's all calm down and ..."

"Calm down?" Sherrelle asked, coming to life, the colors of the room suddenly fixing and becoming more solid. "Calm down? You want me to calm down after I see you sucking my niece's pussy?" She turned suddenly, finding Ayana within range, and slapped her across the face again.

"Fuck!" Ayana screamed. "What the fuck you hittin' me for? It wasn't my fault. Why you act like you care? You in love with Marlin anyway!"

Percy's stance changed. He was deciding if it was safe for him to take the offensive.

"Don't even think about it," Sherrelle warned, giving Percy a quick jab of her finger. She turned to Ayana. "You. You better be gone by the time I get back." Ayana cringed towards the bed as Sherrelle moved past her to lift the camcorder from the mamosan. She faked like she was going to hit Ayana again, smirking when the young seductress flinched, on her way back towards the door

"Babe," Percy muttered with supplication. "Let's talk about this."

She turned on him when she got to the door, the camcorder bouncing against her thigh. "You take her to the bus stop. Not the airport. Put her ass on the bus," she said calmly.

"NO! Auntie, I'm sorry!" Ayana called out after Sherrelle as she stepped through the hallway. She followed Sherrelle into the spare bedroom.

"Trifling ass tramp!" Sherrelle hissed as she flung the closet door open and searched for the Tiffany bags that contained the jewelry she'd bought for Ayana.

"Is that mine?" Ayana asked, stepping aside as Sherrelle walked out the room with four small powder- blue bags. The sense of loss made her fearful.

"Hell naw!" she replied, brushing by her with a hot body.

"I'm sorry," Ayana pleaded as she followed her through the hallway. She'd managed to pull a pair of shorts over her nakedness and slip on a baggy t-shirt.

"I'm sorry too," Sherrelle said over her shoulder as she passed Percy, who stood by the dining room table looking like a lost puppy. He didn't know what to expect from his wife on her return. One thing for certain; he was going to put Ayana on a bus back to Los Angeles.

Sherrelle gave out a rebellious whoop as she stepped with slanging hips down the driveway to her car. She did not hear Ayana's pleas as she stood on the porch while she backed out the driveway. It wasn't until she could no longer see the house that a lone tear rolled down her flushed face. She wiped it away quickly, refusing the ghetto drama a chance to ruin her day of progress.

***

Mary J. Blige provided the powerful words to accentuate the celebratory atmosphere of the penthouse. He couldn't have asked for anything better. His reward had manifested itself after a long struggle.

Lounging in the living room, going over some recent photos of themselves were the beautiful Latinas. Maria and Sophia were wrapped in a glow that competed with the sun streaming in through the floor-to-ceiling window. Dahji had just come from the pool area with a tray of bar-b-que ribs when his house phone rang.

"Marly Marl," he called out to the man that made him an official sports agent. Ebony had Marlin hemmed up in the kitchen, quizzing him about all things related to football as Dahji walked in carrying the food. "I need you to quarterback," he added, gesturing towards the ringing phone.

As Marlin scooped up the receiver Ebony turned her attention to Dahji. "I'm glad I decided to stay. When is Sherrelle coming?" she wanted to know.

Marlin turned to Dahji and announced that there was a woman named Coretta downstairs.

"Let her up," Dahji instructed, before turning his attention to Ebony. "Grab that bowl of potato salad out the frig ... She should be here," he replied as he checked his diamond bezel Rolex. "Marly Marl. Ain't this one delicious like your neighbor?" he asked, gesturing with a quick nod to Ebony," who smiled as if she were in front of a camera.

"No doubt," he agreed.

"So, what y'all gon' do now Marly Marl? Y'all gon' go half on a baby?"

Marlin situated himself on a high stool on the other side of the black marble counter. Ebony watched him curiously, waiting for his answer. "She's married," he responded as a knock came at the door.

"I'll get it," Ebony said, even though she was further away from the door than Marlin. She was around the counter before Marlin could think to get off the stool. Dahji answered the ringing phone.

"Mr. McBeth. There is an Edith here to visit," Gerald announced.

Dahji grinned proudly. It was a special kind of feeling to be chosen by a woman of Edith's pedigree. He rubbed his palms together as he instructed Gerald to send her up."

Coretta entered with a surveying glance. Aryn was at her side and immediately darted into the kitchen and wrapped her arms around Dahji's waist.

"Hi daddy! Daddy, mommy said that we could swim in your pool."

Dahji lifted her into his arms as Coretta made a point of kissing him on the lips as Ebony looked on. He was thankful that Marlin grabbed Ebony's attention with a question about her modeling career.

"Hey you," Coretta said, helping Aryn from Dahji's arms as Ebony spoke on moving to Los Angeles.

"Hey baby girl," he replied before looking into his daughter's bright, brown eyes. "Are you going swimming in that cute dress?"

Aryn shook her head enthusiastically. "No!" she cheered. "You have my bathing suit," she added with a happy laugh and pushed into his stomach.

It's in the downstairs room. Go get changed." He looked up to Coretta, noting how her shapely, petite frame was hugged by a pair of Evisu jeans.

Her breasts bubbled over the soft cotton of a plain white V-neck t-shirt. "You going in with her?"

In response she tapped at the large Coach bag. "Just my feet and maybe a sit in the Jacuzzi. Are you ..." She was stopped short by a soft knocking at the door.

Dahji moved swiftly around Coretta. "Excuse me for a minute," he added with an amused glance.

"I know THAT," Ebony replied after him around a soft giggle.

Edith smiled her proper grin when Dahji opened the front door. Her long, blonde hair fanned down around her face in gentle Shirley Temple curls. Her legs were longer than he'd remembered, encased in a pair of brown jockey riding pants that disappeared into brown leather knee-high boots with low heels. Her creamy breasts were barely visible under the white silk blouse.

"Hi," she said simply.

Dahji was still caught up in the blue of her eyes. Tucked under her arm was a plumed Salvadore Ferragamo pheasant-feather bag. Its earth toned feathers lay over the leather as if the purse would take flight at any moment.

"That's nice," he said after he'd let her into the penthouse. "But what's that?" he asked, pointing to the silver square case in her other hand.

She handed it to him. "This is for you," she replied in her soft voice. *Choosing fee,* Dahji thought to himself.

"Well, sounds good to me." He pointed to the stairway that led to the loft. "Follow those stairs and wait for me up there," he instructed, her eyes following his arms as it stopped at the bright red Gucci comforter covered bed on the loft.

"Okay."

"Here. Take this with you." He handed the case back to her. He watched her take two strides across the hardwood floor before turning to Jon Ansar, who'd been watching the scene unfold. He gave Dahji a subtle head nod and a crooked, diamond toothed grin. The Latinas seemed to straighten their postures and check their makeup with Edith's arrival. They were like candles to Edith's sun.

"Who is that?" Coretta wanted to know as he stepped back into the kitchen.

"That's why so many people in prison now. Everybody wanna know who dat is," he replied sarcastically as he plucked a bottle of Smirnoff Grand Cosmopolitan and two glasses from the wet bar. He ignored Coretta's curious stare as he passed her going into the living room. He stepped with controlled glee. He was in his element. He popped a thumb up beside the Smirnoff bottle to Jon Ansar before turning to Marlin.

"Marly Marl. Quarterback," he instructed.

Edith stood at the tall window, looking out at the Infiniti pool and the city beyond. The silver case was placed in the middle of the now made-up bed. She'd arranged the vintage-scarf pillows along the low wooden head board. "This is nice," she said with a small wave of her arm.

"That's because you're nice," he replied as he handed her a glass. He filled their glasses half way and set the bottle on the wooden edge of the bed.

"Open your gift," she said, her bright blue eyes staring into his for what might be there after he saw what she had for him.

Dahji reached out and pulled the silver case to him. He pressed two silver knobs and with a hissing sound the case parted. He lifted the cool lid slowly. The dull green stacks of money came into view like a sunset. He nodded his agreement as he scanned the neat, ten-thousand-dollar stacks. Five rows across and two rows up, they filled the petite case perfectly. This was the one hundred thousand dollars that he's asked if she could get her hands on. *Yeah, she had promise,* he thought to himself as he looked back to her to show her the glimmer of pleasure in his eyes that her choosing fee called for.

***

The sun spilled into her small apartment when she opened the door. It was the way Bo's hard, dark eyes roamed over her body that reminded her that she was naked beneath the t-shirt. The phone felt light in one hand as she reached the stack of money out to him with the other. It seemed like forever as he slowly accepted the money.

Bam and Drew looked on hungrily, their hawk-like eyes looking from the stack of dirty money to how her shapely figure was making the t-shirt do weird things against her hips and breasts.

"Whas dis?" Bo asked after sifting halfway through the money. He held the halves apart as if to go on any further would only upset him. A shot of fear passed through her, buoyed by an anger that made her breathing grow sharp.

"Ten grand," she replied. Bo nodded as he bowed his head to the money in his palms. He held the halves away from each other as if to measure their significance.

"You had this up here all this time?" he wanted to know, looking back to her. There was some hidden communication in the way he leaned away from her that caused Bam and Drew to take a step in her direction.

"That's all I got," she said quickly as she eased the door across her body, making the open space more narrow.

Peaches watched Bo consider this lie as he looked up the rail and back to her. It was only an instant before he stepped quickly to the door and shoved her inside. Bam and Drew followed quickly, slamming the door so hard behind them that it popped back open.

"This ain't gon' be enough," Bo said casually.

"That's bullshit Bo," she shouted as she stepped out of reach. She knew it was bad to go backwards, but Drew and Bam made it difficult for her to move in any other direction.

Bo was shaking his head as he shoved the money into his pocket. He looked to Bam and Drew with a knowing smirk.

"Tequan sent you here for what Bo?" Peaches asked, fear lacing her words though she tried to sound tough.

He pat his pockets. "This right here ... So, what you gon' say in the courtroom? They ask where you get the product from?" He seemed too big for her apartment.

"WHAT?! Hell naw! They ain't tripping on that and I ain't about to say nothing about it. You should know me better than that Bo." She could feel her skin tingling with fear, her eyes shifting to Drew who was by the fake fireplace mantle looking at pictures of her in frames.

"How can I be sure? You need to let a nigga go on and hit that," Bo suggested, taking another step in her direction.

Peaches chuckled with the absurdity of his request, noticing how it gathered Bam and Drew's attention as if this was spoken of between them on the way over.

"This is hardly the time or the place for ..." she began, but was cut off by his sudden movement towards her. He gripped her arm and looked hard into her face. His fingers dug into her muscle.

"All that stripping and shit! Don't tell me what time it is cuz I already know bitch! You ah hoe just like the rest of these tramp bitches." His dark face was a maniacal sneer.

She snatched her arms from his grip quickly and turned into the hallway. Her heart beat through her chest as she dashed into her room, Bo's laughter following her through the hallway. Just as she tried to close the door behind her it came crashing back against the wall.

"Where the fuck you goin'?" he asked, followed by Bam and Drew. They filled her small room with their hungry scent.

"Don't do this Bo," she pleaded as she backed up to the bed. She saw through his scanning eyes the manila folder of money spread out on the bed. The Louis Vuitton bag was at the headboard. It was then that she remembered that Tequan's 9mm Glock was stashed in the bottom. Her mind worked quickly to find her only solution.

"Oh, you breaded up in here," Bo observed.

"You got your money Bo. Don't be a ..."

"Shut up bitch!" Drew screamed out as he dashed to the foot of the bed. It was the first time he'd spoken. He fumbled with his belt buckle. "You gon' let a nigga fuck or ..." He stopped when Bo held his hand up.

"It ain't gotta be like that Peaches. You the homegirl," Bo began. "Just give a nigga some of that pussy and we out." He was already unzipping his blue khaki pants.

Peaches surveyed her options quickly. They were not going to be denied. The stairwell had grown very dark and the sunlight was further away from her reach. She let out a deep breath of resignation; she was a fool to think that it would be so easy to leave the past behind.

"Okay, but only you Bo."

He shrugged nonchalantly before looking to Bam and Drew as if they would have to miss out. "You got that," he agreed, his menacing eyes, glittering and anticipatory, swinging back to her.

"Just let me clear this bed," she said dejectedly, turning towards the Louis Vuitton bag.

"Leave that cheese on the bed," Bo instructed. "How much is that anyway? I always wanted to fuck on a bed of cheddar." He chuckled as an invitation for Bam and Drew to join in. They were happy to take part in this sordid form of foreplay as they hovered near the door, exchanging dap at what they perceived was a just reward for being loyal hood niggas.

Peaches never turned around. The laughter was loud in her ears. There was no way that they would leave her in peace or allow her to dictate the terms of this jack move. She inhaled deeply, her breath hot with a calm anger. She rubbed her moist palms together to ready them for the cool steel that lay at the bottom her Louis Vuitton bag.

"Not that much," she mumbled in reply, knowing exactly how much money she had spread on the bed, as she reached to the bottom of the soft leather bag.

Bo was making a joke about how she was saving trick money when she turned around with the Glock pointed at his chest. The sinister giggles he'd caused in Bam and Drew were cut short to a nervous chuckle.

"Whas .." Drew stuttered, bringing his arm up to point at the gun clenched tightly in her hand.

Bo snapped his mouth shut as his eyes moved from the barrel to her blazing silver-gray eyes. The fire coming from them said everything that he thought not possible. Tequan said nothing about her having a pistol. He saw the flexing of her forearms before he saw sparks erupt from the barrel.

POP!!

Bam and Drew were frozen in place as Bo swiveled from the impact of the bullet ripping into his muscular shoulder.

POP!! POP!!

With each shot Peaches shut her eyes. Like a silent film reel, Bam and Drew came to life and bumped into each other in their haste to escape through the bedroom door as Bo crashed against the wooden dresser, breaking the mirror and spilling her perfume and stuffed animals to the floor.

POP!! POP!! POP!!

The bullets chased after Bam and Drew with menace. There was no escaping her wrath. She was feeling good now. The scene unfolded below her as she hovered near the ceiling. She could see herself holding the gun and Bo sliding on top of the stuffed animals. He was holding his palms to the two holes leaking blood out of his chest.

"AW SHIT!" Drew screamed as Bam fell to the floor in the hallway. He loosened the fallen man's grip from his leg in an effort to escape.

Peaches walked slowly to the door and popped another shot into a frightened Bam. He'd rolled to his back, the side of his head bleeding, and made a fresh bullet hole in his stomach. He screamed out in agony as he folded into a fetal position.

Drew was at the front door when Peaches reached the living room. She shot one time in his direction, the bullet crashing through the window. He was through the door quickly, slamming it against the wall with his effort. Peaches gave chase. He was nearly at the stairs when she steadied her aim and squeezed the trigger in rapid succession.

Drew's arms flailed into the air and his knees buckled just as he reached the stairway. His khaki shirt billowed out from the bullets ripping through to his body.

In an instant Drew disappeared, tumbling down the stairs, and all was quiet. Peaches had only now realized that her legs were swathed in Bam's blood as he tried to grab her in the hallway. Her chest heaved and swelled with deep breaths. The Glock felt like a hot chunk of iron in her grip. When she turned to walk back to her apartment there were heads peeking from doorways along the concrete walkway. Their wide eyes said more about what happened than Peaches felt for herself. The macabre scene was mirrored in their gasps and shocked glances to the smoking Glock gripped tightly in her hand.

***

Everybody was celebrating. The champagne was flowing and the music was rocking. The Latinas were dancing with sexual seduction in the middle of the living room. They'd peeled Marlin from his place near the wet bar, interrupting Ebony's infatuation, to dance with them. The sun spilled into the open space like a tidal wave of prosperity.

Jon Ansar and Talib lounged near the fireplace with their long, jeweled fingers wrapped around a crystal glass of Hennessy XO. Their gold trimmed, diamond-toothed smiles spoke of their luxurious presence. They cheered Marlin on as Ebony rocked gently on the couch between them.

Prince Sweetwater strolled in from the pool area with Emma Jean, nodding his flowing mane subtly to Mary J. Blige's passionate serenade. Emma jean was glamorous and fabulous as she served Prince Sweetwater a mixed drink of orange juice and Tanqueray. She next moved into the kitchen to make him a plate of bar-b-que chicken, pork & beans, potato salad, and cob corn.

Dahji was still on the loft, giving Edith special instructions and allowing her to feel her way into his space. They leaned onto the railing, exchanging light laughter while observing the scene below. Everything was right with the world. The penthouse was officially his, Marlin made the squad, the Bentley GT was on order, and all that was left was for Sherrelle to arrive and get this HoodSweet jumped off right and make it official. *And where is Peaches?* he wondered, reminding himself to call her after Edith was done telling him about her time in a French boarding school.

Marlin was absorbed with his effort to perfect a sweet two-step Maria was showing him. Sophia was behind him with her hands on his waist. He was sandwiched between them. He had no idea that Prince Sweetwater was at the door until Sherrelle walked into the penthouse. His eyes met hers and his body instinctively followed her silent instruction. There was hurt and passion inking her dark brown eyes. The blood red strap dress fell across her curves like morning dew, stopping at the middle of her thighs. She'd dropped two large duffel bags to her feet. Though she was greeting Prince Sweetwater, her eyes shifted to him with hidden meaning.

"Excuse me," Marlin said to Maria as he moved from Sophia's light touch on his hips.

"Hey ... Homeboy," she greeted him haltingly. Her eyes threatened tears as he grabbed her in his arms.

"You okay, baby" he asked with his hands around her waist. He'd leaned back to look into her dreamy eyes.

"I wasn't, but I am now," she replied with a brave smile.

"That's good to hear. I'm glad you showed up."

"Me too. We have to stop meeting like this though," she said around a short giggle. Seeing Marlin was a pleasant surprise and immediately erased the pain of seeing her niece squatted on her husband's face.

"Maybe we oughta go out on a date," Marlin suggested. "I got these two for one meal tickets for Haitian Jack's." Her laughter was a musical note that soothed his soul. For the moment they were the only people in the room. In the world.

"Two for one, hunh ... Aren't you afraid I might call you cheap?"

"Naw, I ain't worried about that at all. You and me from the same place. We from the dirt. We sneaking food into movies and bringing our own wine to the restaurant."

Sherrelle smiled in agreement. "That's right." She waved to Dahji and shrugged her shoulders when he mouthed an inquiry as to where Peaches might be.

"You talk to her this morning?" Marlin wanted to know.

"Yeah. She had to handle some business real ... But look," she began anew as if remembering a former frame of thought. "Is there somewhere that we can talk?"

Marlin looked around at the beautiful and glamorous people enjoying themselves. "Well ..."

"Come with me," Sherrelle instructed, leaving her duffel bags at the door and grabbing his hand in hers. She led him through the sunlit hallway and made a right into the spare room.

Atop the canopied bed were a little girl's clothes. "Oh, Dahji's daughter came in here to change. She's in the ..." Sherrelle put her finger to his lips as she closed the door behind her.

"I didn't bring you in here to talk about Dahji's daughter." She leaned to him and softly placed her lips over his. "Do you want me?" she asked in a whisper.

"Since day one."

"Good," she smiled and kissed him again as she pulled a strap from her shoulder.

The plasma screen on the wall was rolling credits over a Saturday morning cartoon. The happy music chirped and hopped through the room on a bubble of children's laughter.

"You are absolutely beautiful," Marlin whispered as she let the dress fall to her ankles. Her body was tight and curvaceous, wrapped sensuously in what was her own clothing line of sexy lingerie.

"Mid-day breaking news this morning in a quiet suburb ..." a serious white woman was saying through the plasma monitor.

"Please stop talking, Marlin."

He smiled nervously. This was happening suddenly. He'd dreamed of this very moment from the first day he'd seen her. Now he was acting like a school kid about to lose his virginity.

"Federal agents have been investigating accounting fraud at one of the nation's leading firms ..." the white woman continued.

"Okay," Marlin said as he turned to the television. "Let's turn this off ..." he began.

"WAIT!" Sherrelle whispered loudly in fright as she stepped quickly towards the plasma screen. "Is that my house?"

"Shit ..." Marlin hissed, feeling Sherrelle move into his body. She was looking towards the screen with her fingers over her mouth.

Behind the blonde, proper-sounding white woman was Sherrelle's house. White shirted, clean cut men in ties traipsed through her open door. "Mr. Percival Santiago has been at the center of a multi-billion dollar fraud investigation," she was saying as the camera zoomed in on the front door. Percy emerged under escort, his arms folded behind his back. He looked befuddled and distraught.

"Oh my ..." Sherrelle whispered beside Marlin as he hugged her close to him. After Percy was a man carrying his laptop and the computer Sherrelle used to keep records of her emerging business.

"No ..." She looked to Marlin. "Can they take my computer?" she asked with wide eyes before looking back to the screen.

"We'll go together and see about getting it back," Marlin assured her.

"I have a back-up disc." Her reply was barely a whisper as a new line of suited men emerged from her house.

"Mr. Percival Santiago will be arraigned in Federal Court in a couple of days. Witnesses say that his wife would often return home from lavish shopping sprees ..." the reporter said as the camera now included Marlin's wife in the frame. She had a professional, satisfied look straining her face.

"Beside me is a neighbor who says that Mr. Santiago's marriage was anything but a happy union," the reporter continued as she turned to Stacy with the microphone to her lips.

"I knew something was wrong. His wife liked to look into my bedroom window. I would hear them fighting all the time," Stacy said in her clipped bourgeois manner. Sherrelle's body shook with laughter against Marlin.

"She's fucking her boss. A woman," Marlin said.

Sherrelle looked up to him as he faced the screen. "I didn't want to say anything, but I saw her at a restaurant kissing a white woman."

Marlin nodded. "Classic."

"And I found out that my husband was cheating on me with a white woman. I think he likes to be whipped with a leather strap." Her voice was neutral, as if simply reporting the facts.

"And a multiple homicide has been committed on the south side ..." a man's voice began.

"I figured he was the type," Marlin was saying. Sherrelle slapped him across the shoulder playfully.

"No, you didn't," she replied around a soft giggle.

"When officers responded to shots fired they found a Ms. Helen Adebenro attempting to flee the scene ..."

"NO!!" Sherrelle shouted and nearly collapsed. Marlin held her up and moved her to the bed.

There was a different reporter now. She was a Hispanic woman who was now on the scene. Behind her were black, curious faces. Some of the women were still in rollers and dingy robes; while men were in wife-beaters and sagging jeans. They made gang signs into the camera and laughed amongst themselves at their childish antics.

"There is no word yet as to motive ..." the dark-haired reporter began anew. "But apparently police had the young woman's description and found her attempting to start her car in the middle of the Martin Luther King and Cesar Chavez intersection. Inside police found a duffel bag with an undisclosed amount of money and what they believe is the murder weapon."

Sherrelle began to shake violently as tears streaked down her face.

"From what we have learned on the scene is that she may have been assaulted by the three men found dead in her apartment. She was a popular exotic dancer at ..." She consulted the note pad in her hand. "The

Applebottoms Gentlemen's Lounge." Behind her a cheer of shouts rang out from the excited men.

Sherrelle shook her head sadly into Marlin's shoulder as he held her tightly, tears streaming down her face. Marlin's assurance that everything would be okay felt like a blanket of calm over her. After telling him to turn the plasma screen off she asked him to hold her tightly. She was suddenly very cold.

He joined her and held her to him, whispering encouraging words to soothe her pain. It was as if they were the only people alive and that was all that mattered. She huddled against him and her lips found his in due time. They kissed through her tears and moved into each other as if finding the grooves of each other's body. They were a perfect fit. Together they could get through this; Sherrelle was sure of this more than she was sure that she would take her next breath.

... Sequel coming soon ...

Signature

Peter Mack

SINCE
1889

Apparel

Ayana Cherry & The Tabernacle Glorious

a novel

by

Peter Mack

Reverend Mathias Lovejoy has big plans to build a campus-size cathedral, but a shameful secret threatens everything he's built.

When Ayana Cherry is offered a job and a place to stay at The Tabernacle Glorious, she never imagined that she would play a key role in exposing the womanizing deacon and foiling his plot to blackmail the reverend.

Ayana's power of seduction is in full swing while in the service of Mathias Lovejoy, helping him to realize his dream and free Peaches from jail in the process. Her desire is to use her seductive prowess for good in the hopes her aunt Sherrelle will forgive her past transgressions.

Ayana Cherry & The Tabernacle Glorious

a novel

by

PETER MACK

"If we say that we have no sin,

we deceive ourselves, and the truth

is not in us."

---I John 1:8

---Holy Bible

CHAPTER ONE

It had only been a week since she stepped through this same terminal on her way to what she thought was a new beginning. The hustle and bustle of Indianapolis Airport lacked the same positive energy as it had with her arrival; now this same going to and fro represented dashed hopes. The curious stares of passersby reflected her gloom.

Ayana sat sandwiched between large Louis Vuitton duffel bags as if she were the teary-eyed prize waiting to be peeled from the innards of fine luggage. *How could I have been so reckless?* she asked herself as she uncrossed and recrossed her long legs which were sheathed in pink velour Baby Phat pants. She let her leg swing at the knee, the bright pink Nike shoes bouncing jauntily in the air; the gold Figaro bracelet winded seductively around her thin, toffee-toned ankle with each gentle bounce.

She still had yet to fully recover from the drama that erupted after her fight with Sherrelle. As she thought about it now she recognized that ominous knock; it was the knock of the police. Percy had no clue. He'd gone to the door expecting that it was his wife; maybe she'd forgotten her keys in her anger. Her face still stung from her aunt's angry slap as she watched Percy saunter shirtless to the front door. Her suspicions had been proven correct when she saw the flash of a gold plated badge and those piercing blue eyes of the white man who would eventually question her as to who she was. He'd seemed confused by her appearance, no doubt wondering what had happened just before he and his team arrived. It took all of her strength not to laugh out loud in his face while he questioned her. How could he suspect that her aunt had just caught her sitting on Percy's face?

Added to this – and she smiled even now – Ayana still did not see the reasoning for this disclosure, but it was all she could do to deflect some of Sherrelle's anger, to tell her about the white woman her husband was cheating on her with. It worked for a second, but Sherrelle was beyond mad. It was as if she were somehow glad that it was so. She didn't even give Percy a chance to deny the accusation.

Ayana let out a sigh, lamenting the demise of her suburban experience. Keyshia Cole offered what little solace she could as she sang through the small iPod speakers neatly tucked into her ears.

For a while there she thought it was going to be a nice change of pace. She had to admit to herself that she was going to miss Grump. He had been so nice to her. She wiped a tear from her eye with the thought of him standing on the porch, looking out blindly as Sherrelle watched her get into a taxi cab. Now it was back to the gritty streets of Los Angeles. She would have to face her old friends and try to explain her early return. She dreaded the I-told-you-so look that her mother would give her. This hurt more than everything else.

She'd foolishly believed that her aunt would have forgiven her when she walked into the house later that evening. No amount of pleading or begging would dissuade Sherrelle from her decision to kick Ayana out of her house. Even with Percy's arrest there was no room for reprieve. Oddly, Sherrelle seemed to have been very calm – even rejoicing – at the sudden turn of events. As Ayana thought of this now she suspected that perhaps her aunt had finally been with Marlin in the way she denied herself due to her marriage vows. She wished she could have thought of this sooner; maybe she could have used this knowledge to persuade her aunt to let her stay. It could have been just the two of them. She could have tried harder to put it all on Percy. It could have been the two of them living in the house and having a good time without her cheating husband around. She could have ...

Then someone got her attention. The image of the shiny black, sharply dressed man at the Air France terminal made her forget her private rumblings. They'd made brief eye contact through the milling crowd, and that was all it took to make Ayana take a private inventory of what he must have seen: Breasts bubbling over the v-neck of the HoodSweet shirt as the pink Baby Phat top framed the voluptuous curves, hiding the 'H' and 'T' scrawled across her chest. She'd looked away, pretending to fidget with her iPod, glad for some reason that she'd discarded the hazel- colored contact lenses; her tears made them uncomfortable. Her full lips were glazed with a light sheen of peach gloss and her dark eyes were made more riveting with the thin ring of black eyeliner she'd applied in the bathroom.

The man checked his gold watch. He was tall and confident. He could be a wealthy business man. Who was he waiting for? Maybe it was his wife that had him standing at attention. Ayana adjusted herself in her seat so that his attention was once again drawn to her. She pretended to look to some spot over his head as she reached inside of her Fendi purse. She pulled a small compact from the leather bag and placed it on her lap. He was watching her as she pulled the iPod buds from her ears and deposited the entertainment system into her purse.

Ayana was free for conversation. She quickly traced her wide mouth with the tip of her fingers before the mirror. This gesture seemed to move something in the man as he took a step in her direction

***

Deacon Maceo detested being sent to fetch the reverend's wife. He did not look forward to her coldness. He'd long ago given up trying to get into her good graces. Sometimes he wondered why he stayed around to play second fiddle. After all, wasn't it him that the congregation applauded? Wasn't it he that they really came to hear speak, even if it was a small introductory to the great ... The grand Reverend Mathias Lovejoy?

Being second in command at The Tabernacle Glorious did have its advantages, he thought to himself as he traversed the crowded airport in search of the Air France terminal. He had his pick of women in the congregation and the reverend never questioned his count of the tithes contributed for each of the two Sunday services. This was his private motivation for staying around. He'd managed to accumulate a nice little nest egg for himself.

"So, quit bitching," he muttered to himself. "You couldn't ask for a better situation," he added. But there was still that nagging feeling that he was going to be left behind with this new expansion. Once the church got bigger and a board of trustees was formed to account for the money and the property, then it was going to get harder, if not impossible, to remain relevant. This is what Maceo feared most: That he would be left out in the cold once the church was in bed with the politicians.

There it is, Air France. He looked up at the arrival time and checked his watch. He had nearly ten minutes before her plane landed. No doubt she would have exotic luggage for him to carry. He knew that there was no amount of money he could steal that compared to her monthly trips abroad. And this was another thing: Reverend Mathias and Sophia Lovejoy had the oddest marriage. It was as if they were a business unit; one complimenting the other.

No use in thinking about that, he reasoned as he scanned the seating area. A large family of kente cloth clad Africans took up an entire section in a very prime spot in front of the large plasma screen. Further on were a row of restaurants. The Olive Garden sounded nice; perhaps a chicken salad and a glass of wine. Just as he made this decision his eyes moved back across the room and settled on the image of a beautiful woman in a form-fitting velour track suit. Around her was expensive luggage. Though she appeared to look brave, his training made it possible to see that she was just from a recent cry. Even from this distance he could see that her mind was preoccupied with some disappointment. She *is too pretty to be so troubled,* he assured himself just as she seemed to notice him.

Maceo looked back to the arrival gate as if Sophia Lovejoy would suddenly appear to destroy his intentions. He took a deep breath and reached to grasp the large knot of his silk tie. He was suddenly glad that he'd chosen to wear this blue pinstriped suit and burgundy wing-tips. He didn't have to run his palm across his head to know that his low-cut waves were gleaming under the florescent lighting. One hundred strokes in the morning and at night made his hair the envy of everyone. With his sharp, dark features he was often mistaken for Ving Rhames.

She'd pulled out a mirror from her purse and licked her lips. She had to know he was looking at her. Who was this woman? Was she coming or going? What was her story?

He took a step in her direction and took it as an invitation when she pulled the iPod speakers from her ears and dropped them into her expensive-looking purse. She was watching him now with large, dark eyes. Maceo made an effort to steady himself before her soft appraisal as he approached.

"Excuse me miss," he said, making a noticeable glance to the Louis Vuitton duffel bags framing her and occupying the seats on either side.

Ayana made no move in either direction. Her gaze was still upon him, slightly amused by his obvious play.

He didn't want to be looking down from such a high angle nor did he want to step away from her to the nearest seat which was too far away. He kneeled to the balls of his feet and extended a hand to her.

"My name is Maceo Jenkins."

She let her hand slip into his cold palm smoothly. "Ayana Cherry."

He grinned, exposing the gold cap on a side tooth. It added flavor to his smoky personality. "Nice to meet you Ayana Cherry," he replied in his deep voice, realizing the heat she left on his palm with her gentle departure.

Ayana leaned back in her seat, observing the way he was put together. "Do you play sports,?" she asked, glad to see him smile. She didn't really think he played ball. He was too short for basketball and his shoulders were too narrow for football. The suit couldn't hide his small paunch of a stomach, and when he kneeled his thighs spread like butter. He nearly toppled over with the effort, but his smile said that he took this as a compliment and it was then that she knew she could have him.

"No no no ... I don't play sports." He smiled with this and looked to her in what he hoped was a serious, yet sincere gaze. "I'm the head deacon at The Tabernacle Glorious," he said with a bit of pride.

"Deacon?"

"It's just Reverend Lovejoy and me. You could say that I'm the assistant reverend, but I don't have a degree yet so ..." He shrugged his shoulders, his knees willing him to get up.

The intercom was now loud in his ears with his discomfort. The squeaky female voice was announcing arrivals and departures. He vaguely heard the arrival of Air France and wondered where this beautiful woman before him was headed to.

"Well, that's good. As long as you're serving God," Ayana replied with a generous smile.

"That's all that matters. Yes indeed," he said, absorbing the shock of pain that shot up his straining thigh. Maceo's knees hurt, but he couldn't bring himself to rise from his kneeling position. "So, what time does your flight leave?"

Ayana let a pout live where her sigh died. "In about an hour," she reasoned sadly, seeing immediately an option opening up to her.

"Why you so sad? You going somewhere you don't want to go?" He was genuinely interested in her situation. She at once seemed complicated and vulnerable.

"Well, I just got out here a few days ago, but since my sponsor died I have to go back." Her voice trembled with this last bit of news and her eyes gleamed from a fresh coat of threatening tears.

Maceo was tempted to reach out to her, but any movement would have forced him to the shiny floor.

"Your sponsor?"

Ayana nodded. "Yeah ... I was supposed to go to fashion design school, but then he died, so ..." There was more information this time. More lies. She looked up from her lap and stared into his eyes.

"Where are you from?"

"Watts," she replied dramatically, conjuring up all the ruthlessness of ghetto life in her voice.

"Did he ... your sponsor buy you all this luggage?" Maceo wanted to know. He knew Watts and she didn't seem like a product of that ghetto. But every now and then a rare flower was grown from this concrete jungle. Maybe this would explain why she seemed so distraught. She didn't want to go back. Who would? Her eyes rose above him slowly and he knew without looking that Sophia Lovejoy was standing behind him.

"Pray tell ... Is she the reason you failed to meet me at the gate?" came a feathery voice laced with a husky undertone. Maceo resisted the urge to curse. He hated being in a position where he could be called out. He should have been at the gate. There was no escaping the wince of pain shooting through his knees as he rose to his feet.

Ayana threw away the thought that this was his wife. They were in a different league even though he was dressed well enough. This woman standing before her, who obviously had some control over Maceo Jenkins, was unhurried and unruffled. She oozed money and privilege. If she were a white woman she could easily be mistaken for a dutchess in some rural part of England that no one ever heard of. She was the shade of a black woman who passed for white in the early part of the century. *Maybe she is passing now,* Ayana thought as she observed the way the hazel cat eyes looked to Maceo as he turned to her.

"Mrs. Lovejoy," he replied, smiling graciously as he looked around her for the luggage he knew she must have.

"My luggage is on the carousel Maceo," she stated shortly as if to dismiss him.

Maceo was stuck between his conversation with Ayana and following Sophia's instruction. He'd lost his poise and revealed himself to be no more than a lackey.

"How was your flight?" he asked as a way of restoring some of his dignity.

"My flight was well Maceo, but I am awfully tired. Would you be so kind as to catch my belongings. It would be a shame if they were lost to some thief."

Ayana was amazed by the sight of this slight woman with long sandy brown hair. Her lithe frame was dripped and draped in startling diamonds and platinum. A small red purse with an embossed MCM emblem hung from her slim arm. *She has class,* Ayana thought to herself, nearly afraid to be left alone with her.

"Wait. Don't be rude. Introduce me to your friend?" the expensively coiled woman said, reaching out tenderly to hold Maceo's elbow. He seemed to forget himself for a moment before he turned to Ayana.

"My apologies," he began. "Mrs. Reverend Lovejoy."

"Sophia," the tall woman cut in with her long fingers extended in a way that forced Ayana to rise from her seat. The effect of her voluptuous figure was not lost on the widening eyes of Maceo. Surely, he licked his lips, but Ayana could not be sure as she was held in Sophia's piercing gaze.

"This is Ayana Cherry," Maceo offered, pushed to the side to observe the meeting.

"Ayana Cherry. What a beautiful name," Sophia quipped.

"She just arrived to go to modeling school, but an unfortunate death has interrupted her plans."

Sophia's thin eyebrow arched with Maceo's words. "Family?" she asked.

"No. My sponsor."

A small clucking sound escaped the proper woman's lips. "How unfortunate. Is there no other way you can stay? Any family here?"

"No. All of my family is in Los Angeles," Ayana replied. Maceo was looking from one to the other. He thought it was a smart move for her not to mention Watts.

"Well, I suppose you miss your family and there are so many nice schools on the west coast" Sophia said in her rhetorical way.

"She was hoping to find a way to stay here," Maceo offered, meeting Sophia's gaze evenly before she turned to Ayana.

"Actually there's not much to go home to," Ayana confessed. "But I don't have a choice now," she added with a shrug. She saw the reverend's wife's mind working.

"What do you think Maceo?" she asked the deacon. With this simple question she'd returned the squareness to his shoulders and lifted his chin.

"Well, we could use someone for the elderly food program. Remember ... Monica had to leave."

Sophia smiled slightly with a slow nod of appraisal. "Well, you don't seem to need much in the way of clothes," she observed with a wave of her hand. "If you'd like to stay and see what Indianapolis has to offer you're more than welcome." With this she turned to Maceo. "Do you have an apartment available?"

He nodded before he could get the words out. "We sure do. Freshly painted."

Ayana couldn't believe her luck. Just like that she was back in the game. She would get her own apartment and from what it sounded like she'd be delivering food to old people. She reminded herself to research a few fashion design schools in the area in case she was quizzed later on.

***

The walls were lined in thick, leather-bound theological texts. A large crystal chandelier hung from the ceiling under a slow turning, wooden armed fan. Amber-hued lighting escaped from recessed portals adding to the old-school charm of this private space which spoke of accomplishment, casting its glow across the wall of certificates and plaques. The dim lighting shone across the sumptuous brown-leather chairs, their brass studs gleaming, facing the wide mahogany desk. On the hardwood floor was scattered brightly colored area rugs which testified to global travels and rich, cultural experiences.

Reverend Mathias Lovejoy reclined in a overstuffed leather chair as he puffed on a Cuban cigar. Before him were the architectural designs of a cathedral-sized church to rival that of T.D Jakes. He was on his way. He'd been successful in purchasing large lots of commercial property surrounding his modest-sized Tabernacle Glorious.

Beside the blueprints of his future church was the ledger which enumerated the holdings of The Tabernacle Glorious. He'd done right by the community by providing day care for school-aged children, tutoring, and meals for the elderly. His property holdings included several group homes for boys and girls. He owned several apartment buildings in the city and operated a church-affiliated homeless shelter.

This same portfolio listed his personal corporate stock holdings and bank accounts; these were separated from the financial records he kept that were generated by his pastoral duties at The Tabernacle Glorious.

The ringing phone interrupted his moment of reverie. The caller I.D. showed the rare number that was the key to his future.

"Judge Higginbotham," he cheered into the phone as he let a plume of cigar smoke escape his thin lips.

"Mathias. When are you going to start calling me Roy?" replied the judge, a low chuckle following his southern drawl.

"You got me there Roy. Just feels funny saying so in private, that's all."

He watched the cigar smoke as it eased through the glowing crystals and was separated by the slow- moving ceiling fan. The effect was nearly hypnotizing.

"Yeah. I know what 'cha mean. I nearly called you reverend," Roy responded before continuing. "But with your help you'll have to get used to calling me Congressman." His voice was laced with the wetness of a single malt scotch.

"That'll be a good thing, Congressman. I won't mind that at all. Sophia and I really appreciate how you've shown our best sides to the Senator."

"Aw shucks, that's nothing. We all need each other. You have a growing voice and we're willing to invest in your potential. The upcoming election is critical. Those red-neck republicans plan to take control of Indiana, and we can't allow them to do it!" he hissed in growing anger. Mathias had a vision of the judge sitting in a quiet library much like his own.

"I agree. The people won't stand for it."

"Exactly. The people. It's the people we need on our side, and we're counting on you to make this happen."

"It's a done deal. So, what can I do for you tonight?" Mathias wanted to know.

"Well, me and John will be at your morning sermon tomorrow. We expect that it'll be a good one ..."

"The good Lord has always saw fit to give me good counsel," Mathias replied, sensing that the judge was beating around the bush.

"Yeah, I 'spose so ... I guess it'll have to wait until tomorrow. I'd like to ask a special favor of you."

"Sure. Anything. We can have some privacy in my office."

"Will the wife be joining you?"

"Uhh, yeah, she'll be there, but ..."

"That'll be great!' said the judge, his voice growing buoyant with expectation."

"You're a fine man, Reverend. You'll go far in this town."

"Thanks Roy. God bless."

Mathias let the phone ease into the cradle as he took a small pull of his cigar. *What kind of favor does the judge need?*, he asked himself as he perused the blueprints of his new cathedral. Whatever it is, he is going to make sure the judge is satisfied. He is the link to the raised platform that stood in the center of his mega-church. He'd liked the way Reverend K.C. Price stood aloft as he gave his sermons. There were people all around him as he waved the soft, leather bible in the air to punctuate a serious point. Mathias

Lovejoy wanted this for himself. He wanted the television exposure that was in the works. He would be on TV every Sunday morning.

Yeah, whatever the judge wants, the judge will get. Little did he and the Senator know, they didn't have to promise him the money for the church or the television contracts in return for his political endorsement. It didn't matter to him that they were going to raise taxes. What mattered to him was that they were going to make sure he reaped direct financial benefits and State tax breaks for his ministry. This was going to amount to hundreds of millions of dollars. This would make up for their stance on reducing after-school programs, Medicare benefits, drug-treatment facilities, and increasing sentences on violent offenses. *Shit, if more people were in church they wouldn't have to worry about that stuff,* he thought to himself as he slid his dark hand across the expanse of his future mega-church.

He saw the car lights flash across the high windows of his den before he heard the low crunching sound of gravel. *That's Maceo returning from the Airport with my wife,* the reverend surmised. He was curious as to why the headlights were still emblazoned across the maroon curtains. The outside security lamps had been activated so there was no need to keep the car running. He sat silent, listening for voices. Then he heard the soft clicking of the front door just outside the library. Maceo's voice was a whisper. He was saying something about getting Yaya (who's Yaya?) to the apartment and to give the Reverend his best. *Well, that's good,* Mathias thought to himself as he looked towards the door. He suspected that Maceo had helped to carry Sophia's luggage into the house. The front door closed again and before long the burgundy curtains grew dark with the departing headlights.

There was a soft knock on the heavy library door. "Honey," she whispered from the other side. "I'm home." Her words were a lilting song that stirred his loins. The door opened slowly to reveal the beauty that was his wife.

Mathias grinned broadly, his cream-colored skin blushing. At his temples was a brush of gray strands that contrasted delicately with his oily, black hair that he wore combed away from his forehead. His features were delicate, a testimony to his Creole mother and father who'd been notorious snake oil dealers. It was often joked that he'd inherited his parent's gift of persuasion and oratory. He was a product of hustlers who enjoyed the finer things in life even though they never worked for anyone else but themselves.

"What g'won chyl' whut have fa dada?" Mathias sang as he leaned back in his chair. Sophia glided across the floor as if on a surfboard, her Chanel jogging suit seemed to peel away from her body as if thrown off by some mystical force. By the time she reached him she was barefoot in garter belt, lace panties and bra; her small, pert breasts stood firm and adamant for attention.

Mathias welcomed her onto his lap as she bent to dip her cold tongue into his mouth. She explored him hungrily. She moaned with her exploration as she reached for his growing joint.

"You missed me?" she asked with panting breath, raising up to gaze into his light-brown eyes.

"Sho nuff," he responded as she reached into his silk robe and grabbed a hold of his long joint. She stroked him slowly as she looked into his clouding eyes.

"Maceo picked up a stray," she announced. "Yeah. She's very pretty and I suspect that he's in love with her." She said this with a light chuckle.

"At the Airport?"

"Indeed. Right there in the lobby." She stroked him, enjoying the length of him grow in her palm. "She was surrounded by really nice Louis Vuitton luggage. She said something about her sponsor dying and having to move back to Los Angeles. I hardly believed a word of it, but Maceo was absolutely melting before my very eyes."

"Was she just in the car?"

"Yes, dear. She's harmless really. Couldn't be no more than eighteen years old."

Mathias had grown used to his wife's whims. She had this need to befriend beautiful women. Maybe this was her way of feeling ...

"You're beautiful," he said, echoing his thoughts with barely a whisper. She tightened her grip on his shaft and leaned to nibble on his ear lobe. Her tongue darted across his ear with a rapid stroke in tune with her palm over his joint.

"You always know the right thing to say," she whispered. "Missed you so much," she added as she slid from his lap and fell to her knees. She took him into her mouth expertly. She moved her tongue across the base of him as she slid him to her throat.

"How was Paris?" Mathias asked around a sudden jolt of pleasure.

"Beautiful," she whispered over his swollen dick. She untied her hair and it fell across his lap, giving him a tingling sensation with its many soft strands rolling and dipping across his skin with her movements.

Sophia eased up from her duty and turned away from him. She slid her panties down her long legs. Her ass was a perfect pair of half moons in the dim light. She reached around and spread her cheeks as she backed onto him. The fleshy pink knot was barely visible in the dim light. "I've missed you so ..." she moaned as the tip of his meaty head met her tight hole.

Mathias grimaced with the tight fit. She opened expertly for him and wiggled seductively onto him. His dick pulsed as she allowed him past her opening. He breathed in deeply when he felt the first wetness. She opened more for him, allowing more of his throbbing meat inside of her.

"Ooooohhh!" she moaned as she arched her back and threw her long hair over a bare shoulder. Mathias took hold of her slim waist and guided her onto him snugly.

"Ahhh!" he grimaced just as a soft popping sound signaled he'd gained entry into her private love box. She relaxed onto him and ground the head of his dick against her inner walls. Side to side she moved, fitting him tightly inside of her.

"Missed me?" she asked, feeling his hot breath on her back. His fingers dug into her waist as he neared climax. A low growl was his answer.

Sophia tightened her muscles around his dick as she massaged her swollen mound. She gasped with pleasure as he began to pump inside of her.

Mathias braced himself against the arms of his leather chair and leaned back to watch his dick slide in and out of her ass hole. She was squeezed over him tightly as she flexed and bent away from him.

"Come on baby. Let me have it," she urged him as she tightened her muscles around him. She worked vigorously to reach her own climax as she slid onto him with such tightness that he hissed and grunted with each movement. His hot breath was a signal that he was about to release himself.

With this urging she slid at length to the tip of him and lowered herself dramatically. This move proved too much for him to take. He exploded on cue as she squirted her own pleasure. She slumped against him with exhaustion and pronounced her undying love.

Reverend Mathias Lovejoy accepted the light weight of his beautiful wife with pleasure. He enjoyed the way she lulled onto his shoulder and whispered low against his hot cheek.

Peter Mack was born and raised in Los Angles, California. He is also the author of *Play My Hand: The Sex, Violence, Money and Murder of Raymond Cooks* (Autobiography), and HoodSweet, written under his government name, Isiko Cooks. Since penning his autobiography he has written nearly 20 novels, which are in varying degrees of contract negotiations or submission, which spans popular genres that include crime, romance, and urban fiction. He currently resides near Sacramento, California.

petermackpresents@yahoo.com
www.petermackpresents.com
facebook.com/petermackpresents